WORDSWORTH CLASSICS
OF WORLD LITERATURE

General Editor: Tom Griffith MA, MPhil

NJÁL'S SAGA

Njál's Saga

*Translation
by Carl F. Bayerschmidt
and Lee M Hollander*

*Introduction
by Thorsteinn Gylfason*

**WORDSWORTH CLASSICS
OF WORLD LITERATURE**

For customers interested in other titles from Wordsworth Editions

Visit our web-site at
www.wordsworth-editions.com

Or for our latest list and a full mail order service contact:

Bibliophile Books
5 Thomas Road
London
E14 7BN

Tel: (0044) 020 7515 9222
Fax: (0044) 020 7538 4115
e-mail: orders@bibliophilebooks.com

This edition published 1998 by Wordsworth Editions Limited
8b East Street, Ware, Hertfordshire SG12 9HJ

ISBN 1 85326 785 6

© Wordsworth Editions Limited 1998

1 3 5 7 9 10 8 6 4 2

Wordsworth ® is a registered trade mark of
Wordsworth Editions Ltd

Typeset by Antony Gray
Printed and bound in Great Britain by
Mackays of Chatham PLC, Chatham, Kent

CONTENTS

NJÁL'S SAGA

INTRODUCTION

I

Sagas

Njál's Saga is the greatest and most celebrated of all Icelandic sagas. It has been called one of the great prose works of the world.[1] It was written somewhere in Iceland in the late thirteenth century. We do not know who wrote it.

The Icelandic word 'saga' – like 'histoire' in French, 'Geschichte' in German and 'storia' in Italian – means both *story* and *history*. In English, and many other languages, the Icelandic word has been adopted as a term of art referring to various literary works composed in Iceland in the late middle ages (about 1200–1400), among them the so-called sagas of Icelanders. The sagas of Icelanders are sometimes misleadingly called the Icelandic sagas. But they are quite different from, for example, the equally Icelandic sagas (histories) of Norwegian kings, the most famous of which are contained in the *Heimskringla* of Snorri Sturluson (1179–1241), the sagas (biographies) of Icelandic bishops, the sagas (chronicles) of contemporary events brought together in the collection *Saga of the Sturlungs* (also called *Sturlunga*, named for the clan of Snorri), or the heroic sagas of Scandinavian or Germanic antiquity such as the *Saga of the Volsungs* drawn upon by Richard Wagner in his *Ring of the Nibelung*. Further there are sagas (lives) of saints – the oldest extant Icelandic manuscripts contain such lives – and sagas of knights (romances of chivalry) which belong to a European genre

1 W. P. Ker, *Epic and Romance*, p. 60.

that flourished in Norway and Iceland in the thirteenth and fourteenth centuries and beyond.

In addition to the various kinds of sagas the mediaeval manuscripts of Iceland contain laws, in which the author of *Njál's Saga* took great interest, and a fair amount of scholarship, including the renowned mythology and poetics of Snorri Sturluson's *Edda* (the *Younger Edda* or *Prose Edda*). Last but not least there is a great deal of poetry. The oldest poetry, some of which antedates the settlement of Iceland, is preserved in the *Elder Edda*, a superb collection of anonymous mythological and heroic poems. The Eddaic poems have metres similar to that of the Anglo-Saxon *Beowulf* and the Old High German *Hildebrandslied*, and the heroic poems are similar in subject-matter to the later Middle High German heroic epic such as the *Nibelungenlied*. The *Saga of the Volsungs* is based on this poetic heritage. A poetic tradition different from that of the *Edda* is scaldic poetry. This was composed by known poets (a poet is *skáld* in Icelandic), among them the tenth-century viking poet Egill Skallagrímsson. Scaldic verse has intricate metres and uses elaborate metaphors (kennings), often derived from pagan lore even in the verse of Christian poets. Occasional scaldic stanzas are often attributed to saga characters. Thus *Njál's Saga* contains several examples of scaldic verse, as well as a substantial part of a long poem, 'The Song of the Valkyries', in an Eddaic metre.

The numerous sagas of Icelanders, long and short, fill thirteen volumes in the standard modern edition.[2] They are of two kinds. Some are biographies of individual Icelanders, for instance *Egill's Saga*, the life of Egill Skallagrímsson, now commonly thought to have been written by Snorri Sturluson. The rest are family sagas like *Njál's Saga*, set in a mediaeval society in which the family or clan is the supreme social institution. This society, whether pagan or Christian, was in all essentials the same as that of the rest of mediaeval Europe, with frequent feuds between the clans. The feuds involved the paramount duty to avenge the death of a kinsman. An Icelandic scholar of the eighteenth century said that all the sagas of Icelanders could be summed up in four words: 'Farmers came to blows.'

2 Íslenzk fornrit, Hið íslenzka fornritafélag, Reykjavík. The series was begun in 1933. Vol. XII, *Brennunjálssaga*, appeared in 1954, edited by Einar Ólafur Sveinsson.

The sagas of Icelanders are mainly concerned with people and events of the first hundred and twenty years of the Icelandic commonwealth, from 930 to 1050. But they were written almost three centuries later. Thus *Njál's Saga* is thought to have been composed in the period from 1270 to 1290. It is controversial to what extent these sagas were based on oral traditions going back to the tenth and eleventh centuries, and also to what extent they may, whatever their origins, be used as historical sources about particular people and events, or about the society described and its laws and customs. But even if *Njál's Saga* is partly or largely unhistorical – for example, its detailed accounts of Icelandic law and legal procedure are not always reliable – the early history of Iceland is highly relevant both to the saga itself and to the turbulent times of its anonymous author.

According to most mediaeval Icelandic historians their country had been settled from 870 to 930, mainly by Norwegians resisting the unification of Norway under a single king. In 930 they formed a new state in Iceland by establishing a General Assembly (Althing) with legislative power. The Althing adopted Christianity in 1000. The official conversion is described in some detail in *Njál's Saga* as well as in other sources. A court of law, with 36 judges, was also established. It was later divided up into four courts, one for each quarter of the country. The verdicts of these courts had to be unanimous, which meant that many cases could not be settled. Then a Fifth Court was instituted, a high court that reached its decisions by majority vote. In *Njál's Saga* an account is given of the establishment of the Fifth Court: Njál is said to have proposed it, ultimately for purposes of his own. This tale does not agree with other sources and seems to be a piece of fiction.

In this commonwealth there was no king or other central executive authority and hence, apart from the elected speaker (*lögsögumaður*) of the Althing, no officials nor police. Thus someone who won a case in court would himself have to see to the execution of the sentence against his opponent, each party relying on its clan for support or assistance. This lack of an executive authority is sometimes said to have been the main reason for the collapse of the mediaeval commonwealth in 1262. But the Icelanders, whose commonwealth lasted for over three centuries, did have various ways of managing their kingless society. One of these ways was to maintain a balance of power between the 39 (later 48) chieftains (goði, plural goðar). The chieftains were self-appointed members of the legislature (lögrétta), and also priests of local temples. Farmers were free to switch their allegiance from one chieftain to another.

By the late twelfth century this balance of power had been disturbed. It had always been possible to buy chieftainships (goðorð), as is apparent from Njál's Saga, and now many of them came into the hands of a few men who represented powerful clans. The church contributed to this development through the division of the tithe and its insistence on the separation of secular and ecclesiastical power. The clans' struggle for power led to fierce and often barbaric battles. Sturlunga also tells of the burning of farms, such as that of Flugumýri in northern Iceland in 1253. This seems to have inspired a part of the description of the burning of Bergthórshvál in Njál's Saga. During the first half of the thirteenth century Iceland was almost in a state of civil war. The result was that in 1262 the Icelanders submitted to the King of Norway who had had his eyes on Iceland for a long time. This led to peace.

Njál's Saga was written when the disintegration and collapse of the commonwealth were still vividly remembered in Iceland. It is longer and much more complex than any other saga. At first it may seem to be a mere succession of tales, set in Iceland and abroad, that from time to time is carried onwards mainly by the author's intense pleasure in telling a good story and describing remarkable people. After careful reading, however, the saga will be seen to be woven together so as to form a single whole, with a central plot that culminates, after many bloody feuds and patient attempts to settle or avoid them, in a great crime, the burning of Njál's farm Bergthórshvál. This crime is, for further effect, presented against the background of Iceland's conversion to Christianity.

In Iceland Njál's Saga has been the most popular of sagas since the time it was written. It is preserved in more manuscripts, old and new, than any other saga of Icelanders. Scholars and critics, in Iceland and abroad, have lavished praise on the saga, ever since they began to concern themselves with it in the eighteenth century. In particular, the author is often praised for his style. For the Icelanders, who still speak his language, he is a consummate master, and a constant source of quotations as Shakespeare is for speakers of

English. Some of the elements of his use of language – its terseness and objectivity – are common stylistic features of the sagas of Icelanders or of the historical writings of Snorri Sturluson. Others are peculiar to *Njál's Saga*. In Icelandic the author's sentences and paragraphs are very distinctive, though without a trace of affectation. This does not prevent him from giving each of his main characters, in the numerous dialogues, a voice of his or her own.

The author shows many signs of having been a well-read man. His account of Gunnar's decision to stay in Iceland, after he looks back to his farm, is probably based in part on a description given in a mediaeval French epic by Philippus Galterus, translated into Icelandic by Bishop Brandur Jónsson around 1250, of Alexander the Great viewing the lands of the East from the top of a mountain. A little later, when Gunnar fights his last battle, his wife denies him a lock of her hair to repair his broken bow-string. This incident was probably suggested by tales from ancient Rome of wives who did not fail to give their hair to their husbands for a similar purpose. And these are only two small examples of the author's literary sources. There are also various echoes of the Bible, lives of saints, and knightly romances in the saga.

In earlier times it was common for scholars and critics to regard the sagas of Icelanders as manifestations of the heathen spirit of the old Norsemen, like the *Edda*. In more recent times scholars have detected many signs of Christian influence in the sagas, not least in *Njál's Saga*. But such signs must be considered in the context of the saga as a whole. Professor Peter Foote has wisely observed: 'The author of *Njáls Saga* must have known much translated romance and ecclesiastical literature . . . yet he wrote *Njáls Saga*.'[3]

Obviously the author was a Christian. Iceland had been Christian for almost three hundred years when he wrote. But in his saga the Conversion Episode is primarily a political story with a religious aspect, a monument to human prudence rather than to the new faith, and in the remainder of the saga the religious aspect is mainly a background against which Christians commit an immense crime. The author indicates in many ways that Christianity is as powerless as the wisdom of Njál to stop the horrors of his tale. The Conversion Episode is immediately followed by the revenge of

3 Peter Foote, *The Pseudo-Turpin Chronicle in Iceland*, London 1959, p. v.

Ámundi the Blind and the slaying of Hoskuld. And Hoskuld's
widow Hildigunn incites her uncle Flosi to revenge by saying:

> I call God and all good men to witness that I adjure you by all the
> wonders of your Christ and by your manhood and valour that
> you avenge all the wounds which Hoskuld received on his body,
> or else be called a caitiff wretch before all men. (Chapter 116)

Flosi responds with fury. But before long he will burn Njál's farm
with the blessings of priests.

The author, in his last sentence, gives his work the title
Brennunjálssaga, *The Saga of the Burning of Njál*. The Icelanders, at
least since the sixteenth century, have fondly abbreviated the title
to *Njála*. Other popular sagas have acquired analogous familiar
names: *Egill's Saga* becomes *Egla*, *Grettir's Saga* becomes *Grettla*
and so forth. In what follows I shall observe this Icelandic custom
and refer to our saga as *Njála*.

II

Plot[4]

A prologue (1–17) introduces Hallgerd as a beautiful little girl
with 'a thief's eyes' (1), and later gives an account of her two
early marriages which both end with her henchman killing her
husband (9–17). It also describes her uncle Hrút's travels abroad,
and his marriage to Unn, unconsummated as a result of a curse
(2–8).

First Part: The Tragedy of Gunnar (18–81)

In a prelude to the main action (18–34) the heroic Gunnar of
Hlídarendi and his wise older friend and counsellor Njál of
Bergthórshvál are introduced (18). Njál's sons with his wife
Bergthóra are Skarphedin, Grím and Helgi (25–27). Gunnar is

---

4 The numbers refer to chapters. I follow Einar Ólafur Sveinsson in dividing
the main body of the saga into three parts rather than two ('Gunnar's Saga'
and 'Njál's Saga') as do Lars Lönnroth and Theodore Anderson, or five as
does Denton Fox.

related to Unn, and recovers her dowry from Hrút. Unn marries
Valgard the Grey (21–25). Gunnar then travels abroad (28–32),
and upon his return in glory marries the beautiful Hallgerd (33–
34).

A feud arises between Hallgerd and Bergthóra, involving the
deaths of several members of their households, but their husbands
make a peaceful settlement after each killing. The friendship
between Gunnar and Njál is even strengthened in the process. But
lasting hostility arises between Thráin Sigfússon, Gunnar's uncle,
and the sons of Njál (35–45).

Otkel of Kirkby, a wealthy farmer, refuses to sell Gunnar provisions during a hard winter (47). Hallgerd orders one of her men to
steal food from Otkel. When Gunnar learns of this he slaps his wife
in the face, as her two earlier husbands had also done. Since Otkel
refuses to settle the feud continues until Gunnar kills Otkel. After
this a settlement is made. But Gunnar gets involved in further feuds
with Egil and Starkad (57–66), and then with Thorgeir Starkadsson
and Thorgeir Otkelsson. In each case a settlement is worked out,
with the sound advice and through the good offices of Njál, while
Mord Valgardsson advises Gunnar's adversaries. But after the
second settlement Gunnar is attacked and thus provoked to kill
Thorgeir Otkelsson. The Althing sentences Gunnar to three years
of exile (67–74). In Iceland anyone will be free to kill him as an
outlaw in due course.

As Gunnar is about to leave the country with his brother
Kolskegg he changes his mind and, disregarding Njál's advice and
predictions, returns to his farm at Hlídarendi. There he is attacked
by his enemies. Hallgerd refuses to give him a lock of her hair to
repair his broken bow-string, and he falls after a heroic defence
(75–77). His son Högni and Skarphedin Njálsson avenge his death
(78-80). Kolskegg sails, enters the Varingian Guard in Constantinople and never returns to Iceland (81).

Second Part: The Burning of Njál (82-132)

This central part of the saga begins with a prelude set in the
British Isles and Norway (82-90). One summer Thráin Sigfússon,
Gunnar's uncle, and Grím and Helgi, sons of Njál, go separately
abroad (82–83). During a battle in the Orkneys Grím and Helgi
get to know Kári Solmundsson (83). In Norway Thráin accepts a

bribe from the Icelandic criminal Hrapp, and conceals him from his pursuers led by Earl Hákon. As a result of Thráin's – and Hrapp's – escape to Iceland Grím and Helgi incur the enmity of the earl. But with the help of Kári they too are able to sail to Iceland.

Grím and Helgi demand compensation from Thráin (91). A feud results, and Thráin falls (92). After a settlement has been reached Njál offers to foster the young son of Thráin, Hoskuld, as he would one of his own sons (94).

When Hoskuld Thráinsson is a grown man he proposes, on Njál's advice, to Hildigunn daughter of Starkad, the niece of the chieftain Flosi Thórdarson of Svínafell. For the marriage to be acceptable to Hildigunn Hoskuld has to acquire a chieftainship (goðorð). Njál sees to that, making full use of his legal and political craft (97). But the original settlement of the killing of Thráin is not kept, for Thráin's brother-in-law Lýting kills Hoskuld Njálsson, the illegitimate son of Njál (98). Hoskuld Thráinsson and his foster-father Njál make a settlement (99).

At this point the author interrupts his main tale for a few chapters (100 to 105 – known as 'The Conversion Episode') to tell of a different compromise. Christianity has been preached, with word and sword, in Iceland as in Norway, the Faroes, the Orkneys and Hebrides. The chieftain Thorgeir of Ljósavatn is empowered by the Althing to find a way to reconcile the warring parties. His compromise is accepted. Thus Iceland is peacefully converted to Christianity.

The blind son of Hoskuld Njálsson, granted sight for a miraculous moment, avenges his father's death by killing Lýting. Njál and Hoskuld Thráinsson settle again (106).

The chieftain Mord Valgardsson, whose men are leaving him for the new chieftain Hoskuld Thráinsson of Hvítaness, is encouraged by his heathen father to sow hostility, by means of slander, between the sons of Njál and Hoskuld so that they will kill him (107–10). This plan proves successful. Hoskuld is brutally murdered by his foster-brothers as he is sowing corn, soon after sunrise, in a field at Hvítaness (111).

Once again there are attempts at reconciliation. Flosi Thórdarson of Svínafell, the uncle of Hoskuld's widow Hildigunn, leads the claimants on Hoskuld's side. But he resists Hildigunn's incitation to revenge (116). Njál represents his sons. After a lawful agreement has been reached during a meeting of the Althing, an exchange of insults between Flosi and Skarphedin leads Flosi to refuse to accept any financial compensation for the killing of Hoskuld (113–23).

Flosi instead leads a large group of men to burn the farm of Bergthórshvál at night. Njál, Bergthóra, all their sons, their young grandson Thórd Kárason, and many others perish in the fire. Of the men of Bergthórshvál only one gets away unobserved. He is Njál's son-in-law and little Thórd's father, Kári Solmundsson (124-32).

Third Part: Revenge and Reconciliation (133-159)

The prelude (133–40) begins with Flosi's dream. He takes the dream to mean that many of the burners will die (133). So he rides off to gather support for his cause at the Althing (134). Kári does the same for his cause, and enlists the support of Mord Valgardsson among others (135). Eyjólf Bolverksson becomes Flosi's chief legal adviser (138). In this prelude many new characters are introduced.

At the Althing the burners face a lawsuit which is described in considerable legalistic detail. The proceedings are partly a battle of wits between Eyjólf Bolverksson and the bedridden Thórhall Ásgrímsson, foster-son and pupil of Njál (141–44).

When the lawsuit fails a battle breaks out at the Althing. Many are killed. Hall Thorsteinsson of Sída, an old chieftain on Flosi's side, makes a reconciliation possible by renouncing any claim for compensation for his fallen son. A settlement is made. Only Kári is irreconcilable. No one of Flosi's group is granted compensation for those fallen in the Battle of the Althing, except Hall of Sída who is given fourfold compensation in recognition of his noble renunciation. Many of the burners are exiled, some for good, Flosi for three years (145). Flosi goes abroad (153).

Kári sets about avenging the burning, first in the company of Thorgeir Skorargeir (146–47), then in the company of the braggart Bjorn of Mork who brings comic relief (148–52), and finally abroad (154–55, 158).

Some of the burners fall in the Battle of Clontarf in Ireland (155-57). This battle between heathen and Christian forces is described with great gusto. The description culminates in the blood-drenched

'Song of the Valkyries' ('Darraðarljóð') (157). After the noise of the battle there is a brief soft-voiced coda. Flosi goes to Rome and gets absolution from the pope. A little later Kári turns up shipwrecked at Svínafell, where he is reconciled with Flosi and marries his niece Hildigunn, the widow of Hoskuld of Hvítaness (158–59).

III

Tragedy

The blood-feud, with its motives of honour and shame, provides the author of *Njála* with the basic machinery of the action of many parts of his tale. But the author also treats the feud as a theme over which he weaves a number of variations, some relatively simple and others quite complex. In this way he presents us with numerous parallelisms or analogies. The first extended feud we are told of is that between Hallgerd and Bergthóra. This arises from an exchange of insults and then escalates until several people have been killed. Much later, after the slaying of Hoskuld of Hvítaness, the settlement at the Althing ultimately breaks down for reasons similar to those that led to the first feud between the two housewives. It ends in an exchange of partly the same insults.

The author does not only apply the technique of parallelisms, or of theme and variations, in his accounts of feuds. The various sojourns abroad are also treated in this way. For example, the adventures of Gunnar in Norway are presented as a parallel to the earlier adventures of Hrút. One point of the Conversion Episode is to show us a political settlement parallel to the judicial settlement just arrived at by Njál and Hoskuld Thráinsson. The settlements, whether attempted or achieved, are innumerable. The saga's earliest example of a settlement occurs in Chapter 8 where Hrút gives his ring to a young boy who had insulted him gravely.

On a grander scale, the first two parts of *Njála* present us with partly parallel stories. In both Njál and his family play a central part. The first story is that of Gunnar, a blameless hero whose judgment is clouded at a crucial moment so that he rushes knowingly towards certain death. His life has been dedicated to the cause of law and peace when he is drawn into a feud. Once more a settlement is achieved. It requires Gunnar to spend three years abroad where he is sure to gain further fame. But on the way to his ship he suddenly changes his mind and decides to stay as an outlaw in Iceland. He tells his brother Kolskegg, who was to accompany him on the voyage, that it is the beauty of the landscape that prevents him from going abroad. Icelandic readers of *Njála* have usually taken him at his word, and the chapter in question has become one of their favourite episodes in all the sagas. A wonderful poem – 'Gunnarshólmi' by Jónas Hallgrímsson (1807–45) – is based on this episode and turns it into an intense expression of an Icelander's love of his country.

But all this is to forget that a little later on in *Njála* Gunnar himself tells us, in a stanza he recites from his mound after his death, of a very different motive for his disastrous decision. In the light of that his remark to his brother becomes at best a rationalisation. He was, after all, incapable of giving in to his enemies. Gunnar might have said with the Ajax of Sophocles:

> A noble man should either live finely or die finely.
>
> (*Ajax* 479–80)

In *Njála* Gunnar makes a dreadful mistake in rebelling against the decree of the Althing even if not in wanting to die finely. Ajax went mad and took his own life.

The second part of *Njála* tells the story of a feud between the sons of Sigfús and the sons of Njál. This leads in the end to the slaying of Hoskuld of Hvítaness. The saga indicates in various ways that this was a vicious deed. Even Skarphedin seems to admit this. But it is worth noting that a modern scholar has analysed this feud as related in *Njála*, and argued that the slaying of Hoskuld was an understandable and even an excusable act in the light of the ethic of feuding.[5] Be that as it may, after Hoskuld's death his widow's uncle, the noble Flosi, is reluctantly drawn into the feud. As a result Njál is killed with his whole family by Flosi and others, and Flosi, in being responsible for this, becomes guilty of an heinous crime by the laws of his society as well as by his Christian faith.

But the author is not content with a series of tales of more or less

5 William Miller, 'Justifying Skarphéðinn'.

comparable feuds. He turns these into two parallel tragedies in which noble intentions, first of Gunnar and Njál and later of Flosi, are thwarted by circumstances and ultimately by the traditions of the society in which they live. *Njála* is a saga of the futility of human endeavour. It describes at length the incessant attempts of Njál to maintain the peace, with great wisdom and even a certain amount of foreknowledge. But these attempts are in vain. Njál does not foresee some of the misfortunes, such as the killing of Hoskuld. Some may even be traced to his advice. Thus the feud of Thráin and Njál's sons derives from the marriage of Thráin and Thorgerd with the blessing of Njál. From Gunnar's assistance to Unn, with Njál's support, springs her second marriage and of that is born the evil and envious plotter Mord. Even the death of Gunnar at the hands of his enemies may be traced in part to the counsels of Njál.

The tragedy of Gunnar is mainly a story of an individual hero blinded in a moment of weakness, unless he closed his eyes wilfully. But the saga as a whole can only be regarded as a social tragedy. The author describes Icelandic society and its laws and customs in detail, and he obviously holds in high regard many of its ideals of honour and in particular its respect for the law. But he is also fully aware of its primitive excesses. An Icelandic scholar once remarked that in *Njála* all the passions of humanity run wild, except the love of man and woman. It is true enough that even if the love of man and woman is certainly there – between Gunnar and Hallgerd, for instance, or Njál and Bergthóra – it never runs wild. But what really runs wild in *Njála* is not the passions of humanity but the society of feuding clans. As a social tragedy *Njála* is comparable to the tragedies of such nineteenth century writers as Balzac (*Père Goriot*) or Ibsen (*Ghosts*). It is in this respect not at all like Greek or Shakespearean tragedy, in spite of such common elements as the noble hero who fails through a single fault or flaw, and the presence of the envious plotter who brings down a prominent family, as Iago does in *Othello*.

IV

Fate

In Greek tragedy human beings are the puppets of fate. One of the oldest and most common conceptions of *Njála*, among scholars and critics, is that it expresses a profound fatalism. The nineteenth-century Swedish poet A. U. Bååth thought that the idea of fate held the whole of *Njála* together, for example through omens, premonitions and prophetic dreams.[6] The Icelandic novelist Halldór Laxness has written that *Njála* is above all a book about the fatalism of the pagan Norsemen, from the moment Hrút notices the thief's eyes of Hallgerd until the head is cut off the last burner mentioned in Flosi's dream. Thus the saga is deeply antithetical to Christianity, and the author to be regarded, for all his ecclesiastical learning, as a heathen sage.[7]

Fatalism is the belief that human beings are in the power of a hostile supernatural agency that may interfere in their affairs and turn even their wisest plans against them with the force of necessity. The tragedy of Oedipus is an example of this. He is destined to kill his father and marry his mother, and so he does, for all he and others try to do to prevent this catastrophe. Sometimes the agent of fate is a god, as when Artemis makes it inevitable for Agamemnon to sacrifice his daughter Iphigenia. Sometimes a human curse will do, as when Eteocles, cursed by Oedipus, is compelled to kill his own brother in *Seven Against Thebes*.

There is no fatalism in *Njála*. What may mislead readers, as it misled Bååth, is the occasional occurrence of omens, supernatural foresight – Njál has it and Snorri of Helgafell does not – and prophetic dreams such as Flosi's dream. But these do not add up to any kind of fatalism, any more than similar phenomena in our day do. People today have premonitions and think they have prophetic dreams. Many believe in astrology and even guide their lives by it. Such beliefs may be superstitious, but they certainly need not be fatalistic. For one thing, the hostility of the supernatural plan is

6 Lars Lönnroth, *Njáls Saga: A Critical Introduction*, p. 9.
7 *Brennunjálssaga*, edited by Halldór Kiljan Laxness, Reykjavík 1945, pp. 416–17.

missing, and even the mere idea of a plan. For another, there need not be any idea of necessity involved.

The case is the same with *Njála*. Hallgerd's theft from Otkel is neither planned nor necessitated in any way. All we can say is that it is in character, and that her uncle happened to discover what could be expected of her when she was a child. Character is not fate. Generally speaking, not a single action of any consequence is presented in *Njála* as being necessitated by fate or planned by any external power. The author's characters perform their actions of their own free will, and count as fully responsible for them. To an extent they are victims of chance, such as that of the meeting of Gunnar and Hallgerd which leads to their marriage, or that of the sons of Njál meeting Kári in Scotland. The tragic heroes Gunnar and Flosi do not bow to fate, or 'put on an harness of necessity' like Eteocles or Agamemnon. Their judgment fails, and they bow to the worst traditions of their community, even if they do not fail altogether ignobly, for a kind of honour is their motive. In this respect the author of *Njála* should not be compared to a Greek tragic poet, but to the historian Thucydides as described by Bernard Williams:

> Thucydides certainly believed that the world's course was not governed by supernatural purposes and also that *gnome* [human wisdom] could do something to control it, but he had a powerful sense of the limitations of foresight, and of the uncontrollable impact of chance.[8]

Ideas often associated with the alleged fatalism of *Njála* are those of *gæfa* and *ógæfa*, good and bad luck or fortune. These ideas are easily made to seem strange, for example the view that bad luck is somehow contagious as in the case of Thráin and Hrapp, or that it can be seen in the eyes of the child Hallgerd, or in the countenance and bearing of Skarphedin at the Althing. Such strange views may then be connected with the old Icelandic belief – not prominent in *Njála* even if it does occur – that a man's luck is a supernatural being that guards him and may leave him. In this last respect 'gæfa' may be compared to the Greek word 'eudaimonia' that plays a

8 Bernard Williams, *Shame and Necessity*, p. 150.

fundamental part in Aristotle's *Ethics*. This connotes the presence of a supernatural demon.

But *gæfa* and *ógæfa* are by no means essentially supernatural notions any more than *eudaimonia* is in Aristotle. And the natural elements of these ideas should not really seem strange at all, even in the drastic form they take in Hrút's comment about the thief's eyes of his niece. People do have traits of character over which they have minimal control, and signs of these may sometimes be detected in young children. And as far as contagiousness is concerned, a twentieth-century Justice of the United States Supreme Court – Louis Brandeis – once wrote that crime was contagious.

The words 'gæfa' and 'ógæfa', and various derivative words such as 'gæfumaður' (man of *gæfa*) and its opposite 'ógæfumaður', are alive and well in Icelandic to this day. They are perfectly ordinary words, and have their important uses along with words for happiness, luck, fortune and welfare and their opposites. But they have no exact equivalents in English. Nor does Aristotle's 'eudaimonia', for that matter. One kind of *ógæfumaður* in our day might be a criminal, an alcoholic or a drug addict. In calling him that we are removing from him some, but by no means all, of the blame for the way he has turned out. There may be a hint of *natural* necessity here – if we can say that nothing could have been done to prevent the outcome – but there is no suggestion of a hostile plan. We sometimes know that a love affair of a friend will be a disaster, and yet can do nothing to prevent it. It will just have to take its course. Anything we could say or do would only make matters worse. So whatever happens could not be helped. But this *ógæfa* has nothing to do with fate.

Just as there is no hostile plan for the *ógæfumaður*, there is no suggestion of a beneficent plan for the *gæfumaður*. The key to this notion is that the word 'gæfa' is cognate with the verb 'gefa', 'to give'. It refers to the good things given to you by nature, circumstances or pure chance. Hence *gæfa* is what you are or should be grateful for in life. You have not earned it, nor do you deserve it. Your *gæfa* is your blessings: perhaps your good health, happy marriage, or the fine way in which your children have turned out. For all this you are grateful without having anyone to offer your thanks to. This, of course, leaves room for a lot of gratitude to specifiable people, including yourself. Obviously a good marriage and the raising of children require a lot of effort. Some people will see their blessings and misfortunes in the light of their religious beliefs and thank God for the good things or blame the Devil for the bad. But this is inessential. The notions of *gæfa* and *ógæfa* can stand on their own without any supernatural agencies: for example, the idea that we may be grateful without being grateful to anyone. And there is no fatalism in this. Nor need fatalism enter the picture when we choose to personify the object of our gratitude in poetry, mythology or religion.

This is how the words 'gæfa' and 'ógæfa' are used in modern Icelandic, and they are, moreover, important words in the moral vocabulary of modern Icelanders. The question now arises: can we detect any differences between this usage and the usage of the same words in *Njála*? The answer must be a resounding no. The author of *Njála* conceives of *gæfa* and *ógæfa* in the same ways as we do. Hence it is only through an over-interpretation of his words that scholars have been able to read fatalistic beliefs into them.

In our time most people in the Western world will regard fatalism as a superstition. Yet the power of the Greek tragedies is unmistakable. What they demonstrate, through the operations of fate they describe, is the futility of human endeavour. Thus there is something to be learnt from them, and it is as if the lesson is being taught by a grim teacher. Supernatural fate may even be regarded as the poetic personification of this teacher. Aeschylus seems to think of fate in this way in a chorus from the *Agamemnon*. It is addressed to Zeus,

> Who setting us on the road
>   Made this a valid law –
>   'That men must learn by suffering.'
> Drop by drop in sleep upon the heart
> Falls the laborious memory of pain,
> Against one's will comes wisdom...

> (*Agamemnon* 176–181,
> translated by Louis MacNeice)

On the lesson itself, and even on the teaching by suffering, Aeschylus and the author of *Njála* would have seen eye to eye if they had been able to compare notes on the human condition. They would also have found much to agree on about societies groping their way towards the rule of law, and away from hereditary feuds or tribal war, a matter of great concern in the *Oresteia* as well as in *Njála*. But in the chorus from the *Agamemnon* Aeschylus goes on to say:

> The grace of the gods is forced on us
> Throned inviolably.

These ideas of force and inviolability are nowhere to be found in *Njála*.

V

Honour

This does not mean that the mediaeval Icelanders were not different from us in many ways. For example, they did not have our concept of murder. They had the word – 'morð' is the Icelandic form – and distinguished *morð* from *víg* or *dráp* (slaying, killing). But for them, and in their law, *morð* was only a secret killing, one not publicly acknowledged by the killer. This makes it less surprising than it otherwise would be that they were more prepared to commit what we call murder than we are. But we have our bloody habits too, for example in war. If we regard the mediaeval society of Iceland, as described in *Njála*, as a society in a permanent state of war, of clan against clan, we come to see similarities between them and us, in spite of their alien conceptions of killing. The barbarism of twentieth-century wars – or just of the violence in our films – even surpasses that of the battles in *Njála*.

In *Njála* people kill for the sake of honour. Hallgerd is responsible for the deaths of at least two of her husbands. Both had slapped her face. This was humiliation. Hallgerd's long feud with Bergthóra arises from a humiliating insult. Humiliation is one of the themes that become the subjects of endless variations in the saga. And humiliation and honour go hand in hand, for humiliation is an injury to one's honour. The importance of honour in *Njála* (and other sagas) is often said to reflect a special morality of honour which is sometimes said to be characteristic of shame cultures, for instance that of the Greece of Homer and the tragedians. Shame cultures are then distinguished from guilt cultures with their morality of conscience, regret and forgiveness. Fierce individualism is often supposed to be a further characteristic of shame cultures. Modern cultures are guilt cultures, and the morality of honour is thought to be outmoded in our times, at least in the Western world.

We need not examine the theory of shame cultures and guilt cultures. The idea that honour is an outmoded notion in our time seems reasonable enough at first sight, independently of anthropological conceptions of shame and guilt as cultural phenomena. For example, the duel is an institution which essentially involves honour. Duels are now illegal in our part of the world. And many other institutions of honour have disappeared. A friend told me he once saw a stout Swedish countess accompanied by two maids at a beach. The countess expressed her various wishes in a dignified manner. The two maids observed all the etiquette of the count's palais, with curtsies where appropriate, the only difference being that this was a nudist beach. They were all naked. This little comedy of manners illustrates the fate of much old-fashioned honour in our time.

In English-speaking countries explicit appeals to honour are now rare in ordinary moral discourse, and when they occur they are likely to sound pompous or at least quaint. In Iceland, however, the language of honour and dishonour is perfectly colloquial to this day. We say, as a matter of course, such things as 'My honour demands that I go to that meeting tonight', or 'My honour forbids . . .', or 'Now prepare well for the examination for the sake of your honour.' Sometimes we may translate such appeals to honour into English by saying that what my honour demands is my duty, or required by my conscience or self-respect, or that what my honour forbids is below my standards or beneath my dignity. But none of these are exact translations. In general, Icelandic locutions involving 'sómi' or 'sæmd' (honour) and 'skömm' (shame), and cognate and related words, are not literally translatable into English. They become quaint, like 'See your honour in going to that meeting.' And what is quaint about these is, among other things, the very use of 'honour'.

There seems no reason for saying that the modern Icelanders, with their free use of words like 'gæfa' and 'ógæfa', 'sómi' and 'skömm', in spite of their thousand years of Christianity and their modern welfare state, have a morality different from that of the British or the North Americans. This suggests that the differences between the moral vocabularies of contemporary English and Icelandic are superficial ones. We may then come to notice that even if honour is seldom appealed to in English, everyone knows what shame and humiliation are, and shame and humiliation are notions involving that of honour. Instead of honour in our examples above, we could talk of shame: 'You would be ashamed if you failed the exam.' In addition we might remind ourselves of various, though perhaps not very conspicuous, ideals of honour which are alive and well in our society. Such ideals include professional honour, for instance among doctors. Sometimes professions have a written code of ethics which includes a code of honour.

Now the question arises about *Njála*: is there any difference between the moral vocabulary of the saga and that of contemporary Iceland? Does the author of the saga use words like 'honour' or 'shame' and their cognates differently from us? As with his use of the words 'gæfa' and 'ógæfa', the answer must be a resounding no. The language of honour, like that of luck or fortune, is the same as ours.

'Sæmd' (honour) in *Njála* on occasion has the sense of financial recompensation. The word also occurs in this sense in the oldest Icelandic law. Similarly, 'fortune' in English may mean wealth. Under the rule of Norwegian kings respect, social standing and even honour itself came to be particularly associated with wealth in Iceland. But there are no signs of such ideas in *Njála*. Gunnar, the noblest of men, is at one point reduced to asking for assistance during a famine. This does not affect his honour in the slightest. Then there is the wonderful comedy of Bjorn of Mork in which an insignificant braggart is turned into an honourable man. In this episode it is the various details that count: Bjorn's attitude to his wife, his attitude to the claims of courage, his stand in the battle, his final request to Kári. Bjorn's honour is only partly deserved, as honour usually is. But honour it is.

Honour and shame are social phenomena. In this way, among others, honour is different from self-respect. Honour is interactive and depends on a certain consensus about what is honourable and dishonourable, while any fool can have self-respect. This may be thought to imply that honour and shame essentially depend on the received opinion of a community – on the consideration 'What will people say?' But it does not. There is, in Greek tragedy as well as in an Icelandic saga, plenty of room for a higher honour, independent of received opinion. In our time too. A French ambassador to Iceland was once by mistake given a place at table at a state dinner far below what diplomatic etiquette demanded. When the chief of protocol called on him the next day to apologise, the ambassador said: 'The seat of France is always a seat of honour.'

So there are different levels and types of honour. To many people in *Njála* killing is the only honourable thing to do in a feud. But over and over again we are told how the peaceful settlements entered by disputing parties serve precisely the honour of those concerned. A child who makes an insulting remark will often be scolded or even slapped for it, and the common view, now as in mediaeval Iceland, probably is that this is as it should be. So Hoskuld hits the boy who makes fun of the unconsummated marriage of Hrút and Unn. But Hrút gives the boy a ring with the admonition not to hurt anyone's feelings again. The incident, naturally enough, brings Hrút great honour. After the battle at the Althing Hall of Sída offers to make the sacrifice of asking no reparations for his fallen son. He knows this is humiliating. 'Now I shall show again that I am a humble man,' he says. 'An ignoble man' would be an alternative translation. But precisely this gains him great honour, and this is shown when the settlement is concluded.

The fundamental moral conceptions of *Njála* are shared by us. But the genius of its anonymous author is not.

THORSTEINN GYLFASON
University of Iceland

FURTHER READING

On Icelandic Literature

Theodore M. Anderson, *The Icelandic Family Saga*, Harvard
    University Press, Cambridge, Massachusetts 1967
Peter Hallberg, *The Icelandic Sagas*, translated by Paul Schach,
    University of Nebraska Press, Lincoln 1962
W.P. Ker, *Epic and Romance*, Dover, New York 1957
Jónas Kristjánsson, *Eddas and Sagas*, translated by Peter Foote,
    Hið íslenzka bókmenntafélag, Reykjavík 1997
G. Turville Petre, *The Origins of Icelandic Literature*, Oxford
    University Press, 1953

On *Njál's Saga* and Related Matters

Richard Allen, *Fire and Iron: Critical Approaches to Njáls Saga*,
    University of Pittsburgh Press, 1971
Nigel Balchin, 'Burnt Njal – The Irredeemable Crime', in *Fatal
    Fascination: A Choice of Crime*, Hutchinson, London 1964
Denton Fox, 'Njáls Saga and the Western Literary Tradition',
    Comparative Literature 15 (1963), 289-310
Halldór Kiljan Laxness (ed.), *Brennunjálssaga*, Helgafell, Reykjavík
    1945
Lars Lönnrot, *Njál's Saga: A Critical Introduction*, University of
    California Press, Berkeley 1976
William Miller, *Humiliation*, Cornell University Press, Ithaca
    1993
William Mille, 'Justifying Skarphéðinn', *Scandinavian Studies* 55
    (1983), 316-44
Einar Ólafur Sveinsson (ed.), *Brennunjálssaga*, Hið íslenzka
    fornritafélag, Reykjavík 1954
Einar Ólafur Sveinsson, *Njáls Saga: A Literary Masterpiece*, edited
    and translated by Paul Schach, University of Nebraska Press,
    Lincoln 1971

On Greek Tragedy

Bernard Williams: *Shame and Necessity*, University of California
    Press, Berkeley 1993

All these works have been drawn on in the introduction.

ACKNOWLEDGEMENTS

Many thanks are due to the Arnamagnean Institute of Copenhagen and its members for their hospitality in the early months of 1997, and for much help on various scholarly matters; to Benjamin Arnold of Reading, Bergljót Kristjánsdóttir of Copenhagen, Tom Griffith and Rosalind Hursthouse of Oxford, and Thorvaldur Gylfason, Helgi Hálfdanarson, Kristján Karlsson, Mikael Karlsson, Jónas Kristjánsson, Guðrún Nordal, Baldur Símonarson, Helgi Thorláksson and Örnólfur Thorsson of Reykjavík. Örnólfur Thorsson also prepared the family trees.

T.G.

NOTE ON THE TEXT

Nearly a century ago (1861) Sir George Webbe Dasent published a translation of the *Njáls saga*. This was republished and made more accessible in Everyman's Edition (1912) under the title of *The Story of Burnt Njál*.[1] A new translation seems called for, since Dasent's, though outstanding for its time, bears many earmarks of Victorian style (and prudery) less appropriate for rendering the realistic manner of Icelandic sagas.

The present translation is based on Finnur Jónsson's fine edition (Halle, 1908), which contains an excellent introduction and many valuable footnotes. On certain difficult passages we had the kind assistance of Professor Einar Ól. Sveinsson (Reykjavík), and were able to derive signal benefits from his new monumental Fornritafélag edition (1954) and his research in the origins and textual tradition of this saga. The translation of the skaldic verses was prepared by L. M. Hollander.

A word about the ever present (and insoluble) problem of the proper translation of Old Icelandic names. We have pursued a conservative middle course, translating a few and leaving others in their original form. We have deliberately written the Rangá River,

---

1 As suggested by the last line of the saga, *The Saga of Njál of the Burning* would have been a more accurate translation.

the Kringlumýr Swamp, and others, which, though tautological to the expert, should be no more offensive than, for example, the Rio Grande River or the City of Constantinople.

And a note to the reader: all names should be accented on the first syllable. Vowels have the Continental values; those marked with the acute are long, all others short.

We would express our thanks to the Columbia University Press for permission to reprint (with a few changes) the translation of the 'Song of the Valkyries' which appeared in *Old Norse Poems* (1936); and to the Albert Bonnier Publishing Company (Stockholm) for permission to use the maps prepared for Hjalmar Alving's Swedish translation of the saga. We are also grateful to the members of the Committee on Publications of the American–Scandinavian Foundation for their helpful interest; more especially to Dr Henry Goddard Leach and Mr Erik J. Friis for their energetic offices in seeing the book through to its completion.

C. F. B.
L. M. H.
1955

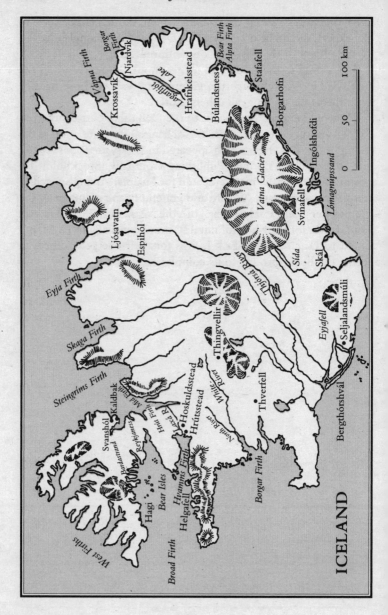

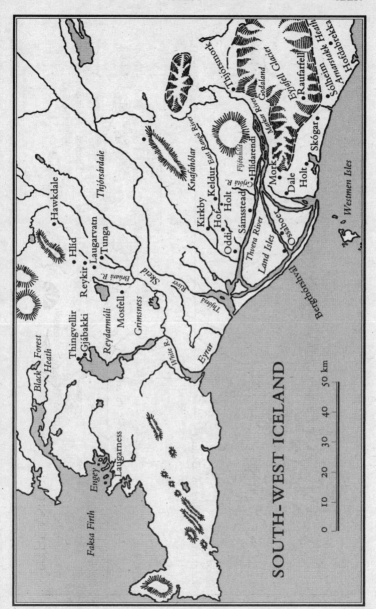

SOUTH-WEST ICELAND

The Family of Njál and Bergthóra

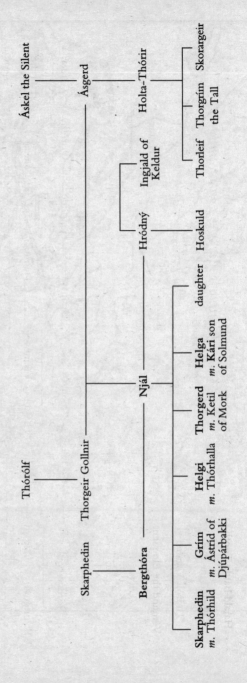

Gunnar's Ancestors and Family

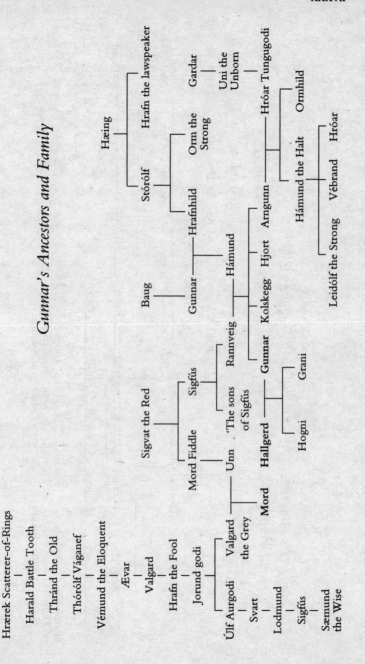

*Hallgerd's Ancestors
and Family*

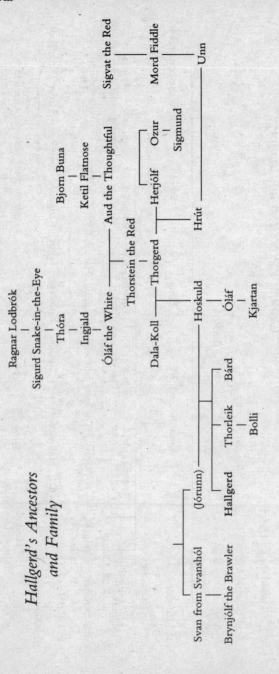

The Descendants of Sigvat the Red

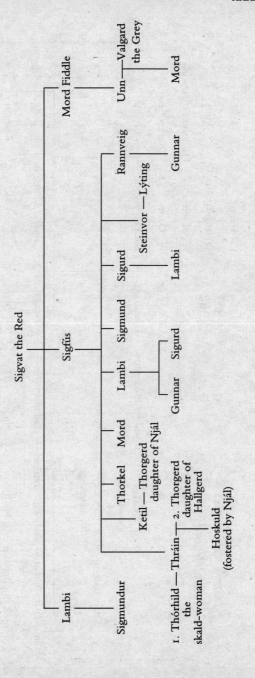

Flosi's Ancestors and Family

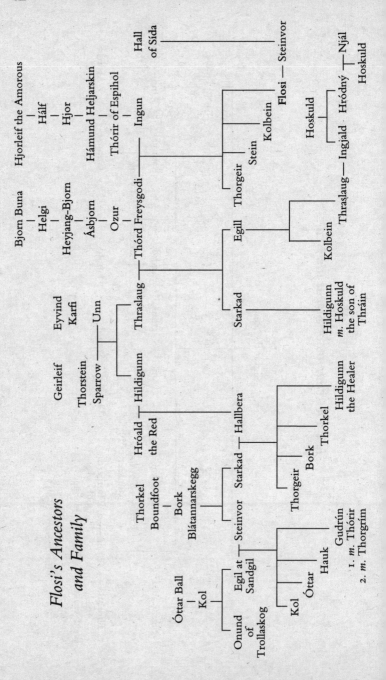

NJÁLS SAGA

I

Mord, Hoskuld, and their Kin

There was a man named Mord who was also known as Mord Fiddle.[1] He was the son of Sigvat the Red and dwelt at the farmstead called Voll in the Rangá River district.[2] He was a mighty chieftain and a man who was of great assistance in the prosecution of lawsuits. So great a lawyer was he that no judgements were considered valid unless he had a hand in them. He had a daughter named Unn. She was a beautiful woman, well bred and gifted, and considered the best match in the entire Rangá River district.

The saga now turns to the west, to the Broad Firth Dales.[3] Here there lived a man named Hoskuld Dalakollsson.[4] His mother was Thorgerd, the daughter of Thorstein the Red, the son of Óláf the White, the son of Ingjald, the son of Helgi. The mother of Ingjald was Thóra, the daughter of Sigurd Snake-in-the-Eye, the son of Ragnar Lodbrók.[5] Thorstein the Red's mother was Aud the Thoughtful, the daughter of Ketil Flatnose, the son of Bjorn Buna.

Hoskuld lived at Hoskuldsstead in Laxárdale. He had a brother named Hrút who lived at Hrútsstead. The latter had the same mother as Hoskuld, but his father was Herjólf. Hrút was a handsome man; he was tall and strong, skilled in arms, and yet of gentle disposition. He was one of the wisest of men; stern toward his enemies, but ready to help his friends in all important matters.

It happened one day that Hoskuld invited his friends to a feast, and his brother Hrút was there and occupied the seat beside him. Hoskuld had a daughter named Hallgerd who was playing on the floor with some other girls. She was beautiful and tall; her hair shone like silk and was so long that it came down to her waist. Hoskuld called to her: 'Come here, my daughter!'

She came to him immediately and he chucked her under the

chin and kissed her. After that she went away again. Then Hoskuld remarked to Hrút: 'What do you think of this girl? Don't you think she's beautiful?'

At first Hrút remained silent. When Hoskuld repeated the question Hrút answered: 'Beautiful this maiden certainly is, and many are likely to suffer for it; but I don't know whence thief's eyes have come into our kin!'

Hoskuld became angry at this remark, and for some time after this the relations between the brothers were strained. The brothers of Hallgerd were Thorleik, the father of Bolli; Óláf, the father of Kjartan;[6] and Bárd.

2

Hrút's Betrothal

It happened once that the two brothers, Hoskuld and Hrút, rode to the Althing;[1] many people were gathered there. Then Hoskuld said to Hrút: 'There is one thing that I would wish, brother, and that is that you marry and thereby better your position.'[2]

Hrút answered: 'I have had that in mind for a long time, but never could come to a decision about it. However, now I will do as you wish. Where do you think we should best turn our attention?'

Hoskuld answered: 'There are many chieftains here at the Assembly now and there is a good selection to choose from, but I have already decided on a certain match for you. The woman's name is Unn and she is the daughter of Mord Fiddle, one of the wisest of men. He is here at the Assembly with his daughter, and you can see her if you wish.'

The next day when court convened[3] they saw some well-dressed women standing before the booth of the men from the Rangá River district.[4] Then Hoskuld said to Hrút: 'There is Unn now, the one I told you about. What do you think of her?'

'I like her well enough,' he answered, 'but I am not so sure that we would be happy together.'

Thereupon they proceeded to the court. Mord Fiddle was

explaining the law and legal procedure, as was his custom, and he then returned to his booth. Then Hoskuld and Hrút arose and went to Mord's booth. They entered and greeted Mord who was sitting toward the rear. Mord arose to meet them and he took Hoskuld by the hand and had him sit down next to him. Hrút sat beside Hoskuld.

After they had talked about many different things, Hoskuld came to the point and said: 'I want to come to an agreement with you about this: Hrút wants to sue for the hand of your daughter, and I have assured him of my support.'

Mord answered: 'I know you are a great chieftain, but I know nothing about your brother.'

'And yet he is a better man than myself,' Hoskuld replied.

To this Mord answered: 'You will have to produce a considerable sum for him, for she is the heiress to everything I own.'

'You shall not have to wait long to hear what I propose to bestow on him,' said Hoskuld. 'Hrút shall have Kambsness and Hrútsstead and the land as far up as Thránd Chasm. He is, furthermore, the owner of a trading ship.'

Then Hrút said to Mord: 'Bear in mind now, freeholder, that my brother has praised me greatly because of his love for me, but if you will take the matter into consideration, I am willing that you name your own terms.'

Mord answered: 'I have already thought over the terms. She shall have sixty hundreds,[5] and that shall be increased by a third when she is married; but if you have heirs, the entire property shall be divided equally between you two.'

Hrút said: 'I accept these terms; now let us name witnesses to the agreement.'

After that they arose and shook hands, and Mord betrothed his daughter Unn to Hrút; the wedding was to take place at Mord's home half a month after midsummer.

Thereupon both parties rode home from the Assembly; Hoskuld and Hrút rode westward by way of Hallbjorn's cairns. Then Thjóstólf, the son of Bjorn Gullberi of Reykjardale, rode out to meet them and reported the arrival of a ship in White River. On board was Ozur, Hrút's uncle; and he urged Hrút to come and meet him as soon as possible. When Hrút learned this, he asked Hoskuld to accompany him to the ship. Hoskuld joined him and

when the two came to where the ship lay, Hrút gave his uncle
Ozur a warm and cordial welcome. Ozur invited them into his
booth to drink with him, and so they took the packsaddles from
the horses and entered and drank.

'Now, kinsman,' said Hrút to Ozur, 'I suggest that you ride
west[6] with me and stay with me this winter.'

'That cannot be, kinsman,' replied Ozur, 'for I have come to
report the death of your brother Eyvind and to inform you that he
named you his heir at the Gula Assembly. And your enemies will
seize this inheritance, if you don't come to claim it.'

'What do you advise me to do about it, brother?' asked Hrút.
'This looks like a difficult matter, now that I have already set my
wedding date.'

'You must ride south and speak to Mord,' Hoskuld answered.
'Ask him to postpone the date which you two have agreed upon.
Let his daughter remain at home for three years as your betrothed.[7]
In the meantime I shall ride home and bring your wares down to
the ship.'

Hrút said: 'It is my wish that you take flour and timber and
anything else you need from the cargo.'[8]

Hrút had his horses brought out and he rode south,[9] but Hoskuld
proceeded home to the west. Hrút rode to the Rangá River district
to Mord's farm and was well received by him. He explained to
Mord the circumstances that had arisen and asked him for his
opinion.

'How much does this inheritance amount to?' asked Mord.

Hrút answered it would amount to two hundred marks,[10] if he
got it all.

To this Mord replied: 'That is a great deal compared to what I
shall leave behind. You should certainly go, if you wish to.'

Thereupon they postponed the wedding date and Unn was to
remain at home for three years as Hrút's betrothed. Then Hrút
rode back to the ship and remained there during the summer until
he was ready to put to sea. Hoskuld brought all of Hrút's wares
down to the ship and Hrút placed in Hoskuld's hands the administration of his property during the time that he was to be abroad.
Thereupon Hoskuld rode home to his farm. Shortly thereafter
they got a favourable wind and set sail. After three weeks they
came to the Herney Islands[11] and they sailed eastward to Víken.[12]

3

Hrút Sails to Norway to Regain his Inheritance.
His Relations with Queen Gunnhild

At that time Harald Greyfur[1] was reigning in Norway. He was the son of Eirík Bloody-Axe, the son of Harald Fairhair. His mother was Gunnhild, the daughter of Ozur Tóti.[2] Gunnhild and her son Harald Greyfur had their residence at Konungahella[3] in the east of Norway.

Now the news was spread about that a ship had come from the west to Víken. As soon as Gunnhild learned of this, she asked what Icelanders there were aboard. She was told that one of them was named Hrút and that he was the son of Ozur's brother. Then Gunnhild said: 'I see plainly that he wants to claim his inheritance, but the fact is that a man named Sóti[4] already has it in his possession.'

Thereupon she summoned her squire, who was named Ogmund, and said: 'I wish that you go to Víken to meet Ozur and Hrút. Tell them that I should like to invite them both to spend the winter here. You may add that they will have a friend in me. If Hrút follows my counsel, I shall support him in the matter of his inheritance and in anything else with which he might be concerned. Furthermore, I shall speak a good word to the king in his behalf.'

With that Ogmund set out and found the two men. As soon as they learned that he was Gunnhild's squire they gave him a warm welcome. He conveyed his message to them secretly, whereupon they discussed their plans by themselves. Then Ozur said to Hrút: 'It seems to me, kinsman, that we have already made our decision.[5] You see, I know Gunnhild's disposition; as soon as we indicate that we do not want to come to her, she will drive us out of the country and take all our goods by force. But, if we go to her, she will render us all such honour as she has promised.'

Ogmund returned and when he came before Gunnhild, he told her of the result of his errand; that is, that the men would come.

Gunnhild said: 'That was to be expected, as Hrút is said to be a sensible man and well bred. Now keep a lookout and let me know when they approach the town.'

Hrút and Ozur went east to Konungahella and on their arrival they were met and welcomed by their kinsmen and friends. They enquired whether the king was in town and they were told that he was. Afterwards they met Ogmund who brought greetings from Gunnhild, adding that she could not invite them to her house before they had seen the king, because of the talk it might stir up[6] – 'and that it does not appear as though I were overeager to have them with me. But I shall put in a good word for them. Tell Hrút to speak up to the king and ask to be one of his retainers.'

'And here,' said Ogmund, 'is a robe of state, which she sends you, Hrút, and in which you must appear before the king.' With that he went away.

The following day Hrút said: 'Let us now go before the king.'

'That we will do,' said Ozur.

So they went, twelve of them in all, kinsmen and friends, and they came into the hall just as the king sat over his drink.[7] Hrút went up first and greeted the king. The king looked the man over carefully and saw that he was excellently apparelled. Then he asked him his name. Hrút told him.

'Are you an Icelander?' asked the king.

Hrút said that he was.

'What has brought you here to me?' asked the king.

'I have come to see you in your greatness, sire,' Hrút answered. 'Furthermore, I have come in the matter of a large inheritance which I have here in this land, and I shall need your help if I am to secure my rights.'

'I have promised every man the protection of the law in this country,' answered the king. 'Have you any other request of me?'

'Sire,' said Hrút, 'I should like to be accepted in your bodyguard and to be one of your men.'

To this the king made no answer, but Gunnhild spoke: 'It seems to me that this man is offering you a great honour, for if there were many such men in your bodyguard, it would in my opinion be very well manned.'

'Is he a clever man?' asked the king.

'He is both clever and energetic,' she answered.

'It seems best to me,' said the king, 'that you be given the rank which you have requested. However, out of respect for my honour and the custom of the land you should return to me after a half-month's time and then I shall make you one of my retainers. In the meantime let my mother look after you. After that interval, however, come back to me.'

Then Gunnhild said to Ogmund: 'Accompany these men to my establishment and have a good feast prepared for them there.'

Ogmund left the king's presence with them and brought them to a hall built of stone[8] which was hung with the most beautiful tapestry. There too was Gunnhild's high-seat. Then Ogmund said: 'Now you will see that what I told you about Gunnhild is true. Here is her high-seat. Sit down in it and keep this seat, even though she herself comes in.'

After that he prepared a feast for them. They had not been sitting there long before Gunnhild entered. Hrút was about to jump up and greet her.

'Keep your seat,' she said, 'as long as you are my guest!'

Thereupon she sat down beside Hrút and they drank together. Later in the evening she said: 'You shall lie with me tonight in the upper chamber, we two alone!'

'It is for you to command,' he answered.

Afterwards they went to her couch and she bolted the chamber door. They slept there that night and in the morning they drank together. Thus the two slept together in the upper chamber every night for the whole half-month. Gunnhild spoke to all those attending her: 'Don't say a word about my relations with Hrút if you value your lives!'

When the half-month was over, Hrút gave Gunnhild a hundred ells of dress material and twelve sheepskins, and she thanked him for the gifts. Hrút in turn thanked her with a kiss and then went away. She bade him farewell. Together with thirty men he went before the king on the following day and greeted him. The king said: 'I suppose you want to hold me to my promise now.'

Thereupon he appointed Hrút as one of his bodyguard. Hrút then asked: 'Where shall I sit?'

'My mother shall determine that,' answered the king.

Thereupon she secured the seat of greatest distinction for him and he spent the whole winter with the king and enjoyed great honour.

4

Queen Gunnhild Equips Hrút to Pursue Sóti

In the spring Hrút received information that Sóti had fared south to Denmark with the inheritance. Then he went to Gunnhild and told her of Sóti's journey.

Gunnhild said: 'I will supply you with two long-ships, fully manned, and along with all that one of the bravest men, Úlf the Unwashed, our supervisor of guests.[1] But in any case go and see the king before you set out.'

Hrút did so and when he came before the king, he told him of Sóti's journey and that he now was of a mind to pursue him.

The king asked: 'What assistance has my mother contributed?'

'Two long-ships and Úlf the Unwashed to command them,' replied Hrút.

'That is a generous gift,' said the king. 'Now I shall give you two additional ships, for you will need all of this force.'

After that he accompanied Hrút to the ship and bade him farewell. Hrút then sailed away to the south with his men.

5

Hrút Overcomes Atli and Recovers his Inheritance

There was a man named Atli, the son of Arnvid,[1] Earl of East
Gotland.[2] He was a great warrior and had had his haunt with a
fleet of six ships to the east in Lake Mälar.[3] His father had held
back his tribute from King Hákon, Aethelstan's foster son, and
then father and son had fled from Jämtland[4] to Gotland. Later Atli
had sailed with his fleet from Lake Mälar through Stock Sound
and then south to Denmark, and at this time was stationed in the
Öresund.[5] He had been outlawed both by the Danish king and
the Swedish king.

Hrút sailed south to the Öresund and found a great many ships
lying there in the passage. Then Úlf said: 'What's the best thing to
do now, Icelander?'

'Hold straight to our course,' Hrút answered, 'for nothing
ventured, nothing won! Ozur and I will go ahead with our ship,
but you can proceed as you wish.'

'Rarely have I made use of others as a shield before me,' said Úlf,
as he placed his galley beside that of Hrút. In this way they sailed
forward together into the sound. Now those deployed in the
sound saw ships advancing and they told Atli. He answered: 'Then
there will be good opportunity for booty.' – Thereupon they made
ready for combat on each ship. – 'But my ship shall be in the
middle of the fleet,'[6] said Atli.

Thereupon the ships advanced. As soon as they were within
hailing distance Atli stood up and said: 'You are not proceeding
very warily. Didn't you see that there were warships in the sound?
What is the name of your leader?'

Hrút gave his name.

'Whose man are you?' asked Atli.

'I am a member of King Harald Greyfur's bodyguard,' answered
Hrút.

'For the longest time there has been no love lost between us and the kings of Norway,' said Atli.

'So much the worse for you,' said Hrút.

To this Atli replied: 'Well, the outcome of our meeting will be that you will not live to tell the tale.' With that he picked up a spear and hurled it at Hrút's ship, and the man it struck fell dead immediately. Thereupon the battle started, but they were not very successful with their attack on Hrút's ships. Úlf advanced bravely, now thrusting and now cutting.

Ásolf was the name of Atli's forecastleman.[7] He leaped aboard Hrút's ship and killed four men before Hrút became aware of him and turned on him. When they met, Ásolf thrust at Hrút's shield and pierced it, but Hrút cut at Ásolf and dealt him his deathblow.

Úlf the Unwashed saw that and said: 'You deal out mighty blows, Hrút, but then you also have much to thank Gunnhild for!'

'It seems to me,' said Hrút, 'that these are the words of a doomed man!'

Right then Atli saw where Úlf was unprotected and hurled a spear through him. Then there was a fierce fight. Atli leaped aboard Hrút's ship and with mighty blows cleared a path for himself. Ozur turned to meet Atli and thrust at him, but he himself fell on his back as another man thrust at him. Hrút then turned to face Atli; he cut at Hrút and split his shield in two. At that moment a stone struck Atli on his hand and the sword fell from his grasp. Hrút picked up the sword and cut off Atli's leg and then dealt him his deathblow. Hrút and his men captured much booty here and they took with them the two best ships. They stayed there only a short while, but in the meantime Sóti and his company slipped by them and sailed back to Norway and landed at the Limgard coast.[8] There he met Ogmund, Gunnhild's man-in-waiting. Ogmund recognised Sóti at once and asked: 'How long do you plan to stay here?'

'Three days,' said Sóti.

'Where do you plan to go after that?' asked Ogmund.

'Out west, to England,' replied Sóti, 'and I'll never return to Norway as long as Gunnhild rules here!'

Ogmund left and sought Gunnhild, because she was not far away at a feast with her son Gudröd.[9] He told Gunnhild about Sóti's plans, and she immediately ordered Gudröd to kill him. Gudröd set out at once and came upon Sóti unawares. He had him brought to shore and hanged, and he took Hrút's inheritance and brought it back to his mother. She had men bring everything to Konungahella, and shortly after she went there herself.

Hrút sailed back in the autumn after he had amassed a great amount of booty. He went to the king immediately and received a hearty welcome. He invited the king and Gunnhild to help themselves to whatever they pleased of his goods, and the king took a third of it all. Gunnhild told Hrút that she had gotten hold of his inheritance and had had Sóti killed. He thanked her and gave her half of everything he had.

6

Hrút's Return and Marriage to Unn

Hrút stayed with the king that winter and was held in very high esteem, but when spring came he became very silent. Gunnhild observed this and asked him once when they were alone: 'Is melancholy plaguing you?'

Hrút answered: 'As the saying goes: "unhappy the man who lives in a foreign land." '

'Do you wish to return to Iceland?'

'That I do,' he replied.

'Is there some woman waiting for you out there?' Gunnhild asked.

'No,' he answered.

'I'm sure there is,' she said, and with that they broke off their conversation.

Later Hrút went before the king and greeted him. The king asked: 'What is it you wish, Hrút?'

Hrút answered: 'I would like to beg leave to go to Iceland, sire.'

'Will you have greater honour there than here?' asked the king.

'Very likely not,' answered Hrút, 'but everyone's course of life is laid out for him.'

'You have an obstinate man to deal with,' said Gunnhild. 'Give him permission to go as he desires!'

Harvests were poor in the land that year; still Gunnhild secured for Hrút as much flour as he wanted to have. Now he and Ozur made ready for the trip to Iceland. When they were all ready, Hrút went before the king and Gunnhild. She took him aside and said to him: 'Here is a gold ring which I wish to give to you.' With that she put it on him.

'Many good gifts have I received from you,' said Hrút.

She put her arms around his neck, kissed him, and said: 'If I have as much power over you as I think I have, then I cast this spell over you: that you may never be able to enjoy the love of that woman in Iceland on whom your heart is set. With other women, however, you may have your will. Both of us are ill bestead now; you did not put full trust in me.'[1]

Hrút laughed at this and left her. Later he went before the king and thanked him. The king was very friendly to him, wished him the best of luck on his voyage, and added that Hrút was one of the doughtiest of men and one who knew how to associate with men of noble birth.

After that Hrút went to his ship, set sail, and with a favourable wind made the Borgar Firth[2] in Iceland. As soon as the ship reached land, Hrút rode home to the west[3] while Ozur had the ship unloaded. Hrút rode to Hoskuldsstead. Hoskuld gave him a warm welcome and Hrút told him all about his travels. After that they sent a messenger eastward to Mord Fiddle with the request that he prepare for the wedding. But the two brothers rode to the ship, and Hoskuld told Hrút how he had administered his property and how it had increased in value while he had been away.

Hrút said: 'Your reward will probably be smaller than it ought to be, but I shall give you as much flour as you will need for your household this winter.'

Then they had the ship rolled up on land and covered up, but all the cargo they took westward to the Dales.

Hrút remained at home in Hrútsstead until six weeks before the beginning of winter.[4] Then the brothers and Ozur together with some sixty men made ready to ride east to Hrút's wedding. When they arrived at the Rangá River district, there were already many wedding guests there. The men were assigned to their seats, and the women to theirs on the dais. The bride was quite downcast. The feast then began and everything went off well. Mord paid out the dowry of his daughter, and she then rode west with her husband and his company. When they arrived at Hrútsstead, she was given the administration of everything within the house, and all seemed pleased with that. However, all winter long there was not much intercourse between the two as man and wife.

Thus things went on until spring. At that time Hrút had to make a journey to the West Firths[5] to collect money for wares which he had sold out there. Before he left, however, his wife asked him: 'Do you plan to return before the men ride to the Assembly?'

'Why do you wish to know?' he asked.

She answered: 'I wish to ride to the Assembly and see my father.'

'You can do that,' he said, 'and I will ride to the Assembly with you.'

'That is fine,' she answered.

Thereupon Hrút rode away to the West Firths, collected the money, loaned it out again, and then rode home. After he had returned from the west, he prepared for the trip to the Althing and had all his neighbours ride with him. Hoskuld, his brother, also rode along. Then Hrút said to his wife: 'If you are just as eager to go to the Assembly as you indicated, then get ready and ride along with me.'

She got ready quickly, and thereupon they all rode to the Assembly. Unn went to the booth of her father where she was warmly welcomed. However, she seemed somewhat depressed, and when her father noticed that, he said to her: 'I have seen you with a happier expression. Is there something weighing on your mind?'

She began to weep, but gave no answer. Then he asked her: 'Why did you ride to the Assembly, if you don't want to confide in me? Don't you like living out in the west?'

She answered: 'I would give everything I own if I had never gone out there!'

Mord replied: 'I'll soon get to the bottom of this.'

He sent out a messenger to fetch Hoskuld and Hrút, and they came immediately. When they arrived before Mord, he arose, greeted them cordially, and asked them to sit down. They talked together for a long time in friendly fashion. Then Mord asked Hoskuld: 'Why is my daughter so unhappy out there in the west?'

'Let her speak out,' said Hrút, 'if she has any complaint to make against me!'[6]

However, she brought no charges against Hrút. Then Hrút had

his neighbours and the members of his household questioned as to his treatment of Unn. They all bore him good witness and said that he gave her free hand to do just as she pleased.

Then Mord said: 'Go home now and be content with your marriage, for everybody speaks better of him than of you.'

After that Hrút and his wife rode home from the Assembly and things went smoothly between them that summer. But when winter came, it was the same old story again, and things grew even worse during the spring. Hrút again had to travel to the West Firths, and he announced that he would not ride to the Althing. Unn had very little to say about this; so Hrút rode away to the West Firths.

7

Unn Divorces Hrút

Now the time for the Assembly drew near. Unn spoke with Sigmund Ozurarson[1] and asked if he would ride to the Assembly with her. He said he would not ride there, if his kinsman Hrút were in any way opposed to it.

'Well,' she said, 'I've asked you because I thought I had more right to ask this of you than of any other man.'

He answered: 'I will make this condition: you must ride back west with me and you must not have any underhand dealings against Hrút or myself.'

She promised that, and thereupon they rode to the Assembly.

Her father Mord was at the Assembly. He welcomed her and asked her to stay in his booth during the meeting of the Assembly. This she did.

Mord asked: 'What do you have to tell me about your husband Hrút?'

She answered: 'I can report nothing but good of him as far as his intentions are concerned.'

Mord was silent for a while and then said: 'You have something on your mind, my daughter, which you don't want anyone else to know but myself, from whom you can best expect help in your troubles.'

Then they went aside where no one could hear them talk.[2] Mord spoke to his daughter: 'Now tell me everything about you two and don't be afraid to tell me the whole story!'

'So it shall be,' she answered. 'I would like to be divorced from Hrút, and I can tell you what particular reason I have for it. He is not able to have marital intercourse with me in any such manner that I can enjoy. In all other respects he has the ways of other excellent men.'

'I don't quite understand,' said Mord; 'be more specific.'

She answered: 'Whenever he comes to me in bed his member is so large that he cannot gratify himself with me; and yet we have tried all ways to have intercourse, but always unsuccessfully. Yet before we part he shows that he is as passionate as other men.'

Mord said: 'You have done well to tell me this. Now I shall give you a bit of advice which will help you, if you follow it and carry it out exactly as I tell you. First ride home from the Assembly; your husband will have come home by that time and will be glad to see you. Be friendly and agreeable to him and he will think things have taken a turn for the better. You must give no indication of displeasure on your part. But when spring comes you must sham illness and take to your bed. Hrút will have no idea of the nature of your illness nor will he scold you at all. On the contrary, he will request all to take as good care of you as possible. After that he will ride out to the West Firths and Sigmund will travel with him. He will bring all his goods from the west and he will be away until far into the summer. But when men ride to the Assembly and all those from the Dales who plan to go have departed, then rise from your bed and summon men to accompany you to the Assembly. When you are ready, step up to your bed with the men who are to accompany you. You shall name witnesses there beside your husband's bed and declare yourself divorced from him by a legal separation.[3] Your declaration must be as correct and precise as possible in accordance with the language of the Althing and the laws of the land. You shall then name witnesses a second time at the main door. After that ride away over the Laxárdale Heath and continue on to Holtavorda Heath, since they will not look for you along the Hrút Firth. Ride on then until you come to me, for I'll take care of this matter; and never again shall you come into his hands!'

Thereupon she rode home from the Assembly; Hrút had already come home and was glad to see her. She returned his friendly greetings in like fashion and acted very kindly toward him. Their relations were good that year. When spring came, however, she fell ill and took to her bed. Hrút rode off to the West Firths, but before he left, he gave orders to the members of his household to take good care of her.

Now when it was time for the Assembly, Unn prepared to leave. She did everything as Mord had told her, and then rode to the Assembly. The people of the district tried to find her, but could not. Mord welcomed his daughter and asked her if she had followed his instructions, and she answered: 'In every respect have I done as you advised.'

Mord then went to the Law-Mount and gave public notice of Unn's divorce from Hrút. This was big news for everyone. Unn returned home with her father and never again went back to the west.

8

Hrút Refuses to Return Unn's Dowry

When Hrút came home and learned that his wife was gone, he was extremely put out. However, he controlled his feelings very well and remained at home this entire summer and the following winter without discussing the matter with anyone. The following summer he rode to the Assembly with his brother Hoskuld and a large following. When he came to the Assembly, he asked whether Mord Fiddle was there, and he was told that he was. Everyone thought they would talk about the divorce, but that was not the case.

One day when the people went to the Law-Mount, Mord named witnesses and announced a money suit against Hrút for the return of the dowry of his daughter, and he set the amount at ninety hundreds. He proclaimed a demand for payment and delivery of this amount and a penalty of three marks if not paid promptly. He made this proclamation in the Quarter Court before which it should come by law, and he made this legal proclamation so that all who were at the Law-Mount might hear it.

After he had spoken this, Hrút answered: 'You are carrying on your daughter's suit more out of desire for strife and greed for gain than in any spirit of good will and manliness. However, I'll counter with this: the money now in my possession is not in your hands yet. I now make this statement, so that all who hear it on the Law-Mount may bear witness: I challenge you to the holm.[1] The whole dowry shall be at stake. Furthermore, I'll put up an equal sum and the entire amount shall belong to the one who defeats the other. However, if you will not fight with me, then you will have to give up all claim to the money.'

Then Mord became silent and took counsel with his friends as to the advisability of accepting the challenge. The *goði* Jorund[2] spoke: 'You don't need any advice from us in this matter, for you know that you will lose both your life and the money if you fight with

Hrút. He is a formidable opponent; he is powerful and very brave.'

Then Mord declared that he would not fight with Hrút, where-upon there was a great amount of shouting and hooting at the Law-Mount, and Mord received the greatest humiliation from this suit. Finally people rode home from the Assembly.

The brothers Hoskuld and Hrút rode west to Reykjardale and stopped off at Lund. At that time Thjóstólf, Bjorn Gullberi's son, lived there. It had rained hard all day, and the men had become wet; so fires were kindled for warming and drying them. Thjóstólf, the master of the house, sat between Hoskuld and Hrút, and two boys, wards of Thjóstólf, were playing on the floor. There was a little girl playing with them and they chattered a great deal, little knowing what they were saying. One of the boys said: 'I'll be Mord and I'll bring suit against you so that you lose your wife on the grounds that you couldn't copulate with her!'

The other boy answered: 'I'll be Hrút and I'll refuse you the money, if you are afraid to fight with me!'

They repeated this several times and thus caused great laughter among the household. Then Hoskuld became angry, took a switch, and hit the boy who called himself Mord. The blow struck the boy in the face and broke his skin.

Hoskuld said to the boy: 'Get out of here and don't make fun of us!'

But Hrút said: 'Come here to me!'

The boy did so, and Hrút took a ring from his finger and gave it to him. 'Go away now,' he said, 'and don't hurt anyone's feelings again!'

As the boy went away, he said: 'I shall never forget your noble-mindedness.'

The incident brought Hrút much praise. After that they went home to the west, and that is the end of the story about Mord and Hrút.

9

Thorvald Sues for the Hand of Hallgerd

Now the saga continues with Hallgerd, Hoskuld's daughter, and how she grew up to be a most beautiful woman. She was of tall stature, whence people called her 'Longlegs'. Her hair was fair and so long that she could cover herself completely with it. She was headstrong and of harsh disposition. Her foster father, who came from the Hebrides, was named Thjóstólf. He was a strong man and well skilled in arms. He had slain many men and had never paid reparations for any one of them. It was said that he was hardly the type of man to improve Hallgerd's character.

There was a man named Thorvald Ósvífrsson who lived at Medalfell Strand[1] at a farm called Under the Fell. He was a wealthy man who owned the islands called Bear Isles, which lie out in the Broad Firth;[2] from there he used to procure his dried fish and flour.[3] Thorvald was strong and well bred, but somewhat quick-tempered.

It happened once that Thorvald and his father were discussing the matter of Thorvald's marriage. It was soon evident that Thorvald was of the opinion that a suitable match could be found not too far away.

Then Ósvíf asked: 'Do you mean to ask for the hand of Hallgerd Longlegs, Hoskuld's daughter?'

'Yes, I do,' he replied.

'You two wouldn't have too easy a time in making a go of it,' said Ósvíf, 'because she is a woman of proud mind, and you are stern and unyielding.'

'All the same I shall sue for her hand,' Thorvald answered; 'so there is no use in trying to dissuade me.'

'Well, you are the one who has most to lose,' said Ósvíf.

After that they set out to press their suit for Hallgerd and came to Hoskuldsstead where they were well received. They immediately discussed their mission with Hoskuld and asked for Hallgerd's hand.

Hoskuld answered: 'I am familiar enough with you men and your position and means, but I would not like to deceive you about the fact that my daughter is of a harsh disposition. As far as her looks and breeding are concerned, however, you can judge for yourselves.'

Thorvald answered: 'Name the conditions, because I will not let her quick temper stand in the way of this bargain!'

Thereupon they discussed the matter; Hoskuld did not ask his daughter for her opinion,[4] because he was eager to marry her off. They agreed to the terms of the match, whereupon Thorvald was betrothed to Hallgerd. After all arrangements had been made, Thorvald and Ósvíf rode home.

10

Hallgerd Marries Thorvald

When Hoskuld told Hallgerd about the match he had made, she replied: 'Now I have the proof of what I have long suspected! You do not love me as much as you always protested you did, since you didn't take the trouble to discuss the matter with me. For that matter, this match isn't as good a one as you have always promised you would make for me.'

It was very evident that she considered herself thrown away in a marriage below her social station.

Hoskuld said: 'Your pride hasn't so much weight with me as to let it stand in the way of the arrangements I have made. It is I who will decide, and not you, whenever we differ!'

Hallgerd replied: 'You and your kinsmen are so filled with arrogance that it isn't a wonder if I have some of it!'

With that she went away. She found her foster father Thjóstólf and told him what had been planned for her, and she was very depressed in spirit.

Thjóstólf said: 'Cheer up! You will be married a second time, and then you shall be asked for your consent; for in all matters I shall do as you ask me to except where your father or Hrút are concerned.' After that they said no more about the matter.

Hoskuld prepared for the wedding feast and rode away to invite guests. He came to Hrútsstead and had Hrút called out of the house to speak with him. When he came out, they went aside and Hoskuld told him all about the suit and invited him to the wedding. – 'I hope you do not take it amiss that I did not inform you when the arrangements were made,' he added.

'I would prefer to have as little as possible to do with it,' answered Hrút, 'for there will be no luck in this match, either for him or for her. However, I shall in any case come to the wedding if you think it will be to your honour.'

'Indeed it will,' said Hoskuld; and with that he rode home.

Ósvíf and Thorvald also invited people to come to the wedding, so that no fewer than a hundred were invited.

There was a man named Svan[1] who lived at a farm called Svanshól in the Bear Firth; Svanshól lies to the north of the Steingríms Firth.[2] Svan, who was the brother of Hallgerd's mother, was a great wizard. He was quarrelsome and very hard to deal with. Hallgerd, however, sent Thjóstólf to Svan to invite him to the wedding. Thjóstólf went and there was very soon a close friendship between him and Svan.

Now the people came to the wedding, and the bride Hallgerd sat upon the cross-bench[3] and was in excellent spirits. Thjóstólf kept coming over to speak to her, but at times he also spoke with Svan, so that people wondered what they might be talking about. The wedding feast went off well and Hoskuld paid out Hallgerd's dowry with the greatest readiness. Then he asked Hrút: 'Shall I add any other gifts to this?'

'You will have opportunity soon enough to lay out money for Hallgerd!' Hrút answered. 'So let that be sufficient for now!'

II

Thorvald is Murdered by Thjóstólf

Thorvald rode home from the wedding, and with him rode his wife and Thjóstólf. The latter rode close to Hallgerd, and the two kept talking together in a low voice. Ósvíf turned to his son and asked: 'Are you satisfied with this match? How did things go when you talked together?'

'Very well,' he answered; 'she was all sweetness to me. You can see that yourself from the way she laughs at every word I say.'

'I don't think so much of her laughter as you do,' said Ósvíf, 'but we shall see what we shall see.'

Thus they rode until they came home. In the evening Hallgerd sat beside her husband and made room for Thjóstólf next to her at her right. There were not many words wasted between the two, Thjóstólf and Thorvald, nor did they have much to do with one another throughout the winter.

Hallgerd was both greedy and wasteful; she kept a big house and lived in great style, and when spring came there was a lack of provisions, and they had run out of both flour and dried fish. Hallgerd came to speak with Thorvald and said: 'You just can't sit around doing nothing! We need both flour and dried fish in the household.'

Thorvald answered: 'I didn't lay in any smaller supply this year than in other years; yet it always used to last until summer.'

Hallgerd said: 'It's of no concern to me if you and your father saved money by starving yourselves!'

Then Thorvald became angry and struck her in the face and drew blood. After that he went away and called his servants to follow him. They launched a skiff and eight of his men jumped in. They rowed out to the Bear Isles where they got their dried fish and flour.

We are told that Hallgerd sat outside, in front of the house, and was very depressed. Thjóstólf came up to her, saw that her face was bleeding, and asked: 'Why have you been mistreated like this?'

'It is my husband Thorvald who has done it,' she said, 'and you were not around at the time, though you would have been, if you cared at all for me.'

'I didn't know anything about it,' he replied, 'but avenge it I will!'

After that he went down to the shore and pushed out a six-oared boat. In his hand he carried a large axe which belonged to him and which had a shaft wound about with gold wire. He stepped into the boat and rowed out to the Bear Isles. When he arrived there, all the other fishermen had gone except Thorvald and his men. Thorvald was busy loading the skiff and his men were carrying the goods down to him. At this moment Thjóstólf came up, jumped on the skiff, and began to help with the loading. Then he said: 'You don't have the necessary strength for this work, and besides you don't know how to load anyway!'

Thorvald answered: 'So you think you could do it better?'

'There is hardly a thing I can't do better than you,' he said. 'The woman who has you for a husband has made a poor marriage, and by rights you shouldn't be together much longer!'

Thorvald picked up a knife, which lay beside him, and stabbed at Thjóstólf. But the latter had raised his axe to his shoulder and now it crashed down on Thorvald's arm, so that the wrist was broken and the knife fell to the ground. Then Thjóstólf raised his axe a second time and drove it into Thorvald's head, so that he fell dead on the spot.

12

Compensation is Paid by Hoskuld

At this moment Thorvald's men came down with their loads. Thjóstólf did not hesitate very long, but wielding his axe with both hands he hewed at the side of the skiff and smashed the planks the length of two thwarts, and then jumped into his boat. The cold blue sea rushed into their skiff and down it went with all its freight. Down also went Thorvald's body, so that his servants could not see what had been done to him; but one thing they knew for certain and that was that he was dead.

Thjóstólf rowed up the fjord, while Thorvald's men cursed him and wished him every kind of bad luck. He didn't answer, but rowed on until he came home. Then he drew the boat up on land and went up to the farm. The axe, which he carried on his shoulder, was all covered with blood. Hallgerd happened to be outside and she said: 'Your axe is bloody! What have you done?'

I have now seen to it,' he replied, 'that you can be married a second time!'

'You are telling me that Thorvald is dead!' she said.

'That's right,' he replied, 'and now think of some way to help me to safety.'

'That I will,' she said. 'I will send you north to Svanshól in the Bear Firth. Svan will receive you with open arms, and he is a man so mighty that no one will try to attack you there.'

He saddled a horse which belonged to Hallgerd, mounted it, and rode north to Svanshól in the Bear Firth. Svan received him with open arms and asked him for news; whereupon Thjóstólf told him about the slaying of Thorvald and how it had come to pass.

Svan said: 'That's what I call a real man, one who doesn't flinch at anything. I'll promise you this: if they attack you here, they will get nothing but the greatest humiliation for their efforts!'

Now to return to Hallgerd: she asked Ljót the Black,[1] a kinsman of hers, to saddle their horses and ride with her – 'because I want to ride home to my father.'

While he prepared for the trip, she went to her chests, unlocked them, called all the members of the household around her, and then gave some gift to each one of them. They were all very sad to see her go. Thereupon she rode home to her father, who was very happy to see her, for he had not yet heard the news. Hoskuld asked her: 'Why didn't Thorvald come with you?'

She answered: 'Because he is dead!'

Hoskuld said: 'I suspect that Thjóstólf did it!'

She said it was so.

'Rarely has it happened that Hrút was wrong in his predictions,' remarked Hoskuld. 'In this case he said that this match would only result in misfortune, but there is no use crying over spilt milk.'

Now to return to Thorvald's men; they had to wait until ships came from the mainland. They reported the slaying of Thorvald and asked to be taken to the mainland. That was done right away and they rowed to Reykjaness,[2] found Ósvíf, and told him the tidings.

He said: 'Ill hap is bound to follow ill counsel! I can see now how it all happened. Very likely Hallgerd sent Thjóstólf to the Bear Firth and she herself probably rode home to her father. We will now gather men and pursue him up in the north.'

This they did; they went about asking for support and were successful in getting many men. They rode to the Steingríms Firth and then to Ljótárdale and Selárdale[3] and finally came to the Bear Firth.

At this time Svan began to yawn a great deal and he said: 'Now the *fylgjur*[4] of Ósvíf are approaching.'

Thjóstólf jumped up and reached for his axe, but Svan said: 'Follow me! This will not require many measures on our part.'

So the two of them went out. Svan took a goatskin and wrapped it around his head[5] and spoke: 'Let there be mist and mischief, and let marvels eke befall all those who as foes seek you!'[6]

Now to tell how Ósvíf and his men rode along the mountain ridge.[7] They were met by a thick fog and Ósvíf said: 'This is Svan's doing, and we shall be lucky if no worse follows.'

A little while later great darkness fell on their eyes, so that they could see nothing. They dropped from their saddles and lost their horses; some fell into bogs and some lost their way in the woods so as to come to harm, and they lost their weapons too.

Then Ósvíf said: 'If I could only find my horses and weapons again, I would turn back.'

As soon as he had said this, they were again able to see somewhat and they found their horses and weapons. Then many of the men urged that they continue with their pursuit. They did so and the same foul play happened again. This went on three times.

Then Ósvíf said: 'Our expedition has not been successful, but now we shall turn back all the same. I shall try something else. I have in mind to go to Hoskuld and demand reparations for the death of my son; for "where honour dwells 'twill be given to all"!'[8]

Thus they rode from there to the Broad Firth Dales, and nothing much occurred before they arrived at Hoskuldsstead. Hrút had just arrived there from Hrútsstead. Ósvíf asked Hrút and Hoskuld to come out and both did so. They greeted him and then they stepped to one side to talk together.

Hoskuld asked Ósvíf where he had come from just then; and he answered that he had gone out to look for Thjóstólf, but had not been able to find him. Hoskuld remarked that he had probably gone north to Svanshól – 'and it isn't an easy matter for just anyone to catch him there.'

'That is the reason I have come here,' said Ósvíf, 'because I mean to ask you for reparations for my son.'

Hoskuld answered: 'I didn't slay your son and neither did I plot his death. Nevertheless, you can't be blamed for looking for reparations somewhere.'

Then Hrút spoke up: ' "Next is nose to eyes!",[9] brother. It is important that we avoid scandal by paying him reparations for his son, and thus mend your daughter's state; because that is the only way to avoid scandal, and it is better all around that there be little talk about this business.'

Hoskuld asked: 'Would you care to make the award?'

'Gladly,' replied Hrút; 'nor shall I deal gently with you in my award, for to say the truth, it is your daughter who is responsible for his death.'

Hrút was silent for a while; then he stood up and said to Ósvíf: 'Take my hand now as a token that you agree to drop the suit.'

Ósvíf stood up and said to Hoskuld: 'It isn't likely to be a settlement satisfactory to both parties if one's brother is to make the award; and yet you have shown such good will, Hrút, that I trust you to make a fair award.'

With that he took Hoskuld's hand and they agreed on the award which Hrút was to make and deliver before Ósvíf went away. Thereupon Hrút made the award and said: 'For the slaying of Thorvald I award two hundreds of silver' – that was then considered a very good wergild for a man[10] – 'and that is to be paid immediately, Hoskuld, to Ósvíf's complete satisfaction.'[11]

This Hoskuld did. Then Hrút said to Ósvíf: 'As a present I wish to give you this good cloak which I brought with me from Norway.'

Ósvíf thanked him for the gift and went home, well satisfied with the way things had gone. Later Hrút and Hoskuld went to Fell for the division of the property with Ósvíf, and here again they settled everything in amicable fashion and then returned home with their share of the property.[12] Now Ósvíf is out of the saga.

Hallgerd asked Hoskuld whether Thjóstólf might come to live at Hoskuldsstead, and he granted her request. For a long time there was still much talk about Thorvald's slaying. Hallgerd's property continued to increase in value and amounted to a considerable sum.

13

Glúm Sues for the Hand of Hallgerd

Three brothers are now introduced in the saga:[1] one was named Thórarin, the second Ragi, and the third Glúm. They were the sons of Óleif the Halt and were men of great distinction and wealth. Thórarin also had the surname Ragi's brother; he was the law-speaker after Hrafn Hœingsson.[2] Thórarin was a very wise man and he and Glúm shared the farm at Varmalœk.[3] Glúm was a tall, strong, and handsome man, and had long lived abroad. Their brother Ragi was known as a great slayer of men. The brothers owned the farms of Engey and Laugarness in the south in common.[4]

Once the brothers Glúm and Thórarin were talking together, and Thórarin asked Glúm whether he planned to go abroad, as was his custom.

He answered: 'I had rather thought of giving up these trading voyages.'

His brother asked: 'What do you have in mind then? Do you wish to get married?'

'Yes, I would like to,' he answered, 'if I could find a good match for myself.'

Thórarin then enumerated the unmarried women in the Borgar Firth district and asked Glúm if he cared to marry any one of them. – 'If you do, I will ride there with you.'

Glúm answered: 'No, I don't care to marry any of these.'

'Then name me one you would like to have,' said Thórarin.

Glúm answered: 'If you want to know, her name is Hallgerd, and she is the daughter of Hoskuld out west in the Dales.'[5]

'The maxim "one man's woe is another man's warning" is not heeded by you,' said Thórarin. 'She has already been married once, and she was the cause of her husband's death.'

Glúm said: 'It may be that such a misfortune will not happen to her a second time. I know for a certainty that she will not cause my death. You will do me great honour, if you accompany me when I ask for her hand.'

Thórarin replied: 'It will be no use trying to prevent this. That which is fated to happen will certainly come to pass.'

Glúm often brought this matter up in talking with Thórarin, but for a long time his brother kept making excuses and putting it off. Finally, however, it did come about that they gathered men and rode westward twenty men strong to the Dales to Hoskuldsstead. Hoskuld gave them a cordial welcome and they stayed there that night. Early the next morning Hoskuld sent for Hrút and he came immediately. Hoskuld was outside as he rode into the courtyard and he told Hrút who had come.

'What do you suppose their errand can be?' asked Hrút.

'As yet they have not brought up any business,' replied Hoskuld.

'Yet their business is likely to be with you,' said Hrút. 'They will probably ask for the hand of your daughter Hallgerd. What will you answer to that?'

'What would you advise?' asked Hoskuld.

'Give them a friendly answer, but tell them all about her vices as well as her virtues,' said Hrút.

While the brothers were conversing, the guests came out of the house. Hoskuld and Hrút went to meet them; Hoskuld greeted them cordially, and Hrút also welcomed Thórarin and his brother. After that the four men conversed and Thórarin spoke: 'I have come here, Hoskuld, with my brother Glúm to ask in his behalf for the hand of your daughter Hallgerd. I can tell you that he is an accomplished man.'

'I know that you and your brother are both very respected men,' said Hoskuld, 'but I would like to tell you frankly that I arranged her first marriage for her and it turned out to be a great misfortune for us.'

Thórarin answered: 'We will not let that stand in the way of our bargain. What happened once doesn't necessarily have to happen again. This time it may work out well, even though it went badly the first time. Besides, it was Thjóstólf who was most to blame anyway.'

Then Hrút said: 'There is one bit of advice I would like to give you, if you will not let that which has already happened to Hallgerd stand in the way of the match, and that is that Thjóstólf does not go to live with her in the south, if the marriage does take place. He should never stay there longer than three days at a time, unless Glúm gives him permission, but should fall at the hands of Glúm as an outlaw, if he stays longer. Of course, Glúm might grant him permission to stay longer, but that would not be my advice. Also, you should not proceed as you did the first time and do this without Hallgerd's knowledge. She should learn all about the suit, see Glúm, and decide for herself whether she wants him or not. Then she won't be able to blame anyone else if it does not work out well. The entire business should be open and above board.'

Thórarin replied: 'Now, as usual, it is best that your counsel should prevail.'

Then they sent for Hallgerd and she came, and there were two women with her. She wore a cloak of blue woven material and beneath it a scarlet skirt and a silver belt about her waist. She sat down between Hrút and her father. She greeted them all with friendly words, spoke frankly and in a forthright manner, and asked what the tidings were. After that she ceased speaking.

Glúm said: 'My brother Thórarin and I have already spoken with your father about a certain matter. It is that I should have you as a wife, Hallgerd; that is, if it is your wish as it is theirs. If you are a woman who knows her own mind, you will now tell us whether this match is to your liking. However, if you are not interested in this marriage, then we will say no more about it.'

Hallgerd said: 'I know that you brothers are men of great worth and I also know that I will be wedded much better this time than before. But first I would like to know what you have already talked about and how far you have already come in the discussion of the matter. I will say this, however: I have the feeling that I might be able to love you, if our temperaments agree at all.'

Glúm himself told her all about the negotiations without deviating from the truth in any way, and he asked Hoskuld and Hrút whether he had repeated it correctly. Hoskuld said that he had.

Then Hallgerd said: 'Since you, father, and you, Hrút, have taken this matter up with so much consideration for me, I will do what you have advised. Let this bargain stand as you have agreed.'

Hrút then said: 'I think it is best that Hoskuld and I name witnesses, but that Hallgerd betroth herself, if that procedure seems correct to you as a legal authority, Thórarin.'

'Correct it is,' answered Thórarin.

After that Hallgerd's property was evaluated. It was then agreed that Glúm put up an equivalent amount, and that they share equally in the entire estate. Thereupon Glúm was betrothed to Hallgerd, and after that the brothers rode back to their home in the south. Hoskuld was to hold the wedding at his home. All was now quiet until it was time to ride to the wedding.

14

Glúm Marries Hallgerd

Glúm and his brothers gathered a large following of well-selected men. They rode west to the Dales and came to Hoskuldsstead where a large crowd had already gathered. Hoskuld and Hrút were seated on one bench and the bridegroom on another. Hallgerd sat on the cross-bench and made a most attractive figure. Thjóstólf went about with his axe on his shoulder and behaved in a most provocative way,[1] but they all pretended not to notice him. When the celebration was over, Hallgerd went away to the south with Glúm and his brothers. Upon their arrival at Varmalœk, Thórarin asked Hallgerd whether she planned to take over the administration of the household.

'No, I do not,' was her answer.

Hallgerd suppressed her bad temper that winter and the people were not dissatisfied with her at all. In the spring the brothers talked about their property and Thórarin said: 'I will give the farm at Varmalœk to you two, for that seems to be the most practical arrangement, and I will go south to Laugarness and live there. Engey, however, we shall own in common.'

Glúm agreed to that; so Thórarin moved south, while Glúm and his wife remained at Varmalœk. Hallgerd added to her servants. She lived in great style and kept a big house. In the summer she gave birth to a girl. Glúm asked what name the child should have.

Hallgerd answered: 'She shall be named Thorgerd after my father's mother, for on her father's side Thorgerd was descended from Sigurd Fáfnir's-Bane.'[2]

The girl was sprinkled with water and given the name Thorgerd. She grew up at Varmalœk and in her looks came to resemble her mother. Glúm and Hallgerd got along quite well together. Thus things went for a while.

About this time tidings came from the Bear Firth in the north that Svan and his men had gone fishing in the spring and that a

great storm had come upon them from the east and driven them
ashore at Veidilausa,[3] so that all had perished. But the fishermen
who lived at Kaldbak[4] believed they had seen Svan go into the
mountain of Kaldbakshorn and that he had been received there
with great joy.[5] Others, however, contradicted this and said there
was nothing to the story. So much all knew, though, and that was
that he was dead. When Hallgerd learned of the death of her
mother's brother, she considered it a great loss.

Glúm suggested to Thórarin that they exchange farms. However, Thórarin didn't wish to do that, and he added: 'If I outlive
you, I plan to have Varmalœk for myself.'

Glúm told this to Hallgerd, and she answered: 'Thórarin has
every right to expect this of us.'

15

Thjóstólf Comes to Hallgerd

Thjóstólf had beaten one of Hoskuld's servants, whereupon
Hoskuld drove him away. He took his horse and weapons and said
to Hoskuld: 'Now I am going away and I will never come back!'

'That will make everybody happy!' replied Hoskuld.

Thjóstólf rode until he came to Varmalœk. He received a hearty
welcome from Hallgerd, and not an unfriendly one from Glúm
either. He told Hallgerd that her father had driven him away, and
he now asked her to help him. She said she could not make him
any promises about staying there until she had spoken to Glúm.

'Are things going well between you two?' he asked.

'Yes, we are very much in love,' she answered.

Then she went to speak with Glúm, put her arms around his
neck and said: 'I have a request to make of you; will you grant it?'

'I will grant it,' he answered, 'if I can do it without dishonour to
myself. What is your wish?'

She answered: 'Thjóstólf has been driven away from Hoskuldsstead, and I would wish that you permit him to stay here.
However, I will not take it amiss if you don't like it.'

Glúm said: 'Since you are so reasonable about it, I will grant your request. But I will tell you this: if he starts any trouble, he will have to leave immediately.'

Thereupon she returned to Thjóstólf and told him what Glúm had said.

He answered: 'That is mighty good of you, but that is just what I expected of you.'

After that he stayed there and he checked his temper for a while, but it was not long before he became the same old troublemaker again. He showed no respect for anyone except Hallgerd; yet she never took his side when he quarrelled with others. Thórarin blamed his brother Glúm for permitting Thjóstólf to stay there. He said that nothing but ill luck would come of it, just as it had once before. Glúm answered in a friendly fashion, but still kept doing just as he pleased.

16

Hallgerd Quarrels with Glúm about Thjóstólf

It happened one autumn that there was great difficulty in fetching the livestock home from the hills, and many of Glúm's wethers were missing. Then Glúm said to Thjóstólf: 'Go up to the mountains with my servants and see if you can locate any of the sheep!'

'Looking for sheep is no business of mine!' said Thjóstólf, 'and another thing: I don't care to chase around after your slaves. Go yourself, and then I might go with you!'

With this they engaged in a violent exchange of words. Hallgerd was sitting in front of the house as the weather was beautiful. Glúm went up to her and said: 'Thjóstólf and I have just had a quarrel, and he won't stay here much longer.'

Then he told her what had happened. Hallgerd spoke up in defence of Thjóstólf, and there were harsh words exchanged. Finally Glúm slapped her and said: 'I shall have no more words with you!' With that he went away.

Hallgerd wept bitterly and she was unable to check her tears, for she loved Glúm very much. Thjóstólf came to her and said: 'You have been badly treated, but that shall not happen again!'

She answered: 'You are not to avenge this, nor are you to interfere in anything which concerns Glúm and myself!'

He said nothing, but he left her, grinning maliciously.

17

Thjóstólf Kills Glúm and is Slain by Hrút

Glúm summoned men to accompany him, and Thjóstólf likewise got ready and went along. They went up through southern Reykjardale, up along Bauga Gorge, and then south to Thverfell. There the men were divided into groups. Some were sent to the Súlur mountains, where they all found a large number of sheep, and the others went to the Skorradale region. And so it came about that the two were left alone, Glúm and Thjóstólf. They went south from Thverfell and found some sheep that had become frightened. They tried to chase them to the ridge, but the sheep got away and escaped to the high mountains. Then each blamed the other and Thjóstólf said that all Glúm was good for was lying with Hallgerd.

Glúm answered: 'A man's worst enemies can be found in his own home; that I should have to take taunts from you, serf in bonds!'

Thjóstólf said: 'You'll soon see that I'm no serf, for I'll never yield an inch to you!'

Then Glúm flew into a rage and thrust at him with his knife, but Thjóstólf blocked it with his axe. The knife struck the broadest part of the blade with such force that it cut into the haft about two fingers deep. Thjóstólf immediately returned the blow with his axe and struck Glúm on the shoulder, so that shoulder bone and collar bone were broken, and the wound bled internally. With his other hand Glúm gripped Thjóstólf with such strength that he was forced to the ground, but he was unable to hold him there, since death came upon him. Thjóstólf then took a gold ring from him and covered the corpse with stones.[1] After that he went straight to Varmalœk. Hallgerd was sitting in front of the house and saw that his axe was covered with blood. Thjóstólf tossed the ring to her.

She asked: 'What tidings do you bring? Why is your axe so bloody?'

He answered: 'I don't know how you are going to like it, but I tell you that Glúm is slain!'

'Then you did it!' she said.

'Right you are!' he answered.

She laughed and said: 'You are a pretty dangerous opponent in any game.'

'What do you advise me to do now?' he asked.

'Go to my uncle Hrút,' she said, 'and let him look after you.'

'I don't know whether this is good counsel,' said Thjóstólf, 'but I'll follow it in any case.'

He took his horse and rode west to Hrútsstead that same night. He hitched his horse at the back of the buildings and then went to the door and knocked loudly. After that he went around to the north side of the house. Hrút had been lying awake; he jumped up quickly, put on his jacket, and pulled on his shoes. Then he took his sword in hand and wrapped a cloak around his left hand and wrist. The people in the house awoke as he went out. He saw a tall man at the rear of the house and recognised Thjóstólf. Hrút asked for tidings, and Thjóstólf answered: 'I report the slaying of Glúm!'

'Who killed him?' asked Hrút.

'I did!' he answered.

Hrút continued: 'Why did you come here?'

Thjóstólf replied: 'Hallgerd sent me to you.'

'Then she has nothing to do with the slaying,' said Hrút, brandishing his sword against Thjóstólf.

Thjóstólf saw this, and not wanting to be caught unawares he immediately levelled a blow with his axe at him. Hrút avoided it deftly and struck the blade of the axe so smartly with his left hand that the axe flew out of Thjóstólf's hand. With his right hand Hrút hacked at Thjóstólf's leg above the knee, so that the leg was all but cut off, merely dangling from the body, and at the same time he rushed at Thjóstólf with such force as to floor him. Then he struck him on the head and that was his end. By that time Hrút's servants had come out of the house and saw what had happened. Hrút had Thjóstólf's corpse carried away and covered with stones. Then he rode to Hoskuld and told him of the slaying of Glúm and of Thjóstólf. Hoskuld considered Glúm's death a great loss, but he thanked Hrút for the slaying of Thjóstólf.

Soon after, Thórarin, Ragi's brother, learned of the slaying of his brother Glúm. With eleven men he rode west to Hoskuldsstead where Hoskuld received him with open arms. That night he stayed there. Hoskuld sent immediately for Hrút and asked him to come to Hoskuldsstead, and he came at once. The following day they spoke at great length about the slaying of Glúm.

Thórarin asked: 'Will you pay me any reparations for my brother? For his death is a great loss to me.'

Hoskuld answered: 'I didn't kill your brother, nor did my daughter plot his death, and Hrút killed Thjóstólf as soon as he learned that he had committed the deed.'

Then Thórarin was silent and matters seemed to have taken an unfavourable turn.

Hrút spoke up: 'Let us make his journey worth his while. He has certainly suffered a great loss, and it will be a credit to us if we make him presents so that he will be our friend for ever after.'

So it was done. The two brothers gave him gifts, and he rode back to the south. He and Hallgerd exchanged farms in the spring; she went south to Laugarness, and he moved to Varmalœk. With this Thórarin is out of the saga.

18

Unn Squanders her Substance

Now it must be told that Mord Fiddle took sick and died. His death was considered a great loss. His daughter Unn, who as yet had not remarried, took over the whole inheritance. She was a very extravagant woman and very careless in the management of her financial affairs. She had soon wasted her goods, so that she had nothing left but her land and personal possessions.

19

Gunnar of Hlídarendi and his Kin

There was a man named Gunnar, who was a kinsman of Unn. His mother was named Rannveig. She was the daughter of Sigfús, the son of Sigvat the Red, who was slain at Sanhóla Ferry. Gunnar's father was named Hámund and he was the son of Gunnar Baugsson, from whom Gunnarsholt (Gunnar's Wood) received its name. The mother of Hámund was named Hrafnhild. She was the daughter of Stórólf Hœingsson. Stórólf was the brother of Hrafn, the law-speaker. The son of Stórólf was Orm the Strong.

Gunnar Hámundarson lived at Hlídarendi in Fljótshlíd. He was tall and strong and well skilled in the use of arms. He could wield the sword and shoot equally well with either hand, and he could deal blows so swiftly that three swords seemed to flash through the air at the same time. He had no equal in shooting with a bow and he never missed his mark. In full armour he was able to leap higher than his own height, and just as far backwards as forwards. He swam like a seal, and indeed there was no sport in which it availed anyone to compete against him. It has been said that no man had been his equal. He was a handsome man with fair skin and a straight nose somewhat turned up at the end. He had sharp blue eyes and a ruddy complexion. His hair was luxuriant and of good colour and texture. He was the most well bred of men, hardy in every respect, generous and even tempered, a faithful friend, but very careful in the choice of his friends. He was well-to-do.

Gunnar had a brother named Kolskegg, who was likewise tall and strong and a noble fellow who knew no fear. A second brother was named Hjort, who at that time was still a child. Another brother of Gunnar was Orm Skógarnef. He was illegitimate and plays no role in this saga. Gunnar had a sister named Arngunn. She was married to Hróar Tungugodi, the son of Uni the Unborn, the son of Gardar who discovered Iceland. The son of Arngunn was Hámund the Halt who lived at Hámundarstead.

20

Njál and his Kin

A man was named Njál, the son of Thorgeir Gollnir, the son of Thórólf. Njál's mother was named Ásgerd and she was the daughter of the chieftain Áskel the Silent. She had come out to Iceland and taken land east of the Markar River between Oldustein and Seljalandsmúli. Her son was Holta-Thórir, the father of Thorlief Crow, from whom the people of Skógar are descended, and of Thorgrím the Tall and of Skorargeir.

Njál lived at Bergthórshvál in the Landeyjar [Landisles].[1] He had another farm at Thórólfsfell.[2] Njál was a wealthy man and handsome, except that he grew no beard. He was so well versed in the law that his equal could not be found anywhere. He was learned and had the gift of second sight. He was benevolent and generous in word and deed, and everything which he advised turned out for the best. He was gentle and noble-minded, and helped all people who came to him with their problems. His wife was named Bergthóra, the daughter of Skarphedin. She was a most excellent and capable woman, but somewhat harsh. They had six children, three daughters and three sons, all of whom play a role in this saga.

21

Unn Seeks Gunnar's Help to Recover her Dowry

Now we revert to what was told before, that Unn had wasted all her substance. She set out for Hlídarendi where she was well received by her kinsman Gunnar. She stayed there that night. The day after they sat outside to discuss their affairs. In the end she told him that she was hard put to it in her affairs.

'That is bad,' he said.

'What help will you lend me in my difficulty?' she asked.

He answered, 'I shall let you have all you need of what I have outstanding.'

'No,' she replied, 'I don't want to waste your substance.'

'Well, then, what do you want?' he asked.

'I would like you to recover my property from Hrút,' she said.

'Easier said than done,' he replied, 'if your father couldn't do it; and he was a great lawyer, whereas I have but little knowledge about the law.'

'Hrút won out more by force than in accordance with the law,' Unn answered. 'Also, my father was an old man, and people thought it best that he should not accept Hrút's challenge. Nor is there anyone among my kinsmen who will take up this case, if you don't have the courage.'

'It isn't the courage I lack to recover your property,' he said, 'but I don't know how to resume the case.'

To this Unn answered: 'Ride to Bergthórshvál and speak with Njál. He will know how to go about it. And he is a great friend of yours.'

'Yes, I certainly can expect that he will give me as sound advice as he gives everyone else,' he replied.

The upshot of the conversation was that Gunnar took over the case, and at the same time gave Unn as much money as she needed for her household; whereupon she returned to her home.

Gunnar now rode to Njál; he was welcomed cordially, and then they discussed the matter.

Gunnar said: 'I have come to you to seek your good counsel.'

Njál answered: 'I have many friends who are worthy of my counsel, but I think I would make the greatest effort to help you.'

Gunnar continued: 'I wish to inform you that I have taken over Unn's suit against Hrút for restitution of her property.'

'That is a very difficult case,' said Njál, 'and one which involves a great risk. Nevertheless, I will outline the procedure which seems to me most likely to succeed. Everything will turn out well, if you abide by what I say, but your life is in danger, if you do otherwise.'

'I shall certainly abide by what you say!' said Gunnar.

Njál kept his peace for a while. Then he said: 'I have been thinking what course to take, and this one is likely to succeed.'

22

Njál Advises Gunnar How to Go about it

'You shall ride from home with two men. Cover yourself with a raincoat and hood and underneath wear a brown-striped woollen cloak. Under all that wear your good clothes, and carry a small axe in your hand. Each of you three must take two horses, one fat and one lean. Take some articles of hardware with you, too. You must ride from here early tomorrow morning, and when you come west over White River, pull your hat down well over your eyes. Then people will ask who this tall fellow is, and your companions shall say that it is the great Huckster-Hedin from the Eyja Firth[1] who is going about selling hardware. They shall add that Hedin is a mean fellow who talks much and thinks he knows everything. Very often he voids a sale after it has already been made, and he attacks people if everything does not go as he wishes. You must then ride west to the Borgar Firth and offer your wares for sale wherever you go. Be sure to void the sales often, so that the rumour will be spread about that Huckster-Hedin is the worst possible man to deal with, and that he is as bad as his reputation. Then ride to North River Dale and continue to the Hrút Firth and to Laxárdale until you come to Hoskuldsstead. Stay there one night and sit near the door and keep your head low. Hoskuld will tell his people not to have anything to do with Huckster-Hedin, because he is a most disagreeable fellow. The next morning you must leave and go to the homestead situated closest to Hrútsstead. Offer your wares for sale there, showing the worst articles you have and minimising their defects. The master of the house will examine the wares and discover their defects. Then snatch the wares from his hands and rail at him. He will say it could hardly be expected that you behave well toward him when you behave so badly toward everyone else. Then you must rush at him, even though that is contrary to your disposition, but check your strength, so that they don't recognise you. They'll send a messenger to Hrútsstead to ask Hrút to do something about separating you. Hrút will then send for you immediately, and you should go to him just as quickly. A seat will be given you on the lower-bench opposite Hrút's high-seat.[2] You must greet Hrút, and he will receive you well. He will ask you whether you are from the north, and you shall say you are from the Eyja Firth district. He will ask you whether there are very many outstanding men there, and you shall answer that there are miserable fellows there and plenty of them. "Do you know Reykjardale?" he will ask, and you must answer: "I know all Iceland." "Are there any great champions in Reykjardale?" he will ask. "There are plenty of thieves and scoundrels there," must be your answer. Hrút will laugh at this and think it great fun. You two will then go on to talk about men in the Eastern Quarter, and you must find something bad to tell about all of them. Then you will talk about the Rangá River district, and you must say that there above all is a dearth of prominent men, now that Mord Fiddle is dead. He will ask how you explain that no one could fill his place, and you must answer that he was so wise a man and so skilful in prosecuting cases that there never was any question about his leadership. He will ask: "Do you perchance know how matters went between him and me?" "Yes, I know," you must say, "that he took your wife from you and you did nothing about it." Then Hrút will answer: "Don't you think that was some disgrace for him that he didn't get her property back, though it was he himself who filed suit for it?" "That is easily answered," you must say. "You challenged him to single combat; but he was an old man, and his friends advised him not to fight against you, and thus the suit was dropped." "Yes, I did challenge him," Hrút will say, "and to stupid people that seemed lawful enough, but actually the suit could have been taken up again at another Assembly, if he had had the courage." "I know that," you must say. Then he will ask you: "Why, do you perchance know anything about the law?" "Why yes, up north people thought I did," you must say, "but you would have to tell me how this suit could be taken up again." Hrút will ask: "What suit do you mean?" "A suit," you must reply, "that doesn't concern me at all: to wit, how Unn's suit for restitution of her property could be taken up again." Then Hrút will say: "I have to be summoned in the suit, and the summons has to be delivered to me personally so that I can hear it, or else it must be made at my lawful domicile." "Recite the summons," you must say, "and I'll say it after you." Then Hrút will summon himself, and you must pay strict attention to exactly what expressions he uses.[3] Hrút will ask you to repeat the summons. This you shall do, but so incorrectly that no more than every other word is right. Then Hrút will laugh and no longer mistrust you. He'll tell you that your summons is full of mistakes. You must blame your companions and say that they confused you. Then ask Hrút to speak the words to you once again and to let you repeat them after him. He will give you permission and will recite the summons himself, but you must repeat the summons right after him, this time correctly. Ask Hrút whether that summons was correctly made, and he will say: "So pronounced it will hold!" Then you must say in a loud voice so that your companions can hear it: "I hereby summon you in this suit, the prosecution of which I have taken over from Unn, Mord's daughter!" Then when all the household is asleep, take your bridles and saddles and tiptoe softly out of the house. Put the saddles on the fat horses in the field and ride away on them, but leave the lean ones behind. Ride up beyond the pastures and stay in the hills three days, for that is about the length of time they will search for you. After that ride home south, travelling only by night and resting during the day. As for ourselves, we will ride to the Assembly and support you in the suit.'

Gunnar thanked Njál and then returned home for the time being.

23

Gunnar Follows Njál's Advice

Two days later Gunnar and the two men set out from home and
rode until they came to the Black Forest Heath. Some men rode
up to them and asked who this tall fellow might be, of whose face
there was so little to be seen. His companions replied that it was
Huckster-Hedin. They remarked that there was slight chance of
encountering a worse customer than this fellow. Hedin immediately acted as if he were going to make for them. But both parties
continued on their way.

Gunnar did everything as had been mapped out for him. He
spent the night at Hoskuldsstead, and from there he rode down
along the valley and came to the farm closest to Hrútsstead. There
he offered his wares for sale and sold three pieces. The farmer
noticed that they were defective and said that the entire deal was a
fraud, whereupon Hedin immediately started to attack him. This
was reported to Hrút, and he sent for Hedin. Hedin came at once
and was welcomed by him. Their conversation followed pretty
much the pattern which Njál had anticipated; Hrút told him how
Unn's suit was to be taken up again, and he recited the summons.
Hedin repeated it after him, but incorrectly, so that Hrút burst out
laughing and, of course, suspected nothing. Then Hedin asked that
Hrút repeat the summons, and Hrút did so. Hedin then spoke the
summons after him, this time correctly, and he called upon his
companions as witnesses that he had summoned Hrút in the suit
which he had taken over from Unn, Mord's daughter.

In the evening he went to bed, as did all the others; but as soon
as Hrút had fallen asleep, Gunnar and his companions took their
clothes and weapons, tiptoed out of the house, mounted their
horses, and rode over the river. They continued along the
Hjardarholt side of the river until they came to the end of the
valley. They remained in the mountains between the valley and
Haukadale Pass at a place where no one could see them, unless he

happened upon them by chance.

At Hoskuldsstead Hoskuld awoke during the early part of the night, aroused his household, and said: 'I have had a dream; I want to tell you all about it. It was as though I saw a large bear issue from the place here, and I know that the equal of this bear for size was not to be found anywhere. And it was followed by two dogs that behaved in friendly fashion to it. The bear made straight for Hrútsstead and entered the house there. Now I wish to ask whether any of you paid particular attention to that tall man [who was here last night].'

One man answered: 'I noticed that from under his sleeve there peeped a piece of gold lace and some red cloth and that he wore a gold ring on his right arm.'

Hoskuld said: 'This bear was the *fylgja* of none other than Gunnar of Hlídarendi. I believe I see it all – now that it is too late. Up, and let us ride over to Hrútsstead!'

This they did. Hrút lay in his locked bedcloset and asked who had come. Hoskuld told him who he was and asked what guests there might be in the house.

Hrút answered: 'Huckster-Hedin is here.'

'No,' said Hoskuld, 'your guest was a more important man than that. My guess is that it was Gunnar of Hlídarendi!'

'If that is the case, he has outwitted me,' said Hrút.

'What happened?' asked Hoskuld.

'I taught him how he should take up Unn's suit,' said Hrút. 'I summoned myself and he repeated the summons after me. Now he will use this summons for the initiation of the suit – and it is correctly worded!'

'He has outwitted us completely,' said Hoskuld; 'but I suspect that Gunnar did not figure that out by himself. It was probably Njál who thought this all out, for there isn't his equal for resourcefulness.'

They looked for Hedin, but he had already disappeared. Afterwards they gathered men and searched for him three days, but still they did not find him. Gunnar rode south down from the mountains to Haukadale; after that he continued east of the pass, and then north to Holtavorda Heath till finally he reached home.

24

Gunnar Compels Hrút to Pay Back Unn's Dowry

Gunnar rode to the Althing. Hrút and Hoskuld also rode there with a large company of men. Gunnar took over the prosecution of the suit at the Assembly; he had summoned the neighbours to bear witness.[1] Hrút and his men had planned to attack him, but they didn't dare. Thereupon Gunnar went before the court of the men of Broad Firth and challenged Hrút to listen to his oath[2] and to his presentation of the case and all testimony. Then he took the oath and presented the charge, after which he had his witnesses testify to the legality of the summons.

Njál was not present at the court. Gunnar prosecuted the suit and then called on the defendant to reply. Hrút then named witnesses and declared that the suit was null and void, because Gunnar had failed to present to the court the three statements made before witnesses: the first, spoken at the bed post, the second before the main door, and the third at the Law-Mount.[3]

By this time Njál had arrived at the court. He explained to Gunnar that the suit was not yet lost – 'if you care to persist with the case in accordance with legal procedure.'

'No,' said Gunnar, 'I don't want to do that. I'll give Hrút the same alternative that he gave my kinsman Mord. Now, are the brothers, Hrút and Hoskuld, close enough so that they can hear me?'

'We can hear you,' said Hrút. 'What do you wish?'

Gunnar spoke: 'May all who are here bear witness to the fact that I challenge you, Hrút, to the holm, and what's more, we'll fight it out today on the island in the Axe River.[4] However, if you are unwilling to fight, then pay back the entire amount this very day!'

After that Gunnar left the court with all his followers. Hoskuld and Hrút likewise returned to their booth, and from that day on nothing further was ever said about prosecuting the suit or defending it.

When Hrút came into his booth he said: 'Never before has

anyone challenged me to the holm and found me unwilling to accept the challenge.'

'You are probably of a mind to fight it out with him,' said Hoskuld, 'but you will not follow my advice, because you will not fare any better against Gunnar than Mord did against you. I think it is best that we both pay back the money to Gunnar.'

After that they asked their following of householders what each would be willing to contribute. They all answered that they would contribute as much as Hrút wished.[5]

'In that case let us go to Gunnar's booth,' said Hoskuld, 'and pay back the money.'

This was reported to Gunnar and he stepped to the entrance of the booth.

Hoskuld said: 'You may now have the money!'

Gunnar said: 'Then pay it; I'm ready to take it!'

They paid back the entire amount and Hoskuld said: 'Enjoy it the way you have gotten it!'

'I'll enjoy it all right,' said Gunnar, 'for this suit was a just one.'

Hrút answered: 'Ill is likely to be your reward for all your trouble!'

'The future will tell!' was Gunnar's reply.

Hoskuld and his men went back to their booth. He was greatly put out and said to Hrút: 'Will this injustice of Gunnar's never be avenged?'

'It will be avenged all right,' said Hrút, 'but the vengeance will not be such as to bring us much advantage. However, most likely he will turn to our own kin for friends when his hour of need comes.' With that they broke off their conversation.

Gunnar showed the money to Njál. 'I see everything went off well,' was Njál's observation.

'Yes, and I have you to thank for that,' answered Gunnar.

Now all the men rode home from the Assembly and Gunnar won great acclaim from the suit. He gave all the money to Unn and refused to keep any of it for himself, but he did say that he had more reason to expect help from her and her kin in the future than from other people. She answered that he had every right to expect that.

25

Valgard Marries Unn. The Sons of Njál

There was a man named Valgard, who lived at Hof by the Rangá River. He was the son of the *goði* Jorund, the son of Hrafn the Fool, the son of Valgard, the son of Ævar, the son of Vémund the Eloquent, the son of Thórólf Váganef, the son of Thránd the Old, the son of Harald Battle-Tooth, the son of Hrœrek Scatterer-of-Rings.[1] The mother of Harald Battle-Tooth was Aud, the daughter of Ívar Widespan, the son of Hálfdan the Bold. The brother of Valgard the Grey was Úlf Aurgodi from whom the men of Oddi[2] are descended. Úlf Aurgodi was the father of Svart, the father of Lodmund, the father of Sigfús, the father of Sæmund the Wise.[3] From Valgard is descended Kolbein the Young.

Valgard the Grey accompanied by his brother Úlf Aurgodi went to woo Unn, and she married Valgard without taking counsel with any of her relatives. This displeased Gunnar as well as Njál and many others, because Valgard was a spiteful and unpopular man. A son named Mord was born to Unn and Valgard; he plays an important part in this saga. When he grew up he treated his kinsfolk badly and Gunnar worst of all. He was a sly and wily fellow and the worst troublemaker.

Now Njál's sons must be named. The oldest was Skarphedin. He was tall, strong, and well skilled in arms. He swam like a seal and he was an excellent runner. Skarphedin was quick in his decisions and absolutely fearless. He spoke trenchantly, [but often] rashly. Yet for the most part he kept his temper well under control. He had brown curly hair and handsome eyes. His features were sharp and he had a sallow complexion. He had a hook nose, his teeth were prominent, and he had a rather ugly mouth, but he looked every bit the warrior. The second son was Grím. He was fair of face and had thick, dark hair. He, too, was tall and strong, but handsomer than Skarphedin. Njál's third son was named Helgi. He was a man of handsome appearance with a fine head of hair. He was strong and well skilled in arms, sensible and even tempered. All the sons of Njál were unmarried. A fourth son of Njál was named Hoskuld; he was born out of wedlock. His mother was Hródny, the daughter of Hoskuld and the sister of Ingjald of Keldur.

One day Njál asked Skarphedin whether he was of a mind to get married. Skarphedin answered that his father should decide that for him. In his behalf Njál asked for the hand of Thórhild, the daughter of Hrafn of Thórólfsfell, and that is how Skarphedin came to own a second homestead there later on. Skarphedin married Thórhild, but continued to live with his father. Njál asked for the hand of Ástríd of Djúpárbakki for his second son, Grím. She was a widow and very wealthy. Grím married her and they both lived with Njál.

26

Ásgrím and his Kin

There was a man named Ásgrím. He was the son of Ellida-Grím, the son of Ásgrím, the son of Ondótt Crow. His mother was named Jórunn and she was the daughter of Teit, the son of Ketilbjorn the Old of Mosfell. The mother of Teit was Helga, the daughter of Thórd Skeggi, the son of Hrapp, the son of Bjorn Buna. The mother of Jórunn was Álof, the daughter of the chieftain Bodvar, the son of Viking-Kári. Ásgrím Ellida-Grímsson had a brother named Sigfús. The latter's daughter was Thorgerd, the mother of Sigfús, the father of Sæmund the Wise. Gauk Trandilsson was Ásgrím's foster brother. He is said to have been one of the most valiant and accomplished men of his day. At that time there was trouble between him and Ásgrím, and [we learn that] he later slew Gauk.[1]

Ásgrím had two sons, both named Thórhall and both promising men. Another son of Ásgrím was named Grím and the name of his daughter was Thórhalla. She was the fairest of women, very well mannered, and an excellent woman in every respect.

One day Njál got to discuss matters with his son Helgi. 'I've thought of a match for you, my son,' he said, 'if you will follow my advice.'

'Of course I will,' he answered, 'because I know you have my best interests at heart, and furthermore, you understand everything best anyway. Of whom have you thought?'

Njál answered: 'We will go and ask for the hand of the daughter of Ásgrím Ellida-Grímsson, since she is a fine match.'

27

Helgi Njálsson Marries Ásgrím's Daughter

Shortly thereafter they set out on their mission. They rode out over the Thjórsá River and continued on until they came to Tunga. Ásgrím was at home and gave them a warm welcome. They stayed there that night and the next day Njál explained the purpose of their trip and asked for the hand of Thórhalla for his son Helgi. Ásgrím answered in very friendly manner and said that there were no men with whom he would rather have dealing than Njál and his sons. After that they discussed the matter, and the result was that Ásgrím betrothed his daughter to Helgi, and the date for the wedding was set. Gunnar was present at the wedding, as were also many other prominent men. After the wedding Njál offered to be the foster father to Thórhall Ásgrímsson. He came to Njál's home and lived there for a long time, and he loved Njál more than his own father.

Njál taught him the law so that he became the greatest lawyer in Iceland.[1]

28

Gunnar Fares Abroad

A ship came out from Norway and landed at the mouth of the
river at Arnarbœli.[1] The master of the ship was Hallvard the
White from Víken. He visited Hlídarendi and spent the winter
with Gunnar. He kept asking Gunnar to travel abroad with him.
Gunnar did not talk about it very much, but he indicated that he
would not be unwilling to travel abroad. In the spring he went to
Bergthórshvál and asked Njál whether he thought it advisable for
him to travel.

'Yes, I should think it advisable,' said Njál. 'You will gain the
friendship and respect of men wherever you go.'

'Would you perhaps care to take over the administration of my
estate while I am away?' Gunnar asked. 'I would want my brother
Kolskegg to travel with me, and I would like you to help my
mother run the establishment.'

'Nothing shall stand in the way of that,' said Njál. 'I'll take care
of everything you wish.'

'I thank you for all your kindness,' said Gunnar, and then he rode
home.

The Norwegian again suggested that Gunnar go abroad with
him. Gunnar asked him whether he had ever sailed to other lands
than Norway. He answered that he had sailed to all the lands that
are situated between Norway and Russia. – 'I have sailed as far as
Permia.'[2]

'Will you take me along to the Baltic?' asked Gunnar.

'That I certainly will,' he answered.

Then Gunnar made ready to sail abroad, and Njál took over the
administration of Gunnar's estate.

29

Gunnar Joins Hallvard

Gunnar sailed abroad, and Kolskegg with him. They made land at the town of Túnsberg[1] and stayed there that winter. There had been a change of rulers in Norway. Both Harald Greyfur and Gunnhild had died, and Earl Hákon,[2] the son of Sigurd, the son of Hákon, the son of Grjótgard, was now ruling. Hákon's mother was named Bergljót and she was the daughter of Earl Thórir. Her mother was Álof Árbot, a daughter of King Harald Fairhair.

Hallvard asked Gunnar whether he wished to attend the court of Earl Hákon.

'No, I don't care to,' he answered. 'Do you have any ships fit for raiding?'

'I have two,' Hallvard answered.

'Then I suggest that we two go out on a raiding expedition and get us men to go along with us,' said Gunnar.

'That we shall,' was Hallvard's reply.

Thereupon they sailed to Víken and made ready the two ships which were there. It was not difficult to secure men, since all had heard so many praiseworthy reports about Gunnar.

'Where shall we sail first?' asked Gunnar.

'East to Hísing[3] to meet my kinsman Olvir,' Hallvard answered.

'What do you want of him?' asked Gunnar.

'He is a fine brave fellow,' said Hallvard, 'and he will very likely contribute something for our journey.'

'Very well, let us go there!' replied Gunnar.

As soon as the ships were ready, they sailed east to Hísing and were welcomed there. Gunnar had not been there very long before Olvir began to admire him greatly. Olvir enquired about the journey, and Hallvard answered that Gunnar wished to go on forays and gather goods for himself.

'That's not a sensible plan,' said Olvir, 'because you haven't the men for such an expedition.'

'Well, you can contribute some,' said Hallvard.

'I plan to support Gunnar in some manner,' answered Olvir, 'and although you are a kinsman of mine, yet I would say that he is the better man of you two.'

'What support will you give us?' asked Hallvard.

'Two warships,' he answered; 'one with seats for twenty oarsmen, and the other with seats for thirty.'

'And where is the crew for them?' asked Hallvard.

'I shall man one ship with my own house servants and the other with farmers,' was Olvir's answer. 'But I have learned that a hostile force has come into the river [to block it], and I don't know whether you will be able to get away.'

'And who are they?' asked Hallvard.

'Two brothers,' said Olvir; 'one is named Vandil and the other Karl, sons of Snæulf the Old from out east in Gotland.'

Hallvard told Gunnar that Olvir had contributed the two ships. Gunnar was happy to hear that, and they then prepared to continue their journey. When they were all ready they went to Olvir and thanked him, but he warned them to be wary of the two brothers.

30

Victorious Battles with Vikings

Gunnar held a course down the river; he and Kolskegg were on one ship and Hallvard was on the other. They saw the vikings' ships before them and Gunnar said: 'Let us be prepared in case they attack us, but if they do not, let us not pick a quarrel with them.'

This course they followed, making ready for anything that might happen. The vikings stationed their ships at a distance from one another leaving a lane between them. Gunnar moved straight ahead between their ships. Vandil threw a grappling hook over to their ships. It lighted on Gunnar's ship and Vandil at once began pulling it over to him.

Olvir had given Gunnar a good sword. Gunnar now drew this sword, and although he had not yet put on his helmet, jumped on the prow of Vandil's ship and immediately struck one man his deathblow. Karl now ran his ship up from the other side and hurled a spear across the ship, aimed directly at Gunnar. Gunnar saw the spear coming toward him, turned around so quickly that no eye could follow him, and caught the spear with his left hand. He then hurled it back at Karl's ship, and the man it struck fell dead at once. Kolskegg picked up an anchor and hurled it at Karl's ship. One prong of the anchor crashed right through the side of the ship, and the deep blue sea rushed in so that all the crew abandoned the large warship and climbed aboard the other ships.

Gunnar now leaped back aboard his own ship. Hallvard joined him and then there ensued a furious battle. All saw now that they had an unflinching leader, and so each one fought his very best. Gunnar was either slashing with his sword or hurling his spear, and many a man met death at his hands. Kolskegg rendered him very valiant assistance. Karl sprang aboard his brother Vandil's ship, and after that they fought there all day long. Once in the course of the day Kolskegg was resting for a moment on Gunnar's ship. Gunnar saw him and said: 'You have treated others better than yourself today, because they don't have to suffer from thirst any more!'

Thereupon Kolskegg took a cup full of mead, drank it, and then continued to fight. Finally Gunnar and Kolskegg leaped aboard the ship of Vandil and his brother, and Kolskegg went along one side of the ship and Gunnar along the other. Vandil turned to meet Gunnar and struck at him, but the blow fell on his shield. Gunnar gave the shield a quick twist, so that the sword, fast in the shield, broke off below the hilt. Gunnar struck back at Vandil and it seemed as though three swords were flashing through the air at once, and Vandil could see no way of avoiding the blow. Gunnar cut off both his legs, and at the same time Kolskegg drove his spear through Karl. After that they took a large amount of booty.

From there they sailed south to Denmark and then east to Småland, and they were victorious wherever they went. They did not return that autumn, and the following summer they sailed to Rafali, where they came upon vikings. They fought with them and were again victorious. Then they sailed east to the island of Ösel and lay there for a while behind a headland.

One day they saw a man coming down from the headland. Gunnar went ashore to meet the man and they spoke together. Gunnar asked him his name, and he said it was Tófi. Gunnar asked him what he wanted.

'I wish to talk with you,' said the man. 'There are two warships at the other side of the headland, and I will tell you what men are in command. Two brothers are their leaders; one is named Hallgrím and the other Kolskegg. I know that they are the greatest of warriors and that one cannot find better arms than the ones they bear. Hallgrím has a halberd on which he has worked a spell, so that no weapon save that halberd itself shall ever inflict a deathblow upon him. Furthermore, one can foretell when a man is going to be slain, for then the halberd makes a loud sound, and it has great power of magic in it. And Kolskegg has a short-sword; you will never find a better weapon. Their forces are a third again as large as yours. They have a vast treasure hidden away on land, and I know exactly where it is. They have sent a ship around the headland to spy on you and they are acquainted with your whereabouts. They are now busy preparing their ships and they plan to attack you as soon as they are ready. Now you must do one of two things: either pull away from here at once, or else make ready as quickly as you can to defend yourselves. If you are victorious, I will direct you all the way to the treasure.'

Gunnar gave the man a gold ring and then returned to his own men and told them that warships were deployed on the other side of the headland – 'and they know all about us. Let us take our arms and make ready, for there is great wealth to be won here!'

This they did, and no sooner were they ready than they saw the ships approaching. Now a battle ensued. They fought for a long time and there was great slaughter. Gunnar himself slew many of the vikings. Hallgrím and his brother leaped aboard Gunnar's ship. Gunnar turned on Hallgrím to parry the thrust of his halberd. There was a boom placed across the ship, and Gunnar had leaped backward over it, but his shield remained in front of the boom, so that Hallgrím's thrust pierced the shield and went into the boom. Gunnar hacked at Hallgrím's arm, and although the sword did not bite, it shattered Hallgrím's arm, so that the halberd fell from his grasp. Gunnar picked up the weapon and thrust it through Hallgrím's body. From that time on Gunnar always carried that halberd as his weapon. The two Kolskeggs fought against each other for a long time, and it was difficult to know which one would finally be victorious. Then Gunnar came up and dealt the other Kolskegg his deathblow. Thereupon the other vikings asked for peace, and Gunnar granted it. He had his men go over the scene of the battle and strip the dead of all their possessions, but let those he spared retain their garments and weapons and return to their homeland. They went away and left Gunnar in possession of their goods.

After the battle Tófi came to Gunnar and offered to lead him to the treasure which the vikings had hidden. He said it was not only larger, but also better than the booty which they had already captured. Gunnar gladly went ashore, and they started for the woods, with Tófi leading the way. They came to a spot where a large amount of wood had been piled together, and Tófi said that the treasure was beneath the pile. They removed the wood and found both gold and silver as well as clothes and fine weapons, all of which they carried back to the ships. Gunnar asked Tófi what reward he would like to have.

Tófi answered: 'I am a Dane and I would wish that you take me to my kinsmen.'

Gunnar asked him what he was doing so far out in the east.

'I was captured by these vikings,' said Tófi, 'and put ashore here at Ösel, and I have been here ever since.'

31

Gunnar Attends the Court of the Rulers of Denmark and Norway

Gunnar took Tófi aboard and said to Kolskegg and Hallvard: 'Now let us head for the northlands!'

They were well pleased to hear that and said they would gladly follow his orders.

Gunnar returned from the east with a great amount of booty. He now had ten ships and with them he sailed for Hedeby in Denmark. King Harald[1] Gormsson sojourned there. He was told about Gunnar and also that there was no man his equal in all Iceland. Harald sent messengers to invite him to come to court, and Gunnar immediately went into his presence. The king welcomed him and assigned him a seat at his side. Gunnar remained there for half a month.

The king made it his sport to let his men vie with Gunnar in various skills, but there was not one who was his equal even in one feat.

The king said to Gunnar: 'It appears that few are your equal anywhere.'

The king offered Gunnar a fitting match and great possessions if he would consent to settle down there. Gunnar thanked the king for his offer – 'but first I wish to sail back to Iceland to see my friends and kinsmen.'

'Then you will never again come back to us!' said the king.

'Fate will decide about that, sire!' said Gunnar.

Gunnar gave the king a good warship and made him many other valuable presents. And the king [on his part] presented him with a beautiful robe, gold-embroidered leather gloves, a fillet with golden tassels, and a Russian hat.

Thereupon Gunnar sailed north to Hísing where Olvir welcomed him with open arms. He returned the ships to Olvir and gave him the cargoes as his share in the enterprise. Olvir accepted the goods and declared that Gunnar was a prince of a man, and he invited him to stay there for a while. Hallvard asked Gunnar whether he cared to attend the court of Earl Hákon. Gunnar answered that he was of a mind to do so – 'since I have now in some measure proved my worth; which was not at all the case when you asked me before.'

They got ready for the journey and sailed north to Drontheim to Earl Hákon who welcomed Gunnar and invited him to stay with him that winter. Gunnar accepted the invitation and he was held in high esteem and honour by everyone. At the Yule festival the earl gave him a gold ring. Gunnar took a great interest in Bergljót, a kinswoman of the earl, and it was evident that the earl would have given her to Gunnar in marriage, if Gunnar had expressed any wish to wed her.

32

Gunnar Returns to Iceland

In the spring the earl asked Gunnar what his plans were; he answered that he wished to return to Iceland. The earl said it had been a bad year for crops in Norway – 'and there will not be many ships sailing out from here, but nevertheless, you shall have as much flour and timber as you wish for your return voyage.'

Gunnar thanked him and soon got his ship ready for the trip. Hallvard and Kolskegg both left with him. They made Iceland at the beginning of summer and landed at the mouth of the river at Arnarbœli shortly before the meeting of the Althing. Gunnar rode home immediately, together with Kolskegg, leaving the men to unload his ship. When they came home, all men were very happy to see them. They were friendly to the members of their household and they had not become overbearing during their stay abroad.

Gunnar asked whether Njál was at home and he was told that he was. So he had his horse saddled and together with Kolskegg rode over to Bergthórshvál. Njál was very happy to see them and invited them to stay there that night. Gunnar accepted the invitation and later on told about his voyages. Njál declared him to be an outstanding man – 'and a well-tested one, too; but you will be tried even more later, for many a man is likely to envy you.'

'I want to be on good terms with everybody,' said Gunnar.

'Many things are likely to bring that about,' said Njál, 'and you will always have to be on your guard against your enemies.'

'In that case it would be well if I have justice on my side,' answered Gunnar.

'That you will have,' said Njál, 'as long as you do not have to suffer for the deeds of others.'

Njál asked Gunnar whether he planned to ride to the Assembly. Gunnar said he had planned to do so and he asked Njál if he would go. Njál said that he would not – 'and I wish that you would not, either.'

Gunnar then set out for home, after he had given Njál good gifts and had thanked him for taking care of his property during his absence. Kolskegg urged Gunnar to ride to the Assembly, saying: 'You will become a man of even greater distinction, for many men will now turn to you.'

'It is not in my nature to boast,' said Gunnar; 'yet it seems right and proper for me to seek the company of excellent men.'

Hallvard had also come to Hlídarendi and offered to ride to the Assembly with them.

33

Gunnar Meets Hallgerd at the Assembly and Asks for her Hand

Gunnar and his company all journeyed to the Assembly. They were so well arrayed that there was no one at the Assembly who could match their splendour, and men came out of every booth to admire them. Gunnar rode to the booth of the men from the Rangá River district and he took quarters there with his kinsmen. Many men came to speak with Gunnar and to ask him for tidings. He was cheerful and friendly to all and he told them everything they wished to know.

One day it happened that Gunnar came from the Law-Mount and went down past the booth of the men of Mosfell. Then he saw some women approaching him and they were all beautifully attired, but the one at the head of them most beautifully of all. As they met she greeted Gunnar at once. He responded politely to her greeting and asked who she might be. She said her name was Hallgerd and that she was the daughter of Hoskuld Dalakollsson. She spoke to him without any shyness and asked him to tell her about his travels, and he answered that he would be glad to do so. So they sat down and conversed. She was dressed in a red gown adorned with much finery. She had a scarlet cloak thrown about her which was trimmed with lace down to her skirt. Her hair, which was both fair and full, came down to her bosom. Gunnar on his part was dressed in the robe of honour which King Harald Gormsson had given him and wore on his arm the gold ring which Earl Hákon had given him. They talked together aloud for a long time, and finally he asked whether she was married. She answered that she was not – 'and there are not many who would risk that.'

'Is it because you cannot find a suitable match?' he asked.

'It's not exactly that,' she said, 'but I am said to be hard to please in the matter of husbands.'

'What would you say if I were to ask you?' he continued.

'You wouldn't be thinking of doing that,' she answered.

'But I am,' said Gunnar.

'If you are of a mind to, then speak with my father,' she replied. With that they ended their talk.

Gunnar went immediately to the booth of the men from the Dales. There he met a man standing before the doorway and he asked him whether Hoskuld was in the booth. The man said he was, and so Gunnar went in. Hoskuld and Hrút both welcomed Gunnar. He sat down between them, and one could not tell from their conversation that there had ever been any enmity between them. Finally Gunnar came to the point and asked how the brothers would answer, if he should ask for the hand of Hallgerd.

'You would receive a good answer,' said Hoskuld, 'if you are really in earnest.'

Gunnar said he was – 'but the last time we parted in such a manner that most people would think it quite unlikely that there should ever be any bonds of kinship between us.'

'What do you think about this, brother Hrút?' asked Hoskuld.

Hrút answered: 'I don't consider this an even match.'

'And why?' asked Gunnar.

Hrút replied: 'I'll answer with the whole truth. You are an excellent man and well regarded, but she is a person who has bad characteristics to go along with her good ones. I would not like to deceive you in anything.'

'May you be thanked for your candid words,' said Gunnar, 'and yet I am inclined to believe that you are still thinking of our old enmity, if you do not agree to the match.'

'No, that is not the case,' said Hrút. 'Rather I see that you are powerless to fight against your inclination. However, even though

Hoskuld and I should not agree to the match, we would still wish to be your friends.'

'I have spoken to her,' said Gunnar, 'and she doesn't seem to have any objections.'

Hrút said: 'Yes, I realise that both of you are foolishly in love. To be sure, it is you two who risk most [if you take such a leap in the dark].'

Without being asked, Hrút then told Gunnar everything about Hallgerd's disposition, and at first it seemed to Gunnar to be plenty and enough that was faulty. Yet, finally they came to an agreement about the match. So they sent for Hallgerd, and the matter was then discussed again in her presence. As before, they let her betroth herself. The wedding was to take place at Hlídarendi. For the time being the matter was to be kept secret, but it turned out that everyone soon learned about it anyway.

Gunnar rode home from the Assembly and came to Bergthórshvál where he told Njál about the arrangements. Njál received the news with great displeasure. Gunnar asked him for what reason he considered this match so ill advised.

'Nothing but trouble will result from her coming east here,' said Njál.

'Our friendship she will never destroy!' answered Gunnar.

'But she will come dangerously near doing so,' said Njál; 'however you will always make amends for what she may do.'

Gunnar invited Njál to the wedding together with all [the members of his household] whom he wished to take along. Njál promised to come. After that Gunnar rode home and then went about the district to invite people to the wedding.

34

The Sons of Sigfús. Thráin at Gunnar's Wedding

There was a man named Thráin. He was the son of Sigfús,[1] the son of Sigvat the Red. He had his farm at Grjótá River in the Fljótshlíd district. He was a kinsman of Gunnar and a man who commanded great respect. He was married to the skald-woman Thórhild. She was a woman with a very sharp tongue who enjoyed mocking and ridiculing people in her verses. Thráin had very little love for her. He was invited to the wedding at Hlídarendi, and his wife together with Njál's wife, Bergthóra Skarphedin's daughter, was to help with the serving at the wedding feast.

Ketil was the name of the second son of Sigfús. He had his farm at Mork east of Markar River; he was married to Thorgerd, Njál's daughter. The third son of Sigfús was Thorkel, the fourth Mord, the fifth Lambi, the sixth Sigmund, and the seventh Sigurd, all kinsmen of Gunnar and great warriors. They, too, were all invited to the wedding. Gunnar had also invited Valgard the Grey and Úlf Aurgodi and their sons Rúnólf and Mord.

The brothers Hoskuld and Hrút came to the wedding with a large company; among them were Hoskuld's sons, Thorleik and Óláf. The bride came with them, too, as well as her daughter Thorgerd. At that time Thorgerd was a most beautiful girl about fourteen years old. With Hallgerd came also many other women. Thórhalla, the daughter of Ásgrím Ellida-Grímsson, and two daughters of Njál, Thorgerd and Helga, were also at the wedding.

Gunnar had invited many guests and he arranged the seating as follows: he himself sat in the middle of the bench, and to his right sat Thráin Sigfússon, then Úlf Aurgodi, then Valgard the Grey, then Mord and Rúnólf, then the other sons of Sigfús, and then Lambi at the extreme end. At Gunnar's left sat Njál, then Skarphedin, then Grím, then Hoskuld,[2] then Hafr the Wise, then Ingjald from Keldur, and then the sons of Thórir from Holt in the east. Thórir himself wished to be seated farthest from the middle on the bench occupied by the men of distinction, because he lent dignity to whatever seat he occupied. Hoskuld[3] sat in the middle of the other bench with his sons to his left and Hrút to his right. We are not told how the other seats were assigned.

The bride sat in the middle of the cross-bench; on one side sat her daughter Thorgerd, and on the other Thórhalla, the daughter of Ásgrím Ellida-Grímsson. [As said before] Thórhild helped in the entertainment and with Bergthóra served the meal.[4]

Thráin Sigfússon kept staring at Thorgerd, Glúm's daughter. His wife Thórhild observing this became angry and spoke this couplet about him:

> Evil is your ogling,
> your eyes are greedy![5]

'You, Thráin!' she said.

He immediately stepped over the table,[6] named witnesses and declared himself divorced from her. — 'I don't want to hear any more of her quips and spiteful innuendos!'

And he was so insistent about this that he would no longer remain at the feast unless she were driven away. And so it came that she left the company.

After that the guests sat, each in his place, and they drank and were merry. Then Thráin spoke: 'I shall not make any secret of what I have in mind. I ask you, Hoskuld Dalakollsson: will you give your granddaughter Thorgerd in marriage?'

'I don't know about that,' he said. 'It seems to me that you have parted in bad fashion from the wife you had before. But what sort of man is he, Gunnar?'

Gunnar answered: 'I don't care to make any statement about him, because he is a kinsman of mine. But you might say something about him, Njál, for everyone will believe you.'

Njál spoke: 'I can say so much about the man: he is wealthy and excellent in every respect. Also, he is a person of great account; so you may grant him his request.'

Then Hoskuld asked: 'What is your advice, brother Hrút?'

'You can agree to the request for her hand, because he is every bit her equal,' answered Hrút.

After that they discussed the terms and agreed on all points. Then

Gunnar and Thráin arose and both went to the cross-bench.
Gunnar asked both mother and daughter whether they consented
to this match. They both said that they could find no fault with it;
thereupon Hallgerd betrothed her daughter. Then the seating
arrangement was changed again, so that Thórhalla came to sit
between the two brides.[7]

The feast now went off in fine fashion. When it was concluded
Hoskuld and his group rode off to the west and the men of the
Rangá River district departed to their homes. Gunnar gave gifts to
many of the guests and that increased his prestige. Hallgerd took
over the supervision of the household at Hlídarendi. She was a very
lavish and domineering person. Thorgerd took charge of the
household at Grjótá River. She proved to be a very good house-
wife.

35

Hallgerd and Bergthóra Fall Out

Because of their close friendship Gunnar and Njál used to
alternate in inviting each other to a winter feast. This time it was
Gunnar's turn to accept Njál's invitation, and so he set out with
Hallgerd to Bergthórshvál. Helgi and his wife were not at home
at the time. Njál gave Gunnar a warm welcome, and after they
had been there a while, Helgi came home with his wife
Thórhalla. Then Bergthóra together with Thórhalla went up to
the cross-bench and said to Hallgerd: 'You'll have to move over
to make room for Thórhalla!'

Hallgerd answered: 'I'll not yield my place to anyone! I'm not an
old poorhouse woman!'

'I give the orders here!' said Bergthóra. Thereupon Thórhalla
seated herself [at the place assigned to her].

Bergthóra went to the table with water for the guests' hands.
Hallgerd took hold of Bergthóra's hand and said: 'There's not
much to choose between you and Njál! You have misshapen nails
on every finger and Njál is beardless!'

'That is true,' said Bergthóra, 'but neither of us reproaches the other because of that. Your husband Thorvald wasn't beardless, and yet you caused his death!'

Hallgerd said: 'What good is it to have married the bravest man in Iceland, if you don't avenge this insult, Gunnar!'

Gunnar stepped over the table and replied: 'I'm going home now, and I think it would be more fitting if you squabbled with your own servants and not under other people's roofs. For that matter I am beholden to Njál for many honours he has shown me, and I am not going to be foolish enough to let myself be egged on by you [against friends]!' After that they went home.

'Remember this, Bergthóra,' said Hallgerd; 'we haven't met for the last time!'

Bergthóra replied that it wouldn't be to Hallgerd's advantage if they should meet again. Gunnar said nothing but went home to Hlídarendi and remained there all winter. Summer came and the time for the Althing approached.

36

Hallgerd Has Svart Killed. Bergthóra Engages Atli

Gunnar rode to the Assembly, but before he left home he said to Hallgerd: 'I want you to get along with folks while I am gone, and not pick any quarrels with any of my friends.'

'The trolls take your friends!' she answered.

Gunnar rode to the Assembly; he saw that he could accomplish nothing by talking with her.

Njál also journeyed to the Assembly, together with his sons.

Now to tell of what happened whilst they were away. Njál and Gunnar had joint ownership of some woodland on the mountain Raudaskridur.[1] They had not divided this land; instead, each was accustomed to cut wood on the property according to his needs, nor did one blame the other for it. Hallgerd had an overseer named Kol. He had been in her service a long time and he was one of the worst of scoundrels. Another man was called Svart; he was a servant of Njál and Bergthóra and they liked him very much. One day Bergthóra told him to go up to Raudaskridur and cut some wood – 'I'll have men fetch the wood home.'

He said he would do as she requested. He went up to Raudaskridur and he was to be there one week.

Some beggars came east to Hlídarendi from Markar River and reported that Svart had been in Raudaskridur and had cut a considerable amount of wood there.

Hallgerd said: 'Quite certainly Bergthóra wants to rob me of as much as she can, but I'll see to it that this fellow will not chop any more wood!'

Rannveig, Gunnar's mother, overheard that and said: 'On this estate we have had good housewives, even though they had no hand in planning deeds against men's lives!'

The night passed; next morning Hallgerd had a talk with Kol and said: 'I have thought of some work for you.' She placed a weapon in his hands and continued: 'Go to Raudaskridur; you'll find Svart there!'

'What about him?' he asked.

'Do you have to ask,' she said, 'you who are the worst scoundrel? You are to kill him!'

'I can do that all right,' he replied, 'but I'll forfeit my own life in the attempt.'

'Coward that you are!' she said, 'and you behave like a poltroon, despite the fact that I have always spoken in your behalf on every occasion. I'll get another man to do it, if you are afraid!'

He was furious, but took the axe and a horse that belonged to Gunnar and rode east until he came to Markar River. There he dismounted and waited in the woods until the other men had carried down the faggots and Svart was left behind all alone. Then Kol rushed at him and said: 'There are more people than you who can do execution with their axe!' With that he crashed his axe upon his head and dealt him the deathblow. Then he rode home and told Hallgerd of the slaying.

She said: 'I'll take care of you so no one will harm you!'

'Maybe you will,' he answered, 'but a dream I had before I killed him pointed in another direction.'

Afterwards the other men went up into the woods again and

found Svart slain and they brought the body home. Hallgerd sent a messenger to Gunnar at the Assembly to report the slaying to him. Gunnar did not speak harshly of Hallgerd in the presence of the messenger, so that people could not tell at first whether he thought well or ill of the deed. A little while later he arose and asked his men to follow him. They did so and they came to Njál's booth. Gunnar sent for Njál and asked him to come out. Njál came out immediately to talk to him.

Gunnar said: 'I have a slaying to report to you; it was my wife who instigated it and my overseer Kol who carried it out, but the victim of the slaying is your servant Svart!'

Njál was silent as Gunnar told him the whole course of events. Then he spoke: 'You will have to see to it that she does not have her way in everything.'

Gunnar replied: 'You shall set the award for reparations yourself.'

Njál said: 'It is going to be difficult for you to atone for all the mischief Hallgerd [is likely to perpetrate]. At some other time there will be still more serious consequences than here where only you and I are involved, and yet even in this case everything is far from being as it should be. We will have to bear in mind the pledges of friendship we have given each other. I know that you will bear yourself honourably, but you will be tried sorely.'

Njál accepted the offer of self-judgement[2] from Gunnar and said: 'I am not going to push this case. Pay me twelve ounces of silver.[3] However, I would like to add this stipulation: I would wish you to be just as lenient and easy in your terms, if anything befall you from our side and you are to make the award.'

Gunnar paid out the money and then rode home. Njál and his sons also rode home from the Assembly. Bergthóra saw the money and remarked: 'This matter has been settled with a very modest payment, but the same amount of money shall be paid for Kol, too, when the time comes.'

When Gunnar came home from the Assembly he rebuked Hallgerd. She said that in many places better men than Svart lay slain without any payment of reparations at all. Gunnar answered that she could start anything she pleased, 'but it is my business to see how these matters are settled.'

Hallgerd was constantly boasting about the slaying of Svart, and it galled Bergthóra very much.

One day Njál and his sons went up to Thórólfsfell to look after their affairs there. The same day it happened that Bergthóra was outside in front of the house when she saw a man riding up on a black horse. She remained standing there and did not go back into the house. The man had a spear in his hand and was girded with a short-sword. Bergthóra asked the man his name.

'My name is Atli,' he said.

She asked him where he came from.

'I am from the East Firth region,' he answered.

'Where are you riding now?' she asked.

'I am out of a [steady] job,' he answered. 'I thought I would look up Njál and Skarphedin and find out whether they would take me in.'

'What work can you do best?' she asked.

'I am a farmer,' he replied, 'and I can do many other things, too, but I will not hide the fact that I am a man of very bad temper, and it has been many a man's lot to bandage the wounds I have struck him.'

'No one can blame you for not being a coward,' she said.

'Have you the authority here to engage people?' Atli asked.

'I am Njál's wife,' she replied, 'and I hire the help just as much as he does.'

'Will you take me in?' he asked.

'I will take you in,' said Bergthóra, 'if you agree to do all the work I ask of you, even if it means going out and killing people.'

'You are so well supplied with men, that you are not likely to need me for that kind of work,' he said.[4]

'I make the conditions, and just as I will!' she said.

'Then we will make the bargain on those conditions,' he said. Thereupon she took him into her service.

When Njál came home with his sons he asked Bergthóra who that man was.

'He is your servant,' she answered. 'I took him in because he said he was handy for all kinds of work.'

'He is likely to accomplish a lot of work,' said Njál, 'but whether all will be good I don't know.'

Skarphedin was very friendly to Atli.

In the summer[5] Njál and his sons rode to the Assembly. Gunnar was also there. Njál took along a pouch full of money.

'What money is that, father?' asked Skarphedin.

'This is the money that Gunnar paid me for our servant,' said Njál.

'We shall very likely find some use for it,' said Skarphedin, and he grinned as he spoke.

37

Atli Slays Kol. Njál Atones for Him

Now it must be told that Atli one day in the absence of the men asked Bergthóra what he was to do that day.

'I have a piece of work all staked out for you,' she said. 'You are to go out and look for Kol until you find him. Because you are to kill him this day if you do what I want you to!'

'That is fitting enough,' replied Atli, 'because both of us are villains; but I shall tackle him in such fashion that one of us will die!'

'Good luck to you!' she said, 'and you will not do this work for nothing!'

Atli took his weapons and his horse and rode up to the Fljótshlíd district and there he met some men who were coming from Hlídarendi. They lived out east in the Mork district. They asked Atli where he was going. He answered that he was riding out to look for an old workhorse. They said that was a rather petty errand for such a stout fellow – 'but it would be best to enquire of those people who have been out all night.'

'Who might they be?' asked Atli.

'Killer-Kol, Hallgerd's manservant, just left the shieling a short time ago, and he has been out the whole night,' they answered.

'I don't know whether I dare to meet him,' said Atli. 'He is very ill-tempered; perhaps I had better let another's hurt be my warning.'

'You don't have the looks of a coward!' they said; and they directed him to Kol.

Then Atli spurred on his horse and rode hard, and when he met Kol he asked: 'How are you getting on tying packsaddles?'

'That's none of your business, you ragamuffin,' said Kol, 'nor of anybody else from over there!'

Atli then said: 'The hardest job is ahead of you, and that is, to die!'

With that Atli hurled his spear at him and pierced him through the middle. Kol swung his axe at him but missed, and then fell off his horse and died immediately.

Atli rode on until he met some of Hallgerd's workmen. He spoke to them: 'Go up to that horse and take care of it; Kol has dropped off the saddle and is dead!'

'Did you kill him?' they asked.

'Well, Hallgerd will hardly believe that he died a natural death!' he answered.

Then Atli rode home and told Bergthóra about the slaying. She thanked him both for the deed and the words which he had spoken.

'I don't know how Njál will like this,' said Atli.

'He will take it well,' said Bergthóra. 'I'll just tell you one thing as an indication that he will: he took with him to the Assembly the money which we were awarded for Svart last summer. That money will now be paid for Kol. However, even though they make a settlement, you must be on your guard, because Hallgerd is not likely to hold herself bound by any agreement they make.'

'Are you going to send anyone to Njál to report the slaying?' asked Atli.

'No,' she answered, 'I would prefer Kol falling on his deed.' Then they broke off.

Hallgerd was told of Kol's slaying and the words which Atli had spoken. She said she would pay Atli back. She sent a messenger to the Assembly to tell Gunnar of Kol's slaying. Gunnar did not say much, but sent a man to tell Njál. Njál, too, remained silent, but Skarphedin said: 'Servants are much more enterprising than they used to be; formerly, they just engaged in fisticuffs, and no one saw any harm in that, but now they are out to kill one another!' And Skarphedin grinned as he said that.

Njál took down the pouch full of money which hung on the wall of the booth and went out. His sons went with him and they came to Gunnar's booth. Skarphedin spoke to a man who was standing at the entrance of the booth: 'Tell Gunnar that my father wants to speak with him.'

The man did so, and Gunnar came out at once and welcomed Njál. Then they went off to the side to speak together.

'Things have taken a bad turn,' said Njál; 'my wife has broken the peace and has had your servant killed!'

'She should not have any blame for that,' answered Gunnar.

'Now it is your turn to fix the amount of the award,' said Njál.

'I shall do that,' said Gunnar. 'I put an equal price on these two men, Svart and Kol; you shall pay me twelve ounces in silver.'

Njál took the money pouch and gave it to Gunnar. Gunnar recognised the money, for it was the same which he had paid to Njál. Njál returned to his booth, and the two men were just as good friends as they had been before.

When Njál came home he rebuked Bergthóra for what she had done, but she answered that she would never yield to Hallgerd. Hallgerd was very angry with Gunnar because he had made a settlement with Njál in the matter of the slaying. Gunnar said he would never break the friendship with Njál and his sons. She continued to rage, but Gunnar paid no attention to her.

Gunnar and Njál took care that nothing untoward happened that year.

38

Brynjólf Avenges Kol. Gunnar Indemnifies Njál

In the spring Njál said to Atli: 'I wish you would betake yourself
to the firths in the east so that Hallgerd may not cause your
death.'

'I'm not afraid of that,' said Atli. 'I will gladly remain here if I
have any choice.'

'That is nevertheless not my advice,' said Njál.

'I would rather lose my life here than change masters,' said Atli.
'There is one request, however, I wish to ask of you: if I am slain,
don't accept a mere slave's price as atonement for me.'

'You shall be atoned for as a freeman!' said Njál. 'Indeed,
Bergthóra will probably make you a promise that she will keep,
and that is, that blood revenge will be taken for you.'

Thus Atli became one of the regular servants.

Now to tell about Hallgerd: she sent a messenger west to Bear
Firth to fetch Brynjólf the Brawler, her kinsman. This was done
without Gunnar's knowledge. Brynjólf was the worst of scoundrels, but Hallgerd said he was well fitted to be her overseer.
Brynjólf came from the west and Gunnar asked him what he
wanted. He answered that he was going to stay there.

'You are not likely to be a great addition to our household,' said
Gunnar, 'to judge from what I have heard about you, but I shall
not turn away any of Hallgerd's kinsmen whom she wishes to have
in her home.'

Gunnar was somewhat cool toward him, but not exactly
unfriendly. The time for the Assembly was now drawing near.

Gunnar rode to the Assembly and Kolskegg rode with him.
When they arrived they met Njál, who was already there with his
sons. They got along well together.

Back in Bergthórshvál Bergthóra said to Atli: 'Go up to

Thórólfs-fell and work there for a week!' He went up there without the knowledge of anyone else and burned charcoal in the woods.

One day Hallgerd said to Brynjólf: 'I have been told that Atli is not at home; he is probably working on Thórólfsfell.'

'What do you suppose he is doing there?' he asked.

'Probably working at some job in the woods,' she answered.

'What am I to do about him?' he asked.

'You shall kill him!' Hallgerd answered.

He fell silent.

'If Thjóstólf were alive,' said Hallgerd, 'he would not hesitate very long to kill Atli.'

'No need to goad me on any more than Thjóstólf,' was Brynjólf's answer.

He took his weapons, mounted his horse, and rode to Thórólfsfell. East of the homestead he saw thick coal smoke. He rode in that direction, dismounted, hitched his horse, and went where the smoke was thickest. There he saw the charcoal pit and a man standing by it. He also saw that the man had thrust his spear into the ground beside him. Under the cover of the smoke Brynjólf went right up to him, but the man was so absorbed in his work that he did not see him. Brynjólf struck him on the head with his axe, but Atli pulled back so quickly that Brynjólf lost his grip on the axe. Atli reached for his spear and hurled it at Brynjólf, but he threw himself on the ground so that the spear flew harmlessly over his head.

'Lucky for you that you caught me unawares!' said Atli. 'Hallgerd will now be very pleased when you tell her of my death. But I am glad to know that you will meet with the same fate soon. You can come over here now and pick up your axe.'

Brynjólf did not answer him nor did he pick up the axe before Atli was dead. Then he rode to the farm at Thórólfsfell and reported the slaying.[1] After that he rode home and reported the slaying to Hallgerd, too. She sent a messenger to Bergthórshvál and had him tell Bergthóra that Kol's slaying was now paid for. Then she sent a messenger to the Assembly to tell Gunnar of Atli's slaying.

Gunnar and Kolskegg both started up and Kolskegg said: 'Hallgerd's kinsmen are likely to prove pretty expensive for you.' Then they went to see Njál.

Gunnar spoke: 'I have come to report to you that Atli has been slain.' He told Njál who had committed the deed – 'and I have come to offer you atonement, and you shall set the amount of the award yourself.'

Njál said: 'We have agreed never to let anything interfere with our friendship; yet I cannot look upon Atli as a mere slave.'

Gunnar answered there was no reason why he should, and he extended his hand and promised to make payment. Njál named his witnesses and they made a settlement on those terms.

Skarphedin said: 'Hallgerd doesn't let our servants die of old age!'

Gunnar answered: 'Your mother will see to it that two can play at this game of revenge!'

After that Njál set the award at a hundred in silver[2] and Gunnar paid out the entire amount immediately. Many who were present thought that the award was set very high. At this Gunnar became angry and said that full wergild was often paid for those who were no better men than Atli.

After that they rode home from the Assembly. When Bergthóra saw the money she said to Njál: 'You think you have kept your promise, but now mine has still to be kept!'

'It's not necessary that you keep it,' answered Njál.

'You probably expected something different, and so it shall be,' she said.

At Hlídarendi Hallgerd said to Gunnar: 'Is it true that you paid a hundred in silver for Atli's slaying and thereby made him out a freeman?'

'He was a freeman before that,' said Gunnar. 'Besides, I wouldn't wish to consider any of Njál's household as outlaws with no right to wergild.'

'You two are alike; you are both cowards!' she answered.

'Time will tell,' he said.

Gunnar was very cool toward her for a long time until she became somewhat more amenable. Now all was quiet the rest of the year. In the spring Njál did not hire any additional men for the farm. In the summer they rode to the Assembly.

39

Thórd Slays Brynjólf

There was a man named Thórd who had the surname Freedmansson. His father was Sigtrygg, who had been the freedman of
Ásgerd and who had drowned in the Markar River. For that
reason Thórd had been living with Njál since that time. He was a
tall, strong man and he had fostered all of Njál's sons. Thórd had
fallen in love with Gudfinna, a kinswoman of Njál and the
daughter of Thórólf. She was a housekeeper at Bergthórshvál and
was then with child.

One day Bergthóra came to speak with Thórd Freedmansson
and she said: 'I want you to go out and kill Brynjólf!'

'I am not the type of person who likes to kill people,' he said.
'But if you want me to I shall do it.'

'I do!' she answered.

After that he went up to Hlídarendi, had Hallgerd called out, and
asked her where Brynjólf was.

'What business is that of yours?' she asked.

'I want him to tell me where he covered up Atli's body,' he
answered. 'I am told he did so poorly.'[2]

She said he was down in Acre-Tongue[3] and she pointed out the
way to him.

'Watch out,' said Thórd, 'that the same thing that happened to
Atli doesn't happen to him!'

'You are not a manslayer; so it doesn't make much difference
where you two meet!' said Hallgerd.

'I have never seen man's blood,' he said, 'and I don't know how
I would feel if I did.' With that he rode swiftly out of the yard and
down to Acre-Tongue.

Rannveig, Gunnar's mother, had overheard their talk and she
said: 'You have challenged his courage, Hallgerd, but I consider
him a man without fear, and your kinsman will find out about that.'

Brynjólf and Thórd met face to face on the beaten track.

Thórd said: 'Defend yourself, Brynjólf, because I don't want to slay a defenceless man!'

Brynjólf rode up to Thórd and struck at him. Thórd struck back at him with his axe and cut in two the handle of Brynjólf's axe just above his hand. Then Thórd at once struck at him again and his axe penetrated the cavity of the chest. Brynjólf dropped from his horse and was dead on the spot. Thórd met one of Hallgerd's herdsmen and reported the slaying as done by his hand, and he told him where the body lay and bade him tell Hallgerd of the slaying. Then he rode to Bergthórshvál and told Bergthóra and the others of the slaying.

'A blessing on your hands that wrought the deed!' she said.

The herdsman reported the slaying to Hallgerd. She was furious when she heard it and said that it would lead to much trouble if she had her way.

40

Njál Atones for Brynjólf

Soon the tidings reached the Assembly. Njál had the messenger repeat it three times before he said: 'More people now become manslayers than I ever expected!'

Skarphedin said: 'But the man certainly must have been fated to die, if he was slain by our foster father, who never before saw man's blood. Most people would rather have held us brothers guilty of the deed, considering our character!'

'You will not have to wait long before it is your turn!' said Njál. 'However, it will then be necessity which will drive you to the deed.'

Then they went to find Gunnar and told him of the slaying. Gunnar said that was no great loss [so far as he was concerned]; — 'still, he was a freeman.'

Njál offered to make a settlement at once. Gunnar agreed and was to set the amount of the award himself. This he did immediately and set the award at one hundred in silver. Njál paid the money then and there, and with that he and Gunnar were reconciled and at peace.

41

Hallgerd Instigates Sigmund to Kill Thórd

There was a man named Sigmund[1] who was the son of Lambi, the son of Sigvat the Red. Sigmund was a great seafarer and was tall, strong, handsome, and well bred. He was of very proud bearing, a good skald, and excellent at most skills. However, he was a most self-assertive man, hard to get along with, and given to mockery. He had returned from foreign parts to Iceland, landing in the Horn Firth in the east. Travelling with him was a man named Skjold; he was a Swede and hard to deal with. They acquired horses and rode west from the Horn Firth and did not interrupt their journey until they came to Hlídarendi in Fljótshlíd. Gunnar welcomed them cordially, as he and Sigmund were close of kin. Gunnar invited Sigmund to stay there that winter. Sigmund replied that he would accept the offer if his comrade Skjold might stay there also.

'I have heard it said of him,' Gunnar answered, 'that he is hardly the type of person to improve your disposition; yet what you need most is someone to help you check your temper. Besides, living at this place might involve certain difficulties; I would advise you and all my kinsmen not to respond if my wife Hallgerd eggs you on to some deed; for she engages in many an enterprise that goes directly contrary to my wishes.'

'Forewarned is forearmed!' said Sigmund.

'Then heed the counsel I give you,' said Gunnar, 'for you will be put to a stern test! However, stay around me always and heed my advice!' After that Sigmund and Skjold joined Gunnar's company.

Hallgerd was friendly toward Sigmund, and in fact went so far as to give him money and was as attentive to him as to her own husband. It was unfavourably commented on, and people wondered what might be behind it all.

One day Hallgerd said to Gunnar: 'I am not satisfied with that one hundred in silver which you accepted for my kinsman

Brynjólf. I'm going to avenge him if I can!'

Gunnar said he was of no mind to bandy words with her and walked away. He met Kolskegg and said to him: 'Go and find Njál and tell him that Thórd must be on his guard in spite of the settlement which we have made, because I don't have too much confidence that this peace will be kept.'

Kolskegg rode off and told Njál, and Njál in turn told Thórd. Kolskegg rode home and delivered to Gunnar Njál's message of thanks for their good faith.

Once it happened that Njál and Thórd were together outside. There was a goat that used to walk up and down in the yard. No one was allowed to drive this goat away. Then Thórd said: 'How strange!'

'What do you see that seems so strange?' asked Njál.

'It seems to me that the goat is lying here in the hollow and is all covered with blood!' answered Thórd.

Njál said that there was no goat or anything else lying there.

'What is it then?' asked Thórd.

'You are a doomed man,' said Njál. 'You have seen your own *fylgja* and you must now be on your guard!'[2]

'It will not help me to be on my guard if I am fated to die anyway,' said Thórd.

[One day] Hallgerd got to talk with Thráin Sigfússon and she said: 'A true son-in-law you would be to me if you would kill Thórd Freedmansson!'

'I'll not do that,' he said, 'since I would then incur the wrath of my kinsman Gunnar. Besides, I would fear the consequences, because that slaying would quickly be avenged.'

'Who is there to take vengeance?' she asked; 'the old beardless fellow, perhaps?'

'No, not he, but his sons,' he answered. After that they talked in a low voice for a long time, and no one knew what plans they made.

One day it happened that Gunnar was away from home. Sigmund and his companion, however, were there, and Thráin had come over from Grjótá River. They sat outside in front of the house with Hallgerd and talked together.

Then Hallgerd said: 'Sigmund and Skjold have promised to slay

Thórd Freedmansson, and you, Thráin, have promised to be present when they do so.'

They all acknowledged that they had made these promises.

'Now I shall advise you how to go about it,' she continued. 'Ride east to the Horn Firth for your wares and don't return until just before the time of the Assembly, for if you are at home before that time Gunnar will desire that you ride to the Assembly with him. Njál will be at the Assembly with his sons, and Gunnar will be there also, and that is the time for you to kill Thórd.'

They all agreed to carry out this plan. After that they set out for the East Firth district, but Gunnar suspected nothing and rode to the Assembly. Njál sent Thórd Freedmansson east to the slopes of Eyjafell and bade him stay there for one day. Thórd rode east, but he was unable to get back to the west bank of the Markar River again, because the water was so high that it could not be crossed on horseback for long distances. Njál waited for him one day, for he had planned that Thórd should ride to the Assembly with him. Then he told Bergthóra that she should send Thórd to the Assembly as soon as he returned. Two days later Thord came home from the east. Bergthóra told him that he should ride to the Assembly – 'but first ride up to the Thórólfsfell farmstead and look after the work there. However, don't stay there longer than one or two days.'

42

Thórd is Slain

When Sigmund and Skjold returned from the east Hallgerd told them that Thórd was still at home, but that he was to ride to the Assembly after an interval of a few days. – 'You have a good chance at him now,' she said, 'but if that does not succeed, you will never have a chance to get at him.'

Some men came to Hlídarendi from Thórólfsfell and told Hallgerd that Thórd was there. Hallgerd went to Thráin Sigfússon and his companions and said: 'Thórd is in Thórólfsfell now and now is your chance to kill him when he returns home.'

'That we will do,' said Sigmund.

Thereupon they took their weapons and horses and went out on the road to meet him.

Sigmund said to Thráin: 'You must not have anything to do with this, for it will not require all three of us.'

'Just as you say,' he answered.

A short time after that Thórd rode up to them. Sigmund said to him: 'Give yourself up, for you must die now!'

'Indeed I won't!' answered Thórd; 'come on and fight me single-handed!'

'Oh no!' said Sigmund; 'we shan't lose the advantage of numbers over you. It is not so strange that Skarphedin is brave, for the saying goes that a man resembles his foster father in a quarter of his ways.' 'You will find out about that,' said Thórd, 'for Skarphedin will avenge me!'

Thereupon they attacked him, but he broke both of their spears, so well did he defend himself. Then Skjold cut off his hand, but he kept them off with his other hand for some time until Sigmund pierced him through the middle. Then he fell dead to the ground, and they covered him with turf and stones.[1]

Thráin said: 'We have committed a wicked deed, and the sons of Njál will take the news of this slaying very badly.'

They rode home and reported it to Hallgerd. She was happy to hear of the slaying, but Rannveig, Gunnar's mother, said: 'Short is the hour of victory,[2] and so it will be in this case. To be sure, Gunnar will settle the matter with a money payment this time, but if ever you swallow Hallgerd's bait again, it will be your death.'[3]

Hallgerd sent a messenger to Bergthórshvál to report the slaying and she sent another to the Assembly to report it to Gunnar. Bergthóra said she would not belabour Hallgerd with abuse about this; that, she said, would not be a fitting revenge for so great a misdeed.

43

Njál Accepts Indemnity for Thórd. His Sons Do Not

When the messenger came to the Assembly to report the slaying, Gunnar said: 'This is a dastardly deed, and no worse tidings could possibly come to my ears. Nevertheless, we shall go immediately to Njál and speak with him, and I expect that he will show his good faith, although this will put him to a stern test.'

They went to see Njál and they called him out for a talk. He came out at once and he and Gunnar spoke together. At first there was no other man present except Kolskegg.

'I have shocking news to report to you,' said Gunnar. 'Thórd Freedmansson has been slain! Now I wish to offer you self-judgement for the slaying.'

Njál was silent for a while and then said: 'It is noble of you to offer that, and I will accept it. I shall certainly be reproached by my wife and sons for doing so, for they will take it greatly amiss. However, I shall risk that, because I know that I am dealing with a man of honour. Nor do I want to be the cause of any break in our friendship.'

'Do you perhaps wish to have your sons present when the award is made?' asked Gunnar.

'No,' replied Njál, 'for they will not break any agreement which I make, but if they are present, it is not likely that they will help us come to such an agreement.'

'Very well,' said Gunnar; 'I shall want you to make the award!'

They shook hands and the matter was settled quickly and to their mutual satisfaction. Then Njál said: 'I set the price of atonement at two hundred in silver, but you will probably consider that very high.'

'No, I do not think it is too high,' said Gunnar; and with that he returned to his booth.

Njál's sons returned to their booth and Skarphedin asked his father how he came to have so much good silver in his possession.

Njál answered: 'Thórd, your foster father, has been slain, but Gunnar and I have made peace in the matter and he has paid a double wergild for the slaying.'

'Who were the slayers?' Skarphedin asked.

'Sigmund and Skjold, but Thráin was standing close by when it happened,' answered Njál.

'They must have thought it necessary to have sufficient help,' said Skarphedin, 'but how far must things go before we are allowed to take matters into our own hands?'

'It will not be long before that time comes,' said Njál, 'and nothing will stop you then. Yet I consider it of the greatest importance that you do not break this agreement.'

'We shall not,' said Skarphedin, 'but if there is any further hostility between us, then we will remember the old quarrel.'

'Then I shall not hold you back,' said Njál.

44

Sigmund's Lampooning Verses

When the Assembly was dissolved, Gunnar rode home and said to Sigmund: 'You are a most ill-starred fellow, and all your gifts you use to evil purpose. However that be, I have made a settlement for you with Njál, but never again let yourself be tricked into doing such a thing! You and I are not of the same disposition; you are given to scorn and ridicule, but that is not according to my nature. You get on so well with Hallgerd because you both are of the same disposition!'

Gunnar continued to berate him for a long time, but Sigmund gave him soft answers and said that he would henceforth follow his counsel more than he had in the past. Gunnar said that would be to his own advantage. Gunnar and Njál maintained their friendship, even though the relationship between other members of their families was quite cool.

It once happened that some beggarwomen came to Hlídarendi from Bergthórshvál. They talked a great deal and had very sharp and spiteful tongues. Hallgerd had a detached room where she often used to sit. Once her daughter Thorgerd was there with her, as were also Thráin and Sigmund and a number of women. Gunnar was not there, nor was Kolskegg. The beggarwomen came into the room, too; Hallgerd greeted them, offered them seats, and asked them where they had spent the night. They answered that they had been at Bergthórshvál.

'What was Njál doing?' Hallgerd asked.

'He was hard at work just sitting still,' they answered.

'And what were Njál's sons doing?' she asked. 'They consider themselves full grown now.'

'They look pretty big when they stand up, but they are still all untried and untested,' they answered. 'Skarphedin was whetting his axe, Grím was fitting a spearhead to a shaft, Helgi was riveting a hilt on a sword, and Hoskuld was reinforcing the handle on a shield.'

'They must be planning some big deed!' said Hallgerd.

'We do not know about that,' the women answered.

'And what were Njál's servants doing?' asked Hallgerd.

'We didn't see what the others were doing, but one of them was carting manure up the hillside.'

'What was he doing that for?' she asked.

'He said it made the hay better there than anywhere else,' they answered.

'Njál is not always equally wise, even though he gives counsel in all matters,' said Hallgerd.

'What do you mean?' they asked.

'I'll mention something which is true,' she answered. 'He didn't manure his beard, to make himself look like other men; so let us call him "the Beardless One," and his sons, "little Dungbeards." You make some verse about this, Sigmund, and let us profit from your being a skald!'

'I'm ready to do that,' he said; and he spoke three or four verses, and all were vicious.

'You are a brick, doing just what I want you to!' said Hallgerd.

At this moment Gunnar came in. He had been standing outside the room and had heard all these words. They were frightened when they saw him enter, and all now became silent, although there had been loud laughter just before. Gunnar was furious and he said to Sigmund: 'You are a fool and haven't sense enough to follow good advice, seeing that you revile Njál's sons, and what is even worse, Njál himself, especially after all the harm you have already done them! These words are likely to cost you your life! But if anyone ever repeats these quips, he will be driven out immediately, and in addition he'll have to reckon with me!' So great was their fear of Gunnar that no one dared to repeat these words.

With that he left them. The beggarwomen made out with one another that they might receive a reward from Bergthóra, if they told her all about this. So they went down to Bergthórshvál, took Bergthóra aside and without being asked, told her everything secretly.

As the men sat at the table Bergthóra said: 'Gifts have been given to all of you, father and sons, and you are not men of honour if you do not pay for them in some way or other!'

'What gifts are they?' asked Skarphedin.

'You, my sons, have all been given the same gift,' she said; 'you have been called "little Dungbeards," and my husband has been called "the Beardless One"!'

'We are not like women,' said Skarphedin, 'that we should fly into a rage about everything.'

'Well, Gunnar became angry in your behalf,' she answered, 'and yet he is supposed to be of a mild disposition. And if you don't avenge this insult, then you can't be counted on to avenge any!'

'It gives our old mother pleasure [to needle us],' said Skarphedin; and he grinned as he said that. And yet the sweat broke out on his brow and red spots appeared on his cheeks, and that was unusual for him. Grím was silent and merely bit his lip. Helgi did not change expression at all.[1] Hoskuld left the hall with Bergthóra; she came in again fuming.

Njál said: 'Slow but sure, mother! And so it is with many things that try men sorely. There are always two sides to a quarrel, even though we avenge this insult.'

In the evening when Njál had gone to bed, he heard an axe strike against the wainscot partition and make a loud ringing sound,[2] and he saw that the shields were gone from another bedcloset where they were wont to hang. He asked: 'Who has taken down our shields?'

'Your sons left with them,' answered Bergthóra.

Njál went out immediately to the other side of the farm and saw his sons on the way up the hill. He asked: 'Where bound, Skarphedin?'

'To look for your sheep,' was the answer.

'You would not be armed,' said Njál, 'if that were your plan. You have some other business in mind.'

'We are going to spear salmon, father,' replied Skarphedin.

'If that were true, it would be best that you not let your catch escape you,' said Njál.

They went their way, but Njál went back to his bed. He said to Bergthóra: 'Your sons were outside, all fully armed. You have probably egged them on to something.'

'I'll thank them from the bottom of my heart, if they tell me of Sigmund's death!'

45

Sigmund is Slain by the Sons of Njál

Njál's sons went up to the Fljótshlíd district and remained there that night, but when it began to dawn they continued on their way to Hlídarendi. That same morning Sigmund and Skjold arose and planned to go out and look after the stud horses. They took bridles with them, mounted horses that were in the yard, and rode away. They found the stud horses between two brooks.

Skarphedin caught sight of them, for Sigmund was wearing bright-coloured clothing, and said: 'Do you see that red elf over there?'[1]

The others looked in that direction and said that they did.

Skarphedin said: 'Don't you take part in this, Hoskuld! You often have to go by yourself without due protection. I want Sigmund for myself; that is a man's job! You, Grím and Helgi, make for Skjold!'

Hoskuld sat down, but the others continued on until they came face to face with Sigmund and Skjold.

Skarphedin spoke to Sigmund: 'Take your arms and defend yourself! That is more called for now than making quips about us brothers!'

Skarphedin waited while Sigmund took up his weapons. Skjold turned to meet Grím and Helgi, and they fought bitterly. Sigmund wore a helmet and had a shield at his side; he was girded with a sword and carried a spear in his hand. He turned against Skarphedin and thrust at him with his spear, and the blow struck Skarphedin's shield. Skarphedin broke the spear shaft in two, then raised his axe and hewed at Sigmund and split his shield down to the handle. Sigmund drew his sword and thrust at Skarphedin, and the sword cut into the shield and stuck there. Skarphedin gave the shield such a quick twist that Sigmund lost his grip on the sword. Thereupon Skarphedin struck at Sigmund with his axe. Sigmund wore a corselet; the axe came down on his shoulder and the shoulder blade was cut right through. At the same time Skarphedin pulled the axe toward himself. Sigmund fell upon both knees but sprang up immediately.

'Now you have gone on your knees to me,' said Skarphedin, 'but you shall fall dead on mother earth before we two part!'

'That would be a bitter fate!' answered Sigmund.

Skarphedin then struck him upon his helmet and after that dealt him the deathblow.

Grím cut off Skjold's foot at the ankle and Helgi pierced him with his sword so that he was immediately killed. Skarphedin had cut off Sigmund's head. Now he saw Hallgerd's herdsman, handed him the head, and told him to take it to Hallgerd. He added that she would know whether that was the head which 'had made lampooning verses about us.'

The herdsman cast the head to the ground as soon as the sons of Njál had departed; he had not dared to do so while they were still there.

The sons of Njál rode on until they came to the Markar River. There they met some men and told them the tidings. Skarphedin declared himself to be the slayer of Sigmund, and Grím and Helgi, the slayers of Skjold. Then they went home and told Njál the news.

He replied: 'A blessing on your hands that wrought the deed! As things now stand, there will be no possibility of self-judgement this time!'

Now to return to the herdsman: he rode back to Hlídarendi and told Hallgerd what had happened. – 'Skarphedin placed Sigmund's head in my hands and told me to take it to you,' he said, 'but I didn't dare to do that, because I didn't know how you would like it.'

'Too bad you did not do it,' she answered. 'I would have taken it to Gunnar, and he would have avenged his kinsman or else stand everybody's scorn.'

Thereupon she went to Gunnar and said: 'I tell you of your kinsman Sigmund's death. Skarphedin slew him and wanted his head brought to me.'

'That is what could be suspected would happen to him,' said Gunnar, 'because ill follows evil counsel! You and he have often enough shown your hate of one another.' With that he walked away.

Gunnar had no steps taken to introduce a suit for manslaughter, nor did he do anything in the matter at all. Hallgerd often reminded him of it and said that he had received no atonement for Sigmund, but Gunnar paid no attention to what she said.

There now elapsed three Assembly meetings at each of which men expected Gunnar to file suit. Then one day there arose a difficulty he did not know how to handle; so he rode over to see Njál, who gave him a warm welcome. Gunnar said: 'I have come to seek your advice in a difficult matter.'

'You are welcome to have it,' said Njál; and he gave him the advice he sought.

Then Gunnar arose and thanked him. Njál took Gunnar by the hand and said: 'Your kinsman Sigmund has lain dead a long time now unatoned.'

'He was atoned for long ago,' answered Gunnar; 'yet I shall not refuse any honourable offer which you might wish to make.'

Gunnar had never spoken any ill of Njál's sons. Njál now insisted that Gunnar make his own award in the matter. This Gunnar did, and he set the award at two hundreds in silver, but for Skjold no wergild was to be paid. Njál and his sons paid the entire amount at once. Gunnar gave notice of the settlement at the Thingskálar Assembly[2] before a great host of people, and he revealed how splendidly Njál and his sons had acted in the matter. He also told of the malicious words which had brought about Sigmund's death. He added that no one should ever repeat them; otherwise he would be liable to fall unatoned.

Gunnar and Njál both declared that they would always settle by themselves any issues which might arise between them. This agreement was well kept afterwards and they always remained friends.

46

Gizur and Geir and their Kin

There was a man named Gizur. He was the son of Teit, the son of Ketilbjorn the Old of Mosfell. Gizur's mother was named Álof; she was the daughter of the chieftain Bodvar, the son of Viking-Kári. Gizur's son was Bishop Ísleif.[1] Teit's mother was named Helga and she was the daughter of Thórd the Bearded, the son of Hrapp, the son of Bjorn Buna. Gizur the White lived at Mosfell and was a great chieftain.

Geir Godi was the name of another man mentioned in the saga. His mother was named Thorkatla and she was the daughter of Ketilbjorn the Old of Mosfell. Geir lived at Hlíd. He and Gizur supported one another in every suit.

At that time Mord Valgardsson lived at Hof in the Rangá River district. He was a sly and spiteful person. His father Valgard was abroad at the time and his mother [Unn] was already dead. Mord was very envious of Gunnar of Hlídarendi. He was wealthy in goods but poor in friends.

47

The Dealings of Gunnar with Otkel

There was a man named Otkel. He was the son of Skarf, the son of Hallkel who fought with Grím at Grímsness and killed him on the holm. Hallkel and Ketilbjorn the Old were brothers. Otkel lived at Kirkby.[1] His wife was named Thorgerd; she was the daughter of Már, the son of Brondólf, the son of Naddad the Faroese. Otkel was a wealthy man. His son was named Thorgeir; he was still young and a very accomplished man.

Another man was called Skamkel. He lived at the other farm called Hof.[2] He too was a wealthy man, but deceitful, overbearing, and difficult to deal with. He was a friend of Otkel. Hallkel was the name of Otkel's brother; he was a tall, strong man, and at that time he was living with Otkel. They had another brother named Hallbjorn the White. The latter had brought with him from abroad a slave named Melkólf. This Melkólf was Irish and a man very much disliked. Hallbjorn went to live with Otkel, as did Melkólf also.

The slave kept saying how happy he would be if he could have Otkel as his master. Otkel was good to him and gave him a knife, a belt, and a complete set of clothes, and the slave did everything just as Otkel desired. Otkel wished to purchase the slave from his brother. Hallbjorn said that he could have the slave as a gift, but he added that he was not so desirable as Otkel believed. But as soon as Melkólf came into Otkel's service he began to do less and less work. Otkel often mentioned to Hallbjorn the White that he thought the slave was doing very little work. Hallbjorn answered that was not even the worst thing about him.

At this time there was a period of great dearth in Iceland,[3] so that there was a lack of fodder and food for people, and that was true of all sections of the country. Gunnar shared hay and food with many men, and all who came to him received supplies as long as they lasted. Finally, Gunnar himself ran out of hay and food. Then he asked Kolskegg to accompany him on a journey, and together with

Thráin Sigfússon and Lambi Sigurdarson they rode to Kirkby and had Otkel called out. He was very friendly in his greeting.

Gunnar said: 'Circumstances compel me to come here to purchase hay and food, if you should have any left.'

Otkel answered: 'I have both hay and food left, but I'll sell neither to you!'

'Will you then give them to me and take the risk of my paying you later?' asked Gunnar.

'No, I don't wish to do that either,' said Otkel.

Skamkel was all the while giving him bad advice on the side.

Thráin Sigfússon then said: 'The proper thing to do would be to take supplies by force and pay you what they are worth.'

Skamkel answered: 'The men of Mosfell would have to be dead and buried[4] if you Sigfússons were to rob them!'

'I'll not go about robbing anyone,' said Gunnar.

'Would you care to buy a slave from me?' asked Otkel.

'I'm not unwilling to do so,' answered Gunnar.

After that Gunnar bought the slave and went home with his mission unaccomplished.

Njál heard about this and said: 'It is a mean thing to refuse to sell to Gunnar, and it doesn't look too promising for others if the likes of Gunnar cannot buy what he wants.'

'Why talk so much about it?' said Bergthóra. 'It would be far more honourable to give him both food and hay, since you do not lack for either.'

'Why, of course,' answered Njál; 'I'll supply him with something or other.'

Then he went up to Thórólfsfell with his sons and they loaded fifteen horses with hay and five others with food. Njál came to Hlídarendi and asked Gunnar to come out. Gunnar greeted them all very cordially.

Njál said: 'Here is hay and food as a present from me. I wish that you never turn to anyone but me, if you ever have need of anything.'

'Your gifts are good,' said Gunnar, 'but of still more worth to me is your friendship and that of your sons.'

After that Njál went home. Spring wore on.

48

Hallgerd Has Melkólf Steal Food

In the summer Gunnar prepared to ride to the Assembly, and a large crowd of men from the Sída district in the east spent the night as guests at Hlídarendi before riding to the Assembly. Gunnar invited them to be his guests again on their return from the meeting. Njál and his sons were also at the Assembly. Nothing of great importance happened there that summer.

Now it is to be told that [when Gunnar was gone] Hallgerd came to speak with the slave Melkólf. 'I have thought of an errand for you,' she said. 'I want you to ride to Kirkby!'

'What am I to do there?' he asked.

'You are to steal enough food to load two horses, and be sure to take butter and cheese and then set fire to the storehouse.[1] They will all believe it happened through carelessness and no one will be thinking of a theft.'

The slave said: 'I have done bad things, but never was I a thief.'

'You don't say!' answered Hallgerd. 'You act as though you were such an honourable man, and yet you have been both a thief and a murderer! And don't you dare to refuse or I shall have you killed!'

He believed he knew her well enough to know that she would do so; so he took two horses, placed packsaddle pads on them, and rode to Kirkby. The dog, recognising him, did not bark but ran up to meet him. Thereupon he went to the storehouse, loaded the two horses with food, and then burned the storehouse and killed the dog. On his return home he was riding up along the Rangá River[2] when his shoe thong broke. He took his knife and repaired it, but then he left the knife and his belt lying there. After that he rode on until he came to Hlídarendi; then he missed the knife, but he did not dare to return. Hallgerd was well pleased with the food which he had brought home.

In the morning when the men in Kirkby came out of the house

they saw the great damage which had been done.[3] A man was sent to the Assembly to report it to Otkel. He took the loss rather calmly and said it was due to the fact that the kitchen adjoined the storehouse. All the others were likewise of that opinion.

When the Assembly dissolved a good many rode to Hlídarendi. Hallgerd set food upon the table and cheese and butter were served. Gunnar knew that they had no such provisions and asked Hallgerd where it came from.

'It makes no difference where it comes from; you may well eat of it,' she answered. 'Furthermore, it is not man's business to be concerned with kitchen affairs!'

Gunnar became angry and said: 'I would hate to be in league with thieves!' – and with that he gave her a slap on the face. She said she would remember that slap and pay him back if she could. Both then left the room. All the food was taken off the tables and meat brought in instead; and all suspected that the reason for this was that it had been acquired in a more honourable manner. Thereupon those who had come from the Assembly went their way.

49

Gunnar Offers to Reimburse Otkel

Now we are told that Skamkel left the farm to look for some
sheep, and as he rode up along the Rangá River he saw something
gleaming on the path. He found a knife and a belt, both of which
looked very familiar to him, and he rode back to Kirkby with
them. Otkel was outside when Skamkel arrived. Skamkel asked:
'Do you by any chance recognise these articles?'

'I certainly do!' said Otkel.

'Whose are they?' asked Skamkel.

'They belong to Melkólf, the slave,' answered Otkel.

'In that case others besides us two ought to see them,' said
Skamkel; 'because now I shall give you some good advice.'

They showed the articles to many men and they all recognised
them.

Then Skamkel asked: 'What do you plan to do now?'

Otkel answered: 'We shall go over to see Mord Valgardsson and
ask his advice.'

Thereupon they went to Hof and showed the things to Mord
and asked whether he recognised them. He answered that he did –
'but what about them? Do you think that you will therefore have
to look for any of your belongings at Hlídarendi?'

'Yes, we do, but we find it very difficult to proceed in this matter
where such powerful men are involved,' said Skamkel.

'That is true,' said Mord; 'yet I may know certain things about
Gunnar's household not known to either of you.'

'We will give you money,' they said, 'if you will investigate this
case.'

'That money will be dearly earned; yet maybe I shall look into
the matter.'

They gave him three marks in silver for his assistance. He advised
them to have women go from house to house with small wares,
give them to the housewives, and see what was given them in

return – 'for all people who have stolen property in their possession have the tendency to give that away first of all. That's the way it may well be in this case, too, if the fire was of any but natural cause. The women shall then show me what has been given them at each place. However, once the evidence is established, I shall want to have nothing more to do with the case.' They agreed to this and then they went home.

Mord sent women out about the country and they were away half a month. After that they returned and brought large packs with them. Mord asked where they had received the most. They said it had been at Hlídarendi and that Hallgerd had been the most generous giver. He asked what they had received there.

'Cheese,' they answered.

He asked to see it and they showed it to him, and there were many large slices of cheese. These he took and kept. Shortly after this Mord went to see Otkel and he asked him to fetch Thorgerd's cheese mould. This was done and Mord placed the slices in it and they fitted the mould perfectly. Then they saw that a whole cheese had been given to the women.

Mord then said: 'Now you can all see that Hallgerd must have stolen the cheese!'

They put together all the evidence. Thereupon Mord declared that he now had nothing further to do with the case, and with that they parted.

Somewhat later Kolskegg came to talk with Gunnar and said: 'I am sorry to tell you, but the story is going the rounds that Hallgerd committed a theft and that she is responsible for the great damage that was done in Kirkby.'

Gunnar said that it was only too likely to be true. – 'But what are we going to do about it?'

Kolskegg replied: 'You as nearest of kin will seem to be the one most obligated to make restitution for what your wife has done. I think the best advice would be to go to Otkel and make him a good offer.'

'That is well spoken,' said Gunnar; 'and that is what I shall do.'

Shortly after Gunnar sent for Thráin Sigfússon and Lambi Sigurdarson and they came at once. Gunnar told them what he planned to do, and they were well pleased at that. In company with eleven others Gunnar rode to Kirkby and called Otkel out.

Skamkel was there also and he said to Otkel: 'I will go out with you; it will now be best to have all our wits about us. I want to be nearest to you when you need it most, as you do right now. I would advise you to put on a high and mighty air.'

Then they went out, Otkel, Skamkel, Hallkel, and Hallbjorn, and greeted Gunnar. Otkel asked him where he was bound.

'No farther than here,' answered Gunnar. 'The purpose of my errand is to speak to you about the great damage that was done here and to tell you that my wife and the slave I bought from you are responsible for it.'

'Just as was to be expected!' said Hallbjorn.

Gunnar continued: 'I wish to make you a good offer, and that is, to let the best men of this district make the awards.'

Skamkel said: 'That's a fine-sounding offer, but a very inequit—able one. You are very well liked by the householders, but Otkel is unpopular.'

'Then I offer to make the award myself and to make it known to you at once. In addition, a promise of my friendship will go with the settlement, and I'll pay the entire sum on the spot, and what is more, I shall offer to pay twice the amount.'

Skamkel said to Otkel: 'Don't accept this offer! It would be simple of you to let him make the award, when it is much more appropriate that you have that right yourself.'

Otkel then spoke: 'No, I'll not let you make the award, Gunnar!'

Gunnar replied: 'I gather that the evil advice of others is at work here. However, they shall get their reward someday. But go ahead and make your own award!'

Otkel leaned over toward Skamkel and asked: 'What shall I answer now?'

Skamkel answered: 'You shall declare that this is a good offer, but leave the decision in the hands of Gizur the White and Geir Godi. Then many people will say that you resemble your grand—father Hallkel who was a man of the greatest valour.'

Otkel said: 'Your offer is a good one, Gunnar, but nevertheless, I wish that you allow me sufficient time to speak with Gizur the White.'

Gunnar replied: 'Do as you like, but people will say that you do not know how to appreciate the honour that is shown you, if you are not willing to accept the offers which I have made you.'

Gunnar then rode home. After he had gone Hallbjorn said: 'Now you can see how great a difference there can be between people! Gunnar made you good offers and you would not accept any of them. How can you expect to measure up to Gunnar in any clash, seeing that there is no man his equal? Furthermore, he is a man of such honour that he will not withdraw these offers, should you wish to accept them later. I think the best advice would be to go and see Gizur the White and Geir Godi at once.'

Otkel had his horse brought and he made ready for the journey. Otkel's eyes were not the best. Skamkel walked along the path with him and said: 'It seems strange to me that your brother did not want to relieve you of this task. I am willing to go in your stead, for I know that these journeys are hard on you.'

'I'll accept that offer,' said Otkel, 'but be sure to stick to the truth!'

'That I promise,' said Skamkel.

Then Skamkel took Otkel's horse and travelling cloak, and Otkel returned home.

Hallbjorn was out in front of the house and said to Otkel: ' 'Tis ill to have a bondsman as one's bosom friend. And we shall be everlastingly sorry that you have turned back. How unwise to let the worst liar go on business on which you may well say men's lives depend.'

Otkel answered: 'How frightened you would be if Gunnar raised his halberd against you, seeing you are so scared right now!'

'I don't know who would be most frightened then,' said Hallbjorn, 'but you may live to see that Gunnar won't lose much time using his halberd once his wrath is kindled.'

Otkel then said: 'All of you are afraid except Skamkel!' – and both were furious.

50

Otkel Summons Gunnar to the Assembly

Skamkel arrived at Mosfell and repeated all of Gunnar's offers to Gizur.

'It seems to me,' said Gizur, 'that these were very fine offers. Why did Otkel not accept any of them?'

'It was chiefly because they all wished to accord you this honour,' said Skamkel, 'and for this reason Otkel wishes to await your decision, and that will be best for both parties.'

Skamkel stayed there overnight. Gizur sent a messenger to fetch Geir Godi, and the latter came over very early in the morning. Gizur told him the entire story and then asked: 'What is to be done now?'

'Just as you probably already advised,' answered Geir; 'and that is, to make that award which is best for both. Now we will have Skamkel repeat his story and see how he tells it this time.'

This they did, and after Skamkel had finished speaking, Gizur said: 'You have probably told this story correctly. Yet I have rarely seen a man more ill-favoured than you. Certainly looks are no guide to character, if you prove to be a man of honour!'

Skamkel returned home and rode first to Kirkby and called Otkel out. Otkel greeted him cordially and Skamkel delivered greetings from Gizur and Geir. – 'There is no secrecy about the fact that both Geir Godi and Gizur the White oppose any friendly settlement. They advise that you issue a summons to Gunnar and sue him for the wrongful use of your goods and Hallgerd for the theft of the same.'

Otkel replied: 'It shall be done as they have advised!'

'The most important factor to them seemed to be that you behaved in such a decisive manner,' said Skamkel. 'And I described you as a man who had shown himself to be courageous in every respect.'

Now Otkel reported this to his brothers and Hallbjorn said: 'It's probably all a big lie!'

Now time wore on till the final days on which a summons to the Althing could be made. Otkel asked his brothers and Skamkel to journey with him to Hlídarendi in order to deliver the summons. Hallbjorn said that he would go along, but he added that they would live to rue the day they went on this journey. They rode, twelve of them altogether, to Hlídarendi. Gunnar was standing outside when they came into the enclosure, but he was not aware of them before they had reached the buildings. He stayed outside, so Otkel recited the summons forthwith in a loud voice. When that had been done, Skamkel asked: 'Well, was that summons made correctly, freeholder?'

'You must know that best yourself,' answered Gunnar, 'but I shall remind you of this errand of yours some day, Skamkel, and of the part you played in it!'

'That will not harm us any,' said Skamkel, 'so long as you don't use your halberd!'

Gunnar was furious. He went in and told Kolskegg. Kolskegg said: Too bad that we were not outside with you! They would have suffered the greatest discomfiture if we had been present!'

'All in its proper time,' said Gunnar. 'But certainly this business will not turn out well for them.'

Shortly thereafter Gunnar went to tell Njál about what had happened.

Njál said: 'Don't be concerned about this, for it will redound to your great honour before the next Assembly comes to an end. We shall all back you zealously with our counsel.'

Gunnar thanked him and rode home. Otkel rode to the Assembly together with his brothers and Skamkel.

51

The Settlement at the Assembly

Gunnar rode to the Assembly together with the sons of Sigfús and Njál and his sons, and no other group there seemed so well equipped and hardy as they. One day Gunnar went to the booth of the men from the Dales. Hrút and Hoskuld were both standing before their booth and they greeted him cordially. Gunnar told them the whole story about the lawsuit.

'What course of action did Njál advise?' asked Hrút.

'He bade me visit you brothers,' said Gunnar, 'and tell you that he would go along with you in any course you saw fit to take.'

'I gather, then, that he wishes me as his kinsman to give my advice first,' said Hrút; 'and so it shall be. You must challenge Gizur the White to the holm if they do not offer to let you make the award; and Kolskegg must challenge Geir Godi. There will be men available to attack Otkel and his band too, as we now have such a large force that you can accomplish anything you wish.'

Gunnar returned to his booth and reported this to Njál. Úlf Aurgodi got wind of their plans and told Gizur. The latter then asked Otkel: 'Who advised you to summon Gunnar to a lawsuit?'

Otkel answered: 'Skamkel told me that it was the counsel of both you and Geir Godi.'

'Where is this miserable scoundrel who told that lie?' asked Gizur.

'He is lying sick in his booth,' answered Otkel.

'May he never rise from his bed again!' said Gizur. 'Let us now, all of us, look up Gunnar and offer him self-judgement. However, I don't know whether he will accept it now.'

Many men cursed Skamkel, and he lay sick during the entire session of the Assembly.

Gizur and his company went to Gunnar's booth. Men saw them approaching and reported it to Gunnar within. Gunnar and his men all came out ready for a fight. Gizur the White came up first and said: 'We wish to offer you the right to make your own award in this suit, Gunnar.'

'In that case it was contrary to your counsel that I was summoned in the first place,' said Gunnar.

'It was neither my counsel nor that of Geir,' answered Gizur.

'Are you prepared to corroborate that with convincing proof?' asked Gunnar.

'What proof do you wish?' asked Gizur.

'That you swear an oath on it,' answered Gunnar.

'I'll do that,' said Gizur, 'if you accept the offer of self-judgement.'

'That was my offer long ago,' said Gunnar, 'but it seems to me that there are other factors which must be taken into consideration in making the award now.'

Njál then said to Gunnar: 'Don't refuse the offer of self-judgement, for the greater the suit, the greater will be your honour if the settlement is put in your hands.'

Thereupon Gunnar said: 'To please my friends I will make the award in the suit. However, I advise Otkel to give me no further cause for complaint.'

Hoskuld and Hrút were then sent for, and they came. Thereupon Gizur and Geir Godi swore their oaths, and then Gunnar made the award without consulting anyone. He declared it as follows: 'This is my award,' he said. 'I will pay you an amount equivalent to the value of the house and the food that was in it, but for the slave I will pay nothing, because you concealed his faults. I return him to you, for "there the ears fit best where they grew."[1] On the other hand I take under consideration that you filed suit against me to disgrace me, and because of that I award myself no less an amount than the value of the house and the stores which were burned in it. However, if you don't agree to this settlement, that is all right with me too; but in that case I have already decided what I shall do, and I shall most certainly carry it through, too!'

Gizur answered: 'We do not ask you to pay anything, but we do beg that you be Otkel's friend.'

'That shall never be as long as I live!' said Gunnar. 'He can have Skamkel's friendship; he has been relying on that for a long time anyway.'

Gizur replied: 'Nevertheless, we wish to have the suit brought to a conclusion, even though you alone have the sole decision as to the conditions.'

Thereupon the settlement was made and hands were shaken on the agreement. Gunnar said to Otkel: 'It is my advice that you move over to your kinsmen,[2] but if you remain in your present home, see to it that you don't get into any trouble with me!'

Gizur said: 'That is good advice, and let him follow it!'

Gunnar won great honour from this suit. After that men rode home from the Assembly. Gunnar remained at his farm, and for a while everything was quiet and peaceful.

52

Rúnólf and Otkel

There was a man named Rúnólf, the son of Úlf Aurgodi; he lived at Dale, east of the Markar River. On his return from the Assembly Rúnólf was a guest of Otkel at Kirkby. Otkel gave him a nine-year-old ox of solid black colour. Rúnólf thanked him for the gift and invited him to his home whenever he cared to come, but the invitation was not accepted for some time. Rúnólf often sent messengers to Otkel to remind him of the invitation and to urge him to come, and each time Otkel promised that he would.

Otkel had two horses, dun-coloured with a black stripe down the back.[1] They were the best riding horses in the district and so fond of each other that one would always follow the other wherever it went.

There was a Norwegian named Audólf who was staying with Otkel. He was very much attached to Signý, Otkel's daughter. Audólf was a tall, strong man.

53

Gunnar is Accidentally Wounded by Otkel and Insulted by Skamkel

One day in spring Otkel said that they would now ride east to accept Rúnólf's invitation, and all were very glad to hear that. In Otkel's company besides Skamkel there were also his two brothers, Audólf, and three other men. Otkel rode one of the dun-coloured horses, and the other ran free at his side. They travelled in an easterly direction to the Markar River, and Otkel galloped ahead of the others. Both horses got out of hand and raced from the path up toward the Fljótshlíd district. Otkel was now riding faster than he cared to.

The same day Gunnar had gone all alone from his home. In one hand he carried a basket with seed and in the other a hand-axe. He went down to his field and sowed the grain there. He had placed his cloak of fine material and his axe upon the ground as he continued to sow for a while.

Now it must be told that Otkel came riding on faster than he wished. He was wearing spurs and he galloped down over the field, and neither of the two men saw the other. Just as Gunnar looked up, Otkel rode down upon him and grazed Gunnar's ear with one of his spurs. That produced a long gash which immediately began to bleed very much. Then Otkel's companions came up.

Gunnar said: 'You can all see that you, Otkel, have inflicted on me a wound which has drawn blood: I consider that a most outrageous offence. First you summon me to the Assembly, and now you trample me under foot and ride over me!'

Skamkel said: 'You took that well, but you were no less outraged the time you managed your suit with the halberd in your hand!'

'The next time we meet you will get to see the halberd!' answered Gunnar.

After that they parted. Skamkel shouted: 'That's certainly brave riding, fellows!'[1]

Gunnar rode home but told no one about the incident, nor did anyone suspect that the wound had been inflicted by any person.

One day, however, it happened that he told his brother Kolskegg about it.

Kolskegg said: 'You must tell this to more people, so that it can never be said that you made any charges against dead men. Your charge will be denied, if you do not secure witnesses who already know what has happened between you two.'

Gunnar then told his neighbours about the incident, but there was little comment made at first.

Otkel arrived east in Dale. He and his men received a warm welcome and they stayed there for a week. Otkel told Rúnólf all that had happened between himself and Gunnar. It occurred to one man to ask how Gunnar had behaved.

Skamkel answered: 'If he were not among the first families, I would say that he wept!'

'Those are shameful words!' said Rúnólf, 'and you will have to acknowledge, when you two meet again, that it isn't in Gunnar's nature to weep. It would be well if better men than yourself do not have to pay for your spite. I think it best that I accompany you when you are ready to ride home, because Gunnar will not harm me.'

'I don't want to do that,' said Otkel, 'because I shall cross the river further down.'

Rúnólf gave him good gifts and said it was unlikely that they would see each other again.[2]

Otkel expressed the wish that Rúnólf remember their friendship and look after his son, if the worst should happen.

54

Otkel and Skamkel are Slain

Now we turn to Hlídarendi again. [One day] Gunnar was outside when he saw his herdsman dashing up. As he rode into the yard Gunnar asked him: 'Why such haste?'

'I wished to be a faithful servant to you,' said the herdsman. 'I saw some men riding down along the Markar River, eight of them altogether, and four of them wore bright-coloured clothes.'[1]

Gunnar said: 'That must be Otkel!'

The herdsman added: 'I have often heard Skamkel use much insulting language [about you]; east in Dale he said that you cried when they rode down on you. I have told you this, because I find the abusive talk of such evil men hard to bear.'

'Well, we must not be too sensitive about such talk,' said Gunnar; 'but from now on you shall work only at that which you choose yourself.'

'Shall I tell your brother Kolskegg about this?' asked the herdsman.

'No, go in and lie down!' said Gunnar. 'I'll tell Kolskegg.'

The herdsman went to his bed and fell asleep at once. Gunnar took the herdsman's horse and placed a saddle upon it. He took his shield and girded himself with his sword, Olvir's gift, put his helmet upon his head, and took his halberd. From the weapon there came forth a loud ringing sound. Rannveig, his mother, heard it. She came up to Gunnar and said: 'You are wrathful now, my son, and I have never seen you like that before!'

Supporting himself on his halberd Gunnar leaped into the saddle and rode away. Rannveig went back into the room where there was much loud talking.

'You are carrying on loudly,' she said, 'but louder still was the sound Gunnar's halberd made when he sallied forth!'

Kolskegg overheard this and said: 'Great tidings are afoot, no doubt!'

'Excellent,' said Hallgerd; 'now they are likely to find out whether Gunnar will cry and run away from them!'

Kolskegg took his arms, looked for a horse, and rode after Gunnar as fast as he could.

Gunnar rode across Acre-Tongue and on to Geilastofnar and from there to the Rangá River, and then down to the ford at Hof. There were some women in the milking pen. Gunnar leaped from his horse and hitched it. By this time the others came riding up. The road up from the ford was covered with flagstones.[2]

Gunnar called out to them: 'Defend yourselves! Now you can find out whether you can make me shed any tears!'

They all leaped from their horses and attacked Gunnar, Hallbjorn foremost.

'Don't you attack!' said Gunnar. 'You least of all would I want to work an injury; but I'll not spare anyone, if it comes to saving my life!'

'There is no help for that now,' said Hallbjorn, 'for you are out to kill my brother, and it would be an [everlasting] shame to me if I merely sat by and looked on.'

Thereupon he thrust at Gunnar with a large spear which he held in both hands. Gunnar quickly brought his shield before the blow and the spear pierced the shield. Gunnar then thrust the shield down with such force that it stuck in the ground,[3] and he reached for his sword with such a quick motion that no eye could follow it, and with it struck Hallbjorn on the arm above the wrist so that the hand was cut off. Skamkel ran up behind Gunnar and lunged at him with a large axe. Gunnar turned around quickly, parried the blow with his halberd, and struck the axe near the base of the blade so that it flew out of Skamkel's grasp and into the Rangá River. Then he thrust at Skamkel a second time with his halberd, running him through with it. He then lifted him up on it and threw him down head foremost on the muddy path. Audólf seized a spear and hurled it at Gunnar, but Gunnar caught the spear in flight and hurled it back immediately. It went right through both the shield and the Norwegian and into the ground. Otkel struck at Gunnar with his sword, aiming at the leg below the knee. Gunnar leaped up high and the blow missed him. Thereupon Gunnar thrust at him with his halberd and drove it through him. At that moment Kolskegg came up and rushed at Hallkel at once and dealt him a deathblow with his short-sword. Gunnar and Kolskegg killed all eight in this fight. A woman who had witnessed the fight ran up to the farmhouse and told Mord and begged him to separate them.

'Very likely they are only such fellows,' he said, 'as may kill each other, so far as I am concerned!'

'No, you can't mean that!' she said; 'Gunnar, your kinsman, and Otkel are among them.'

'Must you always be jabbering, you old hag!' he said. And he remained lying abed while they fought.

After accomplishing this, Gunnar and Kolskegg rode back. As they were riding swiftly up along the river bank Gunnar was thrown from his horse, but he landed on his feet.

'That's brave riding, brother!' said Kolskegg.

'With those same words Skamkel ridiculed me, when I said that they were riding me down,' answered Gunnar.

'But you have avenged that now,' said Kolskegg.

Gunnar replied: 'I don't know whether I am less brave than other men because I dislike killing men more than they.'

55

Njál's Prophetic Counsel

Now these tidings were spread about, and many said that this had not happened any sooner than might have been expected. Gunnar rode to Bergthórshvál and told Njál about the battle.

Njál said: 'You have struck hard, but you were greatly provoked, too!'

'What is likely to happen now?' asked Gunnar.

'Do you wish that I tell you what has not yet taken place?' asked Njál. 'You will ride to the Assembly; there you will follow my advice, and from this affair great honour will be accorded you. This will be the beginning of your many slayings.'

'Will you give me some helpful advice?' asked Gunnar.

'I will do that,' answered Njál; 'never slay more than one man in the same family, and never break the agreements which good men make between you and others, least of all in this affair!'

Gunnar said: 'I should think that there would be greater likelihood of expecting this of others than of me.'

'That may be,' answered Njál, 'but just remember this in your dealings: if you do what I warned you against, then you will not have long to live; otherwise, however, you will live to be an old man.'

Gunnar asked: 'Do you know what will bring about your own death?'

'Yes, I do,' answered Njál.

'What?' asked Gunnar.

'Something that people would expect least of all,' he answered. After that Gunnar rode home.

A messenger was sent to Gizur the White and Geir Godi, for it devolved on them to take over the prosecution in the case of Otkel's slaying.[1] They met and discussed what their procedure should be. They agreed that they should bring suit in all stringency according to the law. The next question was to determine which of the two should take over the prosecution of the suit. However, neither of the two was willing to undertake it.

'It seems to me,' said Gizur, 'that we have two courses open to us: either, one of us will have to take over the prosecution, and this will have to be determined by lot, or else Otkel will lie unatoned. We can also be very certain that this will be a very difficult suit to institute, for Gunnar has many kinsmen and friends. That one of us who does not draw the lot shall give support to the prosecution of the case and not withdraw from it before the case is ended.'

After that they drew lots and it fell to the lot of Geir Godi to take over the prosecution of the suit.

A short time after that they rode east over the rivers and came to that place at the Rangá River where the fight had taken place. They dug up the bodies and named witnesses to the wounds.[2] Then they made known their findings and summoned nine free farmers as witnesses in the suit. They were told that Gunnar was at home with about thirty men. Then Geir Godi asked Gizur whether he wished to ride there with a hundred men.

'No, I do not,' he answered, 'even though the strength of numbers is on our side.' After that they rode back home again.

The news soon spread throughout the entire district that legal proceedings had been instituted in the case, and people said that the meeting of the Assembly was likely to be a stormy one.

56

The Settlement at the Assembly

There was a man named Skapti.[1] He was the son of Thórodd,
whose mother was Thórvor. She was the daughter of Thormód
Skapti, the son of Óleif the Broad, the son of Olvir Barnakarl.
Skapti and his father were both great chieftains and very well
skilled in the law. Thórodd was considered to be deceitful and
tricky. Both father and son supported Gizur the White in every
suit.

A large company of men from Fljótshlíd and the Rangá River
gathered for the Assembly. Gunnar was so well liked that all agreed
to stand by him. Now they all came to the Assembly and set up
their booths.

In the company of Gizur the White were these chieftains: Skapti
Thóroddsson, Ásgrím Ellida-Grímsson, Odd of Kidjaberg and
Halldór Ornólfsson.

One day the men went to the Law-Mount. Geir Godi arose and
gave notice of a suit of manslaughter against Gunnar for the slaying
of Otkel. Another charge of manslaughter he brought against
Gunnar for the slaying of Hallbjorn the White, another for the
slaying of Audólf, and still another for the slaying of Skamkel.
Then he brought a charge of manslaughter against Kolskegg for the
slaying of Hallkel. After he had brought all these charges for
manslaughter, people remarked that he had spoken very well. After
that men went from the Law-Mount.

The Assembly continued in session until the day when the courts
were to gather at their appointed places. Then both parties collected all their forces. Geir Godi and Gizur the White stood to the
south of the Rangá River court, and Gunnar and Njál stood to the
north. Geir Godi enjoined Gunnar to listen to his oath. Thereupon
he took the oath. He then brought the charge and had witnesses
testify that the listing of wounds had been duly made. Then he had
the jury of neighbours seated in their proper places, and he called

on Gunnar to examine the members of the jury carefully.[2] Thereupon he called on the jury of neighbours to utter their findings. The neighbours who had been summoned on the inquest then went before the court and named themselves as witnesses, but they made this reservation concerning the suit involving Audólf, that the lawful prosecutor of it was in Norway, and that they would make no findings in his case. As a jury, therefore, they had nothing to do with that suit. After that they uttered their findings in the case of Otkel and declared Gunnar guilty of the charge. Thereupon Geir Godi called on Gunnar for his defence; he had named witnesses in each step of the prosecution as it was presented.

Gunnar now in turn enjoined Geir Godi to listen to his oath and the defence which he was about to urge.

Then Gunnar took the oath and said: 'I make this defence that in the presence of witnesses I declared Otkel an outlaw for the bloody wound which he inflicted on me with his spur. Geir Godi, I protest your right to prosecute this suit, and I likewise protest the right of the judges to give judgement, and I hereby declare invalid all the measures taken by you in the preparation of this suit. I make this protest on the basis of my legal right, the inviolable and indisputable right which has been granted me according to the law of the Assembly and the law of the land. Furthermore, I'll tell you something else which I plan to do.'

'Is it that you mean to challenge me to the holm, as is your custom, and thus not permit the proceedings to continue in legal manner?' asked Geir.

'Not that,' answered Gunnar, 'but I shall make accusation here at the Law-Mount that you called on neighbours for an inquest in a case which has no bearing on your suit – I mean the slaying of Audólf;[3] and for that reason I declare you guilty and demand the penalty of lesser outlawry.'[4]

Njál said: 'Things must not take this turn, for the only result will be that the feud will be carried on with increasing bitterness. Each of you, it seems to me, has a good deal to be said in his behalf. Some of your slayings, as you cannot contradict, Gunnar, are punishable. On the other hand, you have made out a case against Geir Godi in which he will be found guilty. Also, you should know this, Geir Godi, that there is pending against you a suit calling for a verdict of outlawry. This suit has not even been introduced yet, but it will not be dropped if you do not take my words into account.'[5]

Thórodd Godi then said: 'It seems to me that it would be most conducive to peace if both parties came to an agreement. But why do you say so little, Gizur the White?'

'It seems to me,' answered Gizur, 'that our case needs some more strong support; one can see that Gunnar's friends are standing by him. The most favourable solution for us would be to have sensible men arbitrate the case, if that is agreeable to Gunnar.'

'I have always been ready and willing to make a peaceful settlement,' said Gunnar. 'It is true that much harm has been done for which you should seek redress; yet I consider that I was hard driven to act as I did.'

With the advice of the wisest men it was decided to submit the whole case to arbitration. Six men were to make the award, and it was made right there at the Assembly. It was decided that Skamkel should lie unatoned. One wergild for Otkel's death and the wound which Gunnar had received from the spur were to offset each other. The other slayings were to be paid for according to the worth of each man. Gunnar's kinsmen produced the money, so that all slayings were paid for then and there at the Assembly. Then Geir Godi and Gizur the White went up to Gunnar and gave pledges that they would keep the peace. Gunnar then rode home from the Assembly. He thanked the men for their support and gave presents to many of them. The whole proceedings redounded greatly to Gunnar's honour. He now remained at home, enjoying the greatest distinction.

57

Starkad and his Kin

There was a man named Starkad. He was the son of Bork, surnamed Blátannarskegg, who was the son of Thorkel, surnamed Boundfoot, who had settled around Thríhyrning. He was married to Hallbera, the daughter of Hróald the Red and Hildigunn, the daughter of Thorstein Sparrow. The mother of Hildigunn was Unn, the daughter of Eyvind Karfi and the sister of Módólf the Wise, from whom the Módylfings are descended. The sons of Starkad and Hallbera were Thorgeir, Bork, and Thorkel. Hildigunn the Healer was their sister. They were very proud men, overbearing and difficult to deal with. People in the district were terrorised by them.

58

The Sons of Egil Challenge Gunnar to a Horsefight

There was a man named Egil. He was the son of Kol, the son of Óttar Ball, who had settled between Stotalœk and Reydarvatn. The brother of Egil was Onund of Trollaskóg, the father of Halli the Strong, who was with the sons of Ketil the Smooth-tongued at the slaying of Holta-Thórir. Egil lived at Sandgil. His sons were Kol and Óttar and Hauk. Their mother was Steinvor, the sister of Starkad. Egil's sons were tall fellows, headstrong and overbearing. They always sided with the sons of Starkad. Their sister was Gudrún Nightsun, an excellent and well-bred woman. Egil had taken into his home two Norwegians; one was named Thórir, and the other Thorgrím. They had just made their first trip to Iceland. They were very popular men and wealthy, well skilled in arms and stout in all respects.

Starkad had a good stallion of reddish colour, and it was thought that no horse was its match in fighting. Once it happened that the three brothers from Sandgil were visiting at a farm on the slope of the mountain Thríhyrning. They talked a great deal about all the householders in the Fljótshlíd district, and finally, the sons of Starkad began to ask whether there was anyone who would dare to have his horses fight against theirs.[1] There were some men present who wished to praise them and to win their favour through flattery. They remarked that no one was likely to challenge them and no one, for that matter, who even owned such a horse.

Then Hildigunn spoke up: 'I know a man who will dare to match his horse against yours.'

'Name him!' they said.

'Gunnar of Hlídarendi has a brown stallion,' she said, 'and he will match his stallion against yours or that of anyone else.'

They answered: 'You women seem to think that no one is Gunnar's equal. Even though Geir Godi and Gizur the White were humiliated by Gunnar, it does not follow at all that we shall fare just as badly.'

'You will fare much worse!' she replied; and with that they began to quarrel bitterly.

Starkad said: 'Gunnar is the last man I would want you to fall foul of, because you will find it difficult to match his good luck.'

'But you will give us leave to challenge him to a horsefight?' they asked.

'Yes, I will,' he answered, 'if you do not try to play him any tricks.'

They promised not to. They now rode to Hlídarendi. Gunnar was at home and he went out with Kolskegg and Hjort to greet them and to ask where they were bound.

'No farther than here,' they answered. 'We have learned that you have a good stallion, and we would like to challenge you to a horsefight.'

'I can't say much in praise of my stallion,' said Gunnar. 'He is still young and altogether untried.'

'But we hope you will let us arrange the fight in any case,' they said. 'It was Hildigunn who said you were so proud of your stallion.'

'How did you happen to speak about that?' asked Gunnar.

They answered: 'There were some men who claimed that no one would dare to match his horse against ours.'

'I would dare to do it all right,' said Gunnar, 'but it seems to me the remark was made in a very hostile spirit.'

'May we then consider the matter as settled?' they asked.

'I suppose you will consider yourselves repaid, if I grant you your wish. But I make one request of you, and that is, that we have our horses fight in such manner that we afford pleasure to others without stirring up any trouble for ourselves. And don't try to put me to scorn. Because if you do to me as you do to others, I promise that I will retaliate in a way you will find hard to endure. In other words, I will treat you just as you treat me.'

Thereupon they rode home. Starkad asked how they had fared. They said that Gunnar had granted them their request. – 'He promised to match his horse against ours, and we agreed on the time when the fight should take place. Yet it was very evident that he did not consider himself quite our equal, and he tried to beg off.'

'You will find out that Gunnar is slow to be drawn into a quarrel, but a difficult customer if he can't get out of it,' said Hildigunn.

Gunnar rode to see Njál and told him about the horsefight and what words had passed between them – 'but how do you think the horsefight will turn out?'

'You will have the upper hand,' said Njál; 'yet many a man's death will result from this!'

'Will my death by any chance also result from this?' asked Gunnar.

'Not from this,' answered Njál, 'but they will remember their old enmity – and to this they will add a new enmity, and you will be put into a position where you will have to fight for your life.'

Gunnar thereupon returned home.

59

The Horsefight

About that time Gunnar learned of the death of his father-in-law Hoskuld. A few days later Thorgerd, the wife of Thráin who lived at the Grjótá River farm, gave birth to a son. She sent a messenger to her mother and asked her to decide whether the child should be named Glúm or Hoskuld. Her mother bade her name the child Hoskuld.

Gunnar and Hallgerd had two sons; one was named Hogni and the other Grani. Hogni was capable and of a quiet disposition, circumspect and dependable.

At the time appointed people gathered in great numbers for the horsefight. Gunnar was there, as were also his brothers, the sons of Sigfús, Njál, and all his sons. They came to Gunnar and suggested that they should now bring the horses together. Gunnar agreed to that.

Skarphedin asked: 'Do you want me to lead on your stallion, kinsman Gunnar?'

'No, I do not,' answered Gunnar.

'It would be better in this case,' said Skarphedin: 'they are impetuous, like myself.'

'No,' said Gunnar; 'few words would pass between you before there would be trouble, whereas if I do the goading, quarrels will develop more slowly, though it will all come to the same in the end.'

Thereupon the stallions were brought together. Gunnar got ready to do his own driving as Skarphedin led out the stallion. Gunnar wore a red cloak and had a large horse-staff in his hand. Then the horses went at each other and bit each other for a long time without having to be goaded on, and it proved to be excellent sport. Then Thorgeir and Kol agreed to push their own horse forward just as the horses rushed at each other, to see if they could knock Gunnar down. Now the horses made another rush at each other, with Thorgeir and Kol both at the rump of their horse. Gunnar, on his part, pushed his horse against them, and it happened in a flash that Thorgeir and Kol fell flat on their backs and Gunnar's horse on top of them. Then they leaped up and rushed at Gunnar. Gunnar, however, dodged them, seized Kol, and threw him to the ground with such force that he lay there senseless. Thorgeir Starkadarson struck at Gunnar's stallion and knocked one of its eyes out. Gunnar struck Thorgeir with his horse-staff, so that he, too, fell unconscious. Then Gunnar stepped up to his horse and said to Kolskegg: 'Kill this stallion, for it shall not live as a maimed animal.' Kolskegg thereupon cut off the stallion's head.

At that moment Thorgeir rose to his feet, seized his weapons, and was about to make for Gunnar; but he was stopped as men crowded around the two.

Skarphedin said: 'I'm tired of this aimless jostling. It would be more fitting for men to fight each other with weapons!'

During all this Gunnar remained so calm that one man easily held him, and he never used strong language. Njál tried to bring about a settlement or an exchange of pledges of peace, but Thorgeir said he would neither give nor accept pledges of peace. He would much rather see Gunnar dead because of that blow with the horse-staff.

Kolskegg answered: 'No mere words ever brought Gunnar low, nor will they this time either!'

After the horsefight people dispersed, each one going to his home. No attack was made on Gunnar, and so the year wore on.

The following summer Gunnar met his brother-in-law Óláf Peacock at the Assembly. Óláf invited him to visit him, but he warned him to be on his guard – 'for they will do us as much harm as they can. Whenever you travel, always have as many men as possible with you!'

Óláf gave him much good counsel, and they exchanged vows of the most sincere friendship.

60

Gunnar and Ásgrím Become Friends

Ásgrím Ellida-Grímsson had a lawsuit which he was to prosecute at the Assembly. The defendant in the suit was Úlf Uggason.[1] It so happened that an objection was raised by the defence. It was an unusual experience for Ásgrím that a flaw should be found in any case prepared by him. The objection was that he had summoned five neighbours, whereas he should have summoned nine. His opponents used this fact as a valid objection. Then Gunnar spoke: 'I challenge you to the holm, Úlf Uggason, if you obstruct the course of the law. Njál and my friend Helgi would wish that I defend your cause, Ásgrím, if they could not be here themselves.'

'But you and I have no quarrel!' said Úlf.

'Nevertheless, you will have to reckon with me,' replied Gunnar. The upshot of it was that Úlf had to pay the entire amount involved.

Then Ásgrím said to Gunnar: 'I wish to invite you to my home this summer. In lawsuits I will always be on your side, and never against you.' Gunnar then rode home from the Assembly.

Shortly after this Gunnar met Njál. Njál urged him to be on his guard, as he had heard that the men from the Thríhyrning farm were planning to attack him. He warned him to have the weapons with him at all times and never to go about without a large following. Gunnar promised to follow his counsel. He added that Ásgrím had invited him to his home – 'and I plan to go there this fall.'

'Let no one know when you plan to set out nor how long you plan to stay there,' said Njál. 'But I beg you to let my sons ride along with you.' They agreed upon that.

Now the summer wore on until it was eight weeks before the beginning of winter. Then Gunnar said to Kolskegg: 'Get ready now, for we are going to ride to Tunga to accept Ásgrím's invitation.'

'Shall we not send word to Njál's sons?' asked Kolskegg.

'No,' answered Gunnar, 'I don't want them to be involved in any trouble for my sake.'

61

Starkad Plans to Ambush Gunnar

The three, Gunnar and his brothers, rode together. Gunnar had his halberd and the sword which had been given him by Olvir, and Kolskegg had his short-sword. Hjort, too, was fully armed. They made their way to the farm at Tunga. There they were given a warm welcome by Ásgrím and they remained there for some time. After that they expressed their intention of returning home. Ásgrím gave them fine gifts and offered to ride east with them. However, Gunnar said there was no need of that whatsoever, and so Ásgrím did not ride along.

There was a man named Sigurd Swinehead who had come to the farm at Thríhyrning [as a servant]. He had promised them to report on Gunnar's whereabouts. He now told them of Gunnar's approach and said that they would never have a better opportunity – 'since there are only three of them.'

'How many men shall we need to attack him from ambush?' asked Starkad.

'It will be tough going against him with small fry,' the man said; 'we shall need no fewer than thirty men.'

'Where shall we lie in ambush?' asked Starkad.

'At Knafahólar,' Sigurd answered. 'He will not see us before we attack him.'

'Go to Sandgil,' said Starkad, 'and tell Egil that fifteen of them should get ready and ride from there to Knafahólar; we will join them with fifteen additional men from here.'

Thorgeir said to Hildigunn: 'This hand will show you Gunnar's dead body this very evening!'

'But I rather think,' she said, 'that it will be you who will be coming back from the fray with your head hanging low!'

Starkad together with his three sons and eleven others set out from Thríhyrning and came to Knafahólar where they lay in wait.

Sigurd came to Sandgil and said: 'I have been sent here by Starkad and his sons to tell you, Egil, that you and your sons should set out for Knafahólar and there lie in ambush for Gunnar.'

'How many of us are to go?' asked Egil.

'Fifteen counting me,' he answered.

Kol said: 'Now I mean to try conclusions with Kolskegg.'

'There you will take upon yourself a big venture, it seems to me,' said Sigurd.

Egil asked the two Norwegians to ride along, but they said they had no quarrel with Gunnar. – 'For that matter, you seem to need a great deal of help, seeing that such a host of men is to attack three men!' said Thórir.

Thereupon Egil turned away from them in a rage. But his wife said to the Norwegian: 'My daughter Gudrún did not do well to humble herself to the extent of sleeping with you, if you haven't the courage to accompany your host and father-in-law. You must be a cowardly wretch!'

'I'll go with your husband,' he said, 'but neither of us will return!'

Then he went to his comrade Thorgrím and said: 'Take the keys to my chest, for I shall never turn them again! Take as much of our personal property as you wish and return to Norway, and do not plan to avenge my death; it will be your own death if you do not leave the country.'

He then joined the others.

62

Gunnar's Dream

Now to return to Gunnar. He crossed the Thjórsá River in the east. He had not gone a long way from the river when he became very drowsy. So he bade them stop and let the horses graze. This they did. Gunnar fell fast asleep but was very restless in his sleep.[1]

Kolskegg said: 'Gunnar is dreaming now.'

Hjort replied: 'I would like to rouse him from his sleep.'

'No, don't do that!' said Kolskegg; 'let him have his sleep out and dream his dream to the end!'

Gunnar lay there for a rather long time; he tossed his shield aside, and he had become quite warm.

When he awoke, Kolskegg asked: 'What were you dreaming, brother?'

'I had such a dream,' said Gunnar, 'that I would not have left Tunga in such small company if I had had it before.'

'Tell us about your dream,' said Kolskegg.

'I dreamed that I was riding past Knafahólar, and there, I dreamed, I saw a flock of wolves come down upon me, and they all fell upon me, but I managed to get away from them and to the Rangá River. There they attacked me, but I fought them off. I shot those down who were in the lead, until they pressed so close that I could no longer use my bow against them. Then I took my sword, and with sword in one hand and halberd in the other I struck and thrust at them. I didn't seem to be protecting myself at all, and I really do not know what was protecting me. I killed many wolves, and you helped me, Kolskegg. But Hjort they seemed to have overpowered. They tore open his breast, and one wolf had Hjort's heart in its mouth. Then I seemed to become so enraged that I cut that wolf in two below the shoulder, and after that the other wolves turned and fled. And now I counsel you, brother Hjort, to ride back west to Tunga.'

'That I will not do,' said Hjort, 'and even though I see certain death before me I will follow you!'

Thereupon they proceeded to the east past Knafahólar. Kolskegg said: 'Gunnar, do you see all those spears coming up from behind the hills, and also those men with their weapons?'

'I am in no wise surprised that my dream comes true!' answered Gunnar.

'What do you propose to do?' asked Kolskegg. 'I take it that you don't mean to run away from them!'

'They are never going to poke fun at us on that account,' said Gunnar. 'Let us ride down to the headland by the river; there is a place where we can defend ourselves.'

So they made for that headland and got ready for the fight. As they rode past them, Kol called out: 'Are you going to take to your heels, Gunnar?'

Kolskegg answered: 'Ask that same question later on when the day is over!'

63

The Ambush

Thereupon Starkad urged his men on and they advanced upon the three on the headland. Sigurd Swinehead was foremost; in one hand he had a small round shield and in the other a hunting spear. Gunnar saw him and shot an arrow at him. Sigurd quickly raised his shield when he saw the arrow coming toward him, but the arrow pierced the shield, entered his eye, and came out at the back of his neck. He was thus the first man slain. Gunnar shot his second arrow at Úlfhedin, one of Starkad's overseers. The arrow pierced the middle of his body, so that he fell at the feet of a householder, and the householder on top of him. Kolskegg hurled a stone and struck the householder on the head, so that he, too, was killed.

Then Starkad said: 'We'll accomplish nothing as long as Gunnar can use his bow. Let us advance bravely and briskly against him!'

Then each one urged on the other. Gunnar defended himself with his bow and arrows as long as he could. Then he threw them down and took his halberd and sword and fought with both hands. It was a very bitter struggle, and Gunnar and Kolskegg slew a large number of men. Then Thorgeir Starkadarson said: 'I promised to come home to Hildigunn with your head, Gunnar!'

'She will not place such a great value on that,' answered Gunnar; 'still you will have to come closer if you want to get it!'

Thorgeir said to his brothers: 'Let us all rush up and attack him at once! He has no shield and his fate will thus rest in our hands!'

Bork and Thorkel leaped forward and they were even quicker than Thorgeir. Bork struck at Gunnar with his sword, but Gunnar parried with his halberd with such force that the sword flew out of Bork's hand. At that moment he saw Thorkel standing ready to cut at him from the other side. Gunnar stood with one leg bent. He brandished his sword and crashed it down on Thorkel's neck so that his head flew off.

Then Kol Egilsson said: 'Let me get at Kolskegg! I have always said that we two would be equally matched in battle!'

'That we can find out right now!' said Kolskegg.

Kol hurled his spear at him. Kolskegg had just slain a man and was so occupied that he did not have time to raise his shield in defence, and thus the spear struck the outside of his thigh and pierced the limb. Kolskegg turned around quickly, rushed at Kol, struck him on the thigh with his short-sword, and cut off his leg.

'Well, did I hit you or not?' asked Kolskegg.

'That comes from not being covered with my shield,' said Kol, and stood for a while looking at the stump.

Kolskegg said: 'No need to look! It's just as you thought; the leg is off!' Then Kol fell dead to the ground.

When Egil saw that he rushed at Gunnar and levelled a blow at him. Gunnar thrust at him with his halberd and drove it through his middle, then lifted him up on the halberd and threw him into the river.

Then Starkad said: 'You are a miserable wretch, Norwegian Thórir, to stand by, doing nothing! Egil, your host and father-in-law, has been slain!'

Then the Norwegian in a rage jumped into the fray. Hjort had already killed two men. Now the Norwegian rushed at him and struck him on the breast, so that Hjort fell dead at once.

Gunnar saw this and quickly struck at the Norwegian and cut

him in two at the waist. Shortly after that he thrust at Bork with his halberd. It struck him in the middle, came out through him, and lodged in the ground. Then Kolskegg cut off Hauk Egilsson's head and Gunnar lopped off Óttar's arm at the elbow.

Then Starkad said: 'Let us flee now; we are fighting trolls, not men!'

Gunnar said: 'It will be hard for you to prove that you have been in a battle if you don't bear some marks of it.' And with that he ran at them, inflicting wounds on both father and son.

That was the end of it. Gunnar and his brothers had also wounded many who managed to escape. Fourteen lost their lives in this fight, and Hjort was the fifteenth. Gunnar carried Hjort home on his shield, and he was buried in a cairn. Many men mourned his death, for he had been loved by all.

Starkad came home, and Hildigunn dressed his wounds as well as Thorgeir's and said: 'It would have been well for you two if you had not run afoul of Gunnar.'

'Indeed it would have been,' he answered.

64

Njál Plans Gunnar's Defence

Steinvor at Sandgil asked Thorgrím the Norwegian to manage her property for her;[1] she begged him not to leave Iceland, but to keep in mind the death of his comrade and her kinsmen.

He said: 'My comrade warned me that I would fall at Gunnar's hands, if I remained in this country. And he most likely could foretell that as well as his own death.'

'I would give you my daughter Gudrún in marriage and all my property in addition,' said Steinvor.

'I was not aware that you cared to pay such a high price,' he answered.

So they came to terms. He was to marry Gudrún, and the marriage took place in the course of the summer.

Gunnar rode to Bergthórshvál and Kolskegg with him. Njál and his sons were standing outside and they went to meet Gunnar and gave him a hearty welcome. After that Gunnar and Njál went aside and talked together.

Gunnar said: 'I have come here to seek your help and good counsel.'

Njál answered: 'You shall be welcome to it!'

'I have become involved in great difficulties and have slain many men,' said Gunnar, 'and I wish to know what you think of the matter.'

'Many will say that it was altogether unavoidable for you to do as you did,' said Njál, 'but now you must give me time to think it over.'

Njál went off by himself to reflect on what advice to give. When he returned he said: 'Now I have given some thought to the matter, and I should think that if we proceed with some daring and determination we might succeed. Thorgeir has gotten my kinswoman Thorfinna with child, and I am going to hand over to you the suit for seduction. I am also going to hand over to you another suit of outlawry against Starkad, because he cut wood on my property on Thríhyrning Ridge. You shall prosecute both these suits. Furthermore, you must go to the place where you fought, dig up the dead, name witnesses to the wounds, and declare all the slain outlawed, because they attacked you with the purpose and intention of inflicting wounds on you and your brothers and bringing about your sudden deaths. But if this suit is tried at the Assembly and an objection is raised on the score that you gave Thorgeir the first blow, and therefore may plead neither your own suit nor that of others, then I shall answer this point by saying that I declared you inviolable at the Thingskálar Assembly, so that you could plead not only your own suit but also that of others. That will answer that point. You must also go and look up Tyrfing in Berjaness, and he will hand over to you a suit against Onund in Trollaskóg, on whom it devolves to press suit against you for the slaying of his brother Egil.'

First Gunnar returned home, but a few days later he rode with the sons of Njál to the place where the bodies lay and dug up all that were buried there. Gunnar declared them all outlawed because of their assault upon him after plotting his death. Thereupon he returned home.

65

Measures and Countermeasures

That same autumn Valgard the Grey returned to Iceland and rode
to his home at Hof. Then Thorgeir went to visit Valgard and his
son Mord and protested what an outrage it was for Gunnar to
have declared outlaws all those whom he had killed. Valgard
answered that it must have been Njál's counsel and that it
remained to be seen yet what other schemes he had hatched out
for him. Thorgeir asked father and son for help and support, but
they held out for a long time and demanded a stiff price. Finally it
was agreed that Mord should ask for the hand of Thorkatla, the
daughter of Gizur the White, and that Thorgeir should immediately ride west over the rivers with Valgard and Mord.

The next day they set out, twelve of them altogether, and came
to Mosfell. They were well received and they brought up the
matter of their errand. The result of the discussion was that the
marriage was agreed upon and that the wedding feast was to take
place at Mosfell after a half-month's time. Thereupon they rode
home and in due time father and son invited a large number of
people to go to the wedding with them. There were already many
guests at Mosfell when they arrived, and everything at the wedding
feast went off well. Thorkatla rode home with Mord and took over
the management of the household, but Valgard went abroad again
that summer.

Mord urged Thorgeir to start an action against Gunnar. Thorgeir
went to look up Onund and asked him to take over the prosecution of the suit against Gunnar for the slaying of his brother Egil
and his sons – 'and I shall take over the prosecution of the suit for
the manslaughter of my brothers and for the wounds inflicted on
myself and my father.'

Onund said that he was prepared to do so, and thereupon they
proceeded to give notice of the slayings and summoned nine
neighbours who lived closest to the scene of the fight.

At Hlídarendi they learned of these preparations to bring suit. Gunnar went to see Njál, told him about it and asked what he would suggest that they do.

Njál said. 'Now you must summon your own neighbours as well as those closest to the scene of the fight. Name witnesses and select Kol as the slayer of your brother Hjort, for that is in accordance with the law. Then you must accuse Kol for having committed that slaying, even though he is dead. Then you must name witnesses and summon neighbours to go to the Assembly with you so that they may testify whether or no Kol and his companions were the assailants when Hjort was killed. You must also summon Thorgeir for seduction and press the suit against Onund which you have taken over from Tyrfing.'

Gunnar now did everything just as Njál had counselled. Many men thought this a very strange way to initiate a lawsuit. Now all these suits came before the Assembly. Gunnar rode to the Assembly, as did Njál and his sons and the sons of Sigfús. Gunnar had sent a messenger to his brothers-in-law, asking them to ride to the Assembly with a very large following, because it was a suit in which one would need all possible support. Thus a large band of men came from the west.

Mord journeyed to the Assembly, as did Rúnólf from Dale, the men from the Thríhyrning farm and Onund of Trollaskóg.

66

The Settlement at the Assembly

When they arrived at the Assembly they joined company with Gizur the White and Geir Godi.

Gunnar, the sons of Sigfús, and the sons of Njál all went in one group, and they marched so briskly and in such a closely knit formation, that men who stood in their path had to watch out that they were not bowled over. Nothing at this entire Assembly was discussed so much as this great lawsuit.

Gunnar went to meet his brothers-in-law, Óláf and his brothers, and they received him with open arms. They asked Gunnar about the fight, and he told them everything in a very clear and objective manner. He also told them what he had done in the case since that time.

Óláf said: 'It is of the greatest advantage to you that Njál supports you so firmly with all his counsel.'

Gunnar said that he would never be able to repay Njál for that. He then asked them for their support, and they replied that it was no more than right that he should have it.

Now the suits on both sides came before the court, and each side pleaded its case.

Mord asked how a man like Gunnar, who had already deserved to be outlawed because of the wound he had inflicted on Thorgeir, should be allowed to file a suit.

Njál said: 'Were you at the Thingskálar Assembly last autumn?'

'I certainly was,' answered Mord.

'Did you hear that Gunnar offered him reparations in full?' asked Njál.

'Yes, I did,' answered Mord.

'At that time I proclaimed Gunnar's inviolability and gave him the right to conduct all legal actions,' said Njál.[1]

'That is according to law,' said Mord, 'but how do you justify Gunnar's declaring Kol guilty of the slaying of Hjort, when it was actually the Norwegian who slew him?'

'That was according to law, too,' said Njál, 'because he designated him as the slayer before witnesses.'[2]

'That is probably according to law,' said Mord, 'but why did Gunnar declare them all liable to outlawry?'

'You should not need to ask about that,' answered Njál, 'inasmuch as they all planned beforehand to perpetrate assault and manslaughter.'

'But at any rate Gunnar did not suffer any hurt,' continued Mord.

'But Gunnar's brothers, Kolskegg and Hjort, were there,' answered Njál, 'and one was slain and the other wounded.'

'You have the law on your side,' said Mord, 'although it is hard for me to take it.'

Then Hjalti Skeggjason of Thjórsárdale came forward and said: 'Until now I have never taken sides in your litigations, Gunnar, but I want to know how far you will go [to compose this matter] for the sake of my words and friendship.'

'What would you ask me to do?' said Gunnar.

'This, that you submit the entire business to the judgement of well-meaning men for an equitable and just settlement.'

Gunnar replied: 'I will do so with the condition that you promise never to be against me, whatever men I have to deal with.'

'That I promise,' said Hjalti.

After that Hjalti negotiated with Gunnar's adversaries and brought about a settlement. Each side gave a pledge of peace to the other. Thorgeir's wound was offset by the suit for seduction, and Starkad's wound was cancelled out by his cutting wood on Njál's property. Thorgeir's brothers were atoned for with half penalties; the other half was forfeited because of their attack on Gunnar. Egil's slaying and Tyrfing's suit likewise offset each other. Hjort's slaying was compensated by the slaying of Kol and of the Norwegian, and all the others were atoned for with half fines.

Njál was among those making this arbitration, as were Ásgrím Ellida-Grímsson and Hjalti Skeggjason.

Njál had a considerable amount of money loaned out to Starkad and to the men at Sandgil; he gave all of this to Gunnar to pay his fines. Gunnar had so many friends at the Assembly that he was able to pay the fines for all the slayings immediately. In addition, he gave gifts to the many chieftains who had given him their support. From this suit Gunnar won the greatest honour, and all men agreed that he had no equal in the South Quarter.

Gunnar rode home from the Assembly and was now at peace, but his adversaries greatly begrudged him the great respect he had now.

67

Mord Continues Plotting Against Gunnar

Now we have to tell about Thorgeir Otkelsson; that he grew up to be a big and strong man, honest and upright, but somewhat inclined to follow the advice of others. He was very popular among the best men and much beloved by his kinsmen.

One day Thorgeir Starkadarson went to visit his kinsman Mord. 'I am very much dissatisfied with the result of our suit against Gunnar,' he said. 'Now as matters stand we have assurance from you that you will stand on our side so long as we two live. I wish you would think of some plan to attack Gunnar, but it must be a deep-laid one. I speak so frankly because I know you are Gunnar's greatest enemy, and he yours. I will make it worth your while if you devise such a plan.'

'It is known to everyone that I am always out for money,' said Mord, 'and that's the way it is in this case, too. It will prove very difficult to devise any plan by which you may accomplish your purpose without violating the agreements made. However, I have been told that Kolskegg plans to bring suit and take back a fourth part of Móeidarhvál farm, which was deeded over to your father as atonement for his son. Kolskegg has taken over the suit for his mother, and it is Gunnar's counsel to redeem this land by payment, but not to give it up. Let us wait until he has done so, and then declare that he has broken the agreement made with you. He has also taken a grain-field from Thorgeir Otkelsson, and thus broken the agreement made with him, too. Go and look up Thorgeir Otkelsson and have him make common cause with you, and then attack Gunnar. But if you are unsuccessful in this attempt and are unable to bring him down, then you will simply have to attack him again and again. However, I'll tell you this. Njál has looked into Gunnar's future and made the following prophecy: if Gunnar ever slays more than one man in the same family, and if at the same time it happens that he breaks the settlement subsequently made, then it will lead to his sudden death. That is why you must have Thorgeir Otkelsson involved in this case, because Gunnar has already slain his father; so if you two ever are in the same fight, you must be careful to protect yourself, but Thorgeir will advance boldly and Gunnar will slay him. Then he will have committed the second slaying in the same family, but you shall flee to safety. But if this is to bring about his death he will have to break the agreement [made afterwards]. As to that, we shall have to await developments.'

After that Thorgeir Starkadarson returned home and secretly initiated his father in this plan. They agreed between them that they would proceed with their scheme without anybody else's knowledge.

68

The Two Thorgeirs Plan to Attack Gunnar

Shortly after this Thorgeir Starkadarson went to Kirkby to visit his namesake [Thorgeir Otkelsson]. They went aside and conversed in secret the entire day. And at their parting Thorgeir Starkadarson gave his namesake a spear inlaid with gold, and they exchanged vows of most sincere friendship.

At the Thingskálar Assembly in the autumn Kolskegg brought up his claim to the land at Móeidarhvál; Gunnar named witnesses and offered to redeem this land from the owners of the Thríhyrning farm by payment or by the offer of other land according to the legal evaluation of the property. Thorgeir then named witnesses and charged that Gunnar had broken the agreement which had been arranged between them. With that the Assembly came to an end.

One year passed. The two Thorgeirs were constantly meeting, and the closest friendship existed between them.

One day Kolskegg said to Gunnar: 'I have been told that there is a very close friendship between the two Thorgeirs, and many men say that they are planning something. I would wish that you be very much on your guard.'

'Death will come to me wherever I may be, if it is so fated,' replied Gunnar.

With that they broke off their conversation.

In the autumn Gunnar gave orders that his people should work one week there at home and the following week down in the land-isles,[1] and thus finish the haymaking. He added that all should leave the farm except himself and the women.

Thorgeir from Thríhyrning went to see his namesake, and as soon as they met they began to talk together, as was their wont.

Thorgeir Starkadarson said: 'Let us now take heart and make for Gunnar!'

'Whenever Gunnar has been attacked he has emerged victorious,' said Thorgeir Otkelsson. 'Besides, I have no desire to be called a breaker of settlements agreed on.'

'They broke them, not we!' answered Thorgeir Starkadarson. 'From you Gunnar took your grain-field and from my father and myself he took Móeidarhvál.'

And so they agreed to attack Gunnar. Thorgeir Starkadarson said that Gunnar would be at home all alone after a few days. – 'You with eleven others join me, and I shall have just as many with me.'

After that Thorgeir rode home.

69

Njál Frustrates their Plan

Thorgeir Starkadarson was informed that Kolskegg and his men-servants had been in the land-isles for three days, and he sent word to his namesake to meet him on Thríhyrning Ridge. Thereupon Thorgeir from the Thríhyrning farm set out with eleven men, rode up to the ridge, and waited there for his namesake. Gunnar was now all alone at his homestead. The two Thorgeirs rode into a wood; there a great drowsiness came over them and they could do nothing but sleep.[1] They hung their shields in the branches of a tree, tethered their horses, and laid their weapons down at their sides.

Njál was at Thórólfsfell that night and he was unable to sleep, but kept walking in and out of the house. Thórhild[2] asked Njál why he couldn't sleep.

'Many things are passing before my sight,' he said, 'and I see the attendant spirits of many of Gunnar's enemies. However, one thing is very strange; they seem ravening, yet act aimlessly.'

A short time later a man rode up to the door, dismounted, and went in. It was the shepherd of Thórhild and Skarphedin.

She asked: 'Did you find the sheep?'

'I found something which might be more important,' he answered.

'What was that?' asked Njál.

'I found twenty-four men up in the woods. They had tethered their horses and were fast asleep. Their shields they had hung up in the branches of a tree.'

He had observed them so carefully that he was able to describe the weapons and the dress of all of them. Njál knew exactly who each one was and he said to the shepherd: 'I hired a good man when I hired you, and it would be fine if I had more like you! This service will stand you in good stead, but now I wish to send you on an errand.'

The shepherd answered that he was prepared to go.

'I want you to go to Hlídarendi,' said Njál, 'and tell Gunnar to hurry to Grjótá River and then send out a call for men. I shall go out and meet those others in the woods and frighten them away. This has turned out very well, because they will gain nothing from their undertaking but lose much.'

The shepherd went and reported everything very exactly to Gunnar. Then Gunnar rode to Grjótá River and sent out a call for men.

But as to Njál, he went out to find the two Thorgeirs.

'It is very careless of you to lie here like this,' he said to them. 'What was the purpose of this expedition anyway? Gunnar is not the type of man to be trifled with. The fact of the matter is that you are in for the worst kind of drubbing. And you might as well know that Gunnar is busy gathering forces and will be here soon and slay you all unless you decamp and return to your homes.'

They were greatly frightened and lost no time. They took their weapons, mounted their horses, and rode back to the Thríhyrning farm. Njál went to meet Gunnar and warned him not to disband his company. – 'But I shall go and try to arrange a settlement; they will be properly frightened now. For this attempt on your life the atonement shall not be any less, since they are all involved, than for the slaying of either one of the two Thorgeirs, in case that should occur. I shall keep this money and see to it that it is made available to you whenever you have need of it.'

70

They are Compelled to Pay an Indemnity

Gunnar thanked him for his aid, and Njál went to the Thríhyrning farm and told the Thorgeirs that Gunnar would not disband his company until the matter between them had been settled. They made various offers, because they were sore afraid, and begged Njál to go to him with proposals for an amicable settlement. Njál said he would deliver only such proposals as involved no guile. They begged him to lend his help in making the award and they promised to abide by his decision. Njál said he would make no award except at the Assembly and in the presence of the wisest men. They agreed to that.

Then Njál served as an intermediary and succeeded in having each party give to the other pledges of peace and reconciliation. He also was to make the award and to choose whom he wished to help him.

Shortly after this the Thorgeirs visited Mord Valgardsson. He reproached them very much for having placed the matter in Njál's hands, seeing he was such a close friend of Gunnar. He said that would turn out to their disadvantage.

Now the men rode to the Assembly as usual, and both parties were present. Njál requested silence and asked all the best men who had come to the Assembly what claim, in their opinion, Gunnar had against the Thorgeirs for their attempt on his life. They answered that, in their opinion, a man in Gunnar's place had great and just claims for compensation. Njál asked whether he had a case against all of them or whether only the leaders had to take the blame. They answered that most of it should fall on the leaders, but that all were involved to a large extent.

'Many people will say that it didn't happen without cause,' said Mord, 'since Gunnar himself broke the agreement with the Thorgeirs.'

'That is not breaking an agreement,' said Njál, 'if any man deals lawfully with another; for "with the law our land shall be built up, and by lawlessness destroyed"!'[1]

Thereupon Njál explained how Gunnar had offered land or other payment for Móeidarhvál. Then the Thorgeirs understood that they had been deceived by Mord, and they rebuked him and said that he was responsible for this fine.

Njál named twelve men as judges in this suit. Each man who had accompanied the Thorgeirs had to pay a hundred in silver, but the two Thorgeirs, two hundreds. Njál took the money into his keeping. Each side now gave the other pledges of peace, repeating the words after Njál.

Gunnar then rode west from the Assembly to the Dales as far as Hjardarholt, where he was well received by Óláf Peacock. He remained there half a month. During that time he rode around far and wide in the Dales and was welcomed wherever he came.

At his departure Óláf said: 'I wish to give you three things of value: a gold ring, a cloak which once belonged to Myrkjartan,[2] the king of Ireland, and a dog which was given to me in Ireland. The dog is big and will stand you in as good stead as a strong man. Also, he has human intelligence and will bark at every man whom he recognises as your enemy, but never at your friends, because he can tell from a man's look whether he means you well or ill; he will lay down his life for you. Sám is the dog's name.'

Then he spoke to the dog: 'Now follow Gunnar and serve him in every way you can!' The dog immediately went to Gunnar and lay down at his feet.

Óláf urged him to be on his guard because there were many men who envied him — 'seeing that you are considered the most outstanding man in the whole land.'

Gunnar thanked him for his gifts and good advice and rode home. Now Gunnar remained at home for a while and there was no disturbance.

71

The Two Thorgeirs and Mord Plan a Second Attempt on Gunnar's Life

Shortly after this the two Thorgeirs met Mord, but they were unable to reach any accord. The namesakes were of the opinion that they had lost much money because of Mord and had received nothing in return. They now asked him to devise some other plan which might harm Gunnar.

Mord said that he would do so. – 'It is now my counsel that you, Thorgeir Otkelsson, seduce Ormhild, Gunnar's kinswoman. The consequence of that will be that Gunnar will come to hate you even more bitterly. I shall then spread about the rumour that Gunnar is of no mind to stand that from you. Then, after that, you two must attack Gunnar, but not in his home, for that is out of the question, as long as the dog is alive.'

They agreed to carry out this plan.

Now the summer wore on. Thorgeir Otkelsson began to visit Ormhild quite frequently. This displeased Gunnar and a great animosity developed between the two men. And so it went on all winter. When summer came Thorgeir's secret trysts with Ormhild became ever more frequent. Meanwhile the other Thorgeir and Mord had frequent meetings and planned an attack on Gunnar whenever he should ride down to the land-isles to look after the work done by the servants.

One day Mord learned that Gunnar was on his way down, and so he sent a messenger to the Thríhyrning farm to tell Thorgeir that they now had their best chance to attack him. They set out, twelve altogether, and when they came to Kirkby they found twelve others awaiting them. They decided to ride down to the Rangá River and lie in wait for Gunnar there.

When Gunnar returned from the land-isles Kolskegg rode with him. Gunnar had his bow and arrows and his halberd; Kolskegg had his short-sword and other weapons.

72

Gunnar and Kolskegg Rout their Enemies

As Gunnar and his brother rode up to the Rangá River it happened that a great deal of blood appeared on Gunnar's halberd. Kolskegg asked what that might mean. Gunnar answered that such an omen, when it appeared in other lands, was known as a rain of blood – 'and yeoman Olvir said it always betokened great battles!'

After that they rode on until they saw some men at the side of the river; they had their horses tethered.

Gunnar said: 'This looks like an ambush!'

Kolskegg replied: 'They have been plotting this treachery for a long time. What shall we do now?'

'We'll dash past them up to the ford and make our stand there,' answered Gunnar.

The others saw that and immediately turned on them. Gunnar bent his bow, took his arrows, tossed them on the ground before him, and began to shoot at them as soon as they came within range. In this manner Gunnar wounded very many men and killed some.

Then Thorgeir Otkelsson said: 'We are not accomplishing much here; let us attack more sharply!'

This they did. Onund the Fair, a kinsman of Thorgeir's, was in front. Gunnar thrust at him with his halberd; the blow split his shield in two and the halberd pierced Onund in the middle. Ogmund Shaggyhead sprang at Gunnar from the rear, but Kolskegg saw that and cut off both of Ogmund's legs from under him and hurled him into the Rangá River, where he drowned immediately. The fight now became very bitter. Gunnar cut with one hand and thrust with the other. Kolskegg slew a great many men and wounded many others.

Thorgeir Starkadarson said to the other Thorgeir: 'You certainly don't act as though you had a father to avenge!'

Thorgeir Otkelsson answered: 'True it is that we haven't made much progress, but you haven't even kept pace with me; and I don't need to be egged on by you!'

With that he dashed at Gunnar in great fury and hurled his spear through Gunnar's shield and his arm. Gunnar gave his shield such a quick twist that the spear broke off at the socket. At that moment Gunnar saw that a second man had come within his sword's reach, and he struck at him and dealt him the deathblow. Then he grasped his halberd with both hands. Thorgeir Otkelsson had come close to him with his sword drawn. Gunnar turned on him quickly and in great wrath drove his halberd through his body, swung him aloft, and hurled him out into the Rangá River. The body drifted down the river toward the ford where it hit a boulder. From that time on the place has been called Thorgeir's Ford.

Then Thorgeir Starkadarson said: 'Let us flee! We shall not get the better of them at this rate!' Thereupon they all turned and fled.

'Let us pursue them!' said Kolskegg, 'and you, Gunnar, take your bow and arrows! You might get within range of Thorgeir Starkadarson.'

Gunnar answered: 'Our money purses will be well emptied by the time we have paid atonement for all those who lie dead here!'

'You will not lack for money,' said Kolskegg; 'but Thorgeir will never rest until he has caused your death.'

'More men like him will have to stand in my path before I am afraid!' said Gunnar.

Thereupon they rode home and reported what had happened. Hallgerd was glad to hear what was done and praised it greatly. But Rannveig said: 'Maybe the deed was well done, but I have a premonition that evil consequences will flow from it!'

73

Gizur's Suit at the Assembly

News of these events was spread far and wide, and Thorgeir's death was lamented by many. Gizur the White and his men rode to the spot, gave notice of the slayings, and summoned neighbours to the Assembly, whereupon they returned to their homes in the west.

Njál and Gunnar met and spoke about the fight. Njál said to Gunnar: 'Be on your guard; now you have slain two of the same family. Think of your own welfare and remember that your life is at stake if you do not abide by the terms of the agreement that will be made.'

'I don't mean to break the agreement in any way,' said Gunnar, 'but I shall need the help of you and your kinsmen at the Assembly.'

Njál answered: 'I shall keep my vow of friendship to you till my dying day!' Thereupon Gunnar rode home.

The time for the Assembly drew near and each side gathered a large number of followers. There was considerable discussion at the Assembly as to how the suit would end.

Gizur and Geir Godi discussed the problem as to which one of them should give notice of the suit for the slaying of Thorgeir. The result was that Gizur took over the suit and gave notice of it at the Law-Mount with these words: 'I give notice of a suit for assault, punishable under the law, against Gunnar Hámundarson for his assault, punishable under the law, against Thorgeir Otkelsson, in which he inflicted on him an internal wound which became a mortal wound, as a result of which Thorgeir died. I herewith declare that he should be punished by outlawry, and I insist that he should not be fed or forwarded nor given any help or assistance whatsoever. I declare that his goods and possessions should be forfeited, half to me and half to the men of that Quarter who according to the law are entitled to the confiscated goods and possessions of an outlaw. I give notice of this suit in that Quarter Court to which this charge should be referred according to the law. I give notice according to the law; I give notice so that all men at the Law-Mount may hear me; I give notice of a suit of complete outlawry against Gunnar Hámundarson.'

A second time Gizur named witnesses and gave notice of a suit against Gunnar Hámundarson, because he had inflicted on Thorgeir Otkelsson an internal wound which became a mortal wound, as a result of which Thorgeir died. This was done on the spot where Gunnar made an assault, punishable under the law, against Thorgeir.[1] Then he gave notice of this suit as he had done the first time. After that he asked to which Quarter Court the suit should be referred and in what district the defendant lived.

Thereupon the men left the Law-Mount and all remarked how well Gizur had pleaded his case. Gunnar was composed and said little.

The Assembly continued in session until the time for the courts to proceed to their appointed places. Gunnar stood to the north of the Rangá River Court and Gizur stood to the south. Gizur named witnesses and enjoined Gunnar to listen to his oath, to the presentation of the charge, and to all the proof for it which he intended to present. Thereupon he took the oath, brought the above mentioned charge before the court, had witnesses testify that notice of the suit had been duly given, and finally asked the jury of neighbours to be seated. He then called on Gunnar to exercise his right to challenge the jury.

74

Gunnar is Exiled

Then Njál said: 'Now we can no longer sit here merely as spectators. Let us go up to the jurors!'

So they did and challenged four of the jurors as unqualified,[1] but called on the five remaining ones to testify in Gunnar's behalf as to whether the two Thorgeirs had set out for the fray with the intention of killing Gunnar if they could. Without hesitation they all testified that this had been the case. Njál declared this to be legal defence against the charge and said he would bring up this defence if the other party did not agree to arbitration. Many chieftains joined in this request, and it was agreed that twelve men hand down the award. Both parties stepped forward and shook hands on this agreement.

Then the award was made and the amount of reparations determined. The entire sum was to be paid then and there at the Assembly. In addition, Gunnar and Kolskegg were to leave the land, and they were to be away for three years.[2] However, if Gunnar should not leave the land when he had the opportunity to do so, then he might be slain with impunity by the kinsmen of the man whom he had slain.

Gunnar gave no indication that he was dissatisfied with the agreement. He asked for the money which Njál had administered for him. Njál had loaned out the money at interest and now paid over the entire sum, and it was sufficient to cover the amount which Gunnar had to pay in reparations.

Thereupon the Assembly was dissolved, and Njál and Gunnar rode home together. Njál said to Gunnar: 'See to it, my friend, that you abide by this agreement and remember what I have told you! If your first journey abroad brought you great honour, this one will bring you even greater honour. You will return to Iceland as a man of great renown and will live to be an old man, and no one around here will dare to offer you an affront. But if you do not leave the

country and so break the agreement, then you will be slain here in
this land, and that will be sad news for all your friends!'

Gunnar said he did not intend to break the agreement. He rode
home and told them there of the settlement. Rannveig thought it
would be best if he went abroad; in that case his enemies would
have to find someone else with whom to quarrel.

75

Gunnar Defies the Verdict and Remains in Iceland

Thráin Sigfússon told his wife that he planned to go abroad that
summer. She had no objection, and so he arranged for passage
with Hogni the White. Gunnar and Kolskegg arranged for
passage with Arnfinn from Víken.

Njál's sons, Grím and Helgi, asked their father for permission to
travel abroad. He replied: 'You will have so much trouble on this
journey that it is doubtful whether you will live to tell the tale, and
yet it is possible that you will gain honour and renown. But I
would not be surprised if as a result of this journey difficulties
should arise for you when you return!'

Still they continued to ask for permission to travel, and the
upshot was that he told them they might go if they wished to. They
took passage with Bárd the Black and Óláf, the son of Ketil of Elda.
And now there was considerable talk to the effect that the best men
of the district were leaving.

Gunnar's sons were now full grown. They were of very unlike
temperament; Grani had much of his mother's disposition, but
Hogni was thoroughly upright.

Gunnar had all his wares and those of his brother brought to the
ship. After everything had been brought there and the ship was
almost ready to sail, Gunnar rode to Bergthórshvál to say farewell
and to thank all those who had supported him. The following day
he prepared to ride down to the ship and he told all his people that
he was going abroad for good. They took that much to heart, yet
hoped he would return some day.

When he was ready to leave he kissed them all goodbye; they all went out of the house with him. He took his halberd, thrust it into the ground, leaped upon his horse, and rode away with Kolskegg.

As they were riding down toward the Markar River Gunnar's horse stumbled and threw him. He looked up toward the slope where stood the farmhouses of Hlídarendi and said: 'Fair is the slope, fairer it seems than I have ever seen it before, with whitening grain and the home field mown; and I shall ride back home and not go aboard at all!'

'Don't make your enemies happy by breaking the settlement!' said Kolskegg. 'No one would expect such a thing of you, and if you do, you can expect that all will turn out as Njál predicted!'

'I shall not go abroad at all!' said Gunnar, 'and I wish you would not, either!'

'That shall not be!' answered Kolskegg. 'I will not betray the trust others put in me, neither on this occasion, nor on any other. This is the one and only thing which will separate us. Tell my kinsmen and my mother that I never intend to see Iceland again, because I shall learn of your death, Gunnar, and then I shall have no reason to return.'

With that they parted; Gunnar rode home to Hlídarendi, but Kolskegg rode to the ship and went abroad.

Hallgerd was happy to see Gunnar return, but his mother had very little to say.

Gunnar remained at home that autumn and winter, but did not have many men with him. Óláf Peacock invited Gunnar and Hallgerd to live with him, leaving the management of the farm at Hlídarendi in the hands of Gunnar's mother and his son Hogni. That seemed advantageous to him at first, and he agreed; but when it came to the point, he didn't care to go.

At the Assembly the following summer Gizur the White and Geir Godi proclaimed Gunnar an outlaw at the Law-Mount, and before the meeting came to an end Gizur summoned all of Gunnar's enemies to meet at the Almanna Gorge:[1] Starkad from Thríhyrning and his son Thorgeir, Mord and Valgard the Grey, Geir Godi and Hjalti Skeggjason, Thorbrand and Ásbrand, the sons of Thorleik, Eilíf and his son Onund, Onund of Trollaskóg, and Thorgrím of Sandgil.

Gizur said: 'I propose to you that we make an attack on Gunnar this summer and slay him!'

Hjalti answered: 'I promised Gunnar, when he gave heed to my request at the Assembly, that I would never take part in any attack on him, and I mean to live up to that!'

Thereupon Hjalti left the gathering, but those who were left planned the attack on Gunnar, and by handclasp confirmed that anyone backing out would forfeit his life. Mord was to spy on Gunnar and inform the others when the best opportunity to fall upon him should present itself. There were forty men in this ring. They now considered it a small matter to attack Gunnar, since Kolskegg and Thráin and many other friends of his were away. Thereupon people journeyed home from the Assembly. Njál went to visit Gunnar and informed him that he had been declared an outlaw and that his enemies were planning an attack on him.

'You are a true friend to warn me of this!' said Gunnar.

'Now,' said Njál, 'I would like Skarphedin and also my son Hoskuld to come here and stay at your home; they will lay down their lives for you.'

'No,' replied Gunnar, 'I do not wish that your sons be slain on my account; you deserve better of me than that.'

'It will not make much difference in the end,' said Njál, 'for once you are gone they will turn against my sons.'

'Very likely,' said Gunnar, 'but I would not like that misfortune to happen through me. However, I would have one request to make of you, and that is, that you look after my son Hogni. I'll not say anything about Grani, because he does much which is not to my liking.'

Njál promised to do so and then rode home. We are told that Gunnar attended all gatherings and assemblies, but never did his enemies dare to attack him. Thus Gunnar went about for some time just as though he had not been declared an outlaw.

76

Gunnar's Enemies Move on Hlídarendi

In the autumn Mord Valgardsson sent word that Gunnar would
be at home all alone, because all his people would be down in the
land–isles finishing their task of bringing in the hay. Gizur the
White and Geir Godi rode east across the rivers as soon as they
learned of this and continued on over the Sands to Hof. From
there they sent word to Starkad of Thríhyrning. All those who
were going to attack Gunnar met at Hof and took counsel how
to do it. Mord said that they would not be able to come upon
Gunnar unawares unless they seized the farmer who lived at the
next homestead – his name was Thorkel – and forced him to go
along and catch the dog Sám. He was to go up to the farm alone.

They approached Hlídarendi from the west and sent men after
Thorkel. They seized him and gave him the choice of being killed
or laying hold of the dog. He chose rather to save his life; so he
went along with them.

At Hlídarendi there was a horse shelter sloping down from the
yard toward the houses. Here the attacking party halted. Farmer
Thorkel went up to the buildings. The hound was lying on the
roof, and he lured him down into the creek in the shallow ravine.
But no sooner did the dog see the men there than he jumped up on
Thorkel and bit him in the groin. Onund of Trollaskóg struck the
dog on the head with his axe and the blade sank into his brain. At
that the dog let out a loud howl, the like of which they had never
heard before.

77

Gunnar's Death

Gunnar awoke in the sleeping hall and said: 'Hard have you been dealt with, my brother Sám, and who knows but it is foreordained that the same fate befall me soon!'

Gunnar's sleeping hall was made entirely of wood and covered with clapboards on the outside. There were window openings on either side of the ridgepole with wooden shutters covering them. Gunnar slept in a loft of the hall, as did Hallgerd and also his mother. When his enemies came up to the house they did not know whether Gunnar was at home; so they wanted someone to go up to the building and find out. Meanwhile they sat down outside. Thorgrím the Norwegian climbed up on the roof. Gunnar saw a red coat appear at the window and lunged at Thorgrím with his halberd and struck him in the middle. Thorgrím's feet slipped from under him, he dropped his shield and tumbled from the roof. He then walked over to Gizur and the rest of the group who were sitting on the ground. Gizur looked at him and asked: 'Well, is Gunnar home?'

Thorgrím answered: 'Find that out for yourselves! All I know is that his halberd is!' With that he fell dead to the ground.

Then they began to attack the buildings. Gunnar shot his arrows at them and defended himself so well that they could accomplish nothing. Some climbed up on the roof and tried to attack him from there, but Gunnar was able to reach them with his arrows so that they could not accomplish anything either. Thus it went on for a while. Then they took a short rest and attacked a second time, but still Gunnar shot his arrows at them and they had to withdraw again.

Then Gizur the White said: 'Let us press on more sharply! This won't do!'

They made a third assault and kept at it for a long time, but nevertheless, they were forced to retreat again.

Then Gunnar said: 'There is an arrow lying outside on the wall and it is one of theirs. I'll shoot that one at them; it will be a disgrace to them to fall by their own weapons!'

His mother said: 'Don't stir them up again, now that they have withdrawn!'

But Gunnar reached out for the arrow and shot it at them, and it struck Eilíf Onundarson and wounded him severely. He had been standing off to one side, so that the others did not realise that he had been wounded.

'An arm came out over there,' said Gizur; 'there was a gold ring on it and it picked up an arrow which was lying on the roof. Gunnar would not be looking for supplies outside if there were enough inside. Let us attack again!'

Mord said: 'Let us burn down the house over his head!'

'No, I shall never do that, even though my life depended on it!' said Gizur. 'You ought to be able, such a clever fellow as you are said to be, to devise some stratagem to help us!'

There were some ropes lying on the ground, such as were formerly used for holding down the buildings.

Mord said: 'Let us take these ropes and make them fast to the ends of the gable beams, then secure the other ends to boulders, and let us insert beams as windlasses and wrench the roof off the hall!'

They seized the ropes and carried out this scheme, and before Gunnar knew it they had wrenched the whole roof off the hall. Gunnar kept shooting arrows at them so that they could not get near him. Again Mord said that they should fire the hall.

Gizur answered: 'I don't know why you keep on suggesting something that no one else wants to do; and it shall never be!'

At this moment Thorbrand Thorleiksson sprang upon the roof and cut Gunnar's bowstring in two. Gunnar grasped his halberd with both hands, turned quickly on Thorbrand and drove the weapon through his body and hurled him down to the ground below. Then his brother Ásbrand sprang up. Gunnar thrust at him with his halberd. Ásbrand brought the shield before him; the halberd pierced the shield and ran in between the bones of his forearm. Then Gunnar twisted the halberd so hard that the shield split and the bones in Ásbrand's arm were broken and he tumbled from the wall. Before that Gunnar had wounded eight men and killed two.

At this moment he received two wounds; but people said of him that he minded neither wounds nor death. He said to Hallgerd: 'Give me two strands of your hair,[1] and you and my mother twist them together to make a bowstring for me!'

'Does anything depend on that?' she asked.

'My life depends on it,' he answered. 'Because they will never get at me as long as I can use my bow!'

'In that case I'll remind you of the slap on the face you gave me,' she answered, 'and I don't care whether you hold out a longer or a shorter time!'

'Everyone has something he is proud of,' said Gunnar. 'Nor shall I ask you a second time!'

Rannveig said: 'You behave meanly, and your shame will live long!'

Gunnar defended himself bravely and well and wounded eight other men, many so severely that they lay at death's door. He fought until he fell overcome by weariness. They gave him many deep wounds, and still he got away from them and defended himself for a long time. Yet at the end they killed him. Thorkel Elfara-Skáld composed this verse about his defence:

> Heard we, how with murderous
> halberd in the southland
> Gunnar him fended, 'gainst the
> gold-dispensers[2] battling:
> sixteen sea-steed rulers[3]
> sorely wounded he who
> trounced the tiller-wielders[4]
> twain he gave the deathblow.

Gizur said: 'A great chieftain have we laid low now, and it has cost us dear, and his defence will be remembered as long as men live in this land!'

Thereupon he went to Rannveig and asked: 'Will you grant us a plot of earth so that we may bury two of our men who have died here?'

'Gladly for the two, and more gladly would I for all of you!' she answered.

'Good reason have you to speak so,' he replied, 'because you have lost much.' – And he ordered that there was to be no pillaging nor other damage done there. Then they left the place.

Then Thorgeir Starkadarson said: 'We shall not be able to stay at our farms for fear of the sons of Sigfús unless you, Gizur, or you, Geir, stay here in the south for a while.'

'That is likely to be so,' answered Gizur. They drew lots and it fell to Geir's lot to remain in the district. He went to Oddi and settled there.

Geir had a son named Hróald. He was illegitimate, the son of Bjartey, the sister of Thorvald the Ailing who was slain at Hestlœk in Grímsness. Hróald boasted that he had given Gunnar the deathblow. Hróald was now staying with his father. Thorgeir Starkadarson boasted of another wound which he had given Gunnar.

Gizur remained at home in Mosfell. The slaying of Gunnar made much bad blood throughout the country and his death was lamented by many men.

78

Skarphedin and Hogni Plan Revenge

Njál was very much grieved at the news of Gunnar's death, and so were the sons of Sigfús. They asked Njál whether he thought they should give notice of a suit for the slaying of Gunnar or take up the suit at the Assembly. He said they could not do that because Gunnar was in the state of outlawry, and that it would be more advisable to do them some damage by killing some men in revenge for Gunnar.

They threw up a grave mound over Gunnar and let him sit upright in it. Rannveig did not wish that his halberd be put into the cairn. She said that only he who was prepared to avenge Gunnar might have it. So no one would take it. Rannveig was so embittered against Hallgerd that she came near killing her. She said Hallgerd had been responsible for Gunnar's slaying. Hallgerd fled to Grjótá River[1] and took her son Grani with her. A division of the property was then made: Hogni was to have the land at Hlídarendi and the homestead, but Grani was to have whatever property was leased out to tenant farmers.

It happened at Hlídarendi that a shepherd and a housemaid were driving cattle past Gunnar's cairn. Gunnar seemed to be very merry and was reciting verses in his cairn. They went home and told Gunnar's mother Rannveig what they had seen and heard, and she bade them tell Njál. They went to Bergthórshvál and reported it to Njál, and he had them repeat the story three times. After that he spoke with Skarphedin for a long time secretly. Skarphedin took his arms and with the servants rode to Hlídarendi. He was well received by Hogni and Rannveig, for they were very happy to see him. Rannveig bade him stay there a long time and he promised to do so. Skarphedin and Hogni were always together wherever they went. Hogni was a brave and upright fellow, but distrustful, and for that reason the shepherd and the housemaid had not dared to tell him about the apparition they had seen.

Once it happened that Skarphedin and Hogni were standing outside and to the south of Gunnar's cairn. There was bright moonlight, but now and then it was dimmed by a passing cloud. Then it seemed to them as though the cairn were standing open; Gunnar had turned around in his grave and was looking at the moon. They thought they saw four lights burning in the cairn; yet none of them seemed to cast any shadow. They saw that Gunnar was happy and wore a cheerful expression. He recited this verse, and so loudly that Skarphedin and Hogni could have heard it clearly even if they had been standing farther away:

> Said the gold-ring-giver,[2]
> gladly who in sword-fray
> fought with fearless heart, and
> father was of Hogni:
> he would rather, helm-clad,
> holding to his shield aye,
> fall upon the field than
> flee, thou tree-of-combat,[3]
> than flee, thou tree-of-combat.

Thereupon the cairn closed again.

'Would you have believed this marvel if Njál had told you of it?' asked Skarphedin.

'Yes, if Njál had told me of it, I would believe it,' Hogni answered, 'for it is said that Njál never lies.'

'There is great significance to this apparition,' said Skarphedin, 'for Gunnar, who would rather die than yield to his enemies, has shown himself to us and given us this counsel.'

'I shall be able to accomplish nothing,' said Hogni, 'unless you lend me your support.'

Skarphedin answered: 'I shall always remember how Gunnar conducted himself after the slaying of your kinsman Sigmund. I shall lend you as much support as I can. My father promised Gunnar that he would be of help in any matter which involved you or your mother.'

After that they rode home to Hlídarendi.

79

The Revenge is Accomplished

'Now let us set out this very night,' said Skarphedin, 'for if they learn that I am here they will be much more on their guard.'

'I'll follow your counsel in every way,' answered Hogni.

Then when everybody had gone to bed they took their weapons. When Hogni took down Gunnar's halberd it made a loud ringing sound. Rannveig started up in a great rage and said: 'Who is taking that halberd when I forbade everyone to wield it?'

'I mean to bring it to my father,' replied Hogni, 'so that he can take it to Valholl and use it in combat there.'[1]

'Before that it is you who will be using it to avenge your father,' she said, 'because it is foretelling the death of one man or several!'

Then Hogni went out and told Skarphedin of the words which he had exchanged with his grandmother. Thereupon they set out for the farm at Oddi, and two ravens flew above them the entire way.[2]

They arrived there during the night and drove all the livestock up to the buildings there. Then Hróald and Tjorvi ran out and drove the cattle back into the lanes. Both men were armed.

Skarphedin started up before them and said: 'No need to look more closely; it is just as it seems!' And he dealt Tjorvi the deathblow.

Hróald had a spear in his hand and he lunged at Hogni who rushed at him. But Hogni crashed the spear shaft in two with his halberd and then ran him through with the weapon. After that they left the two dead men lying there and made their way up to the Thríhyrning farmstead. Skarphedin jumped on the roof of the house and began to pluck the grass; those inside thought it was the sheep.[3] Starkad and Thorgeir put on their clothes, took their arms, and went out and started up along the fence. Starkad was frightened when he saw Skarphedin and wished to turn back. But Skarphedin dispatched him by the fence. Then Hogni came face to face with Thorgeir and cut him down with his halberd.

From there they rode to Hof where they found Mord outside in the field.[4] He asked for quarter and offered to make a complete settlement. Skarphedin told Mord of the slaying of the other four men – 'and you will go the same way unless you give Hogni the right to settle on his own terms; that is, if he agrees to that!'

Hogni said that he had not intended to come to any terms with the slayers of his father, but finally he accepted the offer of self-judgement.

80

Njál Effects a Settlement

Njál had a hand in persuading those who had the right and duty to take action against the slayers of Starkad and Thorgeir that they should accept compensation. To that end a district meeting was called and men selected to make the award. All the facts in the case were taken into consideration, even the attack on Gunnar, despite the fact that he had been in the state of outlawry. Mord paid everything, for no final settlement with him was made until the other case had been settled. Thereupon they let one award offset the other.[1] Then they declared themselves to be fully reconciled.

There was a long discussion in the Assembly about the case of Geir Godi against Hogni,[2] but finally they reached an agreement which proved lasting. Geir Godi lived at Hlíd till his dying day, and he is now out of the saga.

Njál asked for the hand of Álfeid, daughter of Vetrlidi the Skald,[3] for his son Hogni, and she was given to him. Their son was Ari who sailed to the Shetland Islands and married there. From him was descended Einar the Shetlander, one of the bravest of men. Hogni maintained his close friendship with Njál, and is now out of the saga.[4]

81

Of Kolskegg

Now to tell of Kolskegg. He came to Norway and remained in Víken that winter. But the following summer he sailed to Denmark and entered the service of King Svein Forkbeard, and there he was accorded great honour.

One night he dreamed that a man appeared to him; he was bathed in a radiant light and it seemed to Kolskegg that the man waked him.

He said to Kolskegg: 'Arise thou and come with me!'

'What do you want of me?' asked Kolskegg.

'I shall obtain a wife in marriage for thee, and thou shalt be my knight!' answered the man.

He dreamed that he assented to this, and then he awoke. He went to a wise man and told him his dream. The man interpreted it for him and said that Kolskegg would travel to southern lands and become God's knight.

Kolskegg was baptised in Denmark but was not happy there; then he journeyed east to Russia and stayed there an entire winter. From there he went on to Constantinople and entered war-service there. The last that was heard of him was that he married there and became a leader of the Varangians.[1] There he stayed till his dying day, and he is now out of the saga.

82

Thráin Wins the Friendship of Earl Hákon of Norway

Now to tell of Thráin Sigfússon. He and his company landed in Hálogaland in northern Norway and then continued south to Drontheim and Lade.[2] No sooner did Earl Hákon learn of their arrival than he sent messengers to them to find out what sort of men there were on the ship. They returned and told them who they were. The earl then sent for Thráin Sigfússon, and he appeared before him. The earl asked Thráin of what kin he was; he answered that he was closely related to Gunnar of Hlídarendi.

The earl said: 'That will stand you in good stead, for I have known many Icelanders, but none his equal!'

Thráin asked: 'Sire, will you permit me to stay at your court this winter?'

The earl accepted him, and Thráin remained there that winter and enjoyed great honour.

There was a man named Kol; he was a viking, the son of Ásmund Ashside of Smáland. He was stationed in the Göta River in Sweden with five ships and a large force of men. From there he sailed out of the river and to Norway and landed at Folden. There he came upon Hallvard Sóti by surprise as he lay in a loft. Hallvard defended himself well until they applied the torch to the house. Then he surrendered, but they slew him, took a large amount of booty and sailed back to Ljódhús [on the Göta River]. Earl Hákon was informed of this and had Kol declared an outlaw throughout his entire realm and had a price set on his head.

On a certain occasion the earl spoke as follows: 'It's a shame that Gunnar of Hlídarendi is now so far away. If he were here he would slay this man whom I have declared an outlaw, but now the Icelanders will slay Gunnar. It is unfortunate that he did not come to join us.'

Thráin Sigfússon replied: 'I am not Gunnar, but I am of his kin and am ready to attempt this undertaking.'

The earl said: 'I gladly consent to that and shall equip you well for the expedition.'³

Thereupon his son Eirík had this to say: 'You make fine promises to many men, but your performance does not always measure up to your promise. This is a very difficult journey, for this viking is a formidable opponent and one very difficult to deal with. You will have to exercise considerable care in selecting both men and ships for this expedition.'

Thráin said: 'I will set out on this expedition, even though success is doubtful.'

Thereupon the earl gave him five ships, and all were well equipped. Along with Thráin there were also Gunnar Lambason and Lambi Sigurdarson. Gunnar was a nephew of Thráin. He had lived with him when he was young and the two loved each other greatly. The earl's son Eirík assisted them, examining both the crew and the supply of arms and making such changes as he thought necessary. When they were ready to sail Eirík procured a pilot for them. They then sailed south along the coast. Wherever they landed the earl put at their disposal anything they needed.

They held their course to Ljódhús. Then they learned that Kol had sailed east to Denmark, and so they followed him there. When they arrived at Helsingborg they met some men in a boat who told them that Kol was in the vicinity and that he would remain there for a while. The weather was good on that day and Kol saw the ships approaching. He said that he had dreamed of Earl Hákon that night and added that these were probably his men. He ordered all his men to take up their weapons. Thereupon they prepared to defend themselves and the fighting began. For a long time the issue remained undecided. Then Kol leaped aboard Thráin's ship and quickly cleared himself a path, slaying men right and left. He wore a gilded helmet.

Thráin saw that this would not do; so he urged on his men to follow him. He himself went foremost to meet Kol. Kol struck at him and the blow crashed against Thráin's shield, splitting it from top to bottom. Then Kol was struck on the hand by a stone, so that his sword fell from his grasp. Thereupon Thráin slashed at Kol, and the blow severed his foot. After that they slew Kol. Thráin cut off his head; the trunk he threw overboard, but the head he kept.

They captured a large amount of booty there and then returned
north to Drontheim where they were well received by the earl.
Thráin showed him Kol's head and the earl thanked him for this
deed. Eirík said it was worth more than mere thanks. The earl
agreed with this and bade Thráin and his men follow him. They
went to the shipyard where the earl was having some good ships
built. One ship among them was not made like a man-of-war. It
was well equipped and adorned with a griffin's head.

The earl said: 'You like fine things and display, Thráin, and you
are just like your kinsman Gunnar in this respect. I wish to give you
this ship which is called 'The Griffin'. With it goes my friendship,
and it is my wish that you stay here as long as you care to.'

Thráin thanked the earl for his generosity and said he did not
desire to return to Iceland, as matters stood. The earl had an
engagement to journey east to the boundary of his land to meet the
Swedish king. Thráin accompanied him throughout the summer
and was the skipper of 'The Griffin'. He sailed his ship so swiftly
that few could keep up with him, and he was greatly envied. It was
evident at all times how highly the earl esteemed Gunnar, for he
sternly rebuffed all those who slandered Thráin.

Thráin stayed with the earl all the following winter. In the spring
the earl asked Thráin whether he wished to remain there or sail to
Iceland. Thráin answered that he had not as yet made up his mind,
and he added that he would first like to await news from Iceland.
The earl said he should do just as he pleased, and so Thráin
remained there with the earl. Then came that news from Iceland
which weighed on all: that Gunnar of Hlídarendi was slain. Then
the earl did not care to have Thráin sail to Iceland, and so he
remained there.

83

Grím and Helgi Go Abroad

Now we have to tell about Grím and Helgi, the sons of Njál. They sailed from Iceland the same summer as Thráin and his men. They had taken passage on a ship which belonged to Bárd and Óláf Elda-Ketilsson. They had such stormy winds from the north that they were driven off their course to the south, and they ran into such a dense fog that they did not know where they were going. After a long time on the high seas they finally came to shallow waters, and it seemed certain to them that they must be near land. The sons of Njál asked Bárd whether he by any chance could tell them to what land they might be closest.

'It is possible that it is any one of several, to judge by the wind and the weather we have had,' he answered. 'It might be the Orkneys or Scotland or Ireland.'

Two days later they saw land on both sides and a strong surf running up into the fjord. They cast anchor outside the surf. The storm began to abate and the following morning there was a calm. Then they saw thirteen ships sailing out toward them.

'What shall we do now?' asked Bárd. 'It looks as though these men were going to attack us!'

They took counsel as to whether they should defend themselves or surrender, but before they could make up their minds the vikings were already upon them.

Each side enquired of the other who they were and who their leader was. The leaders of the merchants[1] gave their names, and in turn asked who the captains of the vikings were. One of them said his name was Grjótgard, and the other, Snækólf, both sons of Moddan of Duncansby in Scotland, a kinsman of the Scotch King Melkólf. – 'We offer you these two choices,' said Grjótgard; 'either go ashore and let us seize your goods, or we will attack you and slay every man we lay hands on!'

Helgi answered: 'The merchants choose to defend themselves!'

Then the merchants said: 'A curse on you for your words! How can we defend ourselves? Life is worth more than money!'

Grím then bethought himself of the ruse of shouting at the vikings so that they could not hear the angry grumblings of the merchants.

Bárd and Óláf said: 'Don't you think that these Icelanders will make a laughing stock of you and your behaviour? Rather, take up your arms and defend yourselves!'

They all took their weapons and vowed to one another that they would never surrender as long as they had the strength to defend themselves.

84

Kári Comes to their Aid Against the Vikings

Thereupon the vikings began to shoot at them. The battle began and the merchants defended themselves bravely. Snækólf sprang at Óláf and ran him through with his spear, but Grím gave Snækólf such a powerful thrust with his spear that he knocked the viking overboard. Helgi now joined Grím and together they repulsed all the vikings as they attempted to board the ship. Njál's sons were always at the spot where they were most needed. The vikings called out to the merchants asking them to surrender, but they answered that they would never do that.

At this moment they looked seaward and saw ships coming up from the south around the headland. There were no fewer than ten ships and they were coming straight toward them as fast as they could. Shields lined the gunwales,[1] and at the mast of the foremost ship there stood a man wearing a silken jacket and a gilded helmet. His hair was long and fair and in his hand he carried a spear inlaid with gold.

He asked: 'Who are the parties in this uneven fight?'

Helgi gave his name and informed him that their opponents were named Grjótgard and Snækólf.

'And who are the skippers of your ship?' he asked.

Helgi answered: 'Bárd the Black – he is still alive; but the other, Óláf, has fallen.'

The man continued: 'Are you Icelanders?'

'Yes, we are,' Helgi answered.

He asked whose sons they were, and they told him. Then he realised with whom he was talking and said: 'Widely known are you and your father!'

'And who are you?' asked Helgi.

'My name is Kári and I am the son of Solmund,' he answered.

'Where are you coming from?' asked Helgi.

'From the Hebrides,' he replied.

'If you wish to help us,' said Helgi, 'you have certainly come at the right time!'

'I'll give you as much help as you need,' said Kári. 'But what would you have us do?'

'Attack the vikings!' answered Helgi.

Kári said that he should have his wish.

Then they advanced toward the vikings and the battle began anew. After they had fought a while Kári leaped aboard Snækólf's ship. Snækólf took him on and struck at him, but Kári jumped backwards over a boom which lay across the ship. Snækólf struck the boom with such force that both edges of his sword were buried in it. Kári then struck at Snækólf and his sword crashed down on his shoulder with such force that the arm was severed from the shoulder. Snækólf died immediately. Grjótgard hurled a spear at Kári, but Kári saw it coming and jumped into the air so that the spear missed him. Just then Helgi and Grím came up to join Kári. Helgi sprang at Grjótgard and ran him through with his sword, and that was his deathblow. Then they began to clear the decks. All the vikings begged for mercy; it was granted them, but all their goods were taken from them. After that they sailed out in the lea of the islands with all their ships.

85

Kári and the Sons of Njál with Earl Sigurd of the Orkneys

Sigurd was the name of the earl who ruled over the Orkneys. He was the son of Hlodvir, the son of Thorfinn Skull-Splitter, the son of Torf-Einar, the son of Rognvald the Earl of Mœre, the son of Eystein Glumra. Kári was a member of the earl's bodyguard, and he had been collecting tribute for him from Earl Gilli in the Hebrides. Kári asked Helgi and his companions to come with him to the island of Mainland, saying that the earl would receive them well. They accepted the invitation and sailed with Kári to Mainland. Kári presented them to the earl and explained who they were.

'How did they happen to meet you?' asked the earl.

'I met them in the Scotch firths, and they were fighting with the sons of Moddan and defending themselves very bravely. They quickly shifted from one side of the ship to the other and were always right there where the fighting was most bitter. I should now like to ask you to accept them among your followers.'

'You shall have your way,' answered the earl, 'seeing how strongly you have laid yourself out for them already.'

Thus they spent the entire winter with the earl and enjoyed great honour at his court.

As the winter wore on Helgi grew depressed. The earl could not imagine what was the matter and asked him why he was so silent and whether he found anything wrong with his treatment at court. – 'Don't you like it here?'

'Oh yes, very well!' he answered.

'Then what is the matter?' asked the earl.

'Don't you have a realm in Scotland to protect?' asked Helgi.

'I certainly do!' answered the earl. 'What about it?'

Helgi said: 'I am thinking that the Scots have killed your steward and intercepted all messages so that none could cross the Pentland Firth.'

The earl asked: 'Do you have second sight?'

'It has not yet been put to the test,' answered Helgi.

'I shall give you even greater honour, if it turns out as you say,' replied the earl; 'otherwise you will pay for this.'

'Helgi is not that kind of man,' said Kári. 'What he says is no doubt true, for his father has second sight.'

Thereupon the earl sent messengers south to Stroma to Arnljót, his steward there, and Arnljót in his turn sent men south across the Pentland Firth to make enquiries. They learned that Earl Hundi and Earl Melsnati had killed Hávard, Earl Sigurd's brother-in-law, at Thrasvík. Then Arnljót sent messengers to Earl Sigurd with a request that he come south with a great force and drive these earls out of his realm. As soon as the earl learned this he gathered a very large army.

86

They Join Sigurd on his Expeditions

Then the earl led his expedition south, and Kári and the sons of Njál went with him. They arrived at Caithness. In Scotland the earl owned these lands: Ross, Morey, Sutherland, and the Dales. Men from these districts joined them and reported that the earls were not far off with a large army. Thereupon Earl Sigurd led his forces that way and they met them above Duncansby Head, and the battle was fought there. The Scots had detached a portion of their forces to fall upon the rear of Earl Sigurd's army, and many of his men fell there before Njál's sons countered and fought against the enemy and put them to flight. Then the battle raged in earnest. Helgi and his brothers advanced by the earl's banner and gave a good account of themselves. Then Kári turned against Earl Melsnati. Melsnati hurled a spear at Kári, but Kári caught the spear and sent it back and through the earl. Then Earl Hundi fled, and Sigurd pursued them until they learned that Melkólf had gathered a large army at Duncansby. The earl took counsel with his men, and all thought it most advisable to turn back and not to fight against such a large army. So they retreated.

But when the earl arrived in Stroma they distributed the booty. Then he sailed north to Mainland, and the sons of Njál and Kári accompanied him. Then the earl arranged a great feast at which he gave Kári a good sword and a gold-inlaid spear, Helgi a gold ring and a cloak, and Grím a shield and a sword. Thereupon he made Grím and Helgi members of his bodyguard and thanked them for their brave actions.

They remained with the earl that winter and also the following summer until Kári went on a foray; then they joined him. The entire summer they were out raiding far and wide and they were victorious everywhere. They fought against Gudröd, the king of Man, defeated him, and then returned with their rich booty. That winter they again stayed with the earl.

In the spring the sons of Njál asked leave to sail to Norway. The earl said that they were free to go whenever they wished, and he gave them a good ship and a crew of brave men. Kári said that he, too, wished to sail to Norway that summer with the tribute[1] for Earl Hákon, and he and the sons of Njál agreed to meet there. Thereupon the sons of Njál set sail for Norway and landed at Drontheim.

87

The Blackguard Hrapp and his Misdeeds in Norway

There was a man from Drontheim named Kolbein Arnljótarson. He sailed to Iceland the same summer in which Thráin and the sons of Njál went abroad. That winter he stayed in Broad Dale in the East Firths, but the following summer he prepared to sail from Gautavík. When everything was shipshape for the journey a man came rowing up, made fast his boat to the ship, and then came aboard to speak with Kolbein. Kolbein asked the man his name.[1]

'My name is Hrapp,' he answered.

'What do you want of me?' asked Kolbein.

'I want you to transport me overseas,' he answered.

'Whose son are you?' asked Kolbein.

Hrapp answered: 'I am the son of Orgumleidi, the son of Geirólf Warrior.'

Kolbein asked: 'What is the urgency?'

'I have slain a man!' he answered.

'Whom did you slay and who are the men who will undertake the prosecution?' asked Kolbein.

'I have slain Örlyg Örlygsson, the son of Hródgeir the White, and it will be the men of Weapon Firth who will be bound to take up the case,' was Hrapp's answer.

'I am thinking,' said Kolbein, 'that whoever takes you along will rue it!'

Hrapp answered: 'I am a good friend to him who is a good friend to me, but hit back when I am hurt.[2] For that matter, I don't lack for money to pay for my passage.' In the end Kolbein took him aboard.

Soon thereafter a favourable breeze sprang up and they gained the sea. Hrapp's supply of food ran out on the journey, and so he helped himself to the food of those who sat nearest to him. They jumped up and cursed him, and the result was that they came to blows, and in almost no time Hrapp had two of them down. This was reported to Kolbein. He then invited Hrapp to share his food, and he accepted.

They made land in Norway and cast anchor off Agdaness. Then Kolbein asked where the money was which he had promised to pay for his passage. Hrapp answered: 'It's out in Iceland!'

'You are going to cheat more men than just me,' said Kolbein; 'yet I am going to let you off for the whole fare.'

Hrapp thanked him for that and then asked: 'But what do you advise me to do now?'

'First of all, to get off the ship and away as fast as you can,' said Kolbein, 'because all Norwegians are going to speak ill of you! My second bit of advice is that you never betray your master.'

Thereupon Hrapp went ashore with his weapons. In his hand he had a large axe which had an iron-bound haft, and he travelled until he came to Gudbrand in the Dales. Gudbrand was one of the closest friends of Earl Hákon. Together they owned a temple which was never opened except when the earl was there. That was the largest heathen temple in Norway with the exception of the one at Lade. Gudbrand had a son named Thránd and a daughter named Gudrún.

Hrapp came to Gudbrand and greeted him politely. Gudbrand asked him who he was; Hrapp gave him his name and said that he was from Iceland. Then he asked Gudbrand to take him into his household.

Gudbrand answered: 'You don't seem to me the kind of man who brings much good luck with him!'

'Then there doesn't seem much truth in what people say of you, for I was told that there isn't the likes of you for generosity. I am going to give that the lie unless you take me in!'

Gudbrand said: 'Very well then; stay here!'

'Where shall I sit?' asked Hrapp.

'On the lower-bench opposite my high-seat,' answered Gudbrand. Hrapp took that seat.[3]

Hrapp was a very good storyteller, and so at first it seemed very amusing and entertaining to Gudbrand and many others to listen to him, but many got tired of his forced jokes. In the end he took to talking to Gudrún in private, so that many expressed the belief that he was trying to seduce her. When Gudbrand became aware of this he scolded her severely for conversing with him and warned her not to talk to him except in the presence of others. At first she promised to do as he wished, but soon they began to talk together again as before. Then Gudbrand got his overseer Ásvard to go with her wherever she went.

One day she asked permission to go to the nut-grove to divert herself;[4] Ásvard went with her. Hrapp caught up with them and took her by the hand, and they went off aside by themselves. Then Ásvard went to look for her and found them both lying together in the bushes. He rushed up with his axe raised and struck at Hrapp's leg, but Hrapp dodged quickly so that he missed him. Then Hrapp jumped to his feet in a trice and seized his axe. Ásvard tried to make his escape, but Hrapp hewed his backbone in two.

Then Gudrún said: 'Now you have done something which will make it impossible for you to stay with my father any longer! But there is something else which will seem even worse to him, and that is, that I am with child!'

Hrapp replied: 'He shan't learn this from others! I shall go and bring him both these tidings myself!'

'Then you will not escape with your life,' she said.

'I'll take that risk,' he answered.

After that he took her to some other women and himself went to the hall. Gudbrand sat in his high-seat, and only a few people were there with him. Hrapp shouldered his axe and stepped before him.

Gudbrand asked: 'Why is your axe so bloody?'

'I cured Ásvard's backache with it!' he answered.

'I don't like the way you say that,' said Gudbrand. 'Have you slain him?'

'I have, for sure!' said Hrapp.

'For what reason did you kill him?' asked Gudbrand.

'You will probably think it a small one,' said Hrapp; 'he wanted to cut off my leg.'

'What had you done before that?' asked Gudbrand.

'Something which was no business of his,' answered Hrapp.

'Well, in any case you can say what it was,' said Gudbrand.

'If you must know,' said Hrapp, 'I lay with your daughter, and he didn't like it.'

'Stand up, men!' cried Gudbrand; 'seize him and kill him!'

'Little advantage to me for being in the family,' said Hrapp.

'However, you don't have the men who can kill me that quickly!'

The men in the hall started up, but he backed away from them. They ran after him, but he got away into the woods so that they could not catch him. Gudbrand collected men and had them comb the woods, but they could not find him because the forest was large and dense.

Hrapp made his way through the woods until he came to a clearing. There he saw a farm building and a man who was outside splitting wood. He asked the man his name, and he answered that it was Tófi. Hrapp in return gave his name in answer to Tófi's question. Hrapp asked the farmer why he lived so far away from other people.

'Because here I won't be bothered by other people,' he answered.

'Aren't we both beating about the bush?' said Hrapp. 'Let me tell you first who I am: I have been with Gudbrand in the Dales, but I ran away from there because I slew his overseer. I know that we are both scoundrels, because you would not be hiding here from other men if you were not outlawed for something. Now I shall give you the choice: either I shall tell people where you are, or else we share what you have got here!'

The farmer said: 'What you have said is true; I carried off this woman who is here with me, and many men have been looking for me since that time.'

After that he led Hrapp into the house, which was small but well built. The farmer told the woman that he was giving Hrapp quarters in his house.

'This man will bring bad luck to most people,' she said, 'but I suppose you will have your way!'

Then Hrapp lived with them. He was always on the go and never home. He always managed to have trysts with Gudrún. Both Gudbrand and his son Thránd tried to ambush him, but they were never able to lay hands on him. And so it went on the whole year.

Gudbrand informed Earl Hákon of the trouble he had had with Hrapp. The earl had Hrapp declared an outlaw and set a price on his head. He even promised to go himself in search of him. However, nothing came of that, because he considered it a very easy matter to catch Hrapp at any time, seeing how carelessly he went about.

88

Hrapp Burns Earl Hákon's Temple.
Thráin Helps him Escape

Now we go back to where the sons of Njál left the Orkneys for
Norway and sold their wares there that summer. Thráin Sigfússon
had been preparing his ship to sail for Iceland and was just about
ready to leave.

At that time Earl Hákon was at a feast at Gudbrand's home.
During the night Killer-Hrapp went to the temple which belonged
to the earl and Gudbrand. He stepped in and saw Thorgerd
Holgabrúd[1] in her seat; she was as tall as a full-grown man. She had
a large gold ring on her arm and a linen hood upon her head. He
quickly pulled off the hood and took the gold ring from her arm.
Then he caught sight of Thór's wain and from Thór, too, he took
a gold ring. A third ring he took from Irpa. Then he dragged all
these images from the temple and stripped them of their vestments.
After that he set fire to the temple and burned it to the ground.
Then he left the place as it began to dawn.

As he walked across a field six armed men sprang up and
attacked him, but he defended himself bravely. The end of the
fight was that he killed three men and mortally wounded Thránd,
and chased the two remaining ones into the woods so they would
not inform the earl.

Then he went to Thránd and said: 'It is now in my power to slay
you, but I do not wish to do that. I shall honour our kinship more
than did you and your father.'

Hrapp was about to turn back into the forest when he saw that
men had come between him and the woods, and so he didn't dare
to flee in that direction. Instead, he lay down in a thicket and
remained there for a while.

Early that morning Earl Hákon and Gudbrand went to the
temple and found it burned down and the three images outside
robbed of all their adornment.

Gudbrand spoke: 'Great might has been given to our gods that they came out of the fire by themselves!'

'It is very unlikely that the gods did that themselves. Somebody probably set fire to the temple and carried the gods out. But the gods do not avenge themselves at once. The man who did this will be driven out of Valholl and never be let in again!'

At this moment four of the earl's men came running up and brought him bad news. They said that they had found three men slain in the field and Thránd mortally wounded.

'Who could have done this?' asked the earl.

'Killer-Hrapp,' they answered.

'Then he must be the one who burned down the temple!' said the earl.

They remarked that one might certainly expect such a deed of him.

'Where do you suppose he is now?' asked the earl.

They answered that Thránd had told them that Hrapp had hidden in a thicket. The earl went to look for him, but he was gone. The earl then gave orders to the others to search for him, but they could not find him either. Then the earl conducted the search himself and bade the others rest a while. He went away by himself, bidding that no one should follow him, and was gone for some time. He fell upon his knees and held his hands before his eyes. Then he returned to the others and said: 'Come with me!'

They followed him; he turned abruptly from the path which they had been following, and they came to a dell. There they flushed Hrapp, for he had hidden there. The earl urged his men to pursue him, but Hrapp was so swift of foot that they could not even get close to him.

Hrapp made his way to Lade; Thráin Sigfússon as well as the sons of Njál were just about ready to sail from there. Hrapp rushed up to the sons of Njál and cried: 'Save me, you good men! The earl wants to kill me!'

Helgi looked at him and said: 'You look like a man who brings only ill luck with him! Best for anyone not to have anything to do with you!'

'Then I would like the worst misfortune to befall you two from me!' said Hrapp.

'I shall be man enough to take my revenge when the time

comes!' answered Helgi.

Hrapp then turned to Thráin Sigfússon and asked him for protection.

'What crime have you committed?' asked Thráin.

'I burned down the earl's temple and killed some of his men,' said Hrapp. 'And he is going to be here soon, for he himself has joined in the pursuit.'

'It is hardly fitting for me to help you,' said Thráin, 'seeing how much the earl has done for me.'

Then Hrapp showed Thráin the precious things which he had taken from the temple and he offered to give Thráin everything. Thráin said that he would not take them unless Hrapp accepted payment of equal value in return.[2]

Then Hrapp said: 'Here I'll stay, and if I am killed before your eyes your name will become a byword!'

At this moment they saw the earl and his men approaching. Then Thráin took Hrapp into his protection, had a boat launched, and with Hrapp boarded his ship.

Thráin said: 'The best way to hide you will be to break the bottoms out of two barrels and have you get inside.'

That they did; Hrapp hid in the barrels, which were then fastened together and lowered over the side of the ship.

Then the earl came up with his company and he asked the sons of Njál whether Hrapp had come that way. They answered that he had. The earl asked which way he had gone, and they answered that they knew nothing about that.

The earl said: 'I shall highly reward him who can give me information about Hrapp!'

Grím said to Helgi under his breath: 'Why shouldn't we tell him? I'm not so sure Thráin will be so thankful for our not telling!'

'All the same, we mustn't,' said Helgi, 'since the man's life is at stake.'

Grím said: 'It may be that the earl will turn his vengeance on us, because he is so furious that he will vent his rage on somebody.'

'That should not concern us,' replied Helgi. 'Still, let us two move our ship out of the harbour and make for the high sea as soon as a breeze springs up.'

They did so and anchored behind an island and there waited for a breeze.

The earl asked all the crew of other boats whether they knew anything about Hrapp, but all denied knowing anything about him.

Then the earl said: 'Now we shall go to my comrade Thráin. He will surrender Hrapp if he knows where he is.'

Thereupon they launched a warship and rowed out to the merchantman. Thráin recognised the earl's ship and stood up to greet him. The earl returned the greeting in friendly fashion and said: 'We are looking for an Icelander named Hrapp; he has done us all manner of harm. We shall ask you to give him up or else tell us where he is.'

Thráin said: 'You know that I slew a man whom you had condemned to outlawry, sire; I risked my life in doing so, and for that reason I received great honour from you.'

'Even greater honour you shall have now,' said the earl.

Thráin pondered for a moment, for he did not know which service the earl would value more highly.[3] But he denied that Hrapp was there and asked the earl to search the ship. The earl did so, although very casually, and then went ashore and off by himself. He was in such a rage that no one dared to speak to him.

The earl said: 'Show me to Njál's sons! I'll force them to tell the truth!'

He was then informed that they had already set sail.

'Then we can't do that,' said the earl. 'But two water butts were floating by the side of Thráin's ship, and a man could very well have hidden in them. If Thráin concealed Hrapp, he is likely to be in them. We'll go and talk with Thráin again.'

Thráin saw that the earl was about to come out to them again and he said: 'If the earl was furious before, he will be twice as furious now. The life of every man on board is now at stake.'

They all promised not to reveal anything, for they were all very much frightened. They took some sacks out of the cargo and put Hrapp in their place. Then some lighter sacks were placed on top of him.

The earl came just as they had finished stowing Hrapp away. Thráin greeted the earl politely, and the earl returned his greeting, but rather coolly, and they all saw that he was in a towering rage.

He said to Thráin: 'Hand over Hrapp, because I know for a certainty that you have concealed him!'

'Where should I have concealed him, sire?' asked Thráin.

'You know that better than I,' answered the earl, 'but I venture a guess that you had him hidden before in these water butts.'

'I would not wish you to consider me a liar,' said Thráin. 'I would much rather have you search the ship.'

The earl boarded the ship and searched, but found nothing.

'Do you free me of the charge now?' asked Thráin.

'Far from it!' said the earl. 'I just can't understand why we cannot find him. I can see it all clearly when I go ashore, but when I come back here I see nothing.'

Then he had his men row him ashore; he was so enraged that no one dared to speak to him. His son Svein, who was with him, said: 'It is a strange thing to vent one's wrath on innocent men.'

The earl again went off by himself, but returned to them at once and said: 'Let us row out to them once again!' This they did.

'Where do you suppose he was concealed?' asked Svein.

'No matter where he was concealed, for he will not be there any longer,' answered the earl. 'There were two sacks lying beside the cargo. Hrapp must have been put into the cargo in their place.'

Thráin spoke: 'They are putting out their ship again and they intend to pay us another visit. Now let's take Hrapp out of the cargo and put something else in his place. The two loose sacks can stay where they are.'

After they had done this Thráin said: 'Now let's put Hrapp in the sail which is furled to the topyard!'

The earl arrived after this had been done. He was furious and said: 'Will you hand over the man now, Thráin? The punishment will now be more severe than before, if you don't!'

Thráin answered: 'I would have handed him over long ago if he were in my keeping. Where could he have been concealed?'

'In the cargo,' answered the earl.

'Then why didn't you search there?' asked Thráin.

'We didn't think of that,' answered the earl. Thereupon they looked for him all over the ship, but could not find him.

'Do you free me of the charge now?' asked Thráin.

'Certainly not,' answered the earl, 'because I know you have concealed the man, even though I cannot find him. However, I would rather that you prove false to me than I to you.'

Then he returned to shore. 'Now I think I understand how it

was,' said the earl; 'Thráin concealed Hrapp in the sail!'

Then a fair breeze sprang up and Thráin and his men put to sea. He spoke these words which have long been remembered:

> Let the Griffin gambol:
> ground gives Thráin never.

When the earl heard of Thráin's words he said: 'It is not so much my lack of insight as their alliance which will prove the undoing of them both.'

Thráin had a short passage and landed in Iceland and went home to his farm. Hrapp accompanied Thráin and stayed with him that year. In the spring Thráin secured a farm for him at Hrappstead and Hrapp lived there. However, he spent most of his time at Grjótá River and caused all kinds of trouble there. Some claimed that he was altogether too friendly with Hallgerd and that he had seduced her, but others contradicted this.

Thráin gave his ship to his kinsman Mord the Careless. It was this Mord who slew Odd Halldórsson out east in Gautavík in Bear Firth. All Thráin's kinsmen now looked upon him as their chieftain.

89

The Sons of Njál are Implicated in Hrapp's Escape and are Captured by Earl Hákon. They Escape with Kári's Aid

Now we go back to when the earl failed to lay hold of Thráin. The earl spoke to his son as follows: 'Let us take four warships and attack Njál's sons and kill them, for they must have been Thráin's accomplices!'

'That is not good counsel,' said Svein, 'to throw the blame on innocent men and to let him escape who is really guilty.'

'It is I who shall decide about this!' said the earl.

They now set out after the sons of Njál, looked for them, and found them in the shelter of an island.

It was Grím who first saw the ships of the earl and said to Helgi: 'Warships are approaching; I can see that it is the earl, and he is not likely to be peacefully inclined.'

Helgi answered: 'There is a saying that a staunch man stands his ground, whoever may assail him. And we too shall stand our ground!'

They all bade him do whatever he thought best, and they took up their arms.

The earl came up and called out to them to surrender. Helgi answered that they would defend themselves as long as they could. The earl offered peace to all who would refuse to defend Helgi, but Helgi was so loved by his friends that they all preferred to die with him. The earl and his men then attacked, but the Icelanders defended themselves well, and Njál's sons were always at that spot where the fight was most bitter. The earl repeated his offer of peace many times, but they always gave the same answer and said that they would never surrender.

Then Áslák of Langey attacked them and managed to board the ship three times. Grím said: 'You are attacking quite sharply, and it would be well if you received a reward for your efforts!'

With that he caught up a spear and hurled it at Áslák. It pierced Áslák's throat and he fell at once. Shortly after this Helgi slew Egil, the earl's standard-bearer.

Then Svein Hákonarson attacked and had his men hem them in on all sides with their shields, and thus they were captured. The earl wished to have them killed immediately, but Svein said they should not do that, because it was night.[1] Then the earl said: 'We shall slay them tomorrow, but secure them strongly tonight!'

'It shall have to be as you say,' said Svein, 'but I have never before seen braver men than these, and it is the greatest pity to lose men like them!'

The earl answered: 'They have killed two of our bravest men; and for that they shall be slain!'

'They were all the braver for that,' said Svein. 'However, it must be as you wish.'

They were then bound and fettered. After that the earl lay down to sleep. After he had fallen asleep Grím said to Helgi: 'If we could only escape!'

'Let us hit on some scheme to do so!' said Helgi.

At that moment Grím observed that an axe was lying there with the edge turned up. He crawled over and succeeded in cutting the bowstring with which he was tied, but in doing so he inflicted bad gashes on his hands. Then he freed Helgi, and after that they crept overboard and swam to shore without the earl or his men becoming aware of it. They knocked off the fetters from their feet and went to the other side of the island. Morning was then just beginning to dawn. They saw a ship there and recognised it to be that of Kári Solmundarson. They rejoined him at once, told him of their shameful treatment, and showed him their wounds. They said that the earl and his men were probably asleep at that moment.

Kári said: 'That is a shame that you had to suffer such ill treatment, as though you were scoundrels. What would you now wish to do most of all?'

'Attack the earl and slay him!' was their answer.

'That is unlikely to happen,' said Kári, 'but you certainly don't lack spirit. In any case let us learn whether he is there now.'

Thereupon they went to where the battle had been, but the earl had already left.

Then Kári sailed in to Lade to meet the earl and brought him the tribute.

'Did you take the sons of Njál into your protection?' asked the earl.

'Certainly!' answered Kári.

'Will you hand them over to me?' asked the earl.

'That I will not!' answered Kári.

'Will you swear that you will never attack me?' continued the earl.

Then Eirík, the earl's son, spoke: 'There is no need of requesting anything like that of Kári. He has always been our friend. Besides, things would not have happened as they did if I had been present. Then the sons of Njál would have been left in possession of what they had, and those who deserved it would have been punished. It would seem to me more appropriate to recompense them for the shameful treatment and the wounds which they have received!'

The earl said: 'Indeed it would, but I don't know whether they will accept reparations.'

Then the earl had Kári enquire whether Njál's sons would accept reparations. Thereupon Kári spoke with Helgi and asked whether he would let the earl make amends.

Helgi answered: 'I will accept them from his son Eirík, but I want no dealings with the earl!'

Kári brought this answer to Eirík.

'So it shall be!' said Eirík. 'He shall receive redress from me, if he so prefers; and tell them that I invite them to my estate, and my father is not to harm them.'

They accepted this offer and went to Eirík's estate and stayed with him until Kári was ready to sail west. Then Eirík prepared a great feast for Kári and gave him and the sons of Njál presents. Thereupon Kári made his way over the sea to Earl Sigurd. He and the sons of Njál were well received there and they stayed with the earl that winter. In the spring, however, Kári asked the sons of Njál to go with him on his forays, and Grím agreed to do that if Kári in his turn would sail to Iceland with him afterwards. Kári promised to do that and they went harrying with him. They raided in the south around Anglesey and about all the Hebrides. Then they made for Kintyre and landed there. They fought against the natives, gathered rich booty, and then returned to the ships. From there they fared south to Wales and raided there. Then they continued to Man where they met King Gudröd of Man and fought against him. They were victorious and slew Dungal, the king's son. There, too, they took a great amount of booty. From there they headed north to the isle of Coll and there met Earl Gilli. He received them well and they stayed with him for a while. The earl sailed with them to the Orkneys to Earl Sigurd. In the spring Earl Sigurd gave his sister Nereid to Earl Gilli in marriage. Then he returned to the Hebrides.

90

Kári and the Sons of Njál Return to Iceland

That summer Kári and the sons of Njál made ready for the trip to Iceland, and when they were prepared to sail they went before the earl. He gave them splendid gifts and they parted in the greatest friendship. Then they set sail. They had a good breeze and after a short passage they landed at Eyrar. They secured horses and rode to Bergthórshvál. All were happy to welcome them home. They had all their goods brought home and had the ship drawn up on land. Kári stayed with Njál that winter.

In the spring Kári asked for the hand of Njál's daughter. Grím and Helgi supported the suit, and the result was that she was betrothed to Kári and the day for the wedding feast set. The feast was held a half-month before midsummer. The couple lived with Njál that winter. Then Kári bought some land at Dyrhólmar east in Mydale and set up his homestead there. They left an overseer in charge because they continued to live at Bergthórshvál.

91

Thráin Refuses to Make Amends to the Sons of Njál.
They are Insulted by Hrapp and Hallgerd

[As was told before,] Hrapp had his farm at Hrappstead, but he was constantly over at Grjótá River and caused much trouble there. Thráin, however, treated him well.

Once it happened that Ketil of Mork was at Bergthórshvál. The sons of Njál spoke about the shameful treatment to which they had been subjected, and they said that they could make large claims for redress from Thráin Sigfússon whenever they had a mind to. Njál said it would be best if Ketil would speak to his brother Thráin about it. This Ketil promised to do. They gave Ketil sufficient time to speak to Thráin.

Shortly after this they asked Ketil about this matter, but he said he did not care to repeat many of the words which had passed between Thráin and himself – 'for it is evident that Thráin thinks I put too much weight on being related to you.'

With that they broke off the conversation, but they rather thought that matters were taking a dangerous turn, and they asked their father what he would advise them to do. They said that they were not satisfied to do nothing about the matter.

Njál answered: 'This case is a particularly difficult one. If they are slain, it will seem as though they were slain without cause. My advice is to get as many as possible to be present when you discuss the matter with them, so that it will be general knowledge if they make ill-tempered replies. In that case Kári is to be spokesman because he is a man of even temper. Then the enmity between you and Thráin will grow, because they will revile you and use abusive language when others discuss the case with them, for they are men with little forethought. People may even say that my sons are slow to act, and you will have to bear with that for a while, because once a deed has been done there will always be two opinions as to whether it was justified or not. Should they make insulting remarks about you, you must not speak up unless you are prepared to take action. If you had asked me for advice in the first place, then the quarrel with Thráin would never have become the subject of so much talk, and you would not have had any humiliation from it. Now you will be put to a severe test, and your humiliation will become so great that you will have no other recourse but to face the difficulty and seek redress with arms. And that is why these long preparations are necessary before you reach your goal.'

With that they broke off their talk, but the matter was the topic of conversation among many men.

One day the brothers suggested that Kári go to Grjótá River. He said that he did not much relish that errand, but that he would go if that were Njál's counsel.

Thereupon he went to see Thráin; they spoke about the case, but neither party saw things in the same light. Kári returned and Njál's sons asked him how things had gone between Thráin and himself. Kári answered that he did not care to repeat the words. – 'It is more than likely that the same remarks will be made sometime when you can hear them yourselves.'

At his farm Thráin had fifteen servants, all trained to fight, and wherever he rode eight of them accompanied him. Thráin was a very ostentatious person; he always rode about wearing a blue cloak and a gilded helmet, and he was armed with a spear which the earl had given him, a beautiful shield, and a sword at his belt. He was always accompanied by Gunnar Lambason, Lambi Sigurdarson, and Grani, the son of Gunnar of Hlídarendi, but the man closest to him always was Killer-Hrapp. Lodin was the name of one of Thráin's servants; he and his brother Tjorvi likewise rode with Thráin at all times. Killer-Hrapp and Grani were the men who spoke most scornfully of the sons of Njál, and it was chiefly their fault that no effort was made to reconcile them.

Njál's sons often asked Kári to ride to Grjótá River farm with them, and finally he agreed, saying that it was best that they themselves hear Thráin's answer. They now made ready, the four sons of Njál and Kári as the fifth, and rode to Grjótá River farm. At Grjótá River farm there was a broad porch before the house where many men could stand side by side. A woman who was standing outside saw the sons of Njál riding up and she told Thráin. He ordered his men to go on the porch and take their arms with them. This they did. Thráin stood in the middle of the doorway, and on either side of him stood Killer-Hrapp and Grani Gunnarsson. Next to them stood Gunnar Lambason, then Lodin and Tjorvi, then Lambi Sigurdarson, and then all the others in close order, for the men were all at home.

The sons of Njál and Kári came up toward them; Skarphedin led the way, then came Kári, then Hoskuld, then Grím, and then Helgi. As they came up there was not a word of greeting from those standing on the porch.

Skarphedin said: 'A welcome to us all!'[1]

Hallgerd was standing on the porch; she had been talking with Hrapp under her breath. Now she said: 'None of us standing here will say that you are welcome!'

Skarphedin answered: 'Your words don't matter, for you are either an old woman fit to sit in a corner or a harlot!'

'You shall pay for these words before you return home!' said Hallgerd.

Helgi said: 'It is you, Thráin, I have come to see, and to learn whether you will make any amends for the shameful treatment which I have suffered in Norway on your account.'

Thráin answered: 'I didn't know that you brothers wanted to turn your manhood into money! How long, I wonder, are you going to keep begging for money?'

'The judgement of people will be,' said Helgi, 'that you ought to offer us redress, seeing that your life was at stake.'

Then Hrapp answered: 'There you can see the difference in luck [between Thráin and you], that he got the blow who deserved it, and that you got the drubbing and not we.'

'It wasn't so lucky for Thráin to break faith with the earl in exchange for you,' said Helgi.

'Don't you believe that you should have some redress from me, too?' asked Hrapp. 'I shall pay you back what I think you deserve!'

'The only dealings we two shall have together,' said Helgi, 'won't be much to your advantage!'

'Let us not bandy words with Hrapp!' said Skarphedin. 'Let us pay him back with a red hide for his grey[2] one!'

Hrapp said: 'Hold your tongue, Skarphedin! I'll not hesitate to bring my axe down on your skull!'

'Events will show,' said Skarphedin, 'who will live to tell the tale!'

'Go home, "little Dungbeards"!' said Hallgerd. 'That's what we'll call you from this day on, and your father we'll call "the Beardless One"!'[3]

The sons of Njál did not leave before all those present except Thráin had involved themselves in guilt by repeating these same words. Thráin had even tried to restrain the others.

The sons of Njál left and rode home. They reported the incident to their father.

'Did you name any witnesses to these words?' asked Njál.

'We did not,' said Skarphedin; 'we do not plan to prosecute this suit anywhere except on the battlefield!'

Bergthóra said: 'No one any longer expects you brothers to have the courage to lift a hand in your defence!'

'Don't bother to egg on your sons any more, mistress,' said Kári; 'as it is, they are likely enough to be more than eager to bestir themselves!'

After that Njál and his sons and Kári spoke together for a long time in secret.

92

The Battle on the Ice. Thráin is Slain

Now there was considerable talk about their clash, and it seemed certain to all that there could be no peaceful settlement after what had happened. Rúnólf, the son of Úlf Aurgodi from out east in Dale, was a good friend of Thráin. He had invited Thráin to his home, and it was agreed that he should come about three weeks or a month after the beginning of winter. The following men rode with Thráin: Killer-Hrapp and Grani Gunnarsson, Gunnar Lambason, Lambi Sigurdarson, Lodin, and Tjorvi. There were eight men altogether. Thorgerd and Hallgerd were to go along too. Thráin also announced that he planned to stay at Mork with his brother Ketil, and he mentioned how many days he planned to be away. They all rode fully armed.

They rode east over the Markar River and met some poor women who begged to be taken to the west bank of the river. This they did. Then they rode to the Dale farm where they were well received. Ketil of Mork was already there. They remained there three days. Rúnólf and Ketil begged Thráin to seek a reconciliation with the sons of Njál, but he declared he would never pay them any money. He gave peevish answers and said that he considered himself a match for the sons of Njál wherever they should meet.

'That may be,' said Rúnólf, 'but it is my opinion that no one is the equal of the sons of Njál now that Gunnar of Hlídarendi is dead. The chances are that this quarrel will bring death to either one of you.'

Thráin said he was not afraid of that.

Then Thráin went up to Mork and stayed there two days. Thereupon he rode down to the Dale farm again. At both places he was presented with fitting gifts on his departure.

The Markar River was flowing between sheets of ice on either side and with ice floes here and there bridging both banks. Thráin said he planned to ride home that evening,[1] but Rúnólf advised against it. He thought it would be more prudent to travel some time later than he had announced.

Thráin answered: 'That would be showing fear, and I shall not follow your advice!'

The beggarwomen, whom Thráin and his men had helped across the Markar River, came to Bergthórshvál, and Bergthóra asked them where they came from. They answered that they were from the east, from the slopes of Eyjafell.

'Who helped you across the Markar River?' asked Bergthóra.

'The most showy people you can imagine,' they answered.

'Who were they?' asked Bergthóra.

'Thráin Sigfússon and his followers,' they answered. 'What displeased us most was that they used such reviling and scornful language in speaking of your husband and sons.'

Bergthóra answered: 'You can't prevent people from talking ill about you.'

Before the women went away Bergthóra gave them presents and asked them when Thráin was expected home. They replied that he would be away from home about four or five days. Then Bergthóra reported this to her sons and her son-in-law Kári, and they talked together for a long time in secret.

The same morning as Thráin and his men rode from the east Njál awoke very early and heard Skarphedin's axe knock against the partition. Njál arose, went out, and saw that his sons and son-in-law were all fully armed. At the head of the group was Skarphedin dressed in a blue jacket. He had a small, round shield and carried his axe on his shoulder. Next to him came Kári; he wore a silken jacket and a gilded helmet and carried a shield on which was painted the figure of a lion. After him came Helgi in helmet and red kirtle;[2] he carried a red shield with a hart as an emblem.[3] All wore dyed clothes.

Njál called to Skarphedin: 'Where are you going, my son?'

'To look for sheep!' he answered.

'That's what you said once before,' said Njál, 'but you hunted men then!'

Skarphedin laughed and said: 'Do you hear what the old man says? He is not without his suspicions.'

'When did you speak of such matters before?' asked Kári.

'The time I killed Sigmund the White, Gunnar's kinsman,' said

Skarphedin.

'Why did you do that?' asked Kári.

'Because he had slain Thórd Freedmansson, my foster father,' answered Skarphedin.

Njál went back inside, and the others proceeded up the slopes of Raudaskridur Mountain and waited there. From here one could immediately catch sight of anyone riding east from Dale. It was a clear, sunny day. Now Thráin and his men came riding down from Dale along the sandy river bank.

Lambi Sigurdarson said: 'Over there on Raudaskridur Mountain I see shields gleaming in the sun, and I suspect some ambush!'

'Then we shall keep on riding down along the river,' said Thráin. 'They will meet us there if they have any business with us.' They now turned to go downstream.

Skarphedin said: 'They have caught sight of us now, for they are turning off their course. There is nothing else to do but run down and meet them.'

Kári said: 'Many an ambush is laid with greater advantage of numbers than is the case here; there are eight of them, and five of us!'

They headed downstream and saw an ice floe spanning the river below, and they planned to cross at that spot. Thráin and his men took their stand on the icy sheet above the floe.

Thráin spoke: 'What can these men want? There are five of them against us eight!'

Lambi Sigurdarson answered: 'I believe they would venture to attack us, even though there were still more on our side.'

Thráin took off his cloak and helmet.

It happened that Skarphedin's shoe thong broke as they ran down along the river, and he was delayed.

'Why are you so slow, Skarphedin?' asked Grím.

'I am tying my shoe thong,' he answered.

'Let's go on ahead,' said Kári. 'I am thinking that he won't be any slower than we!'

They turned down toward the ice floe, running as fast as they could. Skarphedin jumped up as soon as he had tied his shoe thong, and with axe raised he ran down to the river. However, there was no place nearby, either upstream or downstream, where the river could be forded, so deep was it. A big ice floe had been

raised up against the other bank. It was as smooth as glass, and
there in the middle of this floe stood Thráin and his men.
Skarphedin took a running start and leaped over the river from
one icy bank to the other, landed on his feet, and continued to
rush forward in the impetus of his slide. The ice floe was so
slippery that he shot forward with the speed of a bird. Thráin was
just about to put on his helmet as Skarphedin bore down on him
and struck at him with his axe, 'Battle-Troll'. The axe came down
upon his head and split it right down to the jaw, so that his jaw
teeth dropped out on the ice. This happened so quickly that no
one could strike a blow at Skarphedin, and he continued to glide
along on the ice sheet at great speed. Tjorvi threw a shield into his
path, but Skarphedin cleared it with a bound and slid to the end of
the ice floe.

Then Kári and the others met him. 'That's having at them like a
man!' said Kári.

'Now it's your turn!' replied Skarphedin.

Thereupon they all rushed at their opponents. Grím and Helgi
saw Hrapp and immediately went for him. Hrapp struck at Grím
with his axe, but Helgi forestalled him and levelled a blow at
Hrapp's hand and severed it, so that the axe fell to the ground.

Hrapp said: 'There you did a most praiseworthy thing, for this
hand has brought harm and death to many a man!'

'And now we shall make an end of that!' said Grím, and ran him
through with his spear.

Tjorvi set upon Kári and hurled his spear at him, but Kári leaped
up and the spear flew harmlessly beneath his feet. Kári made for
him and dealt him a sword blow which pierced the chest and
penetrated to the vitals. He dropped dead at once.

Skarphedin grabbed hold of both Gunnar Lambason and Grani
Gunnarsson and called out: 'Here I've caught two whelps! What
shall I do with them?'

'It is your chance to kill both if you wish them out of the way,'
answered Helgi.

'I do not have the heart to help Hogni and at the same time to
kill his brother,' said Skarphedin.

'Someday you will wish that you had slain him,' said Helgi,
'because never will he be true to you, nor will any of the others
who are here now!'

Skarphedin answered: 'I have no fear of them!'

Thus they spared Grani Gunnarsson, Gunnar Lambason, Lambi Sigurdarson, and Lodin.

After that they returned home. Njál asked what had happened, and they told him everything exactly as it had taken place.

Njál said: 'These are matters of great import, and it is likely that the end will see the death of one of my sons or worse still!'[4]

Gunnar Lambason carried Thráin's body to the farm at Grjótá River, and there he was buried in a cairn.

93

Njál Effects a Settlement with Thráin's Kin

Ketil of Mork was married to Njál's daughter Thorgerd; but he was also Thráin's brother, and so he found himself in a difficult position. He rode to Njál and asked him whether he perchance wished to make reparations for Thráin's slaying.

Njál answered: 'Reparations I shall make, and such as to satisfy you; and I would want you to approach your brothers, who are to share in the reparations, so that they will agree to accept this redress.'

Ketil said he would be glad to do that. First he rode home, but soon after he summoned all his brothers to Hlídarendi. He discussed the matter with them, and Hogni sided with him on every point. The outcome was that men were chosen to pronounce the verdict and a meeting was arranged. There full wergild was awarded for the slaying of Thráin, and all who had a legal claim shared in the payment. After that pledges of good faith were exchanged and everything possible was done to assure the peace. Njál paid out the entire amount just as he had promised, and after that things were quiet for a while.

One day Njál rode up to Ketil's farm at Mork, and Ketil and he talked together the entire day. In the evening he rode home again, but no one knew what they had discussed. Shortly after that Ketil journeyed to the farm at Grjótá River and spoke to Thorgerd

[Thráin's widow]: 'I have always loved my brother Thráin very much; I wish to show that now by offering to be foster father to his son Hoskuld.'

'That I shall accept,' she answered, 'on the condition that you do everything in your power for this boy after he has grown up, that you avenge him if he is slain, and that you contribute the money for his morning-gift.[1] And you are to swear an oath to that effect!'

Ketil agreed to abide by these conditions. Then Hoskuld rode home with Ketil and lived with him for some time.

94

Hoskuld Thráinsson Becomes Njál's Foster Son

One day Njál again rode up to the Mork farm where he was well received, and he stayed there one night. In the evening Njál called to Hoskuld and the boy came to him immediately. Njál had a gold ring on his finger and he showed it to the boy. The boy took the ring, looked at it, and put it on his finger.

Njál asked: 'Would you like to have the ring as a present?'

'Yes, I would!' said the boy.

'Do you know how your father met his death?' asked Njál.

The boy answered: 'I know that Skarphedin slew him, but we don't have to bear that in mind, for the matter has been settled and full atonement paid.'

'The answer is better than the question!' said Njál. 'I know that you are going to be a good man and true.'

'I thank you for your good opinion of me,' said Hoskuld, 'for I know you have knowledge of the future and never speak an untruth.'

Njál said: 'And now I want you to be my foster son, if you will accept that offer.'

He said he would be glad to accept that as well as any other kindness Njál cared to bestow on him.

In the end Hoskuld journeyed home with Njál to be his foster son. Njál took care that no harm ever befell the boy, for he loved him dearly. The sons of Njál always had him along with them and did everything for his welfare.

And so time passed until Hoskuld was grown. He was tall and strong and had a handsome appearance and beautiful hair. He was friendly in his speech, generous, courteous, and well skilled in arms. He always had a kind word for everybody and was loved by all. Njál's sons and Hoskuld were inseparable.

95

Flosi and his Kin

There was a man named Flosi. He was the son of Thórd Freysgodi,[1] the son of Ozur, the son of Ásbjorn, the son of Heyjang-Bjorn, the son of Helgi, the son of Bjorn Buna. Flosi's mother was Ingun, the daughter of Thórir of Espihól, the son of Hámund Heljarskin, the son of Hjor, the son of that Hálf who was the leader of the band called Hálf's warriors, the son of Hjorleif the Amorous. The mother of Thórir was Ingun, the daughter of Helgi the Lean, who settled around the Eyja Firth. Flosi was married to Steinvor, the daughter of Hall of Sída. She was born out of wedlock, and her mother was Sólvor, the daughter of Herjólf the White. Flosi lived at Svínafell and was a great chieftain. He was big and strong and a most energetic man. A brother of Flosi was named Starkad, but they did not have the same mother. Starkad's mother was Thraslaug, the daughter of Thorstein Sparrow, the son of Geirleif. Thraslaug's mother was named Unn; she was the daughter of Eyvind Karfi, one of the first settlers of Iceland, and the sister of Módólf the Wise. The other brothers of Flosi were Thorgeir, Stein, Kolbein, and Egil.

Starkad, Flosi's brother, had a daughter named Hildigunn, a beautiful and high-spirited woman. Few women were her equal in skilled handiwork. She was of a hard disposition and unforgiving, but a person who could be relied on when the occasion demanded it.

96

Hall of Sída and his Kin

There was a man named Hall, known as Hall of Sída. He was the
son of Thorstein, the son of Bodvar. Hall's mother was named
Thórdís, the daughter of Ozur, the son of Hródlaug, the son of
Earl Rognvald of Mœre in Norway, the son of Eystein Glumra.
Hall was married to Jóreid, the daughter of Thidrandi the Wise,
the son of Ketil Thrym, the son of Thórir Thidrandi of Veradale.
The brothers of Jóreid were Ketil Thrym in Njardvík and
Thorvald, the father of Helgi Droplaugarson. Hallkatla was the
sister of Jóreid. She was the mother of Thorkel Geitisson and
Thidrandi. Hall's brother was Thorstein, also known as Broad-
Paunch. His son was Kol, the one Kári was to slay in Wales. The
sons of Hall of Sída were Thorstein, Egil, Thorvald, Ljót, and
Thidrandi, the one who was said to have been slain by the *dísir*.[1]

Also, there was a man named Thórir, surnamed Holta-Thórir.
His sons were Thorgeir Skorargeir, Thorleif Crow, and Thorgrím
the Tall.

97

Hoskuld Thráinsson Marries Hildigunn.
Njál Proposes a Fifth Court

Now it is to be told that Njál spoke to Hoskuld as follows: 'I would like to provide you with a suitable match, my foster son.'

Hoskuld said that was in accordance with his own wishes, and that he would leave the matter in Njál's hands. He asked whether he had anyone in mind.

Njál answered: 'There is a woman named Hildigunn, the daughter of Starkad, the son of Thórd Freysgodi. She is the best match I know of.'

Hoskuld said: 'You decide, foster father! I shall do as you wish!'

'Then we shall ask for her hand,' said Njál.

Shortly after this Njál summoned men to accompany him. Together with him were the sons of Sigfús, Kári Solmundarson, and all of Njál's own sons. They rode to Svínafell where they were well received. The following day[1] Njál and Flosi met and talked together. Finally Njál said: 'This is the errand that has brought us here: we have come to ask for the hand of Hildigunn, your brother's daughter.'

'And for whom?' asked Flosi.

'For Hoskuld, my foster son,' answered Njál.

'That is an excellent choice,' said Flosi; 'however, there is much outstanding between us. But what have you to say about Hoskuld?'

'I can say only the best things of him,' said Njál. 'Furthermore, I shall pay as much money[2] as you consider fitting, if you are willing to take the matter into consideration.'

'We'll call Hildigunn,' said Flosi, 'and see how she likes the suitor.'

They called her and she came. Flosi told her about the proposal, but she answered that she was a woman of very proud mind – 'and I am not sure how I shall behave in the matter, seeing on the one hand, men of such importance,[3] and what is still more significant, that this man has no position of leadership among men. Did you not tell me that you would not give me in marriage to a man without the office of *goði*?'

'That, indeed, is sufficient reason, in case you do not care to marry,' said Flosi; 'and if so, I shall not consider the matter further.'

'I don't say that I wouldn't marry Hoskuld, if such an office can be secured for him,' she said. 'Otherwise I would not consider it!'

Njál said: 'In that case I would ask for three years' time in the matter.'

Flosi answered that it should be granted him.

'I should like to make one further condition,' said Hildigunn; 'and that is, that we live here in the east, if the marriage takes place.'

Njál said he would let Hoskuld decide that for himself. Hoskuld said that he had faith in many men, but in no one as much as his foster father Njál.[4] Thereupon they returned to the west.

Njál tried to secure a position of leadership for Hoskuld, but there was no one who wished to sell his *goðorð*. Thus the summer wore on until it was time for the meeting at the Althing. There were many lawsuits at the Assembly that summer, and as usual, there were many men who came to Njál for his help. However, to all men Njál gave advice which was not designed to be conducive to the success of their suits, so that both prosecution and defence came to naught. A good deal of wrangling resulted, because many cases could not be adjudicated; and the parties left the Assembly without coming to any agreements.

Time passed till the time for another meeting drew near. Njál attended it. At first it proceeded in orderly fashion, until Njál said it was time for the parties to give notice of their suits. Many men remarked that there was no use in doing that, seeing that no one had made any progress with his suit, though it had been aired before the Assembly. – 'And we would rather,' they said, 'obtain our rights at the point of the sword!'

'That would never do,' said Njál, 'for it would be intolerable to have no law in the land. However, you do have just cause for complaint, and this is a matter which concerns us who know the law and should direct it. It seems most advisable to me that we call together all the chieftains and discuss this problem.'

Thereupon they assembled at the place where legislative sessions were held. Njál said: 'I call upon you, Skapti Thóroddsson,[5] and you other chieftains, seeing that our cases have come to a deadlock in the Quarter Courts, and matters have become so involved that cases may neither make progress nor come to an end. It would seem advisable to me that we institute a Fifth Court and refer to it those cases which cannot be settled in the Quarter Courts.'

'How would you appoint a Fifth Court,' asked Skapti, 'in view of the fact that the four dozen *goðis* of each district already serve as judges in the Quarter Courts?'

'I would remedy that by establishing new *goðorðs*,' answered Njál, 'and by appointing to them the best-qualified men from each Quarter, and permitting anyone who so desires to come under the jurisdiction of one of these new *goðis*.'

'We accept this suggestion,' said Skapti, 'but what difficult cases are to come before this court?'

'All those are to come before it,' said Njál, 'that concern contempt of court as well as those that involve false witness or statement. There shall also come before this court suits in which no unanimous verdict can be reached in the Quarter Courts. All these cases shall be referred to the Fifth Court. There shall also come before this court cases in which a bribe has been offered or accepted. In this court the validity of each oath must be substantiated by two men who shall vouch for the truth of what is sworn. Also, this court is to support the judge who has proceeded correctly in cases where the other judge [in the Quarter Court] commits a technical error. Procedure in this court is to be the same as in the Quarter Court except that the prosecutor of a case and the defendant shall each have the right to challenge six of the four dozen men appointed to the Fifth Court. If the defendant does not wish to do so, then the prosecutor shall challenge six additional judges. But if the prosecutor fails to do so, then the case is quashed, for three times twelve [judges] are to compose the court.'

Thereupon Skapti Thóroddsson incorporated into the law the establishment of the Fifth Court as well as the other proposals urged. Then men went to the Law-Mount in order to establish the new *goðorðs*: in the North Quarter, one for the men of Mel in Mid Firth and one for the men of Laufás in Eyja Firth.

Then Njál asked to be heard and spoke as follows: 'It is widely

known how matters went between my sons and the people of
Grjótá River, and that they slew Thráin Sigfússon. Nevertheless,
we came to terms, and now I have adopted Hoskuld Thráinsson as
my foster son and provided a match for him on the condition that
he secure a *goðorð* somewhere. However, no one is willing to give
up his *goðorð*. I therefore ask you to grant me permission to
establish a new *goðorð* at Hvítaness[6] for Hoskuld.'

This was granted him by unanimous consent, and thereupon he
established the *goðorð* for Hoskuld, who was henceforth known as
Hoskuld Hvítanessgodi.

After that men rode home from the Assembly. Njál remained at
home only a short time before riding east with his sons to Svínafell
to bring up the matter of Hoskuld's marriage. Flosi said that he was
prepared to abide by the promise he had made them; so Hildigunn
was betrothed to Hoskuld and the time for the wedding feast was
agreed on. When the matter had been settled they rode home again.

A second time they rode to Svínafell, this time for the wedding,
and after the feast Flosi paid out generously the entire dowry of
Hildigunn. The young couple returned to Bergthórshvál and lived
there that year, and Hildigunn and Bergthóra got along well.

The following spring, however, Njál bought some land in
Ossabœr and gave it to Hoskuld who then settled there. Njál
provided all the household servants for him. And so close were the
relations between them all that nothing was decided upon by one
household before taking counsel with the other. Thus Hoskuld
lived in Ossabœr for a long time. Njál and Hoskuld each did much
to increase the prestige of the other, and the sons of Njál were
always in Hoskuld's company. So intimate was their relation that
each house invited the other to a feast every autumn, and they gave
each other fine gifts. And so it continued for a long time.

98

Lýting Slays Hoskuld Njálsson.
Hródný Demands Vengeance

There was a man named Lýting who lived at Sámsstead. He was married to Steinvor who was the daughter of Sigfús and the sister of Thráin. Lýting was a big strong man, wealthy in goods, but difficult to deal with.

One day it happened that Lýting was having a feast to which he had invited Hoskuld and the sons of Sigfús, and they had all come. Grani Gunnarsson, Gunnar Lambason, and Lambi Sigurdarson were also there.

Hoskuld Njálsson[1] and his mother had a farmstead at Holt. Hoskuld was accustomed to ride there from Bergthórshvál and his path led through the yard at Sámsstead. Hoskuld had a son named Ámundi; he had been born blind, but he was a tall and powerful fellow.

Lýting had two brothers: Hallstein and Hallgrím. They were great troublemakers and always kept with their brother Lýting, because other people could not get along with them.

Lýting was busy outside that day, coming in once in a while. He was about to sit down when a woman who had been occupied outside came in and said: 'You men should have been outside just now when that coxcomb rode through the yard!'

'What coxcomb are you talking about?' he asked.

'Why, Hoskuld Njálsson,' she answered, 'and he was riding by your home enclosure.'

'He often does that,' Lýting said, 'and I can't say it isn't an aggravation to me. And I herewith offer to ride along with you, Hoskuld, if you will avenge your father and slay Hoskuld Njálsson!'

'That I will not,' said Hoskuld Thráinsson, 'for I would then repay my foster father Njál with evil for the good he has done. Confound you and your invitation!' And with that he jumped up from the table, had his horses brought, and rode home.

Then Lýting spoke to Grani Gunnarsson: 'You were present when Thráin was slain and it must still stick in your memory. And you, too, Gunnar Lambason, and you, Lambi Sigurdarson. I want you right now this evening to ride out with me after him and kill him!'

'No,' said Grani, 'I will not attack the sons of Njál and thus break the peace which good men have made!'

And words to the same effect were spoken by all of them including the sons of Sigfús, and they decided to ride away.

After they had gone Lýting said: 'Everyone knows that I received no atonement for my brother-in-law Thráin. I shall never be satisfied until blood vengeance is taken for him!'

After that he called on his two brothers and three servants to ride with him. They went to the path by which Hoskuld would have to return and hid in a hollow north of the stone fence. There they waited for him until mid-evening. As Hoskuld came riding toward them they all jumped up with their arms and attacked him. Hoskuld defended himself so well that they could not get the best of him for a long time. Finally, however, he was killed, but not before he had wounded Lýting on the hand and had slain two of the servants. They inflicted sixteen wounds on Hoskuld, but did not cut off his head. Then they went into the woods east of the Rangá River and hid there.

That same evening Hródný's shepherd found Hoskuld's body; he returned home and told Hródný of her son's slaying.

She said: 'I trust he is not dead yet; or was his head off?'

'No, it was not,' he answered.

'I'll know when I see him,' she replied. 'Go fetch my horse and cart!'

He got everything ready and then they drove to where Hoskuld lay. She looked at his wounds and said: 'It is just as I thought; he is not altogether dead. Njál can heal worse wounds than these!'

Thereupon they took the body, placed it in the cart, and drove to Bergthórshvál. They drove into the sheepfold and placed the body in an upright position against the wall. Then they both went up to the house and knocked on the door. A servant came to the door, but Hródný immediately pushed her way past him and went up to Njál's bed. She asked Njál whether he was awake. He said that he had been sleeping but was awake now – 'but why do you come here so early?'

Hródný answered: 'Get up from the bed of your concubine and come out! She and your sons should come out, too!'

They all arose and went out.

Skarphedin said: 'Let us take our weapons with us!'

Njál said nothing to this, and so they ran back into the house and returned armed.

Hródný led the way to the sheepfold. She went in and requested them to follow. She raised her lantern and said: 'Here is your son Hoskuld, Njál! He has received many wounds and is in need of your healing powers!'

Njál replied: 'I see only the marks of death on him, but no signs of life. Why did you not close his eyes and nostrils? They are still open.'

'I had Skarphedin in mind for that!' she answered.

Skarphedin stepped up and closed Hoskuld's eyes and nostrils[2] and then asked his father: 'Who do you think killed him?'

Njál answered: 'Lýting of Sámsstead and his brothers must have killed him.'

Hródný said: 'I place the responsibility of avenging your brother upon you, Skarphedin, and I expect that you will make this your particular business, even though Hoskuld was born out of wedlock.'

Bergthóra said: 'You act very strangely, my sons, that you slay men for small cause, but now you hem and haw until nothing comes of it. Soon the news will come to Hoskuld Hvítanessgodi, and he'll offer you atonement and you'll accept it. Now is the time to act without delay, if anything is to come of this.'

Skarphedin said: 'Mother is egging us on and she has the law on her side, too!'

After that they all left the sheepfold. Hródný went into the house with Njál and remained there that night.

99

The Sons of Njál Slay Lýting's Brothers.
Njál Effects a Settlement.

Now to tell about Skarphedin and his brothers: they made their
way up along the Rangá River. Skarphedin said: 'Let us stop here
for a moment and listen!' And then: 'Let us step softly, for I think
I hear men's voices up along the river. How about it, would you
rather tackle Lýting or both his brothers?'

They answered that they preferred to tackle Lýting alone.

'He is the bigger catch, and I would be sorry if he got away,' said
Skarphedin. 'And I trust myself best to prevent his getting away.'

'If we get close enough to him, we'll see to it that he doesn't get
away,' said Helgi.

Then they went in that direction where Skarphedin had heard
the men's voices, and they saw Lýting and his brothers standing by
a stream. Immediately Skarphedin leaped over the stream to the
sandy slope on the other side. At the top of the slope stood
Hallgrím and his brothers. With one hand Skarphedin slashed at
Hallgrím's leg, severing his foot, and with the other hand grabbed
hold of Hallkel. Lýting thrust at Skarphedin, but Helgi brought up
his shield and warded off the blow with it. Lýting picked up a stone
and hurled it at Skarphedin so that he was forced to release his hold
on Hallkel. Now Hallkel scrambled up the sandbank, but could
not manage to get to the top of it except by crawling on hands and
knees. Skarphedin swung at him with his axe and cut his backbone
in two. Then Lýting turned and fled, but Grím and Helgi ran after
him and each one was able to inflict one wound on him. However,
he got away from them, leaped into the river, reached his horses,
and galloped away to Ossabœr.

Hoskuld Thráinsson was at home, and Lýting went up to him
immediately and told him what had happened.

'Things went just as might have been expected!' said Hoskuld,
'and the saying is borne out that "short is the hour of triumph." It

must seem very unlikely to you that you can hold your ground now.'

'It is true,' said Lýting, 'that I barely escaped with my life. But now I wish you to help me make a settlement with Njál and his sons, so that I may be allowed to retain my farm.'

'That shall be done!' said Hoskuld.

Hoskuld had his horse saddled and with five other men rode to Bergthórshvál. Njál's sons had already returned and gone to bed. Hoskuld went up to Njál and the two conferred together.

'I have come here to make a request in behalf of my uncle Lýting,' said Hoskuld. 'He has done you a great wrong, breaking the agreements and killing your son!'

Njál replied: 'Very likely Lýting considers that he has already paid sufficiently with the loss of his brothers. However, he can thank you if I agree to any settlement, and I'll agree only on the condition that Lýting's brothers shall be considered slain as outlaws, and that Lýting himself shall receive no redress for his wounds, but make full atonement for the death of Hoskuld.'

Hoskuld Thráinsson said: 'I wish that you alone make the terms for that.'

Njál answered: 'I'll do that if you so wish.'

'Do you want your sons to be present?' asked Hoskuld.

Njál answered: 'No! If they are present we'll not be any closer to an agreement than we were before. However, they will abide by any agreement I make.'

Then Hoskuld said: 'Let us settle matters then and in behalf of your sons assure Lýting of peace.'

'That shall be done!' said Njál. 'He shall pay two hundreds in silver for the slaying of Hoskuld, but be allowed to remain on his farm at Sámsstead, although I would think it wiser for him to sell his land and move away. Not out of fear of us, for neither I nor my sons will break the pledges of peace given him, but because it seems to me that someone might appear in this district against whom he would have to be on his guard. However, I'll give him permission to stay here, lest it seem as though I were trying to outlaw him from the district. Only, he himself then shoulders the responsibility.'

Then Hoskuld went home. The sons of Njál awoke and asked their father who had been there. He told them that it had been his foster son Hoskuld.

'He probably came to make some request in behalf of Lýting,'
said Skarphedin.

'Yes, he did,' replied Njál.

'That is unfortunate,' said Grím.

'Hoskuld could not have shielded him,' said Njál, 'if you had
killed him as had been your intention.'

'Let us not reproach father!' said Skarphedin.

We are told that the agreement that had been made was kept
ever after.

100

Thangbrand's Missionary Activity

A change of rulers had taken place in Norway.[1] Earl Hákon had
died and Óláf Tryggvason had taken his place. Earl Hákon had
met his death at the hands of the slave Kark who cut the earl's
throat at Rimul in Gaulardale.

At the same time it was learned that there had been a change of
faith in Norway. The old faith had been discarded, and King Óláf
had christianised the western lands also: the Shetlands, the Orkneys, and the Faroe Islands.

Njál heard many people say that it was a great wickedness to give
up the old faith, but he answered: 'It seems to me that the new faith
is much better, and happy he who accepts it. If those who preach it
come here I shall do all I can to further it.'

He often went by himself and prayed.

That same autumn a ship arrived in Bear Firth in the east and
landed at Gautavík. Its skipper was called Thangbrand. He was the
son of Count Vilibald of Saxony. Thangbrand had been sent out by
King Óláf Tryggvason to preach the new faith in Iceland. With him
came an Icelander named Gudleif. He was the son of Ari, the son of
Már, the son of Atli, the son of Úlf the Squinter, the son of Hogni
the White, the son of Ótrygg, the son of Óblaud, the son of Hjorleif
the Amorous, king of Hordaland. Gudleif was a very brave and hardy
man and known as a warrior who had committed many slayings.

Two brothers lived at Beruness; one was named Thorleif and the other Ketil. They were the sons of Hólmstein, the son of Ozur of Broad Dale. They called a meeting and forbade men to have any dealings with the strangers. Hall of Sída, who lived at Thvátta River in Álpta Firth, learned of this. He rode to the ship with thirty men to find Thangbrand and asked him: 'Isn't the trading going well?'[2]

Thangbrand said that it was not; whereupon Hall added: 'I should like to tell you the purpose of my coming: I want to invite you and all your crew to stay with me, and then we shall see whether we can find a market for your wares.'

Thangbrand thanked him and went with him.

One morning during the autumn Thangbrand was early afoot outside. He had a tent pitched and was singing Mass there with great solemnity, for it was a holy day.

Hall asked Thangbrand: 'In whose honour are you celebrating this day?'

'In honour of the Archangel Michael,' he answered.

'What is the nature of this angel?' asked Hall.

'A very blessed one,' answered Thangbrand; 'he will set down all the good things that you do, and he is so merciful that he values especially what seems to him well done.'

'I would like to have him as my friend,' said Hall.

'That may well be,' answered Thangbrand. 'Just surrender yourself to him in God's name this very day.'

'I shall do that,' said Hall, 'with the condition that you vouch for him that he become my guardian angel.'

'That I will promise,' said Thangbrand.

Then Hall and his entire household were baptised.

IOI

Thangbrand Preaches the New Faith

The following spring Thangbrand went about preaching Christianity, and Hall accompanied him. When they came west across
Lónsheath to Stafafell they met a man named Thorkel who lived
there. He spoke strongly against the new faith and challenged
Thangbrand to the holm. Thangbrand carried a crucifix in place
of a shield; yet the result was that he slew Thorkel and won the
victory.

From there they went to Horn Firth and were guests at Borgarhofn west of Heinabergssand. Hildir the Old lived there. His son
was Glúm, who later was to go with Flosi to the burning at
Bergthórshvál. Hildir and his entire household accepted the new
faith.

From there they continued to Fellshverfi and were guests at
Kálfafell. Kol Thorsteinsson, Hall's kinsman, lived there. He and
his entire household likewise accepted the new faith. From there
they went to Broad River where Ozur Hróaldsson, another kinsman of Hall, lived. He let himself merely be marked with the sign
of the cross.[1] From there they went to Svínafell, and Flosi also let
himself be marked with the sign of the cross and promised to
support Thangbrand at the Assembly. Then they fared west to
Skógahverfi[2] and were guests at Kirkby. Here lived Surt, the son of
Ásbjorn, the son of Thorstein, the son of Ketil the Foolish. All
these men had already become Christians. Then they left the
Skógahverfi district and travelled to Hofdabrekka. By that time the
news of their journey and mission had spread far and wide.

There was a man named Sorcerer-Hedin who lived in
Kerlingardale. Heathen men paid him money to put Thangbrand
and his followers to death. Sorcerer-Hedin went up to Arnarstakk
Heath and offered a great sacrifice there. As Thangbrand rode over
the heath from the east the earth burst asunder beneath him, but
he leaped from his horse, climbed up to the edge of the chasm, and

saved himself. But the horse with all its gear was swallowed up by the earth, so that it was never again seen. Then Thangbrand praised God.

Gudleif searched for Sorcerer-Hedin and found him on the heath and chased him down into Kerlingardale. And when he came within range he hurled his spear at him and it pierced him.

102

Úlf Refuses to Oppose Thangbrand. Steinunn Contends with him

From there they continued to Dyrhólmar and held a meeting there. Thangbrand preached the faith, and Ingjald, the son of Thorkel Háeyjartyrdil, became a Christian.

From there they went to the Fljótshlíd district and preached the faith there. Thangbrand met the greatest opposition from Vetrlidi the Skald and his son Ari, and for that reason they killed Vetrlidi.[1] This verse is spoken of Vetrlidi's slaying:[2]

> Turned he his tools-of-warfare
> toward the smithy-of-prayers[3]
> of the warlike weapon-
> wielder, in the southland;
> but swiftly smote the valiant
> swordplay-tester,[4] and with
> murderous hammer[5] hit the
> head-anvil of Vetrlidi.

From there Thangbrand went to Bergthórshvál, and Njál and his entire household accepted the faith. Mord and his father Valgard, however, opposed it with great hostility.

Then they set out west over the rivers and came to Haukadale and baptised Hall,[6] who was just three years old at the time.

Then they went to Grímsness. There Thorvald the Infirm gathered a force against Thangbrand and sent word to Úlf Uggason[7] that he should join him against Thangbrand and slay him. Thorvald spoke this verse:

> Offhand shall I order
> Úlf, the steel-clad warrior –
> this the tried and true one's
> task – the son of Uggi:
> that he thrust the evil-
> throated scoffer down, and
> cast him o'er echoing
> cliffs[8] – and I the other.

Úlf Uggason replied to him with another verse:

> Nowise will I, word though,
> winner-of-Odin's mead,[9] you
> send me, simple-hearted
> swallow the bait you offer;
> nor – mischief is in the making –
> master-of-the-sea-steeds[10] –
> I guard me 'gainst such evils –
> go in the trap you set me.

'And,' he said, 'I don't intend to run a fool's errand for him; and let him beware lest his tongue twist a noose around his neck!'

Thereupon the messenger returned to Thorvald the Infirm and told him of Úlf's words. Thorvald had many men with him and he declared that he would ambush Thangbrand and Gudleif on the Black Forest Heath. As Thangbrand and Gudleif rode up from Haukadale they came upon a man riding down to meet them. He asked for Gudleif and then said to him: 'You can thank your brother in Reykjahólar[11] that I bring you this information. They have set many traps for you, and Thorvald himself is at Hestlœk Brook on Grímsness with his band.'

'All the same we shall try conclusions with him,' replied Gudleif.

Thereupon they turned down to Hestlœk Brook. Thorvald had already come over the stream.

Gudleif said to Thangbrand: 'There's Thorvald! Let's attack him now!'

Thangbrand hurled his spear through Thorvald, and Gudleif hewed off his arm at the shoulder, and that was his death.

Then they rode to the Assembly, and the kinsmen of Thorvald were about to attack Thangbrand, but Njál and the men from the East Firths stood by him. Then Hjalti Skeggjason spoke this verse:

> I'll aye make game of godheads:
> a bitch meseems is Freya.
> Truth of the matter is, either
> Ódin's a dog or else Freya.[12]

Hjalti travelled abroad that summer[13] and Gizur the White went with him. Thangbrand's ship, 'The Bison', was wrecked off Búlandsness.[14]

Thangbrand travelled through the entire West Quarter. Steinunn, the mother of Skald-Ref, came out to meet him. She made a long speech and tried to convert him to paganism. Thangbrand remained silent while she spoke, but when she had finished, he spoke at length and confuted everything she had said.

'Have you heard that Thór challenged Christ to the holm and that Christ did not dare to fight against him?' she asked.

'I have heard that Thór would be naught but dust and ashes if God did not permit him to live,' answered Thangbrand.

'Do you know who wrecked your ship?' she asked.

'What do you have to say about that?' he asked.

'I'll tell you,' she answered.

> Was the boat of the bell's warder –
> beached it angry godheads –
> shattered by the ogres'-offsprings'
> awful-slayer[15] wholly.
> Crushed was the craft, nor saved your
> Christ the iron-hoofed road-steed:[16]
> God in nowise guarded
> Gylfi's-reindeer,[16] ween I.

And she spoke yet another verse:

> Thór thrusted then far-off
> Thangbrand's ship from harbour –
> shook the mast, and shoreward
> shoved it on to sandbanks:

never, ween I, will that
wain–of–Atal's–kingdom[17]
sail the swans'–land after
since by him 't was splintered.

Thereupon Thangbrand and Steinunn parted, and Thangbrand and his men travelled west to Bardastrand.[18]

103

Thangbrand Slays a Berserker

Gest Oddleifsson lived at Hagi on Bardastrand. He was a very wise man who could foretell the fates of men. He prepared a feast for Thangbrand and his company, and they came to Hagi, sixty men altogether. It was reported that two hundred heathens were already there, expecting the arrival of a berserker. This berserker was named Ótrygg, and all were sore afraid of him. Remarkable stories were told of him, as for example, that he feared neither fire nor sword. The heathens feared him greatly.

Then Thangbrand asked whether the people wished to accept the faith, but all the heathens were opposed to it.

'I'll give you the opportunity of testing which faith is best,' said Thangbrand. 'We will kindle three fires. You, heathen men, shall hallow one fire, I will hallow the second, but the third shall remain unhallowed. If the berserker is afraid of the fire which I hallow but walks through your fire, then you shall accept the faith.'

'That is a good suggestion,' said Gest. 'I'll agree to that in behalf of my household and myself.'

After Gest had spoken thus, many others agreed to it also.

Now it was reported that the berserker was coming up to the house, and the fires were kindled, and they burned brightly. The men took their weapons and leaped up on the benches and there awaited his approach. The berserker rushed into the hall fully armed and immediately strode through the fire which the heathens had hallowed. However, when he came to the fire which

Thangbrand had hallowed he dared not stride through it, for he said that he was on fire from head to toe. He aimed a blow with his sword at the benches, but it caught in the crossbeam as he raised it aloft. Thangbrand struck him on the hand with his crucifix, and a great wonder happened: the sword fell from the hand of the berserker. Then Thangbrand thrust his sword through his breast, and Gudleif hewed off his arm. Then many others came up and slew the berserker.

Thereupon Thangbrand asked whether they would accept the faith. Gest answered that he had not promised more than he intended to keep. Thereupon Thangbrand baptised Gest and his entire household as well as many others.

Thangbrand discussed with Gest the advisability of travelling to the firths further west,[1] but Gest advised against it, saying that there lived men who were very hard and difficult to deal with. – 'But if it is ordained that this faith is to gain strength, then it is likely that it will be accepted at the Althing, and all the chieftains from each district will be present there.'

'I have already spoken for it at the Assembly,' said Thangbrand, 'and that is exactly where I had my greatest difficulty.'

'But you are the one,' said Gest, 'who has done most to promote it, even though it may be granted to others to introduce it into the laws. It is just as the saying goes: "A tree will not fall at the first blow!" '

Thereupon Thangbrand received splendid gifts from Gest and then returned to the south, first to the Southlanders' Quarter and then to the East Firths. He was a guest at Bergthórshvál where he received additional fine gifts from Njál. Then he rode east to Álpta Firth and met Hall of Sída. He had his ship repaired, and the heathens called it the 'Iron Basket'.[2] On it Thangbrand and Gudleif left Iceland.

That summer Hjalti Skeggjason was condemned to outlawry at the Assembly for blasphemy of the gods.

104

Gizur and Hjalti at the Assembly

Thangbrand told King Óláf how ill the Icelanders had treated him. He said that they were such great sorcerers that the earth had burst asunder beneath his horse and swallowed it up. That so kindled the king's wrath that he had all men from Iceland seized and thrown into dungeons, and wanted to have them slain. Then Gizur the White and Hjalti stepped forward and offered to go surety for them and to sail to Iceland and preach the faith. The king was pleased to accept that offer, and thereupon all the Icelanders were set free. Then Gizur and Hjalti prepared their ship to sail for Iceland and soon were ready. They landed at Eyrar[1] when ten weeks of summer had passed. They secured horses immediately and had men unload the ship. Then they rode to the Assembly, thirty men altogether, and sent word to all who had been baptised to be prepared to lend them their support. Hjalti remained behind at Reydarmúli because he learned that he had been made an outlaw for blasphemy. However, when the others came to Velland Bight below the farm of Gjábakki, Hjalti came riding after them and said that he did not wish the heathens to think that he feared them.

Many Christians now rode out to meet them, and they went up to the Assembly in battle array. So did the heathens, and the whole assembly was about to come to blows. Still, that did not happen.

105

The New Faith Becomes Law on Thorgeir's Advice

There was a man named Thorgeir who lived at the farm of Ljósavatn. He was the son of Tjorvi, the son of Thorkel the Long. His mother was named Thórunn and she was the daughter of Thorstein, the son of Sigmund, the son of Gnúpa-Bárd. His wife was named Gudríd and she was the daughter of Thorkel the Black of Hleidrargard. His brother was Orm Toskubak, the father of Hlenni the Old of Saurbœr. Orm and Thorkel were both sons of Thórir Snepil, the son of Ketil Brimil, the son of Bjornólf, the son of Grím Lodinkinni, the son of Ketil Hœing, the son of Hallbjorn Half-Troll of Hrafnista.

The Christians set up their booths; Gizur and Hjalti shared the booth of the men from Mosfell. The following day both sides went to the Law-Mount, and Christians as well as heathens named witnesses and declared their former community of laws dissolved. Then there arose such a tumult at the Law-Mount that no one could hear what anyone else said. Then they all left the place of assembly, and the situation seemed to be fraught with the greatest danger.

The Christians chose as their law-speaker Hall of Sída, but he went to Thorgeir,[1] the *godi* of Ljósavatn, and gave him three marks of silver in order that he should proclaim what the law should be. This, however, was a very risky step, because Thorgeir was still a heathen.

That entire day Thorgeir lay with a cloak spread over his head so that no one might speak to him. The following day[2] all assembled before the Law-Mount.

Then Thorgeir asked to be heard and spoke: 'It seems to me that our affairs have come to a dangerous pass if we all do not have one and the same law. If the laws are torn asunder, then security can no longer prevail, and we cannot afford to incur that danger. Now therefore I shall ask both heathens and Christians whether they will abide by the laws which I shall proclaim.'

All agreed to that.

He said he required binding oaths from both parties that they would abide by them. They all agreed to that, too, and he took their pledged faith.

'This is the foundation of our laws,' he said, 'that all men in this land are to be Christians and believe in one God – the Father, the Son and the Holy Ghost – and that they are no longer to worship idols, nor expose children nor eat horse meat.[3] If any man is found guilty of these practices, he shall be condemned to outlawry, but if he carries them on in secret, there shall be no punishment involved.'

However, in the course of a few years all these heathen practices were abolished, so that they were no longer tolerated, whether practised openly or in secret.

He further proclaimed laws about the keeping of the Lord's days and fast days, Yule and Easter, and all the important holy days. The heathens thought they had been grossly defrauded. Nevertheless, the new faith became law, and all people in the land became Christians. And with that, people went home from the Assembly.

106

Ámundi Avenges his Father

Three years later it happened that Ámundi the Blind, the son of Hoskuld Njálsson, was at the Thingskálar Assembly. He had someone lead him from booth to booth until he came to the one which housed Lýting of Sámsstead. He had himself led in to where Lýting was sitting and then he asked: 'Is Lýting of Sámsstead here?'

'What do you wish?' asked Lýting.

'I wish to know what reparations you will pay me for my father's slaying,' said Ámundi. 'I am his natural son, but I have received no reparations.'

'I have paid for the slaying of your father with a full wergild,' said Lýting, 'and your father's father and brothers accepted the money, but no wergild was paid for my own brothers. On the one hand, I deserved it; on the other, my punishment was most severe.'

'I am not asking whether you paid them any reparations, because I know that you are reconciled with them,' said Ámundi. 'I merely ask what reparations you will pay me.'

'None at all!' answered Lýting.

'I cannot understand how that can be just before God, for you have hewn so close to me,' answered Ámundi. 'However, I can tell you this: if I were blessed with sight in both my eyes, I would demand full redress for my father's death or else seek revenge! Yet I shall let God decide between us.'

Thereupon he left the booth, but as he came to the door, he turned around once more. Suddenly his eyes opened and he said: 'Praised be the Lord! I can now see what his will is!'

With that he rushed back into the booth, went up to Lýting, and drove his axe into his head right up to the hammer of the axe and then pulled it out. Lýting fell forward and was dead immediately. Ámundi returned to the door of the booth, and as he came to the same place where his eyes had been opened, they now closed again, and he remained blind the rest of his life. After that he was led to Njál and his sons, and he told them of the slaying of Lýting.

'No one can blame you for what you did,' said Njál, 'because to a large extent it was foreordained; and it is a warning to those who have done a heinous deed not to rebuff those so close of kin.'

Thereupon Njál offered to make a settlement with Lýting's kinsmen. Hoskuld Hvítanessgodi persuaded them to accept reparations, and the matter was then referred to the court for decision. Half of the fine was declared forfeited because of the just claim which Ámundi was found to have against Lýting. After that both parties gave pledges of peace and Lýting's kinsmen vowed not to attack Ámundi. All left the Assembly, and there was quiet and peace for a long time.

107

The Advice of Valgard the Grey

Valgard the Grey returned to Iceland that summer; he was still a heathen. He went to visit his son Mord at Hof and stayed there that winter.

One day he said to Mord: 'I have travelled far and wide in the district, but it no longer seems to me to be the same. I came to Hvítaness and there I saw the walls and the foundations of many new booths, and great changes. I came to the Thingskálar Assembly and there I saw all our booths taken down. What is the meaning of this abomination?'

Mord answered: 'A Fifth Court and new *goðorðs* have been established here, and men have left me and put themselves under Hoskuld's authority.'

Valgard said: 'Badly have you repaid me for the *goðorð* which I entrusted to you and which you have administered so poorly. I wish that you now requite them in such manner that it will be the destruction of them all. And the way to do that is to set them by their ears, one against the other, by slander, so that the sons of Njál will slay Hoskuld. There are many who will take up the prosecution for the slaying of Hoskuld, and thus the sons of Njál will most likely be slain.'

'I don't see how I can get that done,' said Mord.

'I shall tell you how to go about it,' said Valgard. 'Invite the sons of Njál to your home and on their departure present them with gifts. However, do not make any slanderous remarks until a very close friendship has developed between you. Then they will believe you just as much as they believe themselves. In that way you will get even with Skarphedin for having made you pay all that money after Gunnar's death. You will not regain your authority before all of them are dead.'

They pledged themselves to carry out this plan.

Mord said: 'I would that you accepted the new faith, father. You are an old man.'

'Rather would I have you renounce that faith and see what will happen,' Valgard answered.

Mord said he would not do that. Valgard broke the crosses and other holy things which Mord had. Then a sickness fell upon him and he died and was placed in a cairn.

108

Mord Toadies to the Sons of Njál

Some time after this Mord went to Bergthórshvál to visit Skarphedin and his brothers. He used the most honeyed words to them and talked with them all day long and said he wished to be more closely associated with them. Skarphedin listened to this willingly enough, but observed that Mord had not been so anxious about that before. In the end they got to be such close friends that no counsel was taken but all shared in it. Njál always expressed his displeasure when Mord came to see them and always showed his disapproval of him.

One day Mord again came to Bergthórshvál and said to the sons of Njál: 'I have arranged the *arvel*[1] for my father at my place, and to this feast I wish to invite you Njálssons and Kári, and I can promise that you shall not depart from there without gifts.'

They promised to come, and he rode home to prepare for the feast. He invited many householders, and the feast was well attended. The sons of Njál and Kári also came. Mord gave a large brooch of gold to Skarphedin, a silver belt to Kári, and goodly presents also to Grím and Helgi. They came home and praised these gifts and showed them to Njál. He said that they had probably paid dearly enough for them and added: 'Take care that you do not repay him in the manner which he would like!'

109

Mord Sets Hoskuld and the Sons of Njál
at Odds with Each Other

Shortly after this Hoskuld Thráinsson, the *goði* at Hvítaness, and the sons of Njál were to have their annual feast, and the sons of Njál first invited Hoskuld to their home. Skarphedin owned a four-year-old brown horse, a large and splendid-looking animal. It was a stallion and had never yet been tested in fight. Skarphedin gave this stallion together with two mares to Hoskuld. The others also gave gifts to Hoskuld and bespoke his friendship.

Thereupon Hoskuld invited them to his home at Ossabœr. There were many guests assembled there in addition to the many members of his own household. Hoskuld had taken down his sleeping hall, but he had three storehouses, and there he had beds set up for his guests. All the people whom he had invited came, and the feast went off very well. When the guests were about to return home, Hoskuld sought out fine gifts for them and accompanied the sons of Njál a little distance on their way.[1] The sons of Sigfús and all of Hoskuld's household also rode along. Both parties said that no one should ever come between them and spoil their friendship.

Some time after this Mord came to Ossabœr and had Hoskuld called out to talk with him. They stepped aside and Mord said: 'There is a big difference between you and Njál's sons; you gave them splendid gifts, but there is mockery and ridicule in the gifts which they gave you!'

'How do you make that out?' asked Hoskuld.

'They gave you a horse which among themselves they called a foal of possibilities,' he added, 'and they did that in a spirit of mockery, because they considered you untested, too. Let me also tell you that they envy you because of your *goðorð*. Skarphedin assumed it at the Assembly when you did not come to the convening of the Fifth Court, nor does he mean ever to let go of it.'

'That is not true,' said Hoskuld. 'I possessed myself of it again at the autumn meeting of the district.'

'Well, Njál arranged that then,' answered Mord, 'but they broke the settlement made with Lýting.'[2]

'I don't believe we can hold them responsible for that deed,' said Hoskuld.

'You can't deny that an axe fell from under Skarphedin's belt as you two were riding east to the Markar River,' said Mord, 'and that he meant to slay you with it.'

'That was his woodman's axe,' said Hoskuld, 'and I saw him put it under his belt in the first place. And as far as I am concerned, let me tell you right off that I will never believe a single word of whatever ill you speak of the sons of Njál. Even if you were telling the truth and it were a question as to whether I should slay them or they me, I would much rather suffer death at their hands than do them the least harm. You are all the worse man for having spoken these words!'

Thereupon Mord went home. Some time later he visited the sons of Njál and spoke at considerable length with them and Kári. He said: 'I understand that Hoskuld said that you, Skarphedin, broke the settlement made with Lýting, and I am sure that he believes you planned some treachery the time you two rode to the Markar River. Nor was any less treachery involved, I believe, when he invited you to his feast and assigned you sleeping quarters in that storehouse which was farthest away from the main hall. All night long he had wood carried up and he planned to burn you inside. But it so happened that Hogni arrived that night, and so nothing came of their attack because they were afraid of him. Later on he accompanied you on your way with a large following of men. It was then he intended to make another attack and had set Grani Gunnarsson and Gunnar Lambason to fall upon you. But their courage failed them and they did not dare to make an assault on you.'

At first the sons of Njál contradicted what he had said, but finally they began to believe him, and there developed a coolness on their part in their relationship with Hoskuld, and they scarcely spoke to him when they met. Hoskuld, too, avoided them more and more and so things went on for a while.

In the autumn Hoskuld rode east to a feast at Svínafell and he was well received by Flosi. Hildigunn was also there.

Flosi said to Hoskuld: 'Hildigunn tells me that considerable misunderstanding has developed between you and Njál's sons. I am sorry to hear that. I beg you not to ride back west again. I'll secure a homestead for you at Skaptafell and I'll have my brother Thorgeir move to Ossabœr and live there.'

'Some people will remark that I fled from there because I was afraid,' answered Hoskuld, 'and I would not want that.'

'Then it is very likely that a great calamity will be the result,' said Flosi.

'That is very unfortunate,' said Hoskuld, 'for I would rather fall unatoned than cause suffering to many.'

When Hoskuld rode home a few days later Flosi gave him a scarlet cloak ornamented with lace down to the skirt. Hoskuld was so popular and well liked that he had almost no enemies, but the tense relationship between the sons of Njál and himself continued unchanged the entire winter.

Njál had taken into his home Thórd, the son of Kári, as his foster child. He was also the foster father of Thórhall, the son of Ásgrím Ellida-Grímsson. Thórhall was a brisk man, hardy in every respect. From Njál he had learned so much about law that he was accounted one of the three greatest men of law.[3]

110

The Attack on Hoskuld is Planned

Spring came early that year, and the men were already busy sowing their grain.

One day Mord came to Bergthórshvál and at once began to talk with Njál's sons and Kári. He slandered Hoskuld as usual. He had many new things to report and he kept on inciting Skarphedin and the others to slay Hoskuld, saying that Hoskuld would forestall them if they did not fall upon him at once.

'I shall go in on that,' said Skarphedin, 'if you join us and take some part in it.'

'That I am prepared to do,' answered Mord.

They pledged themselves to this agreement, and Mord was to come over that very evening.

Bergthóra asked Njál: 'What are they talking about out there?'

'I am not in on their plans,' replied Njál. 'In the past I was rarely kept out when something good was being considered!'

That evening Skarphedin did not lie down to sleep, and neither did his brothers nor Kári. That same night Mord Valgardsson joined them, and they took their weapons and journeyed till they arrived at Ossabœr. There they waited beside a fence wall. The sun had just risen and the weather was good.

III

Hoskuld is Slain

About that time Hoskuld Hvítanessgodi awoke. He put on his clothes and threw over him the cloak which Flosi had given him. He took a basket with seed grain in one hand and his sword in the other and went toward the enclosure to sow the grain. Skarphedin and his men had agreed that they would all attack him. Skarphedin jumped up from behind the fence, and Hoskuld tried to escape as soon as he saw him. However, Skarphedin rushed at him and said: 'Don't try to take to your heels, Hvítanessgodi!' With that Skarphedin cut at him and the blow struck Hoskuld on the head so that he sank to his knees.

He spoke these words: 'May God help me and forgive you!' Then they all made for him and inflicted wounds on him.

After that Mord said: 'I have a plan.'

'What is it?' asked Skarphedin.

'I shall first ride home, but after that I shall ride up to the Grjótá River farm, report the news to them there, and express great indignation at the deed. I am sure that Thorgerd[1] will ask me to give notice of the slaying, and I'll do that, because that will likely invalidate the entire suit for them.[2] I shall also send someone to Ossabœr and have him find out how soon they[3] plan to take action. And he will learn from them what happened, and I shall act as though I heard it all from them.'

'Do so by all means!' said Skarphedin.

The brothers and Kári returned home and reported the news to Njál.

'Most distressing tidings these are, and harrowing for me to hear,' said Njál, 'for I can truthfully say that I am so saddened that I would prefer to have lost two of my sons and have Hoskuld still alive!'

'You have good reason to say that,' said Skarphedin, 'because you are an old man, and one can understand that this blow has struck very close to home!'

'It is not age so much as that I know better than you what will happen hereafter,' said Njál.

'And what will happen hereafter?' asked Skarphedin.

'My death,' answered Njál, 'and that of my wife and all my sons!'

'What do you prophesy for me?' asked Kári.

'They will find it very difficult to contend against your good luck,' said Njál, 'for you will prove to be too much for all of them.'

This was the one thing which so saddened Njál that he could not speak of it without shedding tears.

112

The Beginning of the Suit

Hildigunn awoke and noticed that Hoskuld had left the bed. She said: 'Bad have been my dreams and they forbode no good! Go and look for Hoskuld!'

They searched for him all over the homestead, but could not find him. By that time she was dressed and with two men she went to the enclosure and there they found Hoskuld slain.

Just then the shepherd of Mord Valgardsson arrived and told her that the sons of Njál had ridden away from there – 'and Skarphedin called out to me and gave notice that he was responsible for the slaying.'

'It would have been a manly deed, if one man alone had done it!' she remarked.

She took the cloak and wiped off all the blood with it and wrapped all the clotted blood in it, folded it together, and laid it in her chest.

Then she sent a messenger to the Grjótá River Farm to report the news. Mord had already been there and had spread the news. Ketil of Mork had also come.

Thorgerd said to Ketil: 'Now we know that Hoskuld is dead. Now call to mind what you promised!'

'Maybe,' said Ketil, 'I promised plenty and enough, because it never entered my mind that such things would come to pass as have happened now. And indeed I am in trouble now, for "nose is closest to eyes", seeing that my wife is Njál's daughter.'

'Is it your wish,' asked Thorgerd, 'that Mord serve notice of the slaying?'

'I don't know about that,' answered Ketil, 'because I believe that he brings people more evil than good.'

But as soon as Mord spoke to Ketil it seemed to him, as it did to others, that Mord was his true friend; and they agreed that Mord should serve notice of the slaying and carefully prepare the suit for the Assembly.

Then Mord rode down to Ossabœr; the nine neighbours who lived closest to the spot also came. Mord himself had ten men along with him. He showed the neighbours Hoskuld's wounds and he named witnesses to the wounds, and for each wound but one he named the man who had inflicted it. He pretended not to know who had inflicted this one wound, for it had been he himself who had dealt Hoskuld that blow. The slaying itself he charged to Skarphedin and the wounds to his brothers and Kári. After that he summoned the nine neighbours as jurors to the Althing and then rode home.

He scarcely ever visited Njál's sons, and when they did meet they were at swords' points. That was part of their scheme.

Hoskuld's slaying was discussed in all sections of the land and called forth bitter comments. The sons of Njál visited Ásgrím Ellida-Grímsson and asked for his support.

'You may be sure that I will support you in all great suits,' he said; 'yet I have evil forebodings about this business, because there are many who will take up the prosecution, and public opinion all over the land is much aroused about it.'

113

Gudmund the Powerful and his Kin

There was a man named Gudmund the Powerful who lived at Modruvellir in the Eyja Firth district. He was the son of Eyjólf, the son of Einar, the son of Audun the Bald, the son of Thórólf Butter, the son of Thorstein Scurvy, the son of Grím Kamban. Gudmund's mother was named Hallbera, the daughter of Thórodd Helm. Her mother was named Reginleif, the daughter of Sæmund of the Hebrides. Sæmundarhlíd in Skaga Firth is named after him. The mother of Eyjólf, the father of Gudmund, was Valgerd, the daughter of Rúnólf. The mother of Valgerd was Valborg, the daughter of Jórunn Óborna, the daughter of King Ósvald the Saint. The mother of Einar, Eyjólf's father, was Helga, the daughter of Helgi the Lean, who was the first settler in Eyja Firth. Helgi was the son of Eyvind the Norwegian and of Raforta, the daughter of Kjarval the Irish king. The mother of Helga, the daughter of Helgi, was Thórunn Hyrna, the daughter of Ketil Flatnose, the son of Bjorn Buna, the son of the chieftain Grím. Grím's mother was Hervor and Hervor's mother was Thorgerd, the daughter of King Háleyg of Hálogaland.

The wife of Gudmund the Powerful was named Thorlaug, the daughter of Atli the Strong, the son of Eilíf Eagle, the son of Bárd of Ál, the son of Ketil Fox, the son of Skídi the Old. The mother of Thorlaug was named Herdís, the daughter of Thórd of Hofdi, the son of Bjorn Butterbox, the son of Hróald, the son of Bjorn Ironside, the son of Ragnar Lodbrók, the son of Sigurd Ring, the son of Randvér, the son of Rádbard. The mother of Herdís, Thórd's daughter, was Thorgerd, and she was the daughter of Skídi and Fridgerd, the daughter of Kjarval the Irish king.[1]

Gudmund was a great and wealthy chieftain; he had a hundred servants in his home. He so bore down on the chieftains in the Northern Quarter that some had to leave their homesteads. Others had to relinquish their *goðorðs* because of him, and still others he

put to death. All the greatest families in the land are descended
from him, such as the men of Oddi, the Sturlungs, the men of
Hvamm, the men of Fljót, Bishop Ketil, and many other notable
men. Gudmund was a good friend of Ásgrím Ellida-Grímsson and
the latter relied on him for support.

114

Snorri Godi and his Kin

There was a man named Snorri, known as Snorri Godi. He lived
at Helgafell until Gudrún,[1] the daughter of Ósvíf, bought the
land from him. She lived there until her old age, but Snorri
moved to Hvamms Firth and lived at Sælingsdalstunga. Snorri's
father was named Thorgrím, the son of Thorstein Cod-Eater, the
son of Thórólf Mostrarskegg, the son of Ornólf Fish-Driver, but
Ari the Wise calls Thórólf the son of Thorgil Reydarsída.

The wife of Thórólf Mostrarskegg was Ósk, the daughter of
Thorstein the Red. The mother of Thorgrím was named Thóra,
the daughter of Óleif Feilan, the son of Thorstein the Red, the son
of Óleif the White, the son of Ingjald, the son of Helgi. The
mother of Ingjald was named Thóra, the daughter of Sigurd
Snake-in-the-Eye, the son of Ragnar Lodbrók. The mother of
Snorri Godi was Thordís, the daughter of Súr, the sister of Gísli.

Snorri was a good friend of Ásgrím Ellida-Grímsson, and Ásgrím
relied on him for support also. Snorri was the wisest of all men in
Iceland not reckoning those who had second sight. He was good to
his friends, but stern toward his enemies.

At the time we speak of there was a large attendance at the
Assembly from all quarters of the land and many lawsuits were
introduced.

115

Flosi Gathers Allies

Flosi learned of Hoskuld's slaying and he was both grieved and angry, but he controlled his feelings very well. He was told of the preparations which had been made in the suit for Hoskuld's slaying, but he said very little about it. He sent word to his father-in-law, Hall of Sída, and to Hall's son Ljót, that they should collect a strong following for the Assembly. Ljót was considered to be one of the most promising young chieftains in the east. It had been prophesied that he would become the greatest as well as the oldest chieftain in his line, if he were to ride to the Assembly three times in succession and return home safe and sound. He had already ridden once to the Assembly and was now planning to ride for the second time.

Flosi sent word to Kol Thorsteinsson, and to Glúm, the son of Hildir the Old, the son of Geirleif, the son of Onund Toskubak, as well as to Módólf Ketilsson, and they all came to join forces with Flosi. Hall, too, promised to come with a large following.

Flosi himself rode to Kirkby to Surt Ásbjarnarson. Then he sent for his brother's son, Kolbein Egilsson, and he, too, joined him. Then he rode to Hofdabrekka. Thorgrím the Showy, the son of Thorkel the Fair, lived there. Flosi asked him to ride to the Assembly with him. He agreed and said to Flosi: 'I have often seen you in a more cheerful mood than now, freeholder, but you have good reason to feel the way you do.'

Flosi answered: 'I would give everything I own if that which has happened had never taken place! An ill seed has been sown, and ill is bound to grow out of it!'

From there they rode to Arnarstakk Heath and came to Sólheim that evening. There lived Lodmund Úlfsson, a good friend of Flosi. Flosi stayed with him overnight. In the morning Lodmund rode with him to Dale, the home of Rúnólf, the son of Úlf Aurgodi.

Flosi said to Rúnólf: 'It is from you that we are going to hear the true story about the slaying of Hoskuld Hvítanessgodi, for you are a truthful man and live close to the spot where the deed took place, and I shall believe everything you can tell me about the reason for their falling out.'

Rúnólf answered: 'There is no need of mincing words; he was slain for less than no cause, and all lament his death, but no one more than his foster father Njál.'

'In that case,' said Flosi, 'they will have difficulty in finding men to support them at the Assembly.'

'That is so,' said Rúnólf, 'if nothing else intervenes which might change the situation.'

'What has been done in the suit thus far?' asked Flosi.

'The jury of neighbours has been summoned,' said Rúnólf, 'and notice of the suit for manslaughter has been served.'

'Who attended to that?' asked Flosi.

'Mord Valgardsson,' answered Rúnólf.

'How far is he to be trusted?' asked Flosi.

'He is a kinsman of mine,' answered Rúnólf; 'but the truth of the matter is that more ill than good comes to people from him. Therefore, I wish to ask you, Flosi, to check your anger and decide upon that course which will lead to the least trouble, for Njál and other most excellent men are likely to make good offers [for a reconciliation].'

Flosi said: 'Ride to the Assembly with me, Rúnólf. Your advice will have great weight with me, unless indeed things turn out worse than they should.' With that they ended their talk and Rúnólf promised to ride along.

Rúnólf sent word to his kinsman, Hafr the Wise, and he joined them at once.

116

Hildigunn Incites Flosi to Avenge Hoskuld

From there Flosi rode to Ossabœr. Hildigunn was out in front of the house and she said: 'Now I want all my men servants to stand outside when Flosi rides into the yard, but the women are to sweep the rooms and put up the hangings and make ready the high-seat for Flosi.'[1]

Shortly after this Flosi came riding into the yard and Hildigunn went out to meet him. She spoke: 'Thrice welcome, kinsman! My heart rejoices at your coming!'

'We shall eat our day-meal[2] here and then ride on,' said Flosi.

Their horses were tethered and Flosi stepped into the sitting-room and took a seat. He thrust the bolster on to the dais and said: 'I am neither king nor earl and require no seat of honour, and there is no need to make mock of me!'

Hildigunn stood near and said: 'I am sorry if this offends you, for no ill was meant.'

Flosi said: 'If you mean well by me, that will come to light, but if your intentions are evil, they will stand condemned by themselves.'

Hildigunn gave a cold laugh and said: 'This is nothing as yet; we shall come to closer quarters before we are through!'

She sat down beside Flosi and they talked together for a long time under their breath.

After that the tables were brought[3] and Flosi and his men washed their hands. Flosi looked at the towel and saw that it was full of holes and that an entire piece was torn off at one end. He threw it down on the bench and would not dry his hands on it, but tore off a piece of the tablecloth, dried his hands on that, and then tossed it to his men. Thereupon he sat down at the table and bade his men eat.

Then Hildigunn came into the room and brushed the hair from her eyes and wept.

Flosi said: 'You are sad of heart, kinswoman; that is as it should be, for you mourn a brave man!'

'What redress then can I expect from you, and what assistance?' she asked.

Flosi answered: 'I shall prosecute your suit until you have received complete justice in accordance with the law, or I shall try to effect a settlement which good men will consider to be in keeping with our honour.'

Hildigunn said: 'Bloody vengeance is what Hoskuld would have wreaked if you had been slain and he had to seek redress for your death!'

Flosi answered: 'Vindictiveness you have aplenty, and it is easy to see what you are after!'

Hildigunn said: 'Less wrong had Arnór Ornólfsson from Forsárskóg done Thórd Freysgodi, your father, and yet your brothers, Kolbein and Egil, slew him at the Skaptafell Assembly.'

Thereupon Hildigunn went back into the hall and unlocked her chest. Out of it she took the cloak which Flosi had given Hoskuld and in which he had been slain, and in it she had preserved all the blood. With this cloak she returned to the room and without saying a word walked up to Flosi. Flosi had finished eating and the table had been cleared. She spread the cloak over Flosi's shoulders, and the clotted blood rattled down all over him.[4]

Then she said: 'This cloak you, Flosi, gave to Hoskuld, and now I want to return it to you. In it he was slain. I call God and all good men to witness that I adjure you by all the wonders of your Christ and by your manhood and valour that you avenge all the wounds which Hoskuld received on his body, or else be called a caitiff wretch before all men!'[5]

Flosi flung the cloak from him and back at her and said: 'You are a very devil! You want us to undertake what would lead to the undoing of us all! Cold are women's counsels!'

Flosi was so agitated that his face was now as red as blood, now as wan as grass, and again as black as Hell itself. He rode away with his men and came to Holtsvad where he waited for the sons of Sigfús and the other men of his party.

Ingjald, the brother of Hródný, the mother of Hoskuld Njálsson,[7] lived at Keldur. He and Hródný were the children of Hoskuld the White, the son of Ingjald the Strong, the son of Geirfinn the Red, the son of Solvi, the son of Gunnstein Berserker-Slayer.

Ingjald was married to Thraslaug, the daughter of Egil, the son of

Thórd Freysgodi. Egil's mother was also named Thraslaug and she was the daughter of Thorstein Sparrow. The mother of Thraslaug was Unn, the daughter of Eyvind Karfi. Flosi sent word to Ingjald to join him, and Ingjald started at once with fourteen men. He was a big man, strong and reserved, a good fighter, and open-handed with his friends. Flosi gave him a hearty welcome and said to him: 'We have come into great difficulty, kinsman, and shall find it hard to find a way out. I shall ask you to support me in this affair till it is brought to a successful conclusion.'

Ingjald replied: 'I have come into a very difficult position myself because of my relationship to Njál and his sons and because of other important considerations which have to be reckoned with in this business.'

Flosi said: 'I had thought, the time I gave you my brother's daughter in marriage, that you promised to assist me in every difficulty.'

'And it is most likely, too,' said Ingjald, 'that I shall do so; first, however, I wish to go home, and from there I shall ride to the Assembly.'

117

Flosi Solicits Allies

When the sons of Sigfús learned that Flosi was at Holtsvad they rode there to join him. Ketil of Mork was there as well as his brother Lambi, Thorkel and Mord, the sons of Sigfús, their brother Sigmund, Lambi Sigurdarson, Gunnar Lambason, Grani Gunnarsson, and Vébrand Hámundarson. Flosi arose to meet them and welcomed them all. Thereupon they went down to the river. From them Flosi heard a true account of what had happened, and their story differed in no way from that of Rúnólf of Dale.

Flosi said to Ketil of Mork: 'I wish to ask you this question: how firmly are you and the other sons of Sigfús resolved to back this suit?'

Ketil answered: 'It would be my wish that a settlement be arranged between the two parties. However, I have sworn oaths not to leave you in the lurch in this business before it is settled, one way or another, and if it meant my life.'

Flosi said: 'Spoken like a man! Men like you cannot be rated too highly!'

Then Grani Gunnarsson and Gunnar Lambason spoke up, both at the same time: 'We want them outlawed and killed!'[1]

Flosi answered: 'It is not so certain that we shall have the chance to do as we please.'

Grani said: 'When they slew Thráin at the Markar River, and afterwards his son Hoskuld, it was in my mind that I would never be fully reconciled with them, because I would like to see them all slain.'

Flosi replied: 'You have been living so close to them that you could have avenged these slayings if you had had the courage and the manhood. I am thinking that you and many others now wish to have something done which you would later give much to have undone. So much is clear: even if we do slay Njál and his sons, they are people of such importance that there will be such action taken against us that we shall have to ask many a man on bended knee to give us assistance before we get out of trouble. And you should be prepared to know that many of you who now are wealthy will become penniless, and that some will lose their fortunes and their lives.'

Mord Valgardsson sought out Flosi and said that he would accompany him to the Assembly with all his followers. Flosi accepted the offer with pleasure and made the proposal that Mord should betroth his daughter Rannveig to his own nephew Starkad of Stafafell. The reason Flosi proposed this was that he wanted to assure himself of Mord's adherence as well as his many followers. Mord was agreeable to the suggestion, but said he would refer the matter to Gizur the White, and he asked Flosi to discuss it with Gizur at the Assembly. Mord was married to Thorkatla, the daughter of Gizur the White. Both Mord and Flosi rode to the Assembly and talked together every day from early till late.

118

Njál and his Party

Njál asked Skarphedin: 'What plans have you now, you and your brothers and your brother-in-law Kári?'

Skarphedin answered: 'We don't ordinarily brood over our dreams,[1] but I can tell you that we are going to ride to Tunga to Ásgrím Ellida-Grímsson, and from there we shall continue to the Assembly. But what about your own plans, father?'

Njál replied: 'I also plan to ride to the Assembly, for it is not in keeping with my honour to abandon you in this business as long as I live. I expect that there will be many men at the Assembly who will lend me a friendly ear. Thus you will derive some benefit from my presence, but no harm.'

Njál's foster son, Thórhall Ásgrímsson, was also present at this conversation. The sons of Njál laughed at him because he wore a coarse brown-striped cloak, and they asked him how long he was going to wear that.

He answered: 'I shall be through wearing it the day I shall have to seek redress for the death of my foster father.'

Njál said: 'You will prove all the more reliable, the more depends on you!'

Now they all made ready to depart, and there were almost thirty men in all. They travelled till they arrived at the Thjórsá River. Then they were joined by Njál's kinsmen, Thorleif Crow and Thorgrím the Tall, the sons of Holta-Thórir. They offered the sons of Njál their men and their support, and this offer was accepted. Then all of them crossed the Thjórsá River and journeyed on till they came to the banks of the Laxá River.[2] There they were met by Hjalti Skeggjason. He and Njál conferred together and discussed matters in a low voice.

Hjalti said: 'I shall always make plain that I harbour no secret plans. Njál has asked me for help and I have agreed and promised him my assistance. He has repaid me and many others in advance by his wise counsel.'

Hjalti told Njál all about Flosi's moves. They sent Thórhall ahead to the farm at Tunga to announce that they would arrive there that evening. Ásgrím made ready at once and was waiting outside when Njál and his company rode into the courtyard. Njál was wearing a blue cape and a felt hood, and in his hand he carried a small axe. Ásgrím lifted Njál from his horse, carried him in, and placed him on the high-seat. Then the others entered, Njál's sons and Kári. Ásgrím went out again. Hjalti was about to leave, thinking there were too many people there already, but Ásgrím took hold of the reins and asked him not to ride away. Ásgrím had the horses unsaddled and then led Hjalti in and gave him the seat beside Njál. Thorleif and his brother sat on the other bench with their men.

Ásgrím sat down on a chair in front of Njál and asked: 'Have you any surmises about the outcome of our business?'

Njál answered: 'Yes, and rather bad ones, because I am afraid that some ill-fated men have a hand in it. Summon all who owe you allegiance in this district and come to the Assembly with me.'

'That is what I had planned to do,' said Ásgrím, 'and I shall promise you, also, to stay with you in your difficulty and never leave you as long as I have any men to follow me.'

All who were in the room thanked him for these words, and they thought that he had spoken like a man.

They stayed there that night, and the following day all of Ásgrím's followers arrived. Then they all rode to the Assembly and put their booths in order.

119

The Attempts of Ásgrím and the Sons of Njál to Win Allies

Flosi had already arrived at the Assembly and had put his booth in order. Rúnólf occupied the booth of the men of Dale, and Mord the booth of the men of the Rangá River district. Of all those present Hall of Sída had come the greatest distance from the east; there were scarcely any other men from that section at the Assembly. However, Hall had gathered a large force from his district. He immediately joined forces with Flosi and begged him to accept redress and to make a peaceful settlement. Hall was an understanding and peace-loving man. Flosi gave him a friendly answer, but made no definite promises. Hall asked him which men had promised him their help. Flosi named among others Mord Valgardsson, and added that he had asked for the hand of Mord's daughter for his kinsman Starkad. Hall replied that the girl was a good match, but that it was ill advised to have any dealings with Mord – 'and you will find that out before this Assembly comes to an end.' That was all they said.

One day Njál and his sons had a long secret talk with Ásgrím. Then Ásgrím started up and said to Njál's sons: 'Let us go and look for friends, so that we shall not be overpowered by the force of numbers, because this business is likely to be pursued with great violence by our opponents.'

With that Ásgrím issued from the booth, and he was followed by Helgi Njálsson, then by Kári Solmundarson, then Grím Njálsson, then Skarphedin, then Thórhall, then Thorgrím the Tall, and then Thorleif Crow. They went to the booth of Gizur the White and entered. Gizur arose to meet them and invited them to sit down and drink. Ásgrím said: 'That is not why we have come. We wish to ask you straight to the point and without any secrecy what help we may expect from you, kinsman?'

Gizur answered: 'My sister Jórunn would certainly not expect me to refuse you my help, and so it shall be; we will share one and the same fate, both now and in the future!'

Ásgrím thanked him and then went away.

Then Skarphedin asked: 'Where shall we go now?'

'To the booth of the men of the Olfus district,' answered Ásgrím.

So they went there and Ásgrím asked whether Skapti Thóroddsson was inside. He was told that he was, and so they entered. Skapti sat on the cross-bench and greeted Ásgrím, who returned the greeting politely. Skapti offered Ásgrím the seat next to him, but Ásgrím replied that he did not mean to stay long. – 'But I have a request to make of you.'

'What is it?' asked Skapti.

'I should like to ask for your help for myself and for my kinsmen,' answered Ásgrím.

'I had rather hoped that you would not come to me with your troubles,' said Skapti.

Ásgrím said: 'It is mean of you to help people least when most depends on it.'

'Who is that man,' asked Skapti, 'the fifth in line, tall and sallow, with the look of one who is ill fated, grim and troll-like?'[1]

'Skarphedin is my name,' he answered, 'and you have seen me at the Assembly often enough. But I must be smarter than you, because I don't have to ask you for your name. You are Skapti Thóroddsson, but formerly you called yourself Bristle-Pate, the time you slew Ketil of Elda. Then you shaved your head and smeared it with tar. Then you paid some slaves to cut a strip of sod for you to creep under at night. Then you fled to Thórólf Loptsson of Eyrar, and he took you in and carried you aboard his ship in flour sacks.'[2]

Thereupon Ásgrím and those with him left the booth.

Then Skarphedin asked: 'Where shall we go now?'

'To the booth of Snorri Godi,' answered Ásgrím.

Thereupon they went to Snorri's booth. A man was standing in front of the booth. Ásgrím asked him whether Snorri was inside, and the man said that he was. Ásgrím and the others then entered the booth. Snorri was sitting on the cross-bench. Ásgrím stepped up to him and greeted him politely. Snorri's greeting was likewise very cordial and he bade Ásgrím be seated. Ásgrím said that he could stay only for a short time, and then he added: 'Yet I have come to talk to you about a certain matter.'

Snorri bade him say what it was.

Ásgrím said: 'I would wish that you come to the court with me and grant me your help, for you are a wise man and one of great enterprise.'

Snorri replied: 'We have difficult suits of our own on our hands right now and many men are offering us stiff resistance, and for that reason we are loath to have a hand in the troubles of those from other parts of the country.'

'That is understandable,' said Ásgrím, 'especially as you are in no wise indebted to us.'

'I know that you are a man of mettle,' said Snorri, 'and I shall therefore promise you that I shall in no wise oppose you or give your enemies any help.'

Ásgrím thanked him for that.

Snorri then asked: 'Who is that man, the fifth in line, with a sallow complexion and sharp features, who has a sneer on his face and carries an axe on his shoulder?'

'My name is Hedin,' he answered, 'but some men call me Skarphedin by my full name. Is there anything else you want to say about me?'

Snorri replied: 'Only this, that you seem to be a bold man and stouthearted. But I believe that your good fortune is mostly behind you and that you do not have much longer to live!'

'That is as it should be,' answered Skarphedin, 'for that is a debt we all have to pay. However, it would be much better for you to avenge your father than to foretell my fate!'

'Many have already told me that,' said Snorri, 'and I shall not resent it.'

Thereupon they left his booth, without getting any assistance from him, and proceeded to the booth of the men of Skaga Firth. This booth belong to Hafr the Wealthy. He was the son of Thorkel, the son of Eirík of Goddale, the son of Geirmund, the son of Hróald, the son of Eirík Bristle-Beard who slew Grjótgard in Sóknardale in Norway. Hafr's mother was named Thórunn, the daughter of Ásbjorn Bald-Skull of Myrká River, the son of Hrossbjorn.

Ásgrím and the others entered the booth. Hafr was sitting in the middle of the booth and was speaking with a man. Ásgrím stepped up and greeted him. Hafr returned the greeting politely and invited him to sit down.

Ásgrím said: 'I should like to ask you to help me and my kinsmen.'

Hafr answered quickly, saying that he would have no part of their troubles – 'but I would like to know who that sallow-faced man is, the fifth in line, who looks as grisly as though he had come out of a sea cliff.'

Skarphedin answered: 'Never mind who I am, you milksop, because I wouldn't be afraid to pass through any place where you are lying in ambush for me, and I would not have the least fear though fellows of your stripe stepped in my way! Besides, you would do better to fetch back your sister Svanlaug, whom Eydís Iron-Sword and Stedjakoll bore away out of your home, and you didn't have the courage to lift a hand against them!'

Ásgrím said: 'Let us go out; there is no hope of any help here!'

Thereupon they went to the booth of the men of Modruvellir and asked whether Gudmund the Powerful was inside, and they were told that he was. Thereupon they entered the booth. In the middle of the booth was the high-seat, and there sat Gudmund the Powerful. Ásgrím went up to him and greeted him. Gudmund received him well and bade him be seated.

Ásgrím spoke: 'I do not care to sit down, but I wish to ask you for your help, because you are a man of great energy and a powerful chieftain.'

Gudmund said: 'I shall not be against you, but if it ever seems expedient to help you, then we may talk about that later.' He was well disposed to their cause. Ásgrím thanked him for his promise.

'There is one man in your group,' continued Gudmund, 'whom I have been looking at for some time, and he seems to me unlike most men I have ever seen!'

'Whom do you mean?' asked Ásgrím.

'He is fifth in line,' answered Gudmund, 'and has chestnut hair and a sallow complexion. He is tall and powerful, and so likely to be a man of great hardihood that I would rather have him in my following than ten others. And yet he does not look like one born under a lucky star!'

'I know that you are talking about me,' said Skarphedin, 'but we

are both men of ill luck, each in his own way. I bear the reproach
of having killed Hoskuld Hvítanessgodi, as stands to reason, but
you have been held up to scorn by Thorkel Bully and Thórir
Helgason, which caused you no end of vexation!'

Thereupon they left the booth and Skarphedin asked: 'Where
shall we go now?'

'To the booth of the men of Ljósavatn,' answered Ásgrím.

That booth belonged to Thorkel. He was the son of Thorgeir
Godi, the son of Tjorvi, the son of Thorkel the Long. The mother
of Thorgeir was Thórunn, the daughter of Thorstein, the son of
Sigmund, the son of Gnúpa-Bárd. The mother of Thorkel Bully
was named Gudríd. She was the daughter of Thorkel the Black of
Hleidrargard, the son of Thórir Snepil, the son of Ketil Brimil, the
son of Ornólf, the son of Bjornólf, the son of Grím Lodinkinna,
the son of Ketil Hœing, the son of Hallbjorn Half-Troll.[3]

Thorkel Bully had been abroad and had become quite famous in
foreign lands. He had slain a robber in the forest of Jämtland[4] and
after that had travelled east to Sweden. Here he joined company
with Sörkvir the Old, and together they harried in the Baltic
shorelands. One evening it fell to Thorkel's lot to fetch water for
the crew east of the Bálagard coast. There he encountered a
fabulous monster and fought it for a long time before he was able to
slay it. From there he travelled east to Adalsýsla[5] where he slew a
flying dragon. After that he returned to Sweden, then to Norway,
and then to Iceland, and had had these feats carved over his locked
bedcloset and on a chair before his high-seat. He and his brothers
also fought against Gudmund the Powerful at the Ljósavatn
Assembly, and the men of Ljósavatn were victorious. It was at that
time that Thórir Helgason and Thorkel Bully defamed Gudmund.
Thorkel had declared that there was no one in Iceland whom he
would not dare to meet in single combat or before whom he
would yield ground. That was the reason why he was called
Thorkel Bully, because he spared no one with whom he had to
deal.

120

Skarphedin Humiliates Thorkel

Ásgrím and those who followed him now went to the booth of
Thorkel Bully. Ásgrím said to his comrades: 'This is the booth of
Thorkel Bully, a great warrior, and it would be of great
importance to us if we could get his help. We must proceed very
carefully, for he is a very self-willed and a difficult man to deal
with. I must ask you, Skarphedin, that you keep out of this
business.'

Skarphedin grinned. He was clad in a dark blue kirtle, blue-
striped breeches, and black boots that came high up on the leg.
About his middle he had a silver belt, and he carried a small shield
and the axe with which he had slain Thráin and which he called
'Battle-Troll'. He wore a silken fillet and had his hair combed
back. He looked every bit the warrior and all recognised him, even
those who had never seen him before. He kept in line, neither
pushing ahead nor walking behind.

They entered the booth and proceeded into the interior. There
sat Thorkel in the middle of the cross-bench with his men at either
side of him. Ásgrím greeted him, and Thorkel made him welcome.

Ásgrím spoke: 'We have come here to ask for your assistance in
going to the court with us.'

Thorkel answered: 'Why should you need my assistance, seeing
that you went to Gudmund? He no doubt promised you his help.'

'We did not receive any support from him,' answered Ásgrím.

To this Thorkel replied: 'So Gudmund must have thought your
case hardly one to win you friends, and that is likely to be so, for a
more dastardly deed never was committed. I know what has
brought you here; you thought I would be less particular than
Gudmund and more inclined to lend my support to an unjust case.'

Ásgrím then kept his peace and thought that things were going
hard with them.

Thorkel continued: 'Who is that tall and grim-looking man, the fifth in line, with the sallow face and sharp features, of unlucky appearance, and wicked looking?'

Skarphedin answered: 'My name is Skarphedin, and you have no cause to rail at me with your mocking words. I have never offered violence to my own father nor did I fight with him as you did with yours. Also, you have rarely attended the Althing and concerned yourself with lawsuits. You are likely to be handier at the dairy business on your farm on the Axe River with the few people you have. It would be better for you to pick your teeth to remove the piece of sausage made out of a mare's guts that you ate before coming to the Assembly. Your shepherd saw it and wondered how you could do something so disgusting.'

Thorkel started up in a great rage and reached for his short-sword and said: 'This sword I got in Sweden; with it I slew the greatest champion, and since then, many another man. As soon as I get to you I shall run you through with it and so repay you for your foul speech!'

Skarphedin stood there with his axe raised and grinned and said: 'This axe I had in my hand when I leaped twelve ells across the Markar River and slew Thráin Sigfússon while eight men stood by and could not lay hands on me. Nor have I ever lifted weapon against a man without its hitting the mark.'

With this he broke away from his brothers and his brother-in-law Kári and made for Thorkel. He spoke: 'Now you either put away your dirk, Thorkel Bully, and sit down, or I shall drive my axe into your head and split it down to your shoulders!'

Then Thorkel sat down and sheathed his sword. Never before or after did such a thing ever happen to him. Thereupon Ásgrím and his men left the booth and Skarphedin asked: 'Where shall we go now?'

'Home to our booth,' answered Ásgrím.

'Then we shall have gone begging for help all to no purpose,' remarked Skarphedin.

Ásgrím turned around to him and said: 'Many a time you were rather too sharp of tongue; but now, as regards Thorkel, you gave him just what was coming to him!'

Then they returned to their booth and reported to Njál everything which had happened. He remarked: 'Let then fate take its course, whatever it be!'

Now Gudmund the Powerful learned of what had happened
between Skarphedin and Thorkel and said: 'You will call to mind
how matters went with us and the men of Ljósavatn, but I never
suffered such ignominy and shame from them as Thorkel experi-
enced from Skarphedin; and I am mighty well pleased.'

Then Gudmund said to his brother Einar[1] of Thverá River: 'I
shall want you to go with all my following and stand by the sons of
Njál when the court convenes. And if they need help next
summer, I myself will go to their assistance.'

Einar agreed to that and told Ásgrím what Gudmund had said.

Ásgrím said: 'Unlike is Gudmund to most chieftains!' And then
he told Njál.

121

The Suit

The following day Ásgrím, Gizur the White, Hjalti Skeggjason,
and Einar of Thverá River met. Mord Valgardsson was also
present. He had now handed over the prosecution of the suit to
the sons of Sigfús.

On this occasion Ásgrím spoke as follows: 'I turn to you first,
Gizur the White, and to you two, Hjalti and Einar, that I may tell
you how our suit stands. As you know, Mord took up the suit in
the first place, but the fact of the case is that Mord himself was
present at the slaying of Hoskuld and inflicted the wound for
which no assailant was named. It seems to me that this case will be
quashed as being against the laws.'

'In that case, let us make that point at once,' said Hjalti.

'No,' replied Thórhall Ásgrímsson; 'it would be unwise not to
keep this secret until the courts convene.'

'Why would it?' asked Hjalti.

'Because if they learn right now that the case was prepared in the
wrong fashion,' answered Thórhall, 'they may remedy matters by
sending a man back from the Assembly immediately and summoning the neighbouring witnesses to the Assembly a second

time; and then the case will have been prepared properly.'

'A shrewd man you are, Thórhall,' they said, 'and we shall follow your counsel!'

Thereupon they all returned to their booths.

The sons of Sigfús served notice of the suit at the Law-Mount and asked about the domicile of the jurors and to which assembly they belonged. The court was to convene on the eve of Friday for the prosecution of the case. Until then there reigned quiet at the Assembly. There were many who sought to arrange a settlement between the two parties, but Flosi was unyielding, and others raised still more objections, so that the outlook for a settlement seemed to be hopeless.

Now the time came, on Friday evening, that the court was to convene, and everyone attending the Assembly went there. Flosi and his party stationed themselves to the south of the Rangá River Court. With him were Hall of Sída, Rúnólf of Dale, the sons of Úlf Aurgodi, and all the others who had promised him their support. To the north of the Rangá River Court were stationed Ásgrím, Gizur the White, Hjalti, and Einar of Thverá River. The sons of Njál together with Kári, Thorleif Crow, and Thorgrím the Tall remained in their booth. They sat there all armed, and their flock looked formidable indeed.

Njál had already asked the judges to convene. The sons of Sigfús now began the prosecution of the suit. They named witnesses and enjoined the sons of Njál to listen to their oath. Thereupon they took the oath and then they preferred their charges. After that they had witnesses testify that notice of the slaying had been given. Then they asked the neighbours acting as jurors to take their seats and called on their opponents to challenge them.

Thórhall Ásgrímsson named witnesses and protested the jury's right to utter a finding for the reason that notice of the slaying had been given by a man who himself was guilty of a breach of the law, and therefore himself ought to be outlawed.

'To whom do you refer by this accusation?' asked Flosi.

Thórhall answered: 'Mord Valgardsson went with the sons of Njál for the purpose of slaying Hoskuld, and it was Mord himself who inflicted that wound for which no assailant was named when witness to the wounds was taken. You cannot dispute this! The suit is invalid!'

122

The Settlement of the Suit

Then Njál stood up and spoke: 'I beg Hall of Sída, Flosi, all the sons of Sigfús, and all our own men not to leave the meeting, but to listen to my words.'

They did as he requested, and he continued: 'Now it seems to me that this case has come to a deadlock, and that with good reason, for it has sprung from an evil root. I want you to know that I loved Hoskuld more than my own sons, and when I learned that he had been slain, it was as though the sweetest light of my eyes had been extinguished. I would rather have lost all my sons and have Hoskuld still alive. Now I ask you, Hall of Sída, and you, Rúnólf of Dale, and Gizur the White, and Einar of Thverá River, and Hafr the Wise, that I be granted the right to make atonement for the slaying committed by my sons, and it would be my wish that those men make the award who are best fitted to do so.'

Gizur and Einar and Hafr, each in turn, spoke at length and begged Flosi to accept reconciliation, and they promised him their friendship in return. Flosi replied in good temper, but promised nothing.

Hall of Sída said to Flosi: 'Will you now keep your word and grant the favour which you promised me at that time when I helped your kinsman, Thorgrím Digr-Ketilsson, to escape from the country after he had slain Halli the Red?'

Flosi said: 'I shall, father-in-law, for I know you will ask only for what is likely to redound to my honour.'

Hall said: 'Then I wish that you quickly accept reconciliation and let well-meaning men arbitrate the case and thereby win for yourself the friendship of eminent men.'

Flosi answered: 'I herewith declare that I will comply with the wish of my father-in-law Hall and of other excellent men in letting him and other eminent men, lawfully chosen from both parties, arbitrate the matter. It seems to me that Njál merits this consideration.'

Njál thanked one and all, and Flosi in particular, and the others present likewise thanked Flosi and said that he had acted very nobly.

Flosi said: 'Now I shall name my umpires: first of all, I name my father-in-law Hall, and then Ozur of Broad River, Surt Ásbjarnarson of Kirkby, Módólf Ketilsson [at that time he lived at Ásar], Hafr, and Rúnólf of Dale. And I think all will agree that these men are best fitted, of all those following me, for this task.'

Then he asked Njál to name his umpires. Njál arose and said: 'First of all, I shall name Ásgrím Ellida-Grímsson, and also Hjalti Skeggjason, Gizur the White, Einar of Thverá River, Snorri Godi, and Gudmund the Powerful.'

Thereupon Njál and Flosi and the sons of Sigfús joined hands, and Njál pledged his word in behalf of his sons and Kári that they would abide by the decision of these twelve men. And it was safe to say that everybody at the Assembly was glad about the turn events had taken.

Messengers were sent to Snorri and Gudmund who had remained in their booths. It was decided then that the arbitrators should proceed to take their seats in the Court of Laws and that all others should leave.

123

The Attempt at a Settlement Fails

Then Snorri Godi spoke as follows: 'We are now the twelve umpires to whom the decision in this suit has been referred. I wish to ask all of you that there be no technicalities raised to prevent the parties from being reconciled.'

Gudmund asked: 'Is banishment from the district your purpose or is it exile?'

'Neither,' answered Snorri, 'for that has often produced bad results, in that men have been slain because of it or have fallen out. On the other hand, I shall impose a wergild so large that the slaying of no man has been as costly as that of Hoskuld.'

His words met with their approval. After that they discussed the case, but they could not agree as to which man should suggest how large the fine should be. Finally they drew lots, and it fell to Snorri to declare the amount of the award.

Snorri said: 'I do not propose to deliberate this any longer, but tell you now what my decision is: that Hoskuld's death be atoned for by the payment of three wergilds or, in other words, by six hundred ounces of silver. It is for you to decide now if you think that is too much or too little.'

They answered that they did not want to make any change.

[Snorri added]: 'This involves also complete payment of the fine here at the Assembly.'

Then Gizur the White said: 'That is hardly feasible, because they are unlikely to have enough cash along to make this payment.'

Gudmund said: 'I know what is in Snorri's mind; and that is, that we umpires all contribute as much as our generosity bids us, and then many will do the same.'

Hall of Sída thanked him for these words and said he would contribute as much as the largest giver. All umpires consented. Thereupon they dispersed after deciding that Hall should proclaim the verdict at the Law-Mount.

Then the bell was rung,[1] and all men went to the Law-Mount. Hall arose and said: 'We have reached a unanimous decision in the suit which has been referred to us; we have set the award at six hundreds in silver. We umpires shall pay half of this amount, and all of it is to be paid here at the Assembly. It is now my prayer to all present that each man contribute something for God's sake.'

The decision was well received by all. Hall named witnesses to the verdict, so that no one might ever break the agreement. Njál thanked them for the decision. Skarphedin stood near and grinned, but kept his peace.

Then people left the Law-Mount and went to their booths. But in the community churchyard the arbitrators brought together the money which they had promised to contribute. The sons of Njál gave whatever they had with them, and Kári did likewise; that amounted to a hundred in silver. Then Njál laid to it what money he had with him, and that was a second hundred ounces. After that all the money was brought together at the Court of Laws, and others contributed so much that not even a penny was lacking. Then Njál took a silken cloak and a pair of boots and placed them on the top of the heap of silver. Thereupon Hall asked Njál to fetch his sons – 'and I shall fetch Flosi, and then each party can pledge faith to the other.'

Njál returned to his booth and said to his sons: 'Now our case has taken a good turn; all the money has been brought together in one place and we are reconciled with our adversaries. Each side must now go and pledge peace and good faith to the other. I beg you not to do anything to defeat this settlement in any way.'

Skarphedin stroked his brow and grinned scornfully. Then they all went to the Court of Laws.

Hall had come to find Flosi and said to him, 'Go to the Court of Laws now, for all the money has been duly paid and is now gathered together in one place.'

Flosi asked the sons of Sigfús to accompany him. They all left their booth and approached the Court of Laws from the east, and Njál and his sons approached from the west. Skarphedin went to the middle bench[2] and took his position there.

Flosi went to the Court of Laws to look at the money and he said: 'This is a large amount of good silver, and well paid out, as was to be expected.'

Then he picked up the cloak and asked who had contributed that, but no one answered. Again he waved the gown about, laughing,[3] and asked who might have contributed it, but still no one answered. Then he asked: 'Is it that no one of you knows who owned this piece of apparel, or is it that no one dares to tell me?'

Skarphedin spoke: 'Who do you think gave it?'

Flosi answered: 'If you must know, I'll tell you. I believe it was your father, the "Beardless One"; for many don't know, looking at him, whether he is a man or a woman!'

Skarphedin said: 'It is wicked to make game of an old man, and no man of mettle has done that heretofore. You may well know that he is a man, for he has begot sons with his wife. And few of our kinsmen have lain unavenged outside our doors.'

Thereupon Skarphedin possessed himself of the gown and tossed a pair of blue breeches at Flosi and said he needed those more.

Flosi asked: 'Why should I need them more?'

Skarphedin answered: 'Because if you are the mistress of the troll in the Svínafell, as they say, then he uses you like a woman every ninth night!'

Then Flosi gave the money a kick and said he would not have a penny of it and that one of two things would happen: either that Hoskuld would lie unatoned or that they would avenge his death. After that Flosi would neither give nor accept any offer of peace, and he said to the sons of Sigfús: 'Let us return to our booth! Let one and the same fate now befall us!'

Thereupon they returned to their booth.

Hall said: 'Mighty ill-starred men have had a hand in this business!'

Then Njál and his sons returned to their booth also.

Njál said: 'Now that has come to pass which I have long surmised, that this case would never end well for us.'

'Not so,' said Skarphedin. 'They will never be able to prosecute us according to the laws of the land.'

'Then that will happen,' said Njál, 'which will bring disaster to us all!'

The men who had contributed the money now spoke about taking it back again. But Gudmund said: 'That shame I shall never be guilty of, to take back what I have given – either here or elsewhere!'

'Well spoken!' they said. And no one wanted to take back his money.

Snorri Godi said: 'I suggest that Gizur the White and Hjalti Skeggjason take the money into their safekeeping until the next meeting at the Althing. I have a feeling that it will not be long before there will be need of this money.'

Hjalti took one half of the money into his safekeeping and Gizur took the other half. Thereupon they all returned to their booths.

124

Preparations for the Attack on Njál and his Sons

Flosi called upon all his followers to meet in the Almanna Gorge and then went there himself. By that time all his men, one hundred in number, were already there.

Flosi asked the sons of Sigfús: 'Now what is your pleasure in this business?'

Gunnar Lambason answered: 'We shall never be satisfied until all these brothers, the sons of Njál, are slain!'

Flosi replied: 'I shall promise you this, sons of Sigfús, that I shall never back out of this business until one or the other of the two parties is crushed. I also wish to know whether there is anyone here who is unwilling to help us in this undertaking.'

All answered that they would stand by the sons of Sigfús.

Flosi said: 'Then let every man step up to me and swear an oath that he will never back out of this affair!'

Then they all came up to Flosi and pledged themselves.

Flosi then said: 'Let us all join hands and pledge that whoever backs out of this shall forfeit both life and property!'

These were the chieftains with Flosi: Kol, the son of Thorstein Broad-Paunch, the son of Hall of Sída's brother; Hróald Ozurarson of Broad River; Ozur, the son of Onund Toskubak; Thorstein the Fair, the son of Geirleif; Glúm Hildisson; Módólf Ketilsson; Thórir, the son of Thórd Illugi of Mortunga; Kolbein and Egil, the kinsmen of Flosi; Ketil Sigfússon and his brother Mord; Thorkel;

Lambi; Grani Gunnarsson; Gunnar Lambason; his brother Sigurd; Ingjald of Keldur; and Hróar Hámundarson.

Flosi said to the sons of Sigfús: 'Choose yourself a leader – one whom you consider best suited to lead us, because someone will have to be our leader in this undertaking.'

Ketil of Mork answered: 'If it were up to us brothers to choose, then our choice is quickly made: that you undertake this task. You come from a great family and are a great chieftain, determined and resourceful. Again, we are of the opinion that you should take charge of this affair for the benefit of all of us.'

Flosi replied: 'It seems reasonable that I yield to your request. I will now map out what course we should take. My advice is that everyone journey home from the Assembly and look after his farm this summer while the haymaking on the home fields is under way. I, too, shall ride home and remain there this summer. But on the Sunday which falls eight weeks before the beginning of winter I shall have a Mass sung for myself at home and then ride west over the Lómagnúp Sand. Each of us is to take two horses. I shall not add to our number any beyond those who have now pledged themselves, because our company is quite large enough if everyone stands his man. I shall ride all day Sunday and the following night, and about mid-evening of the second day of the week I shall arrive at the Thríhyrning Ridge. By that time all who are bound by oath in this undertaking should have gotten here. Let no one be missing on pain of his life, if I have anything to say!'

Ketil said: 'How is it possible for you to leave your home on Sunday and arrive at Thríhyrning Ridge by the second day of the week?'

Flosi answered: 'I shall ride up from Skaptá River Junction, then north of the Eyjafell Glacier, and then down to Godaland;[1] and that can be done if I ride briskly. And now I shall tell you my whole design. When we are all together we shall ride to Bergthórshvál – all of us – and attack the sons of Njál with fire and sword, and not leave the place until they are all dead. You must keep this plan secret, for the lives of all of us depend on it. Now let us take our horses and ride home!'

Then they all went to their booths. Flosi had his horses saddled and then they rode home without waiting for anyone. Flosi did not wish to visit his father-in-law Hall, for he felt very certain that Hall would advise against any violence.

Njál and his sons rode home from the Assembly and they all remained on their farm during the summer. Njál asked Kári whether he cared to journey east to his farm at Dyrhólmar, but Kári answered: 'No, I will not ride east, because one and the same fate shall befall me and your sons!'

Njál thanked him for these words and said they were just what he might have expected of him. Including the servants there were nearly thirty fighting men at Bergthórshvál at all times.

One day Hródný, the daughter of Hoskuld, came to Keldur, and her brother Ingjald bade her welcome. She did not return his greeting, but asked him to step outside. Ingjald did so. They went outside the courtyard, and there she seized him and they sat down.

She asked: 'Is it true that you have pledged yourself to attack Njál and slay him and his sons?'

'That is true,' he answered.

'Why, then you are an archscoundrel,' she said, 'for it was Njál who saved you from outlawry on three different occasions!'[2]

'Matters have now come to such a pass, though,' he said, 'that I'll lose my life if I don't do it!'

'That is hardly so,' she replied; 'you will live on and still be called a man of honour if you do not betray him to whom you owe most.'

From her bag she drew a linen cap; it was tattered and torn and covered with blood. She said: 'Hoskuld Njálsson had this cap on his head when they killed him. It is all the less proper for you to stand in with them who are in league with his slayers.'

He answered: 'Neither will I undertake anything against Njál, come what may, though I know they will make trouble for me!'

She said: 'In that case you can render Njál and his sons a great service if you tell him all about these plans.'

'That I shall not do,' replied Ingjald, 'because I should be regarded by everyone as an arrant wretch, if I revealed what was entrusted to my secrecy. But it is a manly thing to abandon this cause when I know they will avenge themselves on me. However, tell Njál and his sons to be on their guard all summer – for that advice will stand them in good stead – and to have many men about them.'

Thereupon she journeyed to Bergthórshvál and told Njál all that had passed between them. Njál thanked her and said she had done a good deed – 'because for him of all men it would have been the greatest outrage to attack me.' Then she journeyed home. But Njál told his sons what he had learned from her.

There was an old woman at Bergthórshvál named Sæunn. She was wise about many things, and second-sighted, but she was very old then, and the sons of Njál called her an old driveler because she babbled so much. Yet much that she predicted came true. One day she took a cudgel in her hand and went around the house to a pile of chickweed. She hit it and cursed it, miserable thing that it was. Skarphedin laughed about her carryings-on and asked why she was so angry at the chickweed.

The old woman answered: 'This chickweed will be used to kindle a fire, when they burn Njál inside his house, and also my foster child Bergthóra. Take it and throw it into the water or burn it, the sooner the better!'

'No, we'll not do that,' said Skarphedin, 'because other things can be found to kindle a fire, if fate so wills it, even though this pile is not used.'

The old woman kept bickering about that pile of chickweed the entire summer, but nothing was done about it.

125

Hildiglúm's Vision

At Reykir in the Skeid district there lived a man named Rúnólf Thorsteinsson. His son was named Hildiglúm. One Saturday night twelve weeks before the beginning of winter Hildiglúm went outside the house. He heard a crash so loud that it seemed as though both sky and earth shook. Then he looked to the west and thought he saw there a circle of fire, and in that circle, a man on a grey steed. The apparition went by quickly, for the man rode fast and furiously. In his hand he carried a firebrand. He rode by so close that Hildiglúm could see him very distinctly. He was as black as pitch and with a loud voice spoke this verse:

> A horse ride I
> hoarfrost-dewy —
> icy the forelocks,
> evil-boding.
> Blaze the barbed ends,
> bane 's in the middle:
> thus Flosi's plans
> as though flew arrow,
> thus Flosi's plans
> as though flew arrow.[1]

Then it seemed to Hildiglúm that the rider hurled the firebrand toward the mountains in the east, and a huge fire blazed up from it, so that he could no longer see the mountains because of the fire. He thought the man rode eastward toward the fire and vanished there. Thereupon Hildiglúm went back into the house and lay down in his bed and fell into a long faint, after which he regained his senses. He remembered everything about the apparition and told his father about it. And his father asked him to relate it to Hjalti Skeggjason; and so he did.

'You have seen the spirit-ride,' said Hjalti, 'and that is always foreboding of great calamities!'

126

The Meeting of the Conspirators

Two months before the beginning of winter Flosi prepared for his journey west and summoned to him all his men who had pledged themselves to go with him. Each man had two horses and good weapons. They all came to Svínafell and stayed there that night. Early on Sunday morning Flosi had Mass sung for himself and then sat down to the table. He told each member of the household what he was to do during his absence, and then he mounted his horse.

Flosi and his company first rode west to Sand. He told his men not to ride too headlong, for they would get there soon enough, and that all should wait for anyone who lagged behind. They rode west to the Skógahverfi district and came to Kirkby. Flosi bade all his men go to church there and pray for themselves, and they did so. Thereupon they mounted their horses and rode into the mountains and came to the Fiskivotn Lakes. They rode past the lakes and then continued in a westerly direction to Sand, keeping the Eyjafell Glacier on their left. From there they descended into the Godaland district, and thus came to the Markar River. They arrived at the Thríhyrning Ridge early in the afternoon of the second day, and there they waited until mid-evening. By that time all had arrived except Ingjald of Keldur. The sons of Sigfús were loud in their condemnation of him, but Flosi asked them not to say anything ill about Ingjald in his absence – 'but we shall pay him back later!'

127

The Portents at Bergthórshvál

Now we have to speak about what happened at Bergthórshvál. Helgi and Grím told their father that they would not be home that evening, and then they rode to Hólar[1] where some foster children of theirs lived. They stayed at Hólar the entire day. Some poor women came there and said they had come a long way. They were asked for news of any importance, but they said they had none to tell – 'but one little thing we can tell you.'

They were asked what it was and to tell all about it. They said they would: 'We were coming down from the Fljótshlíd district and saw all the sons of Sigfús riding fully armed. They were headed up to the Thríhyrning Ridge, fifteen of them. We also saw Grani Gunnarsson and Gunnar Lambason in a group of five men and they were headed in the same direction. One might say that everyone is on the move now.'[2]

Helgi Njálsson said: 'In that case Flosi must have come from the east and they are probably all going to join him. You and I, Grím, should now be where Skarphedin is.'

Grím agreed and so they rode home.

That same evening Bergthóra said to the members of her household: 'This evening let each one of you choose the food he likes best, because this will be the last time I shall serve the food for us all!'

'Far be that!' said all who heard her.

'It will be, nevertheless,' she answered; 'and I could tell you much more if I wished to, and just let this be the proof of it: Grím and Helgi will come home this evening before people have had their fill. And if that comes true, then other things will happen as I foretell.'

After that she set the food upon the table.

Njál said: 'I have a strange vision. When I look about the room it seems as though both the table and the food were gone and everything were covered with blood!'

All were greatly perturbed except Skarphedin. He asked them

not to put on a sad face or otherwise behave in unseemly fashion so that people would point with fingers at them – 'for we shall be judged more strictly than others and are expected to show a manly bearing, and that is the way it should be!'

Grím and Helgi came home before the tables were removed and all were greatly startled at that. Njál asked why they were in such a hurry to return, and they told him what they had learned. Njál said that all should stay up and everyone should be on his guard.

128

The Attack on Bergthórshvál

Flosi spoke to his followers: 'Now let us ride to Bergthórshvál and get there before nightfall!'

This they did. There was a depression in the knoll on which the farm was located. They rode up into it, hitched their horses there, and waited until it became quite dark.

Flosi said: 'Let us now go up to the buildings at a slow pace, keeping close together, and see what they propose to do!'

Njál and Kári and all the menservants had come out and were arrayed on the pavement in front of the house; there were almost thirty of them. Flosi halted and said: 'Let us watch and see what they propose to do, because I don't believe we shall ever get the better of them if they remain outside.'

'Our expedition would be an ignominious one if we did not dare to attack them,' said Grani Gunnarsson.

'Nor will that be the case,' said Flosi. 'We will attack them even though they stand outside. However, the price we pay will probably be so great that not many will remain to live to tell who gained the upper hand.'

Njál asked his men: 'How many men do you believe they have?'

'They have a large and well-knit band,' said Skarphedin, 'and yet they are making a halt now because they realise that they will have a hard struggle to overcome us.'

'That is hardly so,' said Njál. 'It is now my wish that all go inside, because they had a very difficult time in conquering Gunnar at

Hlídarendi, even though he was all alone against them. These buildings are just as strong as were his and they will not be able to take them.'

'That doesn't follow at all!' said Skarphedin. 'Those who attacked Gunnar were chieftains of such noble mind that they would have preferred to turn back rather than burn him in his house. But these here are just as likely to set fire to our houses at once if they cannot get at us any other way. They will resort to every possible means to overcome us. I dare say they consider it will be their death if we escape – and that is not unlikely. Nor am I eager to be stifled like a fox in his hole!'

Njál said: 'Now, as has often been the case, my sons, you will override me and not follow my counsel. When you were younger it was not like that, and things went better then.'

Helgi said: 'Let us do as father wishes; that will be the best for us.'

'I'm not so sure of that,' answered Skarphedin, 'because he is marked for death now. However, I shall gladly do it to please my father and be burned to death inside with him, because I am not afraid to die.'

Thereupon he said to Kári: 'Let us stay close together, brother-in-law, so that we shall not be separated one from the other!'

'That is what I had meant to do,' said Kári; 'but if fate wills it otherwise, then it will be so and we cannot do anything about it.'

'Avenge us, and we shall avenge you if we escape with our lives!' said Skarphedin.

Kári promised to do so. Thereupon they all went in and stood guard in the doorways.

'Now they are doomed, for they have gone indoors,' said Flosi. 'Let us now advance quickly and post ourselves before the doors in large numbers and watch that no one escapes, neither Kári nor the sons of Njál, or else it is our death!'

Flosi and his men now advanced to the houses and placed themselves around them to prevent escape if there was some secret exit. Together with his men he went up to the front of the buildings. Hróald Ozurarson ran up to where Skarphedin stood and hurled his spear at him. Skarphedin hewed the point off the shaft and dealt him a blow with his axe. The axe struck Hróald's shield and dashed it against him, but the upper edge struck him in the face, so that he fell back dead on the spot.

Kári said: 'They didn't manage to get away from you, Skarphedin! You are the stoutest of us all!'

'I don't know about that,' answered Skarphedin, drawing back his lips in a grin.

All three, Kári, Grím, and Helgi, hurled many spears at them, and wounded many of those attacking, so that Flosi and his men were unable to accomplish anything.

Flosi spoke: 'We have suffered great losses among our men, with many of us wounded and that man slain whom we could least afford to lose. It is quite clear now that we can't subdue them with arms. There is many a man here who does not show as much fight as he boasted he would. But now we shall have to hit on another plan. There are two alternatives for us, and neither is good: either to turn back, and that will mean our certain death; or else to set fire to the house and burn them inside, and that is a great responsibility before God, for we too are Christians. However, that is the course we must take; so let us set fire to the place at once.'

129

The Death of Njál and his Family in the Fire

Then they kindled a fire and made a great blaze before all doors.

Skarphedin said: 'You have kindled a fire, you fellows! What do you propose to cook?'

'So it is,' answered Grani Gunnarsson, 'and you'll not need a hotter fire to roast in!'[1]

Skarphedin said: 'You repay me just as one might expect from the likes of you, seeing that I avenged your father – and you consider that your duty which really concerns you less.'[2]

The women then poured whey into the flames and put out the fire.

Kol Thorsteinsson said to Flosi: 'I have an idea. I noticed that there is a loft in the sleeping hall above the crossbeams. Let us kindle the pile of chickweed up there above the house and throw it blazing into that loft!'

Then they took the pile of chickweed and set fire to it, and before the people in the house were aware of it the entire hall was ablaze over their heads. Flosi's men made large fires before all the doors. Then the women within began to whimper and cry.

Njál spoke to them: 'Be of stout heart and speak no words of fear, for this is but a passing storm and it will be a long time before another like it comes![3] Put your faith in God! He is merciful and will not let us burn both in this life and in the life to come!' With such exhortations and with other words even more indomitable he encouraged them.

Now the entire house began to blaze. Njál went to the door and asked: 'Is Flosi close enough to hear my words?'

Flosi said he could hear him.

Njál asked: 'Would you possibly consider coming to an agreement with my sons or else allow any of us to leave the house?'

Flosi answered: 'No, I will not come to any agreement with your sons! We are going to settle matters now, and we shall not leave the place until all of them are dead. However, I shall give the women, the children, and the menservants permission to leave.'

Njál went back into the house and spoke to the members of his household: 'Now all those who have been given permission may leave the house. And you too, Thórhalla, daughter of Ásgrím, go out, and likewise all you others who have been granted permission!'

Thórhalla answered: 'Different is this parting from Helgi from what I had expected. However, I shall make it my business to urge my father and brothers to avenge the slayings committed here.'

Njál said: 'You will be acting as you should, because you are a noble woman!'

Thereupon she left the house together with many of the household. Ástríd of Djúpárbakki said to Helgi Njálsson: 'Come out with me! I'll throw a skirt over you and put a kerchief on your head!'

Helgi would not do it at first, but then he yielded to their entreaties. Ástríd wrapped a kerchief around his head and Thórhild threw a skirt over him, and thus he went out between the two. Njál's daughter Thorgerd and her sister Helga together with many of the people of the household then went out. When Helgi came out Flosi said: 'That is a tall woman and broad about the shoulders who came out there! Seize her and hold her!'

But when Helgi heard that he threw off the skirt. He had been holding a sword under his arm. He now struck at one of the men and the blow cut off the lower point of the shield, and with it, the man's leg. At that moment Flosi came up and with one blow severed Helgi's neck. Then Flosi went to the door and said that he wished to speak to Njál and Bergthóra. Njál came out.

Flosi said: 'I want to offer you permission to leave the house, for you do not deserve to be burned inside.'

Njál answered: 'No, I will not come out, for I am an old man and little fit to avenge my sons, and I do not want to live in shame.'

Flosi then said to Bergthóra: 'You come out, mistress of the house, for under no conditions do I want to burn you inside.'

Bergthóra replied: 'As a young woman I was married to Njál and vowed that one fate should befall us both!'

Thereupon both went in again.

Bergthóra asked: 'What shall we do now?'

'Let us go to our bed and lie down,' answered Njál.

Then Bergthóra said to the boy, Thórd Kárisson: 'I want you to be carried out, for you are not to burn in the house!'

'But you promised me, grandmother, that we two should never part, and that's the way I want it to be,' answered the boy. 'I prefer to die with you rather than live after you!'

Then Bergthóra carried the boy to her bed.

Njál spoke to one of his stewards: 'Now observe where we lie down and how I cover us up, because I shall not budge from here, however much smoke and fire distress me. Thus you may know where to look for our bones.'

The steward said he would do as Njál requested. An ox had recently been slaughtered, and its hide lay there in the hall. Njál ordered the steward to spread the hide over them, and this he promised to do. Then Njál and Bergthóra lay down on the bedstead and laid the boy between them. They made the sign of the cross over themselves and the boy and commended their souls to God. These were the last words they were heard to say. The steward took the hide, spread it over them, and then went out. Ketil of Mork was at the door, waiting for him, and snatched him out. He questioned him closely about his father-in-law Njál and the man told him everything just as it had happened.

Ketil said: 'Fate has been most unkind to us, that such misfortune should befall both of us!'

Skarphedin had observed that his father had taken to his bed and what dispositions he had made. Then he said: 'Father is retiring early, and that is only natural, for he is an old man.'

Skarphedin, Kári, and Grím seized the flaming timbers just as quickly as they came down, and tossed them out on those outside. And so it went for a while. Then they hurled spears against those inside, but Kári and the others caught them in flight and returned them. Thereupon Flosi told them to cease doing that – 'because we shall always come off worse in every exchange of arms with them. You may as well wait for the fire to overcome them.'

This they did. Then the great beams began to fall down from the roof.

Skarphedin said: 'Father is probably dead now; I heard neither groan nor cough from him.'

Then they went to the end of the hall. There the crossbeam had fallen down from above; it was almost burned through in the middle.

Kári said to Skarphedin: 'You run out upon it! I shall lend you a hand and then run right behind you! Both of us may escape if we manage it that way, because all the smoke is drifting in that direction.'

Skarphedin said: 'You run ahead, and I shall follow you at your heels!'

'No,' said Kári. 'That is not the best way, because I can easily get out some other place if I cannot get out here.'

'No, I don't want to do that,' said Skarphedin. 'You run out first, and I shall follow you at your heels!'

Kári replied: 'It is everyone's right to try to save his life while he may, and so I shall now. But very likely there is going to be a parting of the ways for us now, so that we may never see each other again, for if I now escape from the fire I may not have the courage to return into it to join you, and then each of us will have to go his own way.'

'It makes me laugh, brother-in-law, to know that you will avenge us, if you escape,' said Skarphedin.

Then Kári seized hold of a flaming brand and ran up the cross-beam and jumped out. He slung the brand down from the roof, and it fell among those who were standing outside and they scattered. By that time all of Kári's clothing was on fire and even his hair. He plunged down from the roof and ran along with the smoke.

Then someone who stood nearest said: 'Didn't a man just now jump down there from the roof?'

'Nothing of the kind,' said another. 'It was Skarphedin throwing a firebrand at us.'

After that they no longer suspected anything.

Kári ran until he came to a small watercourse. There he threw himself down and quenched his burning clothes. Then he ran, still under the cover of the smoke, and came to a hollow and rested. And since that time this place has been called Kári's Hollow.

130

Skarphedin's Death. Flosi and his Band Depart

Now we must tell about Skarphedin. He ran up along the crossbeam right after Kári, but when he came to the spot where the beam was almost burned through, it gave way beneath him. He managed to land on his feet and at once took another run up the wall. Then the ridgepole came down upon him and he tottered back.

Then Skarphedin said: 'I see now what fate wills.'

Thereupon he went along the side wall. Gunnar Lambason climbed up on the side wall on the outside and caught sight of Skarphedin. He asked: 'Are you crying now, Skarphedin?'

'Not so,' answered Skarphedin, 'though it is true that my eyes do smart. But am I right in thinking that you are laughing?'

'Right you are,' said Gunnar, 'and it is the first time I have laughed since you killed Thráin at the Markar River.'

'Here's a keepsake from him for you,' said Skarphedin. Then he took out of his purse a jawtooth which he had knocked out of Thráin's jaw and threw it at Gunnar. It hit him in the eye so that the eye ran out on his cheek. And with that Gunnar fell down from the roof.

Then Skarphedin went over to his brother Grím. They joined hands and stamped out the fire. But when they came to the middle of the hall Grím fell down dead. Then Skarphedin went on to the gable end. Then there was a great crash as the roof fell down on him. Skarphedin was pinned between the roof and the gable wall and could not budge from there.

Flosi and his men stayed by the fire until it was bright dawn. Then a man came riding up to them. Flosi asked him his name and he answered that he was Geirmund, a kinsman of the sons of Sigfús.

'A mighty deed you have done!' he said.

Flosi said: 'Both a mighty deed and an ill deed people will call it. But it is done now!'

'How many persons of note have perished here?' asked Geirmund.

'Njál and Bergthóra have perished here,' answered Flosi, 'and all their sons, Thórd Kárisson, Kári Solmundarson, and Thórd the Freedman. There were also others whom we don't know, and so we do not know for certain how many people perished.'

Geirmund said: 'You count one as dead who escaped and with whom we spoke only this morning.'

'Whom do you mean?' asked Flosi.

'Kári Solmundarson,' answered Geirmund. 'My neighbour Bárd and I met him, and Bárd gave him his horse. Kári's hair and clothes were all singed off him.'

'Did he have any weapons with him?' asked Flosi.

'He had the sword 'Fjorsváfni' with him,' answered Geirmund, 'and one of its edges had become blued by the fire, and we said that it had probably lost its temper, but he replied that he would harden it in the blood of the Sigfússons or of others among the incendiaries.'

Flosi asked: 'What did he say about Skarphedin or Grím?'

Geirmund answered: 'He said that both were still alive when they parted, but that they were probably dead now.'

'You have told us things,' said Flosi, 'which do not bode us rest or peace, for that man has escaped who comes closest to Gunnar of Hlídarendi in all respects. You may as well realise, you sons of Sigfús, and others of our men as well, that such action will be taken for this burning that many a one is likely to lose his head, and some all their property. I dare say that none of you Sigfússons will risk staying on your farms, and that is quite understandable. Now I shall invite you all to come and stay with me in the east, and let one fate befall us all.'

They thanked Flosi, and Módólf Ketilsson spoke this verse:

> One still lives of weapon-
> wielders, when fire swept through –
> 't was Sigfús' sons who had
> set it – Njál's dwelling.
> Now Thorgeir's son[1] suffered –
> swirled the flames skyward –
> for hapless Hoskuld's slaying;
> high burned the flames to heaven.

'Let us boast of other things than having burned Njál in his house,' said Flosi, 'for there is no glory in that.'

Thereupon Flosi went up to the gable wall, and Glúm Hildisson and some others with him.

Then Glúm said: 'I wonder whether Skarphedin is dead?'

The others answered that he must have been dead for some time. The fire sometimes blazed up and sometimes died down again. Then they heard this verse spoken from down in the fire before them:

> Scarce then could the coffers'-
> keeper[2] her tears hold back, as
> steed-of-the-sea-steerers[3]
> strove in war together;
> where carrion-craving ravens
> caw about their feeder –
> Ygg's gift shape I[4] – and gore did
> gush from sword-gashed bodies.

Grani Gunnarsson said: 'I wonder whether Skarphedin spoke this verse alive or dead?'

'I'll not venture any guess about that,' answered Flosi.

'Let us look for Skarphedin and others who are burned to death within,' said Grani.

'No, we'll not do that,' said Flosi, 'and only fools like you would want to, because men may be gathering all over the district. It is likely to be the death of him who tarries here; and he who does will be so scared that he will not know which way to run. My advice is that we all ride away from here as fast as we can.'

Then Flosi and his men quickly made for their horses. Flosi asked Geirmund: 'Do you know whether Ingjald is at home at Keldur?'

Geirmund answered that he believed he was.

'That is the man,' said Flosi, 'who has broken his oath and all pledges he gave us.' Thereupon Flosi said to the sons of Sigfús: 'What shall we do with Ingjald? Shall we forgive him or seek him out and kill him?'

They all answered that they wanted to seek him out and kill him.

Then Flosi leaped on his horse, and the others did likewise, and they rode away.

Flosi headed them as they rode up in the direction of the Rangá River and along its course. Then he saw a man riding down along it on the other bank, and he knew him to be Ingjald of Keldur. Flosi called to him, and Ingjald stopped and rode down to the river bank.

Flosi said to him: 'You have broken your pledge with us and so have forfeited life and property. Here are the sons of Sigfús; they would like to kill you, but it seems to me that you had got into a difficult position, and so I shall spare your life if you will award me self-judgement.'

Ingjald replied: 'Rather than award you self-judgement I shall be riding to find Kári; and as to the sons of Sigfús, my answer to them is that I am not more afraid of them than they of me!'

'Wait, then,' said Flosi, 'if you are not a coward, and I'll send you a gift!'

'I'll wait all right!' answered Ingjald.

Thorstein Kolbeinsson, Flosi's brother's son, rode forward past him with a spear in his hand. He was one of the bravest men in Flosi's band and one of the most highly valued. Flosi snatched the spear from him and hurled it at Ingjald. It struck Ingjald on his left side and passed through the shield below the handle, splitting it in two. The spear passed into Ingjald's shank and then into the saddletree, and there it stopped.

Flosi then asked Ingjald: 'Well, did it hit you?'

'It hit me all right,' answered Ingjald, 'but I call that a scratch, not a wound!'

Then Ingjald pulled the spear from the wound and said to Flosi: 'Now you wait if you are not a coward!'

With that he hurled the spear back over the river. Flosi saw the spear coming right at him and pulled back his horse, so that the spear flew past in front of the horse and missed him. However, it struck Thorstein in his middle and he fell from his horse and was dead. Thereupon Ingjald galloped into the woods and escaped from them.

'Now we have suffered a great loss,' said Flosi to his men; 'and now that this has happened, we can see that ill luck has dogged us. It is now my advice that we ride to the Thríhyrning Ridge. From there we can overlook the whole district and see who is moving against us, for by now they are likely to have collected a considerable force and are probably thinking that we have ridden from the Thríhyrning Ridge east into the Fljótshlíd district, and from there east into the highlands and down into our home districts. Very likely the greater number of their men will be riding that way after us. But some will go to Seljalandsmúli along the shore, even though they will believe there is less chance of finding us there. I'll now make this suggestion: it is, that we ride up on Thríhyrning Mountain and wait there until the sun has set three times.'

This they did.

131

Kári's Measures

Now to tell about Kári: he left the depression where he had rested and walked till he met Bárd, and he and Bárd had such words together as Geirmund had told Flosi. From there Kári rode to Mord Valgardsson and told him what had happened. Mord made great lament, but Kári said there were more manly things to do than to weep about the dead, and requested him rather to collect men and come with them to Holtsvad.

Then Kári rode to Thjórsárdale to find Hjalti Skeggjason, and when he had gone a way up the Thjórsá River he saw a man riding fast after him. Kári waited for the man and recognised him as Ingjald of Keldur. He saw that his thigh was all bloody and asked him who had wounded him, and Ingjald told him.

'Where did you two meet?' asked Kári.

'By the Rangá River,' answered Ingjald, 'and he flung his spear at me across the river.'

'Did you do anything in return?' asked Kári.

'I flung the spear back,' answered Ingjald, 'and they said it struck a man and that he was killed on the spot.'

'Do you know who it was?' asked Kári.

'It looked like Thorstein, Flosi's nephew,' answered Ingjald.

'A blessing on you for that!' said Kári.

Thereupon they both rode to Hjalti Skeggjason and told him what had happened. He was greatly incensed about what had been done and said it was absolutely necessary to pursue and kill them all. Thereupon he gathered forces, summoning all the men of the district.

Then Kári and he together with their men journeyed to join Mord Valgardsson, and they met him at Holtsvad. Mord was waiting for them with a large force. Then the search parties divided. One party rode by the seaward route to Seljalandsmúli, another up to the Fljótshlíd district, and the third over the

Thríhyrning Ridge down into the Godaland district. From there they rode north to Sand. Some rode as far as the Fiskivotn Lakes and turned back there. Some few took the seaward route to Holt and reported the news to Thorgeir. They asked whether Flosi and the others had ridden by there.

Thorgeir said: 'Consider: though I may not be a great chieftain, Flosi would think twice before riding past me in plain sight after killing my uncle Njál and my cousins. The only thing for you to do is to turn back, for you have been searching too far afield. But tell Kári to ride this way and to stay with me if he wishes. But even though he may not want to come east here, I shall be looking after his farm at Dyrhólmar, if he has no objection. Tell him that I will give him such help as I can and that I will ride to the Althing with him. He probably is aware also that we brothers are the chief prosecutors in this suit and that we mean to follow it up in such fashion that they will all be outlawed, if we have our way, and that there will then be blood revenge. However, I am not going with you now, because I know it will be of no avail. They are now going to be as wary as they possibly can be.'

They now rode back, and they all met at Hof, and admitted that they had received a discomfiture in not coming upon Flosi and his party, but Mord said that was not the case at all. Then some men urged that they ride to the Fljótshlíd district and seize on the property of all those who had taken part in the burning, but the final decision in this matter was left to Mord. He said that would be the worst mistake they could make. They asked him why he thought so.

'Because,' he said, 'if we leave their farmsteads undamaged they will come to visit them and their womenfolk, and there will be a chance to hunt them down when the time comes. Now I don't want you to doubt that Kári can rely on me in every respect, because my own safety is involved.'[1]

Hjalti told him to stick to his promises and invited Kári to come and stay with him, and Kári agreed to do so for the time being. He was told what Thorgeir had offered him, but he said he would make use of that invitation later on, and also that he had fair hopes of success if there were many such men.

Thereupon they let their company disperse.

Flosi and his men had seen all that had happened from where they were on the mountain.

He said: 'Now let us fetch our horses and ride away, for now it is safe to do so.'

The sons of Sigfús asked whether he thought it was all right for them to go to their farms and see after the work there.

'Very likely,' said Flosi, 'Mord is counting on your going to visit your womenfolk, and I surmise that his plan is to let your home-steads stand unharmed. My advice is that we all stay together, and that all ride east with me.'

They all accepted this council and rode north of the glacier[2] and continued east to Svínafell. Flosi sent out men immediately to procure supplies, so that nothing would be lacking.

Flosi never boasted of what he had done; neither could anyone observe that he was afraid. He stayed at home the entire winter until Yule had passed.

132

The Bodies of Njál and Bergthóra are Found

Kári asked Hjalti to go and search for Njál's remains – 'because everybody will believe what you say you have seen.'

Hjalti said he would gladly remove Njál's remains to the church.[1]

He left his farm with a company of fifteen men, and they rode east over the Thjórsá River, summoning men as they went, until they had a hundred men, including Njál's neighbours.

They arrived at Bergthórshvál about high noon. Hjalti asked Kári under which part of the house Njál might be lying, and Kári showed them to the spot. There was a large heap of ashes to be removed. Underneath they found the oxhide all shrivelled up from the fire. They lifted it up, and underneath the two lay there unburned. All praised God for that, for it seemed a great miracle. Then they took up the boy who had lain between them. One of the fingers which he had stuck out from under the hide was burned off. Njál was carried out, as was Bergthóra, and they all went to view their bodies.

Hjalti asked: 'What impression have you of these bodies?'

They answered: 'We would like to hear your opinion first.'

Hjalti said: 'I shall tell you my opinion without reservation. The body of Bergthóra appears to me as might be expected under the circumstances, yet well preserved. But Njál's body and entire appearance seem to me so radiant as I have never seen any dead person's body before.'

All confirmed his opinion.

Then they searched for Skarphedin. The servants showed them to the place where Flosi and his men had heard the verse spoken. There the roof had tumbled down by the gable wall, and there Hjalti told them to dig. They did so and found Skarphedin's body there. He had stood upright by the gable wall, and the lower part of his legs was burned up to about his knees, but nothing else. He had bitten down on his moustache, his eyes were open and not swollen, and he had driven his axe into the gable wall so hard that it had sunk in to the middle of the blade, and it had not lost its temper. Then the axe was pulled out. Hjalti took it up and said: 'A remarkable weapon and one that few will be able to wield!'

Kári said: 'I know the man to wield it!'

'And who is he?' asked Hjalti.

'Thorgeir Skorargeir,' said Kári. 'Him I regard as foremost in this clan now!'

Then Skarphedin was stripped of his clothes, for they were not burned. He had laid his arms crosswise, with the right one over the left. Two marks they found burned on him – one between his shoulders and the other on his chest – both in the shape of a cross, and it was the opinion of men that he had branded himself with them. All were agreed that it was less eerie to stand by the dead Skarphedin's body than they had thought, for no man was afraid of him.

Thereupon they looked for Grím and found his remains in the middle of the hall. Opposite him under the side wall they found Thórd the Freedman, and in the weaving-room they found the old woman Sæunn and three other people. Altogether they found there the remains of eleven persons. Thereupon they brought these bodies to the church. Then Hjalti rode home and Kári rode with him.

Ingjald's leg became inflamed and swollen. He went to find Hjalti and was healed by him, but he walked with a limp ever after.

Kári rode to Tunga to visit with Ásgrím Ellida-Grímsson. Thórhalla had already arrived there and told her father what had happened. Ásgrím received Kári with open arms and asked him to stay there the entire year. Kári said he would do so. Ásgrím also asked all the people who had lived at Bergthórshvál to stay with him. Kári said that was a generous offer – 'and I shall accept it in their behalf.' Then all the servants were moved over there.

When Thórhall Ásgrímsson was told that his foster father Njál was dead and had been burned in his house, he was so wrought up that his entire body swelled and there burst forth from both his ears a stream of blood, and it could not be stopped. He fell in a faint, and then the flow of blood stopped. Then he got up and said that he had behaved in an unmanly fashion – 'but I only wish I could avenge what has just happened to me on some of those who burned Njál in his house!'

But other people present said that no one would regard what had happened to him as a disgrace, but he replied that he could not prevent people from talking about it.

Ásgrím asked Kári what support he might expect from those east beyond the Markar River. Kári answered that Mord Valgardsson and Hjalti Skeggjason would give him as much help as they could, and so too would Thorgeir Skorargeir and all the other brothers. Ásgrím said that was a considerable force of men.

'And what assistance shall we have from you yourself?' asked Kári.

'All that I can possibly give,' answered Ásgrím, 'and I shall do it at the risk of my own life!'

'Do that!' said Kári.

'Also, I have induced Gizur to join us in the suit,' said Ásgrím, 'and I have asked his advice as to how we should go about it.'

'That's good!' replied Kári. 'What advice did he give?'

Ásgrím answered: 'He suggested that we should let everything rest until spring, but that we then ride east and prepare legal action against Flosi for the slaying of Helgi and cite neighbouring witnesses, and at the Assembly give notice of the action for incendiarism and cite the same witnesses as a jury before the court. I also asked Gizur who should plead the suit for manslaughter, and he answered that Mord should do so, whether he liked it or not. He is to be assigned the hardest task because he has behaved the

worst in the whole matter. And Kári is to be in an angry passion
whenever he meets Mord, and this together with my efforts will
make him amenable to our wishes – so said Gizur.'

Then Kári said: 'Your advice we shall follow as long as you will
give us the benefit of it and be our leader.'

It is told that Kári could not sleep nights. One night Ásgrím
awoke and noticed that Kári was awake. 'Can't you sleep of
nights?' he asked.

Then Kári spoke this verse:

> Never, warrior, at nightfall
> neareth sleep – for always
> mournful am I, mindful
> e'ermore – my eyelids,
> since the buckler-bearers
> burned in fall – forever
> harp I on this harm – in his
> homestead Njál's household.

Of no men did Kári speak so often as of Njál and Skarphedin.
However, he never spoke ill of his enemies nor did he utter any
threat against them.

133

Flosi's Dream[1]

One night at Svínafell it happened that Flosi slept very restlessly.
Glúm Hildisson aroused him from his sleep, but it was a long
time before he was fully awake.

Then Flosi said: 'Call Ketil of Mork here!'

Ketil came there and Flosi said: 'I wish to tell you my dream.'

'Do so!' said Ketil.

'I dreamed that I was at Lómagnúp,' said Flosi. 'I went out and
looked up to the cliff above, and it opened up, and a man came
out. He was clad in a goatskin and had an iron staff in his hand. He
went about, calling and summoning my men, some earlier some

later, calling them by name. First he called Grím the Red and Árni Kolsson. Then a strange thing seemed to happen: I thought he summoned Eyjólf Bolverksson and Ljót, the son of Hall of Sída, and some six other men. Then he was silent for a while. After that he called five men of our band, and among them were the sons of Sigfús, your brothers. Then he called another five men, and among them were Lambi and Módólf and Glúm. Then he called three men, and last of all he called Gunnar Lambason and Kol Thorsteinsson. After that he came up to me. I asked him what events had taken place. He said that he could [indeed] tell of such. Then I asked him his name, and he said it was Járngrím. I asked him which way he was going, and he answered that he was going to the Althing.

' "What will you be doing there?" I asked.

'He answered: "First I shall challenge the jurors, then the judges, and then I shall clear the battlefield for the combatants."

'After that he spoke this verse:

> Will one rise to weave the
> web-of-arrows:[2] soon will
> doomed men's heads drop in the
> dust throughout these folk-lands;
> waxes the din of war-play
> wild upon the mountains:
> rivers of red soon will
> run down gashed men's bodies.

'He struck the ground with his staff, and there was a great crash. Then he went back into the mountain. Now I want you to tell me what this dream signifies.'

'I much suspect,' said Ketil, 'that all those who were called are doomed to death. It would be my advice, as matters now stand, that we tell no one of this dream.'

Flosi said that he agreed with that. The winter wore on until it was past Yuletide.

Then Flosi said to his men: 'I think it is time now to leave here, because I rather think we shall have no more peace here. Let us now go and look for assistance. It is likely to come to pass as I forewarned you, that we shall have to approach many a one on bended knee before there is an end to this business.'

134

Flosi's Attempts to Win Allies

Thereupon they all prepared to leave. Flosi was clad in trousers and hose in one piece, because he intended to go on foot.[1] He knew that it would then seem less toilsome to the others to walk. They made Knappavoll the first day, and the next evening they got to the Broad River farm and from there they continued to Kálfafell. From there they journeyed to Bjarnaness in the Horn Firth district and on to Stafafell in the Lón district, and finally to Thváttá River farm where Hall of Sída lived. Flosi was married to Steinvor, Hall's daughter. Hall gave them a warm welcome.

Flosi said to Hall: 'I shall ask you, father-in-law, to accompany me to the Assembly together with all your henchmen.'

Hall answered: 'Now things have turned out the way the saying has it, that but a short time is the hand fain of the blow.[2] The very same men in your company now hang their heads who before urged you on to take an evil course. But my help I am bound to lend you, so far as lies in my power.'

Flosi asked: 'What course would you advise me to take now, as things now stand?'

Hall replied: 'Go north all the way to Vápna Firth and ask all the chieftains for their support. You are likely to have need of it from every one of them before the meeting at the Assembly comes to an end.'

Flosi stayed there three nights and rested. Then he journeyed east to Geitahellur, and then to Bear Firth. There they stayed overnight. From there they journeyed east to Haydale in the Broad Dale district. Hallbjorn the Strong lived there. He was married to Oddný, the sister of Sorli Brodd-Helgason, and Flosi received a warm welcome there. Hallbjorn asked many questions about the burning and Flosi gave him an exact account of everything. Hallbjorn asked Flosi how far among the firths in the north he planned to go, and he answered that he planned to go as far as

Vápna Firth. Then Flosi took a bag full of money from his belt and said he wished to give it to Hallbjorn. Hallbjorn accepted the money, but said that Flosi was under no obligation to pay him anything – 'but I would nevertheless like to know how you wish that I repay you.'

'I am not in need of money,' said Flosi, 'but I would request you to ride to the Assembly with me and stand by me in my suit, though I am aware that I have no claim on you whether by blood or marriage.'

Hallbjorn said: 'I promise to ride to the Assembly with you and to stand by you in your suit just as I would stand by my own brother.'

Flosi thanked him. From there Flosi journeyed to Broad Dale Heath and on to Hrafnkelsstead. Here there lived Hrafnkel,[3] the son of Thórir, the son of Hrafnkel Hrafnsson. Flosi was well received here, and he asked Hrafnkel to ride to the Assembly with him and to stand by him. For a long time Hrafnkel sought to excuse himself, but at length he did promise that his son Thórir would ride with all their henchmen and that he would lend as much assistance as any *goði* of his district.

Flosi thanked him and then continued on to Bersastead. Hólmstein Spak-Bersason lived there and he received Flosi well. Flosi asked him for help. Hólmstein said that Flosi had long ago made up for any help he would lend him. From there they went to Váldjofsstead. Sorli Brodd-Helgason, the brother of Bjarni Brodd-Helgason, lived there. He was married to Thórdís, the daughter of Gudmund the Powerful of Modruvellir. Flosi and his men were well received there. The following morning Flosi brought up the question whether Sorli would accompany him to the Assembly, and offered money as an inducement.

'I don't know,' he said, 'as long as I don't know on which side Gudmund the Powerful, my father-in-law, stands, because I am going to support him on whichever side he stands.'

Flosi answered: 'I can see from your answer that you are under the thumb of your wife.' Thereupon Flosi arose and told his men to take their clothes and arms; they went away without receiving any help there.

They journeyed on and crossed the lower end of Lagarfljót Lake, then over the heath to Njardvík. Two brothers lived there,

Thorkel the Very Wise and his brother Thorvald. They were the
sons of Ketil Thrym, the son of Thidrandi the Wise, the son of
Ketil Thrym, the son of Thórir Thidrandi. The mother of Thorkel
the Very Wise and of Thorvald was Yngvild, the daughter of
Thorkel the Very Wise. Flosi was well received there. He gave the
brothers the reason for his errand and asked for their support.
However, they refused until he gave them each three marks of
silver for their help; then they agreed to stand by Flosi. Yngvild,
their mother, was present as they promised to ride to the Assembly,
and she wept.

Thorkel asked: 'Why are you weeping, mother?'

She answered: 'I dreamed that your brother Thorvald was
wearing a red coat, and this coat seemed to be so tight as though it
were sewn to his body. Below, he seemed to be wearing red hose
wound about with shabby tapes. It hurt me to see that, for I knew
he felt uneasy about it, but I couldn't do anything to help him.'[4]

They laughed at this, calling it so much nonsense, and they said
that her babble would not prevent them from riding to the
Assembly.

Flosi thanked them kindly, and from there they went to Hof in
the Vápna Firth district. Here there lived Bjarni Brodd-Helgason.
Brodd-Helgi was the son of Thorgils, the son of Thorstein the
White, the son of Olvir, the son of Eyvald, the son of Ox-Thórir.
The mother of Bjarni was Halla, the daughter of Lýting. The
mother of Brodd-Helgi was Asvor, the daughter of Thórir, the son
of Graut-Atli, the son of Thórir Thidrandi. Bjarni Brodd-
Helgason was married to Rannveig, the daughter of Thorgeir, the
son of Eirík of Goddale, the son of Geirmund, the son of Hróald,
the son of Eirík Bristle-Beard. Bjarni received Flosi with open
arms. Flosi offered Bjarni money for helping him.

Bjarni said: 'Never have I sold my manhood nor my support for
bribes, but now that you are in need of help I shall act like a friend
to you and ride to the Assembly with you and stand by you just as
I would stand by my own brother.'

'Then you put me under obligation to you,' said Flosi, 'but I
expected that from a man like you.'

Thereupon Flosi went to Krossavík. Thorkel Geitisson had
always been a good friend of his. Flosi told him what his business
was, and Thorkel answered that it was his duty to stand by Flosi

with all the means at his disposal and not to forsake him in his difficulty. At their parting Thorkel gave Flosi good gifts.

Flosi then went north [from] Vápna Firth and up into the Fljótsdale district where he stayed with Hólmstein Spak-Bersason. Flosi told him that all supported his request for help except Sorli Brodd-Helgason. Hólmstein said that the reason for this was that Sorli was not a man who relished violence. Hólmstein gave Flosi good gifts.

Flosi journeyed up along the Fljótsdale Valley and from there south over the mountains and across the Öxarhraun lava flow, then down Svidinhornadale and seaward along the west side of Álpta Firth, and continued till he came to the Thváttá River and his father in-law Hall. There Flosi and his men stayed a half-month and rested. Flosi asked Hall what measures he would now advise him to take and how he should proceed.

Hall answered: 'My advice is that you and the sons of Sigfús stay at your home and that they send men to look after their home-steads. Go home for the time being, but when you ride to the Assembly you must all ride together and not scatter your band. Then the sons of Sigfús can visit their wives. I shall ride to the Assembly with my son Ljót and all our henchmen, and I shall give you as much help as stands in my power.'

Flosi thanked him. When they parted Hall gave him good gifts.

Flosi then left Thváttá River and there is nothing to report of his journey until he came home to Svínafell. He now stayed at home the rest of the winter and the following summer until the time came for the meeting at the Assembly.

135

Mord Introduces the Suit

One day Thórhall Ásgrímsson and Kári Solmundarson rode over to Mosfell to see Gizur the White. He received them with open arms, and they stayed there a very long time.

One day when Gizur and they were talking about the burning of Njál Gizur remarked that it was a good piece of fortune that Kári had escaped. Then this verse came to Kári's lips:

> Out did the hard-helmet-
> hewer[1] issue unwilling:
> loath I 'scaped the swirling
> smoke of Njál's dwelling,
> when Bergthóra's brave sons
> burned within its ruins.
> Let all men remember
> my great loss and hardship.

Thereupon Gizur said: 'One can understand that your mind reverts to this, but let us not touch on it any more now.'

Kári said that he wished to ride home. Gizur said: 'Now let me give you some frank advice. Don't ride to your home, but journey east beyond the Eyjafell Mountains to visit Thorgeir Skorargeir and Thorleif Crow. Let them journey with you to the Assembly, for the responsibility for taking action is theirs. Thorgrím the Tall, their brother, should go with them. You all should look up Mord Valgardsson and deliver my message to him: that he is to introduce the suit against Flosi for the slaying of Helgi Njálsson. If he shows any sign of objecting to this, then fly into a towering rage and act as though you would brain him with your axe. Add, too, that he can be sure of my enmity if he pretends not to be able to attend to the matter. You can also tell him that I would fetch my daughter Thorkatla back home in that case. But he won't let it come to that, because he loves her like the apple of his eye.'

Kári thanked him for this counsel. He said nothing to him about lending his support at the Althing, because he knew that Gizur would prove himself his good friend in this respect as in everything else.

From there Kári and his men rode eastward, crossing the rivers to the Fljótshlíd district, and from there on over the Markar River to Seljalandsmúli. From there they continued east to the Holt farm. There Thorgeir received them with the greatest cordiality. He told them of Flosi's journey and how much help he had been able to get in the East Firths. Kári said that Flosi had good reason for soliciting assistance, in view of the many charges that would be levelled against him.

Thorgeir said: 'The worse they fare, the better I like it!'

Kári told Thorgeir of Gizur's advice. After that they rode west to Mord Valgardsson in the Rangá River district. He received them well. Kári delivered the message of his father-in-law Gizur. Mord was reluctant to do what Gizur wanted him to and said that it was more difficult to prosecute Flosi than ten other men.

Kári said: 'Your bad character shows plainly; you are both timid and fainthearted, and the consequence will be that you will get just what you deserve, which is, that Thorkatla will return to her father!'

Thorkatla got ready immediately and said that she had long been prepared to part from Mord. Thereupon Mord quickly changed his tune and begged them not to be angry with him, and at once declared himself ready to take on the case.

Kári said: 'Now you have taken over the case, and you had better prosecute it fearlessly, for your life depends upon it!'

Mord promised to exert every effort to accomplish the task well and honourably.

After that Mord summoned the nine neighbours who lived closest to the scene of the burning. Mord then took Thorgeir by the hand and named two witnesses – 'to witness that Thorgeir Thórisson has handed over to me the suit for manslaughter against Flosi Thórdarson, to prosecute him for the slaying of Helgi Njálsson with all the evidence appertaining to the accusation. And you herewith cede to me the right to prosecute this case, to come to terms about it, and to make use of all the evidence even as though I were the rightful plaintiff. You herewith cede this case to me in accordance with the law, and I take it over in accordance with the law.'

A second time Mord named witnesses – 'to testify that I give notice of a suit for assault punishable by law, against Flosi Thórdarson, forasmuch as he inflicted upon Helgi Njálsson a brain wound, or else an internal wound, or else a marrow wound,[2] which proved a mortal injury and which brought about Helgi's death. I serve notice of this before five neighbours' – and he named them all – 'I serve notice according to the law, and make known that this suit has been ceded to me by Thorgeir Thórisson.'

And again Mord called witnesses – 'to testify that I give notice of a suit against Flosi Thórdarson for a brain wound, or else an internal wound, or else a marrow wound, which proved a mortal injury and which brought about Helgi's death, and to wit, on that spot where Flosi Thórdarson made unprovoked attack, punishable by law, on Helgi Njálsson. I serve notice of this before five neighbours' – then he named them all by name – 'I serve notice in accordance with the law, and make known that this suit has been ceded to me by Thorgeir Thórisson.'

Thereupon Mord summoned witnesses – 'to testify,' he said, 'that I summon all these nine neighbours who live closest to where the slaying occurred' – and he named them all by name – 'to ride to the Althing and to state as a jury whether Flosi Thórdarson made unprovoked attack, punishable by law, on Helgi Njálsson, and to wit, on that spot where he inflicted upon Helgi Njálsson a brain wound, or else an internal wound, or else a marrow wound, which proved a mortal injury and which brought about Helgi's death. I call upon you for all the findings you are required by the law to make appertaining to this suit, and which I shall require you to adduce. I herewith serve summons so that you may hear yourselves, and summon you in the suit legally ceded to me by Thorgeir Thórisson.'

Mord named witnesses – 'to testify that I summon these nine neighbours who live closest to where the slaying occurred to ride to the Althing and to state as a jury whether Flosi Thórdarson inflicted upon Helgi Njálsson a brain wound, or else a marrow wound, or else an internal wound, which proved a mortal injury and which brought about Helgi's death, and to wit, on that spot where Flosi Thórdarson made unprovoked attack, punishable by law, on Helgi Njálsson. I call upon you for all the findings you are required by the law to make appertaining to this suit, and which I shall require you to adduce. I herewith serve summons so that you may hear yourselves, and summon you in the suit legally ceded to me by Thorgeir Thórisson.'

Mord said: 'Now proceedings have been instituted, as you have requested of me. I should now like to ask you, Thorgeir Skorargeir, to visit me on your way to the Assembly. Thus we two can ride together, each with his own following, and stay as close together as possible. My following will be ready by the beginning of the Assembly, and you can trust me in all matters.'

They expressed their satisfaction with what he had done so far, and they pledged each other to stay together in this business until released by Kári, and to lay down their lives, one for the other. Thereupon they parted in friendship and agreed to meet at the Assembly.

Then Thorgeir rode to his farm, but Kári rode west over the rivers until he came to Ásgrím at Tunga. Ásgrím made him cordially welcome, and Kári reported to him everything which Gizur the White had counselled as well as Mord's institution of the suit.

Ásgrím said: 'I had expected that Gizur would act like a man of honour, and this confirms my view.' He added: 'What news from the east of Flosi?'

Kári answered: 'He went all the way up to Vápna Firth and almost all the chieftains have promised to ride to the Althing with him and to help him. They also expect help from the people in the districts of Reykjardale, Ljósavatn, and the Axe Firth.'[3]

They discussed this at length. The time for the Althing now drew near.

Ásgrím's son, Thórhall, had such a bad sore on his foot that the leg above the ankle was as swollen and large as a woman's thigh, and he could not walk except with a cane. Thórhall was a tall and powerful man with dark hair and complexion, composed in his speech, and yet of hot temper. He was one of the three greatest lawyers in Iceland.

Now the time was approaching for people to journey to the Assembly. Ásgrím said to Kári: 'I should like you to be at the Assembly at its very beginning and prepare our booths for occupation, and I want my son Thórhall to go with you, for I know you will treat him with the greatest care and consideration, seeing that he limps badly. But we will stand in the greatest need of his help at the Assembly. With you two there shall go twenty other men.'

After that they made ready for their journey and went to the Assembly, made the booths ready for occupation, and had everything shipshape.

136

Flosi Visits Ásgrím at the Althing

Flosi journeyed to the Althing from the east, and with him there rode those one hundred men who had been with him at the burning. They continued on their way until they arrived in the Fljótshlíd district. The sons of Sigfús then looked after their homesteads and stayed there that day, but in the evening they rode west over the Thjórsá River and slept there that night. Early in the morning they took their horses and rode on.

Flosi said to his men: 'Now we will ride to Ásgrím at Tunga and have it out with him!'

They considered this a good suggestion, and so they rode until they were not far from Tunga. Ásgrím was standing before the house with some of his men. Ásgrím's men said: 'It's probably Thorgeir Skorargeir.'

Ásgrím answered: 'I am by no means of that opinion, because these men are coming with laughter and unseemly merriment, whereas Njál's kinsmen, such as Thorgeir, will never laugh until some vengeance has been taken for the burning. On the contrary, however unlikely that may seem to you, I am thinking that it is Flosi and those who were with him at the burning, and they probably mean to have it out with us. Let us all go inside!'

This they did. Ásgrím had the floors swept, the hangings put up, the tables set, and the food brought in. He also had additional rows of benches placed alongside the usual ones throughout the entire hall.

Flosi rode into the yard and told his men to dismount and go in.

This they did, and Flosi and his men entered the room. Ásgrím sat on the cross-bench. Flosi glanced at the benches and observed that everything which one might need was completely prepared for their entertainment. Ásgrím offered them no greeting, but said to Flosi: 'The tables are set, so that food is at the disposal of those who need it.'

Flosi and all his men sat down at the tables, and placed their weapons against the wall. Those who could find no room on the inner benches sat on those placed beside them, but four armed men stood guard over Flosi while they were eating.

Ásgrím remained silent during the meal, but his face was as red as blood. When they had finished eating, some of the women cleared the tables and others brought in basins of water to wash their hands. At the corner of the cross-bench lay a carpenter's axe. Ásgrím grasped it with both hands, leaped on to the edge of the cross-dais, and aimed a blow at Flosi's head. Glúm Hildisson saw what he was up to. He started up and managed to grasp the axe above Ásgrím's hands and turn the edge on Ásgrím himself, for Glúm was a powerful man. Then many other men made for Ásgrím, but Flosi said that no one was to do him any harm – 'for we have tried him sorely and he acted only as he should have, and showed thereby that he is a dauntless man.'

Then Flosi said to Ásgrím: 'We'll part now for the time being, but we shall meet again at the Assembly and have a showdown!'

'That we shall!' answered Ásgrím, 'and if things go the way I wish, you will not be holding your head quite so high when this Assembly is over!'

Flosi said nothing to this. Thereupon they left the house, mounted their horses, and rode away. They journeyed on till they came to the Laugarvatn farm and they stayed there overnight. The following morning they continued to the plains of Beitivellir and rested there. Many hosts of men joined them there; among them were Hall of Sída and all the men from the East Firths. Flosi welcomed them all and told them about his journey and his dealings with Ásgrím. Many praised Flosi and said that he had acted in a manly fashion.

Hall said: 'I do not look upon this matter the same way you do; I think it was a foolish step. They are likely to be thinking of their grievances, even if they are not reminded of them anew, and those who bait others in such a provoking manner are only inviting trouble for themselves.' It was quite plain that Hall thought Flosi's action ill considered.

The whole flock journeyed on from there until they arrived at the upper Assembly grounds. There they put their men in battle array and then rode down to the Assembly proper. Flosi had the so-called fortified booth put in order before he had ridden to the Assembly. The men from the East Firths went each to their own booths.

137

The Plaintiffs Arrive at the Assembly

Thorgeir Skorargeir came from the east with a large following. His brothers, Thorleif Crow and Thorgrím the Tall, were with him. They rode until they came to Mord Valgardsson at Hof, and they waited there until he was ready. Mord had summoned up every man who could bear arms, and they were convinced that he could be relied on in every respect.

They journeyed on and crossed the rivers. After that they waited for Hjalti Skeggjason, and he came after they had waited for a short time. They welcomed him, and then all together they rode to Reykir in Byskupstunga. There they waited for Ásgrím Ellida-Grímsson, and he came to join them. Then they rode west over the Brúará River. Ásgrím told them all about what had taken place between Flosi and himself.

Thorgeir said: 'I wish that we might put their bravery to the test before this Assembly comes to an end!'

They rode on until they came to Beitivellir Plains. There Gizur the White joined them with a large following. They talked together for a long time. They then rode to the upper Assembly grounds, put their men in battle array, and then rode to the Assembly proper.

Flosi and his men all rushed to take up their arms, and they were on the verge of coming to blows, but Ásgrím and his men would have no part in this and rode to their booths. After that everything remained quiet that day without any friction between the two parties.

The chieftains had arrived from all Quarters of the land, and as far back as one could remember there had never been an Assembly so well attended.

138

Flosi Wins the Support of Eyjólf Bolverksson

There was a man named Eyjólf. He was the son of Bolverk, the son of Eyjólf the Grey of Otradale, the son of Thórd Gellir, the son of Óleif Feilan. The mother of Eyjólf the Grey was Hródný, the daughter of Mid Firth-Skeggi. Eyjólf was a highly respected man and so well versed in the law that he was counted one of the three greatest lawyers in Iceland. He was a very handsome man, tall and strong, and he gave every promise of becoming an eminent chieftain. Money had a great attraction for him as for other kinsmen of his.

One day Flosi went to the booth of Bjarni Brodd-Helgason. Bjarni received him with open arms and Flosi sat down beside him. They talked about many things.

Flosi asked Bjarni: 'What counsel would you give now?'

Bjarni answered: 'I am thinking that it is a difficult matter to know what to do in this case, but it would seem most advisable that you try to win more support, for they are gathering forces against you. I also wish to ask you, Flosi, if your group has any first-class lawyer, because now only two alternatives are open to you: either you must ask whether they will accept atonement – and that would seem an excellent course to take – or else you must make some good legal defence, if you have any, even though you may be thought to be very obstinate in the matter. It seems to me that this course is the one you should choose. Though you might be thought to be mighty brazen in so doing, it would seem to me ill befitting for you to climb down now.'

Flosi answered: 'Since you ask about a lawyer in our group, I can tell you right now that there is none in our band, nor do I know of anyone to count on except Thorkel Geitisson, your kinsman.'

'No, we cannot count on him,' said Bjarni. 'Although he is versed in the law, he is also very wary. Let no one depend on shielding himself behind him! However, he will back you as bravely as any one of the best, for he is a man of dauntless courage. I'll tell you this: it will be the death of that man who will take it upon himself to defend you in the suit for the burning of Njál in his house, and I would not want that to happen to my kinsman Thorkel. You will therefore have to look around for someone else.'

Flosi answered that he had no idea who the best lawyers were.

Bjarni said: 'There is a man named Eyjólf Bolverksson. He is the best lawyer in the Western Quarter. To be sure, he will have to be well paid if you want him to take up the case, but that should make no difference to us. Also, we should always go armed to the court and always be on our guard, but not attack them unless we are forced to do so in self-defence. Now I will go with you to seek help, because it seems to me that we cannot sit idle any longer.'

After that both left the booth together and went to the men from the East Firths. Bjarni spoke with Lýting and Blæing and Hrói Arnsteinsson and quickly got everything he asked of them. Then they went to see Kol, the son of Víga-Skúta, and Eyvind Thorkels-son, the son of Áskel the *goði*, and asked them for their support. They were evasive for a long time, but in the end they accepted three marks of silver to make common cause with them.

Then they went to the booth of the men of Ljósavatn and stayed there for some time. Flosi asked the men of Ljósavatn for their support, but they were stubborn and difficult to win over. Flosi grew furious and said: 'You are sorry people! At home in your own district you are greedy and unjust, and at the assemblies you do not help men when they ask you for assistance. And you will be held up for shame at assemblies for not bearing in mind the insults heaped upon you men of Ljósavatn by Skarphedin.'[1]

But after a while he took them aside, offered them money for their support, and won them over with honeyed words. In the end they promised him their support, and they put on such a bold front that they said they would fight on his side if it came to that point.

Bjarni said to Flosi: 'Excellently done! You are a great chieftain, bold and determined, and a very prince of a man!'

After that they went west over the Axe River and continued to the booth of Snorri Godi. They saw many men outside before the booth. There was one man who had a scarlet cloak over his shoulders and a gold fillet around his head and who carried a silver-adorned axe in his hand.

'Most fortunate!' said Bjarni. 'Here is Eyjólf Bolverksson right now!'

Then they went up to Eyjólf and greeted him. Eyjólf recognised Bjarni immediately and welcomed him. Bjarni took Eyjólf by the hand and led him up to the Almanna Gorge. Bjarni asked Flosi to follow him with his men; Eyjólf's men also went along with him. They were told to stay up there at the edge of the gorge and be on the lookout from there. Flosi and the other two men, however, went on until they came to the place where the path leads down from the upper edge of the gorge. Flosi said that was a good place to sit and see far and wide. Then they sat down. There were four of them,[2] and no more.

Then Bjarni said to Eyjólf: 'It is you whom we have come to see, friend, for we are sorely in need of your help in every respect.'

Eyjólf answered: 'There are a great many excellent men to choose from here at the Assembly, and it will be an easy matter for you to find men who will be of greater help to you than I can be.'

Bjarni replied: 'No, that is not so! You have many qualities in which no man here at the Assembly can surpass you. In the first place, you are of noble birth just as are all those who are descended from Ragnar Lodbrók. Your forebears have always had a share in all the great and important affairs, at the Assembly as well as at home in their own district, and always had the upper hand. It seems to us, therefore, that you will be just as successful in litigation as your kinsmen.'

'You speak handsomely,' said Eyjólf, 'but I don't propose to have anything to do with any business of yours.'

Flosi said: 'It is hardly necessary to point out what we have in mind. We wish to ask you to support us in this business of ours, go to the court with us, and seize on any points of defence, if any present themselves, plead them in our name, and stand by us at the Assembly in everything which may come to pass.'

Eyjólf started up in a fury and said that no man should presume to have him run a fool's errand or use him as a cat's-paw to do what he did not want to – 'and now I see,' he said, 'what was the real reason for those fine words which you spoke to me!'

Hallbjorn the Strong took hold of him and made him sit down between Bjarni and himself and then said: 'No tree falls at the first blow, friend; so just sit there a while with us.'

Flosi then drew a gold ring from his arm and said: 'I wish to give you this ring, Eyjólf, for your friendship and help, and in order to show you that I will not play you false. You can well afford to accept this ring, because there is no man here at the Assembly to whom I have ever given such a gift.'

The ring was so large and well made that it was worth twelve hundred yards of brown-striped homespun. Hallbjorn placed the ring on Eyjólf's arm.

'Since you behave so generously, it is only reasonable of me to accept the ring,' said Eyjólf. 'And you can also take it for granted that I shall take up the defence in your case and do everything that is required.'

Bjarni said: 'Now both of you behave as you should, and there are men present like Hallbjorn and myself who are well suited to be witnesses to the fact that you are taking charge of this case.'

Eyjólf and Flosi then arose and took each other by the hand, and Eyjólf had the charge of defending the case transferred entirely to him as well as the prosecution of any suit which might arise from this defence, because it often happens that what is a defence in one suit becomes a plaintiff's point in another.[3] And for that reason he took over all the evidence bearing on the case, whether it was to be presented before the Fifth Court or the Quarter Court; Flosi ceding the case, and Eyjólf taking it up, according to the law.

Thereupon he said to Flosi and Bjarni; 'Now I have taken over the defence of this suit as you requested of me, but it is my wish that you keep the matter secret for the time being. If the suit comes before the Fifth Court, you must be particularly careful not to mention that you have paid me for my help.'

Thereupon Flosi and Bjarni and the others arose. Flosi and Bjarni each went to his booth, but Eyjólf went to the booth of Snorri Godi and sat down beside him. They had a long discussion.

Snorri Godi took hold of Eyjólf's arm, turned up the sleeve, and saw that he had a large gold ring on his arm. Then Snorri asked: 'Was this ring bought or was it given to you?'

Eyjólf was embarrassed and said nothing.

Snorri said: 'I see clearly that you must have received it as a gift, and I hope this ring will not prove to be the death of you.'

Eyjólf started up and left the booth, not wishing to talk about the matter, but as he was leaving Snorri said: 'Most likely, when the court's sentence has been handed out, you will find out what sort of a gift you have accepted!'

Then Eyjólf went to his booth.

139

The Plaintiffs Deliberate and Seek Additional Support

Now we take up the story where Ásgrím Ellida-Grímsson and Kári Solmundarson met with Gizur the White, Hjalti Skeggjason, Thorgeir Skorargeir, and Mord Valgardsson. Ásgrím said: 'There is no need to be stealthy in our proceedings, for here are only men who can trust one another. Now I wish to ask you whether you know anything of the plans of Flosi and his men. It seems to me that we, too, must decide on a plan of action.'

Gizur the White answered: 'Snorri Godi sent a messenger to me to tell me that Flosi had received strong support from the men of the Northern Quarter, and also that Eyjólf Bolverksson, his kinsman, had received a gold ring from someone, but that he was trying to keep it secret. It was Snorri's belief that Eyjólf Bolverksson had been selected to lead the defence and that he had received the ring for this reason.'

They all agreed that this probably was so.

Gizur spoke to them. 'My son-in-law, Mord Valgardsson, has now taken over the case likely to be the most difficult of all, that is, the one against Flosi. Now I would like you to divide the other suits among yourselves, because it will soon be time to give notice of the suits at the Law-Mount. Also it will be necessary to look about for more support.'

Ásgrím answered: 'Yes, that we shall do. But I would like to ask you to be along when we ask for support.'

Gizur promised to do so. Thereupon he selected the wisest men from his following to accompany him: they were Hjalti Skeggjason, Ásgrím, Kári, and Thorgeir Skorargeir. Then Gizur said: 'Now we shall go first of all to the booth of Skapti Thóroddsson.'

This they did. Gizur went first, then came Hjalti, then Kári, then Ásgrím, then Thorgeir Skorargeir, and then his brothers. They stepped into the booth of Skapti Thóroddsson. He was sitting on the cross-bench, and when he saw Gizur he arose, welcomed him and all the others, and bade Gizur sit down beside him. Gizur sat down and then said to Ásgrím: 'Now you present to Skapti our request for support, and I shall add whatever remarks I think necessary.'

Ásgrím said: 'We have come here for the purpose of requesting your support and help, Skapti!'

Skapti answered: 'You considered me difficult enough to win over the last time[1] when I didn't wish to become involved in your troubles.'

Gizur replied: 'Things are different now. This time it is a question of prosecuting in behalf of farmer Njál and his wife Bergthóra, both of whom were burned in their home, though they had done no one any harm, and also in behalf of Njál's three sons and many other brave men. And you can't want to refuse help and support to men related to you by blood and by marriage!'[2]

Skapti answered: 'That is exactly what I then had in mind when Skarphedin said that I had smeared tar on my head and cut out a strip of turf under which to hide, and also, that I had been so scared that Thórólf Loptsson had to carry me aboard his ship in his flour sacks and so get me back to Iceland. I then made up my mind that I would never have anything to do with any case in his behalf.'

Gizur said: 'No need to remember that now, because he who said that is now dead. I am thinking that you will lend your support to me at least, even though you may be unwilling to do anything for the others here.'

Skapti answered: 'This whole affair really does not concern you at all unless you really want to become involved in it.'

Gizur then became furious and said: 'Mighty unlike you are to your father; though he was considered somewhat underhanded, yet he always came to the help of men when they needed it badly!'

'We are of unlike disposition,' answered Skapti. 'You two think you have accomplished great deeds: you, Gizur the White,[3] because you fell upon Gunnar at Hlídarendi, and you, Ásgrím, because you slew your own foster brother Gauk!'

Ásgrím replied: 'Naturally you bring up the worst you know about me.[4] Yet many will be of the opinion that I slew Gauk when there was no way out. I can understand that you may have reasons for not wishing to help us, but your heaping reproaches on us is inexcusable. I wish that before this Assembly comes to an end you will suffer the greatest discomfiture from this business and that no one will offer to help you out of it!'

Then Gizur and the others arose and left for the booth of Snorri Godi. As they entered they found Snorri sitting on the cross-bench. He recognised the men immediately, arose to meet them, bade them welcome, and made room for them to sit down beside him. After that they asked one another about news of general interest.

Ásgrím said to Snorri: 'My kinsman Gizur and I have come here to ask you for support.'

Snorri answered: 'You have every reason to push the prosecution of the suit in behalf of such men as your brothers-in-law. Much good counsel did we receive from Njál, even though few are mindful of that now. But I do not know what sort of help you need most.'

Ásgrím replied: 'Most of all we need support in case a fight breaks out at the Assembly.'

Snorri said: 'It is very true that you have much to lose there. I can see it coming that your side will prosecute the case with the greatest vehemence, and they will defend themselves in the same manner, and neither side will make any concessions to the other. You will not put up with that but will attack them; nor will there be any other alternative, for they will attempt to add insult to injury and only rebuff you on top of doing away with your kinsmen.' It was clear that he urged them on in every respect.

Then Gizur said: 'Well spoken, Snorri! You always comport yourself in a most excellent and chieftainlike fashion when most is at stake!'

Ásgrím said: 'I should like to know what sort of help you will give us if things turn out as you have said.'

Snorri replied: 'I shall give you proof of my friendship which will redound to the honour of you all. But I shall not go before the court with you. And if a fight breaks out at the Assembly you must not attack unless you feel certain that you can hold your own, because you are contending against powerful opponents. And in case you yield ground you may retreat this way, because I shall have my men here in battle array ready to stand by you. On the other hand, if it should turn out that they retreat before you, then I surmise they will be wanting to make for the vantage ground in the Almanna Gorge; and if they manage to get there, you will never be able to attack them successfully. I shall take it upon myself to bar their way with my men and keep them from gaining that stronghold, but we shall not follow them up, whether they turn north or south along the river. And when you have slain about as many of their men as I think you will be able to pay compensation for without being forced to lose your *goðorðs* or be driven from your homes, then I shall rush up with all my men and separate you. You will then comply with that, if you wish me to do as I propose.'

Gizur thanked him and said that Snorri had given them the advice which was in the best interest of all. Then they all left Snorri's booth.

'Where shall we go now?' asked Gizur.

'To the booth of the men of Modruvellir,' answered Ásgrím. So they went there.

140

They Win the Support of Gudmund the Powerful

As they came into the booth they saw Gudmund the Powerful sitting and talking with Einar Konálsson, his foster father. Einar was a wise man. They went up to Gudmund, and he welcomed them and made room for them to find seats in the booth. After they had exchanged news Ásgrím said: 'We have come to ask for your unqualified support.'

Gudmund replied: 'Have you already approached any other chieftains?'

They said they had approached Skapti and Snorri, and in a low voice they told him how they had fared with each of them.

Gudmund said: 'The last time[1] you approached me I acted rather shabbily and made difficulties. This time I shall show all the less hesitation the more difficulties I made before: I shall go to court with you together with all my followers and stand by you to the best of my ability and go to battle with you, if necessary, and lay down my life for you. I shall also pay back Skapti by having his son Thorstein Holmuth fight on our side, because Thorstein will not dare to do anything but what I wish since he is married to my daughter Jódís. Thus Skapti will be most likely to part us.'

They thanked him and after that they continued to talk for a long time out of earshot of the others. Gudmund advised them not to bend their knees before any other chieftain – he said that would be cringing – 'we'll take our chances with the men we now have. Always be armed when you go to the court for any dealings, but don't fight as things now stand!'

Then they all went back to their own booths. For the time being all this was known only to a few men. The Assembly meanwhile continued.

141

The Suit is Instituted

One day men went to the Law-Mount, and this was the position
of the chieftains: Ásgrím Ellida-Grímsson, Gizur the White,
Gudmund the Powerful, and Snorri Godi were above, beside the
Law-Mount, whereas the men from the East Firths stood further
below. Mord Valgardsson stood beside his father-in-law Gizur.
Mord was most eloquent. Gizur indicated to him that he was
now to serve notice of the suit for manslaughter and requested
him to proclaim it with so loud a voice that all might hear him
distinctly.

Mord summoned witnesses for the suit and said: 'I summon
them to testify that I serve notice of a suit punishable under the
law, against Flosi Thórdarson, forasmuch as he rushed at Helgi
Njálsson on that spot where Flosi Thórdarson attacked Helgi
Njálsson, and inflicted on him an internal wound, or else a marrow
wound, which proved a mortal injury and which brought about
Helgi's death. I herewith declare that for this cause he should be
condemned to outlawry and declared proscribed, neither to be fed
nor forwarded, and not to be given any aid or assistance whatever.
I declare forfeit all his goods and possessions, the half to me, and the
other half to the men of the Quarter who according to the law are
entitled to the goods and possessions of an outlaw. I serve notice of
this suit for manslaughter in that Quarter Court to which this
charge should come according to the law. I serve this notice
according to the law, and serve it so that all men at the Law-Mount
may hear me. I serve notice of total outlawry this summer against
Flosi Thórdarson. I serve notice of this suit, conducted by me as
proxy for Thorgeir Thórisson.'

There followed loud applause at the Law-Mount, because he
had prosecuted the case well and with authority.

A second time Mord began to speak. 'I summon you to testify,'
he said, 'that I serve notice of a suit against Flosi Thórdarson,

forasmuch as he inflicted on Helgi Njálsson an internal wound, or else a marrow wound, which proved a mortal injury and which brought about Helgi's death, and to wit, on that spot where Flosi Thórdarson made unprovoked attack, punishable under the law, on Helgi Njálsson: I herewith declare that you, Flosi, for this cause should be condemned to outlawry and declared proscribed, neither to be fed nor forwarded, and not to be given any aid or assistance whatever. I declare forfeit all your goods and possessions, the half to me, and the other half to the men of the Quarter who according to the law are entitled to the goods and possessions of an outlaw. I serve notice of this suit for manslaughter in that Quarter Court to which this charge should come according to the law. I serve this notice according to the law, and serve it so that all men at the Law-Mount may hear me. I serve notice of total outlawry this summer against Flosi Thórdarson. I serve notice of this suit, conducted by me as proxy for Thorgeir Thórisson.' Thereupon Mord sat down.

Flosi listened carefully but said not a word all the time.

Thorgeir Skorargeir arose and summoned witnesses: 'I summon them to testify that I serve notice of a suit against Glúm Hildisson because he struck fire, brought it to a blaze, and threw it into the buildings at Bergthórshvál, the time they burned in their house Njál Thorgeirsson and Bergthóra Skarphedin's daughter and all the people who perished there. I declare that for this cause he should be condemned to outlawry and declared proscribed, neither to be fed nor forwarded, and not to be given any aid or assistance whatever. I declare forfeit all his goods and possessions, the half to me, and the other half to the men of the Quarter who according to the law are entitled to the goods and possessions of an outlaw. I serve notice of this suit in that Quarter Court to which this charge should come according to the law. I serve this notice according to the law, and serve it so that all men at the Law-Mount may hear me. I serve notice of total outlawry this summer against Glúm Hildisson.'

Kári Solmundarson brought suit against Kol Thorsteinsson, Gunnar Lambason, and Grani Gunnarsson, and people observed that he spoke exceedingly well. Thorleif Crow brought suit against all the sons of Sigfús, and his brother Thorgrím the Tall brought suit against Módólf Ketilsson, Lambi Sigurdarson, and Hróar

Hámundarson, the brother of Leidólf the Strong. Ásgrím Ellida-Grímsson brought suit against Leidólf, Thorstein Geirleifsson, Árni Kolsson, and Grím the Red – and they all spoke well. After that the others gave notice of their suits and a great part of the day was spent in doing so. Then the men went back to their booths.

Eyjólf Bolverksson went with Flosi to his booth; they stepped to the east side of the booth. Flosi asked whether he could detect any flaws in these suits.

'None,' answered Eyjólf.

'What counsel shall we take now?' asked Flosi.

'I shall give you this counsel,' said Eyjólf. 'You must now transfer your office of *goði* to your brother Thorgeir and declare yourself a member of the Assembly of Áskel the *goði*, the son of Thorkel of Reykjardale in the Northern Quarter. And if they don't get to know it, then maybe they will commit a fatal error in that they will plead their suit in the court of the East Quarter when they should be pleading it in the court of the Northern Quarter.[1] They are likely to overlook this point and a Fifth Court charge will be lodged against them if they plead their suit in any court but the correct one. We shall press this charge then, but not before it is absolutely necessary.'

Flosi said: 'It looks as though we shall be repaid for the ring.'

'I don't know about that,' answered Eyjólf, 'but I will give you every possible legal help so that it will be conceded that nothing more could have been done. Now you must send for Áskel, and Thorgeir and one other man must also come here immediately.'

A short time later Thorgeir came. He took over the office of *goði*. Then Áskel also came. Thereupon Flosi declared himself Áskel's man. This came to the knowledge of no one but themselves.

142

Actions at the Quarter Court

Nothing further happened before the courts were going to convene. Both sides then made ready and armed themselves and put war-tokens on their helmets.

Thórhall Ásgrímsson spoke: 'Don't be hotheaded in anything, but behave as correctly as possible! If you run into any difficulty, let me know as quickly as you can and I shall advise you.'

Ásgrím and the others looked at him, and his face was as red as though it were covered with blood, and a hail of tears poured from his eyes. He asked them to bring him his spear; Skarphedin had given it to him, and it was a most precious weapon.

As they went on their way Ásgrím said: 'My son Thórhall was not in good spirits[1] as we left him behind in the booth. I do not know what he proposes to do now. Let us now proceed to the court with Mord Valgardsson and act as though we were concerned with nothing but the case he makes out against Flosi, because in him we shall make a better catch than in many others put together.'

Ásgrím sent a messenger to Gizur the White and Hjalti and Gudmund. They all came together and went immediately to the court of the East Quarter. They approached the court from the south, whereas Flosi together with all his men from the East Firth region approached the court from the north. With Flosi there were also the men from Reykjardale and Ljósavatn. Eyjólf Bolverksson was there too. Flosi looked at Eyjólf and said: 'The outlook seems good and it may be that you were not far wrong in your surmise.'

'Don't say too much about that!' said Eyjólf. 'The time will probably come when we may benefit from our plan.'

Mord Valgardsson summoned witnesses and proposed that all those who had to institute cases of outlawry before the court should cast lots to determine who should prosecute his case first, who second, and who last. He summoned them to the court with a legal citation in the hearing of the judges. Thereupon lots were cast as to the order of the suits, and it fell to his lot to institute his first.

Then Mord Valgardsson summoned witnesses a second time. – 'I summon witnesses to testify that I reserve for myself the right to exclude all errors in the words of my pleading in case my statements are excessive or erroneous. I reserve for myself the right to amend all my statements until my suit has received its due rights according to the law. I summon these witnesses for myself or for others who are to derive furtherance or benefit from this testimony.'

Mord continued: 'I summon witnesses to testify that I herewith require Flosi Thórdarson or anyone else who has legally taken over the defence for him to listen to this my oath and indictment and all the proofs therefore which I aim to produce against him. I herewith issue a lawful summons to the court so that the judges may hear it, one and all.'

Mord continued: 'I herewith summon witnesses to testify that I swear this oath on the book,[2] a lawful oath, and I declare before God that I shall prosecute this suit in the most truthful and most just manner and in accordance with the law, and I shall execute everything as prescribed by law as long as I have anything to do with this suit.'

After that he spoke as follows: 'I have summoned Thórodd as my first witness and Thorbjorn as my second. I have summoned these witnesses to testify that I have served notice of an assault, punishable under the law, against Flosi Thórdarson on that spot where Flosi Thórdarson attacked Helgi Njálsson with an assault, punishable under the law, when Flosi Thórdarson inflicted on Helgi Njálsson an internal wound, or else a marrow wound, which proved a mortal injury and which brought about Helgi's death. I have declared that for this cause he should be condemned to outlawry and declared proscribed, neither to be fed nor forwarded, and not to be given any aid or assistance whatever. I declared forfeit all his goods and possessions, the half to me, and the other half to the men of the Quarter who according to the law are entitled to the goods and possessions of an outlaw. I served notice of this suit in that Quarter Court to which this charge should come according to the law. I served this notice according to the law, and served it in the hearing of all men at the Law-Mount. I served notice of total outlawry this summer against Flosi Thórdarson. I served notice of this suit, conducted by me as proxy for Thorgeir Thórisson. In my notice I made use of the same words as I have now used in the declaration of my suit. I now make known this suit for outlawry in this form before the court of the East Quarter in the presence of Jón[3] and with the same words which I used when I served notice.'

Mord spoke: 'I have summoned Thórodd as my first witness and Thorbjorn as my second. I have summoned these witnesses to testify that I served notice of a suit against Flosi Thórdarson, forasmuch as he inflicted on Helgi Njálsson an internal wound, or else a marrow wound, which proved a mortal injury and which brought about Helgi's death, and to wit, on that spot where Flosi Thórdarson made unprovoked attack, punishable under the law, on Helgi Njálsson. I declared that for this cause he should be condemned to outlawry and declared proscribed, neither to be fed nor forwarded, and not to be given any aid or assistance whatever. I declared forfeit all his goods and possessions, the half to me, and the other half to the men of the Quarter who according to the law are entitled to the goods and possessions of an outlaw. I served notice of this suit in that Quarter Court to which this charge should come according to the law. I served this notice according to the law, and served it in the hearing of all men at the Law-Mount. I served notice of total outlawry this summer against Flosi Thórdarson. I served notice of this suit, conducted by me as proxy for Thorgeir Thórisson. In my notice I made use of the same words as I have now used in the declaration of my suit. I now make known this suit for outlawry in this form before the court of the East Quarter in the presence of Jón and with the same words which I used when I served notice.'

Then the witnesses to the fact that Mord had served notice of the suit went before the court and spoke these words, with one repeating the testimony and then both confirming it. – 'Mord summoned Thórodd as his first witness and me as his second. My name is Thorbjorn.' – Then he gave his father's name.[4] – 'Mord summoned us as witnesses to testify that he served notice of an assault, punishable under the law, against Flosi Thórdarson, forasmuch as he attacked Helgi Njálsson on that spot where Flosi Thórdarson inflicted on Helgi Njálsson an internal wound, or else a marrow wound, which proved a mortal injury and which brought about Helgi's death. He declared that for this cause Flosi should be condemned to outlawry and declared proscribed, neither to be fed nor forwarded, and not to be given any aid or assistance whatever. He declared forfeit all his goods and possessions, the half to him, and the other half to the men of the Quarter who according to the law are entitled to the goods and possessions of an outlaw. He served notice of this suit in that Quarter Court to which this charge should come according to the law. He served this notice according to the law, and served it in the hearing of all men at the Law-Mount. He served notice of total outlawry this summer against Flosi Thórdarson. He served notice of this suit, conducted by him as proxy for Thorgeir Thórisson. In his notice he made use of the same words which he used in the declaration of the suit, and which we have now used in our testimony. We have now presented our testimony according to the law, and we both agree in everything. This testimony that notice of the suit has been served we present in this form before the court of the East Quarter in the presence of Jón, and with the same words which Mord used when he served notice.'

A second time they presented to the court their testimony that notice of the suit had been served; this time they referred to the wounds first and to the assault last, but all other words were the same as they had used before, and this testimony that notice of the suit had been served they presented in this form before the court of the East Quarter in the presence of Jón, and with the same words which Mord had used when he had served notice.

Then the witnesses to the fact that the suit had been handed over to Mord went before the court; one repeated the testimony, and then both confirmed it, and they declared that Mord Valgardsson and Thorgeir Thórisson had summoned them as witnesses to testify that Thorgeir Thórisson had handed over to Mord Valgardsson a suit for manslaughter against Flosi Thórdarson for the slaying of Helgi Njálsson. – 'He handed over to him this suit with all the proofs of the accusation appertaining to the suit; he handed over to him the right to prosecute the case, to come to terms about it, and to make use of all the evidence just as though he were the real prosecutor of the suit. Thorgeir handed over the suit in accordance with the law and Mord took it over in accordance with the law.'

This testimony, that the suit had been handed over and that Thorgeir and Mord had summoned them as witnesses to that fact, they presented in this form before the court of the East Quarter in the presence of Jón.

They made all their witnesses as well as the judges swear oaths before they gave testimony.

Again Mord Valgardsson summoned witnesses – 'to testify,' he said, 'that I call upon these nine neighbours, whom I summoned in this case which I brought against Flosi Thórdarson, to take their seats on the west bank of the river, and I bid the defence challenge this jury. I call upon them in the hearing of the judges and I ask them in accordance with the law to come before the court.'

Again Mord summoned witnesses – 'to testify that I call upon Flosi Thórdarson, or anyone else who has taken over the defence from him, to challenge the jury which I have had seated on the west bank of the river. I call upon him in the hearing of the judges and I ask him in accordance with the law to come before the court.'

Again Mord summoned witnesses – 'to testify,' he said, 'that all the principal proofs of the accusation appertaining to the suit have now been presented: the summons to hear my oath has been served, the oath has been taken, the suit has been declared, testimony has been presented that notice of the suit has been served and that the suit has been handed over, the jury has been seated, and the defence has been called upon to challenge the jury. I summon these as witnesses to the proofs which have now been presented as well as to the fact that the suit is not to be considered abandoned, even though I should leave the court to seek further evidence or for any other reason.'

Then Flosi and his men went to the place where the jury of neighbours was seated. Flosi said to them: 'The sons of Sigfús will probably know whether these men who have been summoned are the rightful neighbours to the scene of the slaying.'

Ketil of Mork answered: 'There is one neighbour here who held Mord Valgardsson at the baptismal font and another who is a second cousin of his.'

Thereupon they reckoned up his kinship and confirmed it with an oath. Eyjólf summoned witnesses and proposed that the jury should remain seated until all were examined. Again Eyjólf summoned witnesses – 'to testify,' he said, 'that I challenge the right of these two men to sit on the jury' – and he named them as well as their fathers by name – 'on the grounds that one of them is a second cousin of Mord and the other stands in spiritual relation to him, for which reason they are legally disqualified from sitting on the jury. According to the law you two have no right to sit on the jury, since a valid legal objection has now been raised against you. I therefore challenge you in accordance with the accepted usage of the Althing and the law of the land. I disqualify you as jurors in the suit handed over to me by Flosi Thórdarson.'

Now all the people spoke up and declared that Mord's suit had been quashed, and all agreed that the defence was in a stronger position than the prosecution.

Then Ásgrím said to Mord: 'They haven't won this suit yet, even though they think they have delivered a sharp blow. Now someone must go and look up my son Thórhall and find out what counsel he has for us.'

Then a trusty and reliable man was sent to Thórhall to tell him precisely how the suit stood, and that Flosi and his men were of the opinion that they had disqualified the jury.

Thórhall spoke: 'I'll see to it that you'll not lose the suit for that reason. Tell them not to be taken in, even though an artful dodge has been practised on them, because this time that wiseacre Eyjólf has slipped up on something. Go back to them as quickly as you can and say that Mord Valgardsson should go before the court, summon witnesses, and declare that their challenge was invalid' – and he told him precisely how they should proceed.

The messenger went and repeated to them Thórhall's advice. Mord Valgardsson then went before the court and summoned witnesses – 'to testify,' he said, 'that I declare invalid Eyjólf Bolverksson's challenge. I declare this on the grounds that he disqualified them not because of their kinship to the actual plaintiff, but because of their kinship to him who pleaded the suit. I summon these witnesses for myself and for all those who are to derive benefit from this testimony.'

After that he had the witnesses testify before the court. Thereupon he went to the place where the jury of neighbours sat and said that those who had got up should sit down again, because they were rightful jurors according to the law.

Then all said that Thórhall had the best of it, and now all were of the opinion that the prosecution was in a stronger position than the defence.

Flosi asked Eyjólf: 'Do you consider this in accordance with the law?'

'I certainly do,' he answered; 'we certainly have committed a blunder. However, we shall fight it out with them a bit longer!'

Eyjólf summoned witnesses – 'to testify,' he said, 'that these two men are disqualified from sitting on the jury' – and he named them both – 'because you are men who neither own nor rent land. I deny you the right to sit on the jury, because a valid legal objection has been raised against you. I therefore disqualify you in accordance with the accepted usage of the Althing and the law of the land.'

Eyjólf then said that he would be very much surprised if they could refute that. All were of the opinion that the defence was now in a stronger position than the prosecution, and they all praised Eyjólf and said that no one could venture to cope with him in the knowledge of the details of the law.

Mord Valgardsson and Ásgrím Ellida-Grímsson sent a man to Thórhall to tell him how the suit stood. When Thórhall heard this he asked what property the jurors owned. The messenger answered that one of them made his living from his dairy stock of cows and ewes and that the other owned a third of the land on which he and the tenant farmer lived. He supplied his own means of subsistence, but had one hearth and one shepherd in common with the man who leased the land.

Thórhall said: 'They have slipped up on something just as they did before, and I will refute that challenge immediately, even though Eyjólf made a boast of this being in accordance with the law.'

Thórhall then informed the messenger precisely how they should proceed. The messenger returned and told Mord and Ásgrím what advice Thórhall had given. Mord went before the court and summoned witnesses – 'to testify that I declare invalid Eyjólf Bolverksson's challenge on the grounds that he disqualified men from serving on the jury who had a right to be there. The law is that every man who owns three hundreds or more [ells of homespun worth of] land is qualified to sit on a jury, even though he owns no dairy stock, and likewise he who makes his living from his dairy stock is qualified to sit on a jury, even though he leases the land.'

Thereupon he had the testimony brought before the court. He

then went to the place where the jurors were and told the two to be seated, since they had the right to sit on the jury. Then there arose a great hue and cry, and all said that the cause of Flosi and Eyjólf had received a damaging blow, and all agreed that the prosecution was now in a stronger position than the defence.

Flosi asked Eyjólf: 'Is this in accordance with the law?'

Eyjólf answered that his information was insufficient for him to be sure. Thereupon they sent a messenger to Skapti, the law-speaker, to ask whether it was in accordance with the law.[5] He sent back word that it was indeed, although there were few men who knew it. This was reported to Flosi and Eyjólf. Eyjólf then asked the sons of Sigfús about the other neighbours who had been summoned. They answered that there were four of them who had been summoned illegally – 'for there are some who are staying at home who lived closer to the scene.'

Eyjólf summoned witnesses to the fact that he disqualified all four from sitting on the jury, and he used the correct legal formulation for his challenge. After that he said to the five remaining jurors: 'You are obligated to render lawful justice to both sides. Now go before the court when you are called and testify that you are prevented from giving any verdict, since only five of you have been called whereas there should have been nine. If Thórhall can refute this he can win the whole suit!'

Their whole demeanour showed that Flosi and Eyjólf were jubilant, and now there was a chorus of voices to the effect that the suit for the burning was quashed and that the defence was now in a stronger position than the prosecution.

Ásgrím said to Mord: 'They had better wait until we have consulted Thórhall before they boast so much. Njál told me that he had taught Thórhall so much law that he would prove to be the best lawyer in all Iceland, if it ever came to the test.'

Then a man was sent to Thórhall to tell him how things stood and of the boasting of their opponents and the generally voiced opinion that Mord's suit had been quashed.

'That is all very well,' answered Thórhall, 'but as yet they will not derive much advantage from this. Go and tell Mord that he should summon witnesses and swear an oath that the majority of the jury was summoned legally. Let him then produce this testimony before the court and thus save the case for the prosecution.

He will have to pay three marks for each man he has summoned illegally, but he cannot be prosecuted for that at this meeting of the Assembly.'

The messenger returned and repeated all of Thórhall's words as exactly as possible. Mord went before the court, summoned witnesses, and swore an oath that the majority of the jury had been summoned legally. He said that he had herewith saved the case for the prosecution – 'our adversaries may glory in other things, but not in our having committed any great blunder.'

Then the general opinion was that Mord had handled the suit very well, but that Flosi and his men were using mainly tricks and technicalities.

Flosi asked Eyjólf whether this could be in accordance with the law. He answered that he did not know for a certainty, but that the law-speaker would have to clarify the situation.

Then Thorkel Geitisson went to the law-speaker in their behalf and told him how things stood and asked whether there was a legal basis to what Mord had said.

Skapti answered: 'There are more great lawyers nowadays than I had thought. I tell you that it is legally correct in every respect, and so much so that not a single objection to it can be raised; yet I thought I was the only one who knew this article of the law, now that Njál is dead, for so far as I know, he was the only man who knew it.'

Thorkel then returned to Flosi and Eyjólf and told them that it was legally correct.

Then Mord Valgardsson went before the court and summoned witnesses – 'to testify,' he said, 'that I bid these neighbours whom I have summoned in this suit which I have brought against Flosi Thórdarson to render a verdict, and to render it either for him or against him. I make this request in accordance with the law so that the judges may hear it, one and all.'

Then the neighbour witnesses on Mord's jury went before the court; one presented the verdict – and all confirmed it – and he spoke as follows: 'Mord Valgardsson summoned nine of us freemen on this jury; five of us stand here, but four have been disqualified. Testimony has been presented which prevented the four from rendering a verdict together with us. The law now obligates us to render a verdict. We were summoned to declare whether Flosi Thórdarson attacked Helgi Njálsson with an assault punishable under the law, on that spot where Flosi Thórdarson inflicted on Helgi Njálsson an internal wound, or else a marrow wound, which proved a mortal injury and which brought about Helgi's death. He summoned us to make such deposition which the law requires us to make and to declare before the court and which concerns this suit. He summoned us in accordance with the law; he summoned us in our hearing; he summoned us in the suit which was handed over to him by Thorgeir Thórisson. We have now all sworn oaths and formulated our verdict and we are all agreed: we render our verdict against Flosi and declare him guilty in this suit. We nine jurors present the verdict to this effect before the court of the East Quarter in the presence of Jón, as Mord summoned us to do. This is the verdict of all of us,' they said.

A second time they presented their verdict; this time they referred to the wounds first and to the assault last, but all other words were the same as they had used before. They rendered this verdict against Flosi and declared him guilty in the suit.

Mord Valgardsson went before the court and summoned witnesses to the fact that the jury of neighbours, which he had summoned in this suit, instituted by him against Flosi Thórdarson, had rendered a verdict and had found Flosi guilty of the accusation brought against him. He summoned these witnesses for himself or for others who were to derive furtherance or benefit from this testimony.

A second time Mord summoned witnesses. – 'I summon witnesses to testify that I call upon Flosi Thórdarson, or anyone else who has taken over the defence for him, to present his defence in the suit which I have brought against him, because all proofs appertaining to the suit have now been presented in accordance with the law: all testimony has been brought forward, the verdict of the jury has been given, and witnesses to the verdict and to all the proofs have been summoned. However, I reserve the right to maintain this suit if anything arises in their defence action which I may use in my accusation. I make this request in accordance with the law in the hearing of all the judges.'

'I must laugh, Eyjólf,' said Flosi, 'when I think of the wry faces they will make and the way they will scratch their heads when you present the defence.'

143

Eyjólf's Defence

Eyjólf Bolverksson went before the court and summoned witnesses – 'to testify that a lawful point of defence in this suit is the fact that the case was pleaded in the court of the East Quarter, whereas Flosi [previously] declared himself a member of the Assembly of the *goði* Áskel. Here now are witnesses who can testify that they were present and who can bear witness to the fact that Flosi transferred his office of *goði* to his brother Thorgeir and then declared that he had put himself under the protection of *goði* Áskel. I summon these witnesses for myself or for others who are to derive benefit from this testimony.'

A second time Eyjólf summoned witnesses. – 'I summon witnesses to testify,' he said, 'that I call upon Mord who is prosecuting this suit, or upon anyone else who is the leader of the prosecution, to listen to my oath and to the presentation of the defence which I shall bring forward, and to all the proofs which I shall present. I make this request in accordance with the law in the hearing of all the judges.'

Again Eyjólf summoned witnesses. – 'I summon witnesses to testify that I swear this oath on the book, a lawful oath, and I declare before God that I shall defend this suit in the most truthful and most just manner and in accordance with the law, and I shall execute everything which devolves upon me at this meeting of the Assembly.'

Eyjólf spoke: 'I summon these two men as witnesses that I present as a legal point of defence the fact that this suit was pleaded in a Quarter Court other than the correct one. I therefore claim that this suit is quashed. I present this defence in this form before the court of the East Quarter.'

Thereupon he had all testimony appertaining to the defence brought forward. Then he summoned witnesses to all the proofs of the defence and to the fact that all had now been duly presented.

Eyjólf summoned witnesses. – 'I summon witnesses to testify that I declare the judges incompetent to pronounce a verdict in the suit of Mord against Flosi, because a lawful defence has now been presented to the court. I declare this with a lawful protest, with an absolutely full and firm protest, as it is my right to protest in accordance with the accepted usage of the Althing and the law of the land.'

After that he called upon the court to pass judgement on his defence.

Ásgrím and his men then introduced the other suits for the burning, and the litigation took its regular course.

144

The Suit Before the Fifth Court

Ásgrím and his men now sent a messenger to Thórhall and had him informed of the difficult position into which they had got.

Thórhall answered: 'I see I have been too far away from the scene. This suit would not have taken this course if I had been present. I understand their tactics now; they are probably planning to bring you before the Fifth Court for presenting the case before the wrong court. And they probably also plan to bring about a division of the court[1] in the matter of the burning so that no judgement can be given, for now they have entered on a line of conduct such that they will not refrain from any malpractice. You must now go back as quickly as possible and tell Mord to cite both Flosi and Eyjólf for giving and accepting a bribe[2] and to demand the penalty of the lesser outlawry.[3] After that he must cite them a second time because they presented testimony which was irrelevant to the suit and thereby offended against the accepted regulations of the Assembly. Tell them that I say this: if two sentences of lesser outlawry have been pronounced on a man he is thereby condemned to complete outlawry. Your party must bring forward your suit first, because then it will be tried and judged first.'

Then the messenger went back and reported this to Mord and Ásgrím. Thereupon they went to the Law-Mount. Mord Valgardsson summoned witnesses. – 'I summon witnesses to testify that I herewith cite Flosi Thórdarson for bribery, in that he has paid money to Eyjólf Bolverksson for his assistance while here at the Assembly. I hereby declare that for this offence he should be sentenced to the lesser outlawry, not to be forwarded nor granted asylum unless life-money or sustenance-fee[4] be paid after the confiscation of his goods by the court of execution,[5] but that he otherwise be condemned to complete outlawry. I herewith declare that all his goods and possessions are forfeit, half to me and half to the men of that Quarter who according to the law are entitled to the goods and possessions of an outlaw. I call this suit before the Fifth Court to which it should come in accordance with the law; I call this suit before the court and I demand complete outlawry; I declare this in accordance with the law, and I declare it in the hearing of all men at the Law-Mount.'

A like citation he issued against Eyjólf Bolverksson for having accepted the bribe. This suit too he brought to the Fifth Court.

Again he charged both Flosi and Eyjólf with having presented at the Assembly testimony which according to the law was irrelevant to the suit. In doing so they brought on a mistrial, which would draw down upon them the penalty of lesser outlawry.

Thereupon they betook themselves away and to the court of laws just as the Fifth Court was being seated.

After Ásgrím and Mord had left, the judges in the Quarter Court were unable to agree as to how they should give judgement; some wished to give judgement in favour of Flosi, and others in favour of Mord and Ásgrím. Then Flosi and Eyjólf tried to establish a division of the court, but in doing so they were held up while Mord was issuing his citations. Shortly after, Flosi and Eyjólf were told that they had been cited to appear at the Law-Mount before the Fifth Court, and that two citations had been issued against them.

Eyjólf said: 'It is most unfortunate that we have allowed ourselves to be delayed here, so that they have anticipated us with their citations. That shows Thórhall's cleverness, and indeed no one is his equal for adroitness. Now it is their turn to plead their case in court, and that was all-important for them. Nevertheless we shall go to the Law-Mount and file suit against them, even though that may be of little avail now.'

Thereupon they went to the Law-Mount where Eyjólf cited them for bringing about a mistrial. After that they went to the Fifth Court.

When Mord and Ásgrím had arrived at the Fifth Court, Mord summoned witnesses and demanded a hearing for his oath and the presentation of his suit and of all the testimony which he planned to adduce against Flosi and Eyjólf. He called upon them with a lawful summons to come before the court; he called upon them in the hearing of all judges present.

In this Fifth Court co-jurors were to substantiate all oaths and swear oaths as to the truth of their own statements. Mord summoned witnesses. – 'I summon witnesses,' he said, 'to testify that I swear a Fifth Court oath. I pray to God that he may help me in this life and in the next as surely as I shall prosecute this suit impartially, in a just and truthful manner and in accordance with the law. I declare Flosi guilty in this suit, if my charges prove valid. I have not introduced money into this court in order to bias the court in this suit, nor will I do so; neither have I received money, nor will I do so, whether for purposes lawful or unlawful.'

Mord's two co-jurors then went before the court and summoned witnesses – 'to testify that we swear an oath on the book, a lawful oath; we pray to God that he may help us in this life and in the next as surely as we as free and freeborn men give our word of honour that we believe that Mord will prosecute this suit impartially, in a just and truthful manner and in accordance with the law. He has not introduced money into this court in order to bias the court in this suit, nor shall he do so; neither has he received money, nor shall he do so, whether for purposes lawful or unlawful.'

Mord had summoned as a jury nine neighbours[6] who lived near the Thing Plain. Then Mord summoned witnesses and presented the four charges which he had introduced against Flosi and Eyjólf, and he used the same words in the presentation of the charges which he had used in the summons. These suits for lesser outlawry he presented before the Fifth Court in the same form which he had used in the summons. Mord summoned witnesses and asked the nine neighbours to take their seats on the west bank of the river. Mord summoned witnesses and called upon Flosi and Eyjólf to challenge the jury. They came up to challenge the jury, looked at them carefully, but were unable to offer formal objection to anyone, and retired ill pleased.

Then Mord summoned witnesses and asked these nine neighbours whom he had summoned on the jury to give their verdict, either for or against.

Then Mord's jurors went before the court; one presented the verdict, and all confirmed it. They had all sworn a Fifth Court oath and found Flosi guilty in the suit, and gave their verdict against him. They presented their verdict in this form before the Fifth Court in the presence of the judge before whom Mord had declared his suit. Thereupon they gave verdicts in all the suits, as they were obligated to do, and everything took its legal course. Eyjólf Bolverksson and Flosi made every effort to find some flaw in the proceedings, but they found nothing.

Mord Valgardsson summoned witnesses. – 'I summon witnesses,' he said, 'to testify that these nine neighbours whom I have summoned in these suits which I have brought against Flosi Thórdarson and Eyjólf Bolverksson have now given their verdict and have declared them guilty in these suits.' – He summoned these witnesses for himself.

Again he summoned witnesses. – 'I summon witnesses,' he said, 'to testify that I call upon Flosi Thórdarson, or anyone else to whom he has handed over the legal defence, to come forward with his defence, because now all the testimony has been presented: the summons to hear my oath has been given, the oath has been taken, the suit has been declared, testimony has been presented that the summons was issued, the jury has been seated, the defence has been called upon to challenge the jury, the verdict has been given, and witnesses to the verdict have been summoned.' – He summoned witnesses to all the testimony which had been presented.

Thereupon the judge in whose presence the suit had been presented arose and summed up the case. First he summed up how Mord had called upon them to listen to his oath, to the declaration of his suit, and to all the testimony. Next he summed up how Mord and his co-jurors had taken their oaths. Then he summed up how Mord had pleaded his suit, and he used the same words in his summary as Mord had used in his declaration and summons – 'and in this form,' he said, 'he presented the suit before the Fifth Court, and he used the same words in his summons.' Then he summed up that men had presented testimony that the summons had been issued, and he repeated all the words which Mord had used before in his summons, and which they had used in presenting their testimony – 'and which I,' he said, 'have used in my summary. And they presented their testimony in this form before the Fifth Court with the same words as he had used when he had issued the summons.' After that he summed up how Mord had selected the jury. Then he summed up how Mord had called upon Flosi – or anyone else to whom he had handed over the defence – to challenge the jury. Then he summed up how the jury of neighbours had gone before the court, had given their verdict, and had found Flosi guilty in the suit – 'and this nine-man verdict,' he said, 'they presented in this form before the Fifth Court.' Then he summed up how Mord had cited witnesses to testify that the verdict had been given. Last he summed up how Mord had cited witnesses to all the testimony and had called upon the defence to reply.

Mord Valgardsson cited witnesses. – 'I cite witnesses,' he said, 'to testify that I forbid Flosi Thórdarson, or anyone else to whom he has handed over the defence, to raise any further objections, because now all testimony appertaining to the suit has been presented with this summing up, and the proofs for the prosecution have been brought forward.'

Thereupon the foreman of the court summarised this testimony.

Mord cited witnesses and asked the judges to render a verdict in the suit.

Then Gizur the White said: 'You will have to do more than this, Mord, because four twelves cannot render a verdict.'

Flosi asked Eyjólf: 'What counsel shall we take now?'

Eyjólf answered: 'We must make the best of a difficult situation. We shall have to bide our time, but it is my guess that they will make a mistake in the prosecution, because Mord asked for an immediate decision in the case. They are supposed to exclude six men from the court, and after that they are supposed to call upon us before witnesses to exclude six others. However, we shall not do that, because in that case they will have to exclude these six men too, and they are likely to overlook that. Their entire suit falls to the ground if they fail to do that, for the verdict in any suit is to be given by a court of only three dozen.'

Flosi said: 'A clever man you are, Eyjólf and there are few likely to get ahead of you!'

Mord Valgardsson summoned witnesses. — 'I summon witnesses,' he said, 'to testify that I exclude these six men from the court' — and he named them all — 'I deny you the right to sit in the court. I exclude you in accordance with the accepted usage of the Althing and the law of the land.'

After that he called upon Flosi and Eyjólf before witnesses to exclude six other men from the court, but Flosi and Eyjólf refused to do so.

Mord then had the court give judgement in the suit. When the judgement was given, Eyjólf summoned witnesses and declared that the decision was invalid, as was also everything else which they had done in the suit. His grounds were that three and one-half twelves had given judgement, whereas only three twelves should have done so — 'and now we will press our Fifth Court suits against them and declare them outlaws.'

Gizur the White said to Mord: 'You have overlooked an important point! This is a great misfortune! What are we to do about it, kinsman Ásgrím?'

Ásgrím answered: 'We shall send a messenger to my son Thórhall and find out what he advises us to do.'

145

The Battle at the Althing

When Snorri learned what turn matters had taken in the suits he began to draw up his forces in battle array between the Almanna Gorge and his booth,[1] and he told his men beforehand what they were to do.

The messenger now came to Thórhall and told him what had happened: that Mord Valgardsson and all the men on his side would be outlawed and that the entire suit for manslaughter against Flosi had fallen to the ground.

When Thórhall heard this he was so shocked that he could not speak a single word. He jumped up from his bed, reached with both hands for the spear which Skarphedin had given him, and drove it through his foot. Flesh and the core of the boil clung to the spear as he drew it out from his foot, and a torrent of blood and matter poured out along the floor like a brook. Then he issued from the booth without limping and he walked so fast that the messenger could not keep pace with him. He went on until he came to the Fifth Court. There he met Grím the Red, a kinsman of Flosi's, and as soon as they met, Thórhall hurled his spear at him. The blow struck the shield and split it in two, but the spear passed right through him, so that the point came out between his shoulders. Then Thórhall yanked the spear from his dead body.

Kári Solmundarson caught sight of this and said to Ásgrím: 'Your son Thórhall has come here and has at once slain a man. It would be an everlasting shame if he alone had the courage to avenge the burning!'

'Nor shall that be!' answered Ásgrím. 'Let us at them!'

Then there was a loud outcry in the multitude and a mighty battle cry raised. Flosi and his men made a stand against them, and both sides urged on their men vigorously. Kári Solmundarson rushed against Árni Kolsson and Hallbjorn the Strong. No sooner did Hallbjorn see Kári than he slashed at him, aiming at his leg, but

Kári leaped up, so that Hallbjorn missed him. Kári turned on Árni Kolsson and struck at him. The blow fell on his shoulder, shattering both shoulder blade and collarbone, and pierced the breast. Árni immediately fell down dead.

Thereupon Kári cut at Hallbjorn; the blow struck the shield, pierced it, and cut off Hallbjorn's big toe. Hólmstein hurled a spear at Kári, but he caught it in mid-air and hurled it back, and it brought death to a man in Flosi's following.

Thorgeir Skorargeir came up to face Hallbjorn the Strong. Thorgeir thrust at him with one hand, and with such force that Hallbjorn fell, and only with great difficulty was he able to regain his feet and escape. Then Thorgeir faced Thorvald Thrumketilsson and levelled a blow at him with the battle-axe 'Battle-Troll' which had been Skarphedin's. Thorvald brought his shield before himself; Thorgeir's blow cut it in two, and the upper point of the axe-head entered the chest, penetrating the inner organs, and he fell dead at once.

Now to tell about Ásgrím Ellida-Grímsson, his son Thórhall, Hjalti Skeggjason, and Gizur the White: they attacked Flosi, the sons of Sigfús, and the others who had been at the burning. There was a very bitter fight, and as a result of their determined attack Flosi and his men gave ground. Gudmund the Powerful, Mord Valgardsson, and Thorgeir Skorargeir made their attack on the position of the men from the Axe Firth, the East Firths, and Reykjardale, and there, too, was bitter fighting.

Kári Solmundarson made for Bjarni Brodd-Helgason. He seized a spear and thrust at Bjarni, striking his shield. Bjarni twisted his shield aside, else the spear would have pierced him. He returned the blow, aiming at Kári's foot, but Kári jerked it back, turning on his heel, so that Bjarni missed him. Kári immediately hewed at him with his sword. At that moment a man ran up and put his shield in front of Bjarni. Kári's blow split the shield from top to bottom and the point of his sword struck the man's thigh and ripped open the entire leg. He fell immediately and was a cripple all his life. Then Kári gripped a spear with both hands and hurled it at Bjarni. Bjarni had no other choice but to throw himself sidewise to the ground to avoid the blow, and as soon as he regained his feet he made good his escape.

Thorgeir Skorargeir attacked Hólmstein Spak-Bersason and Thorkel Geitisson, and in the end both Hólmstein and Thorkel fled. Then the men of Gudmund the Powerful hooted at them with loud shouts of derision.

Thorvard, the son of Tjorvi of Ljósavatn, received a serious wound on his arm, and it was thought that it was the spear of Halldór, Gudmund the Powerful's son, which had inflicted the wound. Thorvard received no reparations for the wound as long as he lived.

Now there was a great tumult of battle, and though the story tells of some exploits, many more are not recorded.

Flosi had instructed his men to head for the stronghold in the Almanna Gorge if they should be overpowered, for there they could be attacked from only one side. Now the band under the leadership of Hall of Sída and his son Ljót had withdrawn before the attack of Ásgrím and his son Thórhall and had gone down along the east bank of the Axe River.

Hall said: 'It will be a terrible misfortune if all people in the Assembly come to blows! If I have my way we shall ask for help to part them, even though there will be some people who will reproach us for that. Wait here at the head of the bridge while I go down to the booths and ask for help.'

Ljót replied: 'If I see that Flosi and his following need help from our men, then I will hurry to them immediately.'

'You may do just as you think best,' said Hall, 'but I beg you to wait for me!'

Now the ranks of Flosi's men broke in flight and they all fled to the west bank of the Axe River, but Ásgrím and Gizur the White with their entire host pursued them. Flosi and his men made their way up between the river and the fortified booth. There Snorri Godi had drawn up his men in such tight array that they could not pass. Snorri Godi called to Flosi: 'Where are you going in such a hurry? Who is chasing you?'

Flosi answered: 'You are not asking this because you do not already know! Isn't it you who is hindering us from getting through to the stronghold in the Almanna Gorge?'

'No, it isn't I,' answered Snorri, 'but I do know which men are to blame, and I can tell if you want to know; they are Thorvald Curly-Beard and Kol.'[2] At that time both men were already dead, but they had been the worst scoundrels among Flosi's men.

Then, turning to his men, Snorri said: 'At them now! Thrust and chop at them and drive them away from here! They will hold out for only a short time here if the others attack from below. In that case don't pursue them, but let them fight it out with one another.'

A son of Skapti Thóroddsson was Thorstein Holmuth, as was written before.[3] In this battle Thorstein fought on the side of Gudmund the Powerful, his father-in-law. As soon as Skapti learned of this, he went to the booth of Snorri Godi, planning to ask Snorri to go with him to part them. But he had not quite got to the door of Snorri's booth when the battle raged most fiercely. Ásgrím and his men were just then advancing from below.

Then Thórhall called to his father Ásgrím: 'There is Skapti Thóroddsson now, father!'

'So I see, my son!' Ásgrím answered. With that he hurled his spear at Skapti. It struck him just below the thickest part of the calf and pierced both legs. Skapti fell from the blow and could not get up again. Those standing by him did not know what to do except drag him flat on his back into the booth of a certain sword-furbisher.[4]

At that moment Ásgrím and his men attacked so vigorously that Flosi and his men gave ground, retreating south along the river to the booth of the men from Modruvellir. A man named Solvi was standing in front of a booth. He was boiling meat in a large kettle; he had just taken the meat out and the broth was seething at a great rate. Solvi caught sight of the fleeing East Firthers who had come up quite close to him. He said: 'I wonder if all those East Firthers fleeing here are cowards! Even Thorkel Geitisson is taking to his heels! It is a big lie if so many people say of him that he is all courage; but now he is running faster than anyone!'

Hallbjorn the Strong happened to be nearby and said: 'You won't come to say that all of us are cowards!' And with that he grabbed him, raised him aloft, and pitched him head first into the cauldron. Solvi died immediately. Right then Hallbjorn was set upon and had to make off.

Flosi hurled a spear at Brúni Haflidason. It struck him in the middle and he fell dead. He was one of the men in Gudmund the Powerful's band.

Thorstein Hlennason drew the spear from the wound and hurled it back at Flosi. It struck his leg and he received such a bad wound that he fell, but he got up again immediately. Then they turned to the booth of the men from Water Firth.

At that time Ljót and Hall had crossed the river from the east with all their men. When they got up on the lava bed a spear came hurtling from the direction of Gudmund the Powerful's band. It struck Ljót in the middle and he fell down dead at once. It was never learned who had caused his death.

Flosi and his men now made their way up past the booth of the men from the Water Firth. Thorgeir Skorargeir then said to Kári Solmundarson: 'There is Eyjólf Bolverksson now in case you want to pay him back for the ring!'

'I think that is very much in order,' said Kári, and he took a spear from one of the men and hurled it at Eyjólf. It struck Eyjólf in the middle, going right through him, and he fell down dead.

Then there was a short lull in the battle. Snorri Godi came up with his band at that moment. Skapti was there with him, too, and they ran between the two parties so that they could not fight. Hall, too, joined them with the intention of separating them, and a provisional truce was arranged for the duration of the Assembly. The dead bodies were laid out and carried to the church,[5] and the wounds of the injured were bandaged.

The following day men went to the Law-Mount. Hall of Sída stood up and asked to be heard; permission was granted immediately. He spoke: 'Serious events have taken place here, both in slayings and in litigations. Now I shall again show that I am a humble man. I wish to ask Ásgrím and the other men who are the leaders in these suits to grant us a settlement acceptable to both sides.' – And he pleaded with them with many eloquent words.

Kári said: 'Even if all others come to an agreement between them, nevertheless I shall accept no such settlement! You probably want to offset the burning with these slayings, but we will not stand for that!' And Thorgeir Skorargeir concurred in that.

Then Skapti Thóroddsson stood up and said: 'You would have done better, Kári, not to run away from your relatives[6] than now to except yourself from this settlement!'

Kári then spoke three verses:

> How, pray, canst thou, hero,[7]
> heap reproaches on me –
> for lesser cause oft crossed were
> keen swords – that I bolted?
> You who, flinching, forthwith
> fled and were borne to shelter
> when that the hilts'-tongue-blades[8]
> whined aloud, you red-beard?
>
> Little longed he e'er to[9]
> lay strife down, but rather –
> scarce he risked his scalp e'er –
> Skapti urged men to it;
> when by cooks his carcass
> was carried, for shame, lengthwise,
> all a-tremble with terror,
> to the booth of the juggler.[10]
>
> Gay and gamesome thought it
> Grím's and Helgi's slayers –
> wrong the deed and reckless –
> in ruins to lay Njál's dwelling;
> though, after the Thing, me-
> thinks, will on the mountain-
> heights many spear-hurlers
> hear a tune that is different.

This was greeted with loud laughter.[11] Snorri Godi smiled and spoke in a low voice, but so that many, nevertheless, were able to overhear it:

> Spares not Skapti to spoil all;[12]
> his spear hurled but now Ásgrím,
> nowise gives way Hólmstein;
> unwillingly fights Thorkel.

This was followed by even louder laughter.[13]

Hall of Sída spoke: 'All men know what great grief I have suffered in the loss of my son Ljót. Very likely some will think that of all the men who perished here he is the one for whom the greatest fine should be demanded. However, to bring about a settlement I will make the sacrifice of asking no reparations for my son, and at the same time I am prepared to offer my adversaries pledges of peace. I ask you, Snorri Godi, and other excellent men to effect a settlement between us.'

After that he sat down. His words were received with loud approval, and all praised his good will. Then Snorri Godi arose and made a long and eloquent speech, and he asked Ásgrím and Gizur as well as the other leaders on their side to agree to a settlement.

Ásgrím said: 'When Flosi made his entrance into my home I was of a mind never to come to terms with him, but now, Snorri Godi, I wish to do so because of your words and those of other friends of ours.'

Thorleif Crow and Thorgrím the Tall said the same thing – that they wished to make a settlement – and in every way they urged their brother Thorgeir Skorargeir also to agree to a settlement, but he refused and said that he and Kári would never part.

Thereupon Gizur the White said: 'It now depends on Flosi whether he will agree to a settlement, considering that some men intend not to be included in it.'

Flosi said that he would be willing to do so – 'and the fewer good men I have against me,' he said, 'so much the better!'

Gudmund the Powerful spoke: 'As far as I am concerned, I wish to join hands in a settlement for the slayings which have taken place here at the Assembly on the condition that the suit for the burning be not dropped.'

Gizur the White, Hjalti, Ásgrím, and Mord Valgardsson all concurred in this. Thereupon a settlement was brought about. They agreed to refer the matter to twelve men for decision; Snorri Godi together with other good men and true were to pronounce the award. The decision was that the slayings were to offset each other, man for man, and money atonements were to be paid for any slayings on the one side which had no counterparts on the other. An award was also made in the suit for the burning. Njál was to be atoned for with a triple wergild, and Bergthóra with a double wergild. The slaying of Skarphedin was to offset that of Hoskuld Hvítanessgodi. Grím and Helgi were each to be atoned for with a double wergild, and a single wergild was to be paid for each person burned to death at Bergthórshvál. There was nothing in the settlement about the slaying of Thórd Kárisson.[14]

Furthermore, Flosi and all the Burners were to be banished from the country, but they did not have to leave that same summer unless they wished to do so. However, if they had not left by the time three winters had passed, then he and all those involved in the burning were to be declared condemned to total outlawry. It was also decided that the sentence of outlawry should be published either at the autumn Assembly or at the spring Assembly, whichever was preferred. Flosi's exile was to be limited to three years, but that of Gunnar Lambason, Grani Gunnarsson, Glúm Hildisson, and Kol Thorsteinsson was to be permanent.

Then Flosi was asked whether he wished any settlement made for the wound inflicted on him, but he answered that he did not want to make money out of that.

Eyjólf Bolverksson was declared to have fallen on his trickery and perversion of justice.

This settlement was now confirmed by a clasping of hands and it was well kept ever after. Snorri Godi had great honour from these proceedings and received fine presents from Ásgrím and his kinsmen. No award was given Skapti for his injury.

Gizur the White, Hjalti, and Ásgrím invited Gudmund the Powerful to their homes. He accepted the invitations, and each of them gave him a gold ring. Then Gudmund rode home to the north and was praised by all for his conduct in these proceedings.

Thorgeir Skorargeir asked Kári to accompany him, but first they kept company with Gudmund all the way north to the height of the mountains, and at their parting Kári gave Gudmund a gold buckle, and Thorgeir gave him a silver belt, both splendid gifts. They parted in the greatest friendship. Thereupon Gudmund rode to his home in the north, and he is now out of this saga. Kári and Thorgeir rode south from the mountains to the Hreppar district, and from there to the Thjórsá River.

Flosi and all the Burners rode east to the Fljótshlíd district. There Flosi permitted the sons of Sigfús to look after their farms. Then he learned that Thorgeir and Kári had ridden north with Gudmund the Powerful, and so the Burners believed that Kári and his men probably planned to remain in the northland permanently. The sons of Sigfús asked for leave to go to the east slope of the Eyjafell Mountain to collect money which they had outstanding at Hofda-

brekka. Flosi gave them permission, but warned them to be on
their guard and to return as soon as possible. Flosi himself rode up
into the Godaland district, then over the mountains and north of
Eyjafell Glacier, nor did he stop until he came home to Svínafell.

And now it remains to be told that after Hall of Sída had
foregone any reparations for his son, in order to effect a settlement,
everybody at the Assembly contributed toward a gift to him. It
amounted to eight hundred ounces of silver, that is, a fourfold
wergild. But all the others who had been with Flosi received no
compensation for their torts, and they were incensed about that.

146

Kári Attacks the Sons of Sigfús

The sons of Sigfús stayed at home two days, but on the third day
they rode east to the Raufarfell farm and stayed there overnight.
There were fifteen of them altogether and they gave no thought
to any danger. From there they rode away late and planned to be
at Hofdabrekka by evening. They rested and let their horses graze
in Kerlingardale and afforded themselves a long sleep there.

That same day Kári Solmundarson and Thorgeir Skorargeir rode
east over the Markar River and continued to Seljalandsmúli; there
they came upon some women. The latter knew them and said:
'You are not in such high spirits as the sons of Sigfús; yet you, too,
proceed unwarily!'

Thorgeir asked: 'Why are you concerned about the sons of
Sigfús? What do you know about them?'

'They stayed at the Raufarfell farm last night,' they answered,
'and they planned to be in Mydale this evening, and we were glad
to see how much they were in fear of you, and they asked when
you might be expected home.'

Then the women continued on their way, but Kári and Thorgeir
spurred on their horses.

Thorgeir asked: 'What you do propose we should do? What
would you prefer? Do you think we should pursue them?'

Kári answered: 'I have no objections to riding after them, but I don't care to say what I would like most, for as the saying goes: "a long life is often granted those who are slain with words." However, I know what you have in mind; you plan to take on eight men. Yet, that would be less of an exploit than when you slew seven men in the gorge and had to lower yourself down to them with a rope.[1] However, that is the way it is with you and your kin; you want to win glory in everything. Now I can't do less than be an eyewitness in order to tell afterwards what happened. So let us two alone ride after them, because I see that is what you have in mind.'

Thereupon they rode east by the upper route, but did not touch on Holt farm, because Thorgeir did not wish to implicate his brothers in what might happen. Then they rode east to Mydale where they met a man who was leading a horse with crates of peat on its back. That man addressed them: 'All too few are with you, brother Thorgeir!'

'What do you mean by that?' asked Thorgeir.

'I mean that you might bag a big catch,' he answered. 'The sons of Sigfús rode past here and are probably sleeping all day, east in Kerlingardale, because they did not plan to go any farther this evening than to the Hofdabrekka farm.'

Thereupon Kári and Thorgeir continued on their journey up on to Arnarstakk Heath, and nothing particular happened until they arrived at the river in Kerlingardale. It was running high. They rode up along the river, for there they saw saddled horses. They rode up to them and saw some men sleeping in a hollow; their spears were stuck in the ground just above them. They took the spears and threw them into the river.

Thorgeir asked: 'Would you wish us to wake them?'

Kári answered: 'You ask as though you had not already made up your mind not to attack men in their sleep and thus commit shameful manslaughter!'

Thereupon they shouted at the men; they all awoke and reached for their weapons. Kári and Thorgeir did not attack them before they were armed. Thorgeir Skorargeir made a dash at Thorkel Sigfússon. At that moment a man ran up to Thorgeir from behind, but before he could do him any injury Thorgeir raised his axe, 'Battle-Troll', with both hands and drove the axe-hammer into the head of this man who stood behind him, so that his skull was shattered to bits. He fell dead immediately. Swinging his axe forward Thorgeir struck Thorkel on the shoulder and hewed off his entire arm. Mord Sigfússon, Sigurd Lambason, and Lambi Sigurdarson rushed at Kári. Lambi attacked Kári from the rear and threw his spear at him. Kári caught sight of him and jumped up just as he thrust at him, spreading his legs apart as he did so. The spear lodged in the ground, and Kári leaped upon it and broke it in two. He had a spear in one hand and a sword in the other, but he had no shield. With his right hand he thrust at Sigurd Lambason; the blow struck his breast and the spear came out between his shoulders. He fell dead immediately. With his left hand Kári cut at Mord Sigfússon and struck his groin, severing both groin and backbone. Mord fell flat on his face and died immediately. After that Kári turned around on his heel like a top and made for Lambi Sigurdarson; the latter saved himself by flight.

Then Thorgeir faced Leidólf the Strong; each struck at the other at the same moment, and Leidólf's blow was so powerful that it cut off clean that part of the shield which it struck. Wielding his axe 'Battle-Troll' with both hands Thorgeir dealt him a blow so that the lower point of the blade struck Leidólf's shield, splitting it, and the lower point cut his collarbone and went into his chest. Just then Kári came up and slashed off Leidólf's leg between hip and knee; Leidólf fell dead at once.

Ketil of Mork said: 'Let us run to our horses! We cannot hold our own against these terrible fighters!'

So they ran to their horses and leaped into the saddle.

'Shall we pursue them?' asked Thorgeir. 'We could still slay a few more!'

'The one riding hindmost,' said Kári, 'is one whom I should not like to slay. It is Ketil of Mork. Our wives are sisters,[2] and furthermore, in our quarrels until now he has behaved most decently.'

Then they mounted their horses and rode until they came to the Holt farm. Thorgeir had his brothers go east to the Skógar farm, owned by them too, because he did not want them implicated in any breach of truce. After that Thorgeir kept many armed men with him, never less than thirty. They were all in high spirits. By general consent both Kári's and Thorgeir's prestige had grown considerably, and people often called to mind how those two had attacked fifteen, killing five, and putting to flight the ten who escaped.

To return to Ketil and those with him: they rode as fast as their horses could carry them until they got to Svínafell where they reported how badly they had fared. Flosi said that he expected as much – 'and this is a warning to you,' he said, 'and you are not to go about like that in the future!'

Flosi was a man of the most pleasant disposition and a most gracious host, and he is said to have had the qualities of a chieftain in most respects. He remained on his farm that summer and also the following winter. However, that winter after Yule, Hall of Sída and his son Kol came from the east to see him. Flosi welcomed him, and they often spoke about the litigation at the Assembly. Flosi said that they had already paid dearly for it. Hall replied that his surmise concerning the outcome of their suit had been close to the truth. Flosi asked his advice as to what seemed best to him.

Hall answered: 'My advice is that you make a settlement with Thorgeir, if that is at all possible. However, he is not likely to be easily amenable to a settlement.'

'Do you believe that the slayings will then be at an end?' asked Flosi.

'No, I do not,' answered Hall, 'but you will have to contend with fewer men if Kári stands alone. However, if you do not come to terms with Thorgeir, it will mean your death!'

'What terms shall we offer him?' asked Flosi.

'The terms which he will accept will seem hard to you,' answered Hall. 'He is likely to agree to a settlement only on the condition that he pay nothing for what he has already done, and that he receive as atonement for Njál and his sons that third to which he is entitled.'[3]

'Those are hard terms,' said Flosi.

'For you the terms are not so hard,' said Hall, 'because it is not your obligation to bring suit for the slaying of the sons of Sigfús. His brothers have that obligation, and it is the business of Hámund the Halt to bring suit for the slaying of his son.[4] But as for you, you are likely to come to an agreement with Thorgeir, because I shall go there with you, and he will most probably receive me well. However, none of the men who have to bring suit will dare to remain at their farms in the Fljótshlíd district if they do not share in this settlement, for that would prove to be their death. With Thorgeir's frame of mind that is just what may be expected.'

The sons of Sigfús were now sent for and the matter was presented to them. The result of their talk, thanks to Hall's persuasive words, was that they agreed to everything which he suggested and expressed their wish to make a settlement.

Grani Gunnarsson and Gunnar Lambason said: 'If Kári is left out of the settlement, it will be easy for us to make him fear us no less than we him.'

'Rather not talk that way,' said Hall. 'You will have to pay dearly if you have anything to do with him, and you will suffer heavy blows before matters are settled between you.'

With that they broke off their talk.

147

Flosi and Thorgeir Come to Terms

Hall of Sída, his son Kol, and four others rode west over Lómagnúp Sand, and from there they went west across Arnarstakk Heath, and did not stop until they came to Mydale. There they asked whether Thorgeir was at home at Holt, and they were told that he probably was. Hall was asked where he planned to go.

'To Holt,' he answered.

They said that he was without doubt on a good mission. He stayed there for a time and they let their horses graze. Then they saddled them and rode to Sólheim in the evening and stayed there overnight. The following day they rode on to Holt.

Thorgeir was out in front of the house, as were Kári and his men, for they saw the horsemen coming and recognised Hall. He wore a blue cape and in his hand he carried a small axe adorned with silver.

When they had arrived in the home field Thorgeir went to meet him and lifted him from the saddle. Both Thorgeir and Kári kissed him and led him in between them into the sitting-room, placed him in the high-seat on the dais, and asked him for all the news. He stayed there that night.

The following morning Hall brought up the matter of the

settlement with Thorgeir and told him what reparations they offered him, and he talked about the matter with many well-chosen and conciliatory words.

Thorgeir replied: 'You probably know that I did not want to come to any terms with the men involved in the burning.'

'Conditions were very different at that time,' answered Hall. 'You were still wrought up after the fight. For another matter, you have committed many slayings yourself since that time.'

'I suppose that is so,' said Thorgeir; 'but what reparations do you offer Kári?'

'Such terms of settlement will be offered him which will seem honourable to him, if he is willing to accept a settlement,' answered Hall.

Kári said: 'This I would ask of you, Thorgeir, that you agree to a settlement, because your present good position can hardly be improved.'[1]

'I would like it ill,' said Thorgeir, 'for me to accept a settlement and so draw away from you if you don't also accept it.'

'No, I will accept no reconciliation,' said Kári, 'though I consider that now we have avenged the burning; but my son is still unavenged, and that vengeance I aim to accomplish myself, however I get it done.'

However, Thorgeir would accept no reparations until Kári threatened to fall out with him unless he did so. Thereupon Thorgeir by a handshake assured Flosi and his men of peace until arrangements for a reconciliation were made, and Hall did likewise upon the assurances of Flosi and the sons of Sigfús.

Before parting Thorgeir gave Hall a gold ring and a scarlet cloak, and Kári gave him a silver necklace with three golden crosses on it. Hall thanked them kindly for the gifts and rode away highly honoured, nor did he stop till he arrived at the Svínafell farm. There Flosi gave him a cordial welcome. Hall told Flosi all about his business and the discussion which he had had with Thorgeir, and also that Thorgeir would not accept any agreement until Kári had threatened to fall out with him unless he did so. — 'But as for Kári himself, he would not come to terms.'

Flosi said: 'There are few men like Kári, and I would gladly be like him in mind and character!'

Hall and his men stayed there for a time. Then at the appointed time they travelled west to the meeting arranged for the settlement, and both parties met at the Hofdabrekka farm, as had been agreed upon. They then discussed the settlement and everything proceeded just as Hall had predicted. Thorgeir agreed to a settlement on the condition that Kári be allowed to live with him forever, if he so chose – 'and neither party is to harm the other at my home. Also, I don't care to collect the fines from each and every one of them, but would prefer that you, Flosi, be responsible for collecting them from your followers. I furthermore insist that the pact made at the Assembly about the burning be upheld in every detail, and that you, Flosi, pay me the third awarded to me in full.'

Flosi quickly agreed to all this. Thorgeir gave up neither his demand for banishment nor for outlawry from certain districts then imposed. Then Flosi and Hall rode home east.

Hall said to Flosi: 'Abide faithfully by the terms of this settlement, son-in-law, both with regard to going abroad, the pilgrimage to Rome,[2] and the payment of the fines. If you carry out everything manfully, you will earn the reputation of being a man of mettle, even though you did become involved in this unfortunate feud.'

Flosi said he would do so. Then Hall journeyed home to Svínafell and remained there for the time being.

148

Kári Meets Bjorn and his Wife

Thorgeir Skorargeir rode home from the meeting for the arrangement of the settlement. Kári asked whether a settlement had been effected. Thorgeir said that they were now completely reconciled. Kári took his horse and meant to ride away.

'No need for you to ride away,' said Thorgeir, 'because it was stipulated in the settlement that you be allowed to live here forever, if you so wished.'

Kári said: 'No, cousin, it can't be that way, because as soon as I commit a slaying, people will say I was in collusion with you, and that I don't want to happen. However, I do wish that you let me entrust my property to you and that it be assigned to you and to my wife Helga, Njál's daughter, and to my three daughters. Then it will not be confiscated by my enemies.'

Thorgeir agreed to everything which Kári asked of him, and had Kári's property made over to him by shaking hands. Thereupon Kári left. He had with him two horses and his weapons and clothes and some valuables in gold and silver. He rode west around the Seljalandsmúli promontory and then up along the Markar River and continued up into the Thórsmork district.

In that region there are three farms, all called At Mork. In the middle one there lived a man named Bjorn, who was called Bjorn the White.[1] He was the son of Kadal, the son of Bjálfi. Bjálfi had been the freedman of Ásgerd, the mother of Njál and of Holta-Thórir. Bjorn was married to Valgerd, the daughter of Thorbrand, the son of Ásbrand. Her mother was Gudlaug, who was a sister of Hámund, the father of Gunnar of Hlídarendi. Valgerd was married to Bjorn because of his money and did not love him much, but they did have children together. They had an abundance of everything at their farm. Bjorn was given to praising himself, much to the displeasure of his wife. He was keen of eye and quick of foot.

Kári went there to stay overnight, and the two received him with open arms. He remained there that night, but the following morning he said to Bjorn: 'I wish that you would permit me to stay here, for I think I would be well taken care of here. I would like to have you along on my journeys, because you are keen of eye and swift of foot, and I also believe you are good in a fight.'

'I won't deny that I am keen of sight, nor do I lack courage for doing bold deeds,' said Bjorn. 'However, you have probably come here because you have no other place to go. But since you request it, Kári, I shan't treat you like anybody or everybody. I shall certainly help you in everything you ask of me.'

His wife said: 'The devil take your boasting and bragging! Don't make yourself and him believe such nonsense! But gladly shall I give Kári food and other such good things which, as I know, may be of use to him. But don't you depend on Bjorn's hardihood, because I'm afraid you'll find it will turn out differently from what he says!'

Bjorn said: 'You have often scolded me, but I have so much confidence in myself that I know I shall show my heels to no one. And proof of this is that there are few men who will pick a quarrel with me, for the reason they don't dare to.'

Kári stayed in hiding there for a time, and this was known only to a few. People believed that Kári must have gone to the north to visit Gudmund the Powerful, because Kári had Bjorn tell his neighbours that he had met Kári on the road and that he was riding up to Godaland and on to Gásasand[2] to find Gudmund the Powerful at Modruvellir. This account was spread throughout the countryside.

149

Flosi and his Men Prepare to Leave the Country

Now Flosi spoke to his comrades, the Burners: 'The time has not yet come for us to sit in peace and quiet. We shall have to be thinking of going abroad and paying our fines and fulfilling the conditions of the settlement as manfully as possible. Let each secure passage for himself wherever seems best to him.'

They asked him to make the arrangements.

Flosi said: 'We shall ride east to Horn Firth because there is a ship laid up ashore there which belongs to a man from Drontheim, Eyjólf Nose. He wishes to get married, but can't marry the woman he has in mind unless he settles here in Iceland. We will buy the ship from him, because we shall have little cargo but many men. It is a large ship and it will take us all.'

They said no more about this for the time being, but shortly thereafter they rode east and journeyed on till they came to Bjarnaness in Horn Firth. There they met Eyjólf, for he had wintered over there. Flosi was well received there, and he and his company stayed there overnight. The following morning Flosi asked Eyjólf what kind of payment he would accept for the ship. The Norwegian was not unwilling to sell the ship if he could get for it the price he wanted. He said he wanted land, but it had to be close to where he was now. Eyjólf gave Flosi the details of his negotiations with the farmer with whom he stayed. Flosi said that he would co-operate in bringing about the marriage and after that buy the ship from Eyjólf, and the Norwegian was greatly pleased to have him do that. Flosi offered him land in the Borgarhofn district. The Norwegian then took up the negotiations with the farmer in the presence of Flosi, and Flosi used his influence in his behalf, so that the matter was settled between them. Flosi gave a piece of land at Borgarhofn to the Norwegian, and by handshake took over ownership of the ship. Flosi also bought from him twenty hundreds worth of wares, which was included in the bargain.

Thereupon Flosi rode home. He was so esteemed by his followers that he could receive wares from them either on loan or as a
gift, whichever he wished. Flosi now rode home to Svínafell and
stayed there for a while. He sent Kol Thorsteinsson and Gunnar
Lambason east to Horn Firth. They were to stay there with the
ship, prepare everything for sailing, set up booths, pack the wares
in sacks, and collect everything that was necessary for the trip.

Now we must tell that the sons of Sigfús informed Flosi that they
intended to journey to the Fljótshlíd district, there to look after
their farms and to fetch from there wares and other commodities
which they needed. – 'We do not have to be on our guard
against Kári any longer,' they said, 'if he is in the north.'

Flosi answered: 'I do not know how much truth there is to such
rumours of Kári's whereabouts. It seems to me that things observ-
able at closer range than this have often turned out to be untrue.
My advice is that you travel in large numbers, separate from one
another as little as possible, and be very much on your guard. And
you, Ketil of Mork, should bear in mind the dream of which I told
you; you requested that we two keep it secret, for there are many
in your company who were called at the time.'

Ketil replied: 'Everything in man's life must happen just as it is
bound to happen! But I know you mean the best with your
warnings.' After that they spoke no more about it.

Thereupon the sons of Sigfús and all those detailed to go with
them got ready for their journey, eighteen altogether. At their
departure they kissed Flosi. He bade them farewell and said that he
would never again see some of those who were riding away.
However, they did not let themselves be deterred, but went their
way. Flosi had told them to fetch his wares in Medalland and carry
them east and to do the same in Landbrot and in the Skógahverfi
district.

They rode to the Skaptá River Junction and then along the
mountain way north of the Eyjafell Glacier, and continued down
into the Godaland district, skirting the woods, into the Thórsmork
district. Bjorn of Mork caught sight of the company of horsemen
and at once went up to meet them. They greeted each other in
friendly manner, and the sons of Sigfús enquired after Kári
Solmundarson.

'I met Kári,' said Bjorn, 'but that is a very long time ago. He was riding from here to Gásasand on his way to Gudmund the Powerful, and I rather thought at the time that he was afraid of you all. He felt himself quite friendless.'

Grani Gunnarsson said: 'He is likely to be still more afraid of us later! He will find that out when he comes within spear range of us! We don't stand a bit in awe of him, now that he is alone!'

Ketil of Mork asked him to be quiet and not to use such big words. Bjorn asked them when they would be coming back.

'We shall stay in the Fljótshlíd district about a week,' they answered. They told him when they would be riding back over the mountain route. With that they parted.

The sons of Sigfús rode to their homes where they were welcomed by their servants. They stayed there a week.

Bjorn came home, met Kári, and told him all about the journey and plans of the sons of Sigfús. Kári said that he had shown great fidelity to him in this business.

Bjorn said: 'I should think there is greater risk of anyone else but myself not being dependable, once I pledged you my protection and care.'

His wife remarked: 'You are bad enough as it is without becoming a traitor, too!'

Kári stayed there the following six days.

150

The Second Encounter Between Kári and the Sons of Sigfús

Kári now said to Bjorn: 'We shall ride east over the mountains and down to Skaptá River Junction and travel stealthily through the district of Flosi's followers, because I plan to board ship in Álpta Firth and leave the country.'

Bjorn said: 'That is an extremely risky journey, and few would have the courage to take it beside us two!'

His wife said: 'If you don't stand by Kári faithfully, I want you to know that you shan't ever get into bed with me again, and my kinsfolk will see to a division of our goods between us!'

'More likely, wife,' he said, 'that you will have to find some other cause for separation than that, because I shall have witness borne for me how bold and dauntless I am when it comes to fighting!'

That same day they rode east into the mountains, but never along the usual route, down into the region of the Skaptá River Junction, skirting the upper boundaries of all farms till they got to the Skaptá River. They led their horses into a depression, but they remained on the lookout and posted themselves so that they could not be seen themselves.

Kári now asked Bjorn: 'What shall we do if they ride down on us from the mountains?'

'Aren't there two alternatives?' said Bjorn. 'One would be to ride away from them to the north along the slope and let them ride past, and the other, to wait and see if any lag behind, and then fall upon them.'

They talked a long while about this, and one moment Bjorn was all for fleeing as fast as he could, and the next he was all for waiting and fighting it out with them, and Kári found it extremely diverting.

The sons of Sigfús left their farm that day, as they had told Bjorn. They went to Mork, knocked on the door, and wanted to speak with Bjorn. His wife came to the door and greeted them. They asked for Bjorn at once, but she told them he had ridden down the valley toward the Eyjafell Mountains and on to Seljalandsmúli promontory and on east to Holt – 'for he has money outstanding there,' she said.

They believed this for they knew that Bjorn did have money outstanding there. After that they rode east from there into the mountains and they did not stop until they came to Skaptá River Junction. They rode down along the Skaptá River and let their horses graze, just as Kári and Bjorn thought they would. Then they split up. Ketil of Mork rode east to Medalland, and eight men went with him; the others lay down to sleep and were aware of no danger until Kári and Bjorn came upon them. A small tongue of land projected into the river. Kári went out on it and asked Bjorn to stand behind him and not to expose himself too much to danger – 'but give me all the help you can!'

'I had never thought to use anyone to shield me,' said Bjorn, 'but as matters stand, I suppose it is best you have your way. But with my cleverness and dash I may still be of service to you and do our enemies no little damage.'

By that time they had all jumped up and ran to attack the two. Módólf Ketilsson was ahead of them all and he thrust his spear at Kári. Kári had his shield before himself, so that the blow struck the shield and the spear stuck fast in it. Kári then twisted the shield so hard that the spear broke off. Then he drew his sword and cut at Módólf. Módólf struck back, but Kári's sword struck the hilt of Módólf's sword, glanced off to his wrist, and severed his hand, so that both hand and sword fell to the ground. Kári's sword went in Módólf's side between his ribs, so that he fell and was dead immediately.

Grani Gunnarsson grasped a spear and hurled it at Kári who had thrust his shield into the ground so that it stood fast.[1] With his left hand he caught the spear in flight, hurled it back at Grani, and then took up the shield again in his left hand. Grani held his shield before him. Kári's spear struck it, passing right through it and into Grani's thigh below the groin, pinning him to the ground. Grani could not free himself from the spear until his comrades pulled him away from it, and covering him with their shields they brought him into a little depression.

A man rushed up and aimed to cut off Kári's leg. He managed to get to his side, but Bjorn cut off that man's arm and then sprang back again behind Kári, so that no one could do him any harm. Kári made a sweep at that same man with his sword and cut him in two at the waist.

At that moment Lambi Sigurdarson rushed at Kári and struck at him with his sword. Kári caught the blow on the flat of his shield and the sword did not bite. Then Kári lunged at him with his sword and struck his breast, so that the sword point came out between his shoulders and that was his death.

Then Thorstein Geirleifsson rushed at Kári intending to attack him from the side. However, Kári caught sight of him and slashed at him with his sword and cut him in two at the shoulders. Shortly after that he dealt a mortal blow to Gunnar of Skál, a worthy free-holder.

Bjorn had wounded three men who had meant to attack Kári, and yet he was at no time so far forward that he was in any danger. Neither he nor Kári was wounded in the encounter, but those who escaped were all wounded. They all then leaped on their horses and rode out into the Skaptá River as fast as they could, and they were so frightened that they did not stop at any farm, nor did they dare to report what had happened. Kári and Bjorn shouted at them in derision as they rode away. They rode east to the Skógahverfi district and did not stop until they came to Svínafell. Flosi was not at home when they arrived, and therefore no attempt was made to pursue Kári and Bjorn from there. It seemed to all that their journey had brought them the greatest shame.

Kári rode to Skál and served notice of the slayings committed by himself. He reported the death of the master of the house and of five others as well as the injury inflicted upon Grani, and told them it would be advisable to bring Grani home if he was to survive. Bjorn said he had not had the heart to slay him, although he had deserved it, but those who answered said that few had bitten the dust through him. Bjorn replied that he was now in a position to make as many of the men of Sída bite the dust as he wished. They said that would be bad indeed.[2] Thereupon Kári and Bjorn rode away.

151

The Third Clash with the Burners

Kári asked Bjorn: 'What counsel shall we take now?'

Bjorn answered: 'Don't you think it is of the greatest importance that we be as clever as possible?'

'Yes, certainly!' said Kári.

'Then we don't need to think long,' said Bjorn. 'We'll fool them like so many stupid giants. We'll pretend to be riding north into the mountains, but as soon as the hill conceals us from their view, we'll turn back and ride down along the Skaptá River and hide at the most convenient place as long as the search is at its hottest; that is, if they pursue us.'

Kári answered: 'That's what we shall do! That is just what I had planned, too!'

'Now you can see,' said Bjorn, 'that I am not the man to fall short, in mind any more than in bravery!'

Then Kári and Bjorn rode down along the Skaptá River, as they had planned. There a branch of the river flowed to the south-east. They turned down along the middle branch and did not stop until they came to Medalland at a swamp called Kringlumyr. There was lava rock all about it. Kári asked Bjorn to take care of the horses and to stand guard – 'because I am very sleepy.'

Bjorn watched the horses and Kári lay down to sleep, but slept but a short time before Bjorn waked him. He had brought their horses together and they were now standing near them. Bjorn said: 'You certainly do need me! Any other man, if he were not as stouthearted as I, might well have run away from you, because now your enemies are coming at you, so that you must get ready!'

Kári then went and took his stand under a projecting crag and Bjorn asked: 'Where shall I stand now?'

Kári answered: 'You can choose one of two things: either stand behind me and use your shield to protect yourself, if necessary, or else mount your horse and ride away as fast as you can!'

'That I don't want to do,' said Bjorn, 'and for a number of reasons! In the first place, if I ride away, malicious tongues might say that I left you in the lurch out of cowardice, and in the second place, I know what a catch they think they have in me, so two or three would pursue me. But then you would have to do without my help. No! I prefer to stand by you and defend myself with you.'

They did not have to wait long before pack horses were driven by around the swamp, and there were three men with them.

Kári said: 'These men do not see us.'

'Then let them ride by,' said Bjorn.

Thereupon the three rode on past them, but the other six then came riding at them. They immediately leaped from their horses and made for Kári and Bjorn. Glúm Hildisson was the first to rush at Kári and to hurl his spear at him. Kári turned around quickly on his heel, so that Glúm missed him and the blow struck the rock. Bjorn saw this and immediately hewed off the point of Glúm's spear. Standing on slanting ground Kári struck at Glúm and his sword caught Glúm's leg above the knee and severed it high up. Glúm died at once.

Then Vébrand and Ásbrand, the sons of Thorfinn, attacked Kári. Kári rushed at Vébrand and plunged his sword through his body and then cut off both Ásbrand's legs from under him. At that same moment both Kári and Bjorn were wounded. Ketil of Mork rushed at Kári and thrust his spear at him, but Kári jerked his leg up and the spear ran into the ground. Kári leaped on the spear shaft and broke it in two. Then Kári took a firm hold on Ketil. Bjorn rushed up and wanted to kill him, but Kári said: 'No, let him be! I shall offer Ketil peace! Even though it should often come to pass that I have the power of life and death over you, Ketil, I shall never slay you!'

Ketil made not much reply, but rode away with his comrades and told the tidings to those who had not already heard them. They also reported the news to the men of the district, who immediately collected a great force of armed men and went along all the waterways and so far north into the mountains that they were on the search for three days. After that they returned to their homes, but Ketil and his comrades rode east to Svínafell and reported the news there.

Flosi was little moved by what had befallen them; in fact, he said he was not so sure whether that was the end of it – 'for no man alive now in Iceland is Kári's equal.'

152

Kári Rewards Bjorn

Now we must tell of Kári and Bjorn that they rode to the place called Sand.[1] There they led their horses below a sandy hill grown with beachgrass. They cut some of this for their horses so they would not perish of hunger. Kári estimated the time so correctly that he left there just when the others gave up their search for him. He rode by night up through the district, and after that to the mountains, and then along the same route which they had followed when they had ridden east. They did not stop until they came to Mork.

Now Bjorn said to Kári: 'Now you must show that you are my good friend when you talk to my wife, because she will not believe a single word of what I say. However, for me this is very important. Repay me thus for the good help which I have rendered you!'

'I shall do that,' said Kári.

Thereupon they rode up to the farm. Bjorn's wife asked for the news and welcomed them home.

Bjorn answered: 'Things are getting worse and worse, old girl!'

She did not say much, but merely smiled. Then she asked: 'How did Bjorn conduct himself?'

Kári answered: 'Bare is the back without brother behind it![2] Bjorn conducted himself well. He wounded three men and received wounds himself and stood by me the best he could.'

They stayed there three days and then rode to Holt to see Thorgeir and told him in private of what had occurred, for the news had not reached there yet. Thorgeir thanked Kári, and it was quite plain that he was pleased. He also asked Kári what still was undone of what he planned to do.

Kári answered: 'I am to slay Gunnar Lambason and Kol Thorsteinsson, if the chance presents itself. Then we shall have slain fifteen men, counting the five we two killed together. And now I have one more request to make of you.'

Thorgeir said that he would do whatever he requested

'I wish that you take this man into your protection,' said Kári. 'His name is Bjorn and he has been with me in these slayings. I wish that you exchange his home for a well-stocked farm near you. And protect him so that no vengeance be taken against him. And that is well befitting you, the generous chieftain!'

'So it shall be,' answered Thorgeir.

Then he secured for Bjorn a well-stocked farm at Ásólfsskáli, and he himself took over the farm at Mork. Thorgeir himself moved the inmates and the stock of Bjorn's farm to Ásólfsskáli. He also helped Bjorn to come to terms with his enemies, so that he was at peace with everybody. Thereafter Bjorn was regarded as much more of man than he had been before.

Then Kári rode away and did not stop until he came west to Ásgrím Ellida-Grímsson at Tunga. There Kári received a hearty welcome. Kári told him all the incidents of the fight. Ásgrím was well pleased with the outcome and asked what Kári now planned to do.

Kári answered: 'I plan to go abroad on their track and to lie in wait and slay them if I can get at them.'

Ásgrím said that there was no man who was the equal of Kári in courage.

Kári stayed there a few days and then rode to Gizur the White, who received him with open arms. Kári stayed there for a time and then told Gizur that he was about to journey to Eyrar. At their parting Gizur gave Kári a good sword. Kári then journeyed to Eyrar and took passage with Kolbein the Black. Kolbein, who was from the Orkneys, was an old, trusted friend of Kári and a man of great valour. He welcomed Kári cordially and declared that he would share his fortunes.

153

Flosi Becomes the Retainer of Earl Sigurd of the Orkneys

Flosi now rode east to Horn Firth and most of his followers with him. They brought along their wares and other supplies and baggage which they had to take abroad with them. After that they fitted out the ship for the journey. Flosi then stayed by the ship until it was ready, and as soon as there was a fair wind they put to sea. They had a long passage and stormy weather and lost their bearings completely.

One day it happened that some great waves, as big as three seas together, broke over the ship. Then Flosi said that they probably were near land and that these were breakers on a shoal. There was a thick fog, and the weather grew worse till it blew a gale. One night, before they knew it, they were driven ashore. The crew was saved, but the ship was wrecked completely and the cargo could not be saved. Then they had to look about for shelter and warmth for themselves. The following day they went up on a hill. The weather was now fine. Flosi asked if anyone knew what land this was. Two of them had been there before and said they knew it for certain. – 'We have come to Mainland in the Orkneys.'

'We might have done better to land elsewhere,' said Flosi, 'because Helgi Njálsson, whom I slew, belonged to the retinue of Earl Sigurd Hlodvisson!'[1]

Then they looked for a hiding place and spread moss over themselves and lay there for a time, but it was not long before Flosi said: 'We shall not lie here any longer, but get up before the inhabitants discover us hiding!'[2]

Then they arose and took counsel. Flosi said to his men: 'Let us all go and put ourselves in the power of the earl, because we have no other choice, since he can do with us whatever he will, if he so wishes!'

Thereupon they all left that place. Flosi warned them not to tell anyone what had happened or anything of their journey before he told the earl himself. Then they went on until they met some men who directed them to the earl. They went before the earl, and Flosi and all the others greeted him. The earl asked who they might be, and Flosi gave his name and informed him from which section of Iceland he had come. The earl had already learned of the burning, and so he immediately knew who the men were. He then asked Flosi: 'What can you tell me about Helgi Njálsson, my retainer?'

'I can tell you this,' said Flosi, 'that I cut off his head!'

The earl ordered his men to seize them, and this was done. At that moment, Thorstein, the son of Hall of Sída, came forward. Flosi was married to Steinvor, Thorstein's sister.[3] Thorstein himself was one of Earl Sigurd's retainers. When Thorstein saw Flosi being seized, he went before the earl and offered him all his possessions for Flosi's life. The earl was exceedingly furious for a long time, but thanks to the intercession of Thorstein and other well-meaning men – for Thorstein had many friends who joined in his plea – it finally came about that the earl agreed to a settlement and gave Flosi and his followers quarters. The earl followed the generous custom of great lords in that he let Flosi fill the same position in his retinue which Helgi Njálsson had held.[4] Thus Flosi became Earl Sigurd's retainer and soon he became a great favourite with the earl.

154

The Meeting of the Chieftains

Kári and Kolbein the Black put to sea from Eyrar half a month later than Flosi and his followers had done from Horn Firth. They got a fair wind and were out at sea only a short time. They landed at Fair Island which lies between the Shetlands and the Orkneys. There a man by the name of Dávid the White received Kári into his home. He told Kári all that he had learned about the journeys of Flosi and his men. Dávid was a very good friend of Kári, and gave him shelter during the winter. They got news of everything that happened on the island of Mainland and in the west.

Earl Sigurd had extended an invitation to his brother-in-law, Earl Gilli of the Hebrides, to celebrate Yule with him. Gilli was married to Svanlaug, Earl Sigurd's sister. There also came to Earl Sigurd a king of Ireland who was named Sigtrygg. He was the son of Óláf Kváran; his mother was Kormlod. She was a most beautiful woman and showed the best qualities in all matters that were not in her own power, but in all those that were, people said she showed herself of an evil disposition. She had been married to a king named Brján, but now they were divorced, for he was a king of the noblest qualities. He lived in Kankaraborg in Ireland. His brother was named Úlf Hreda, a great champion and warrior. A foster son of Brján was named Kerdjálfad. He was the son of King Kylfir who had fought many battles against King Brján, but who had left the land, fleeing before him, and had entered a monastery. But when King Brján had gone south on a pilgrimage he had met King Kylfir and become reconciled with him; whereupon King Brján took King Kylfir's son Kerdjálfad into fosterage and loved him more than his own sons. Kerdjálfad was already grown to manhood at the time the events to be told here took place, and was a most valiant man.

Dungad was the name of one of King Brján's sons; a second was named Margad, and a third Tadk, for which we say Tann. Tann was the youngest, but the elder sons of King Brján were full grown and very brave men. Kormlod was not the mother of King Brján's children. She was so filled with hate for King Brján after her divorce that she would have wished to see him dead. King Brján forgave all whom he had outlawed three times for the same misdeed, but if they transgressed more often, he had them judged in accordance with the law. From this one may gather what kind of king he was.

Kormlod was forever egging on her own son Sigtrygg to slay King Brján and she sent him to Earl Sigurd to ask for his support. Sigtrygg came to the Orkneys before Yule, and Earl Gilli likewise came there at the same time, as we wrote before. In Earl Sigurd's hall they were seated as follows: King Sigtrygg sat on the high-seat in the middle, and on each side of him sat one of the earls. The followers of King Sigtrygg and Earl Gilli sat close by them, and farther away from Earl Sigurd sat Flosi and Thorstein Hallsson. The whole hall was filled to capacity.

King Sigtrygg and Earl Gilli wished to learn the circumstances surrounding the burning of Njál and also of what had taken place since that time. Gunnar Lambason was selected to tell the story and he was given a chair.

155

The Slaying of Gunnar Lambason and Sigtrygg's Preparations for Battle

It was at this time when no one expected it that Kári and Kolbein and Dávid the White came to the island of Mainland. They went ashore immediately, leaving only a few men to guard the ship. Kári and his comrades went straight to the residence of the earl and arrived at his hall while men were sitting at table and drinking. It was just then that Gunnar was telling the story, and Kári and the others stood outside and listened. It was on the Yule day.

King Sigtrygg asked: 'How did Skarphedin stand up under the burning?'

'Well enough, at the beginning,' answered Gunnar; 'yet at the end he cried.' The whole story he told with bias and many lies.

Kári could not stand that. He dashed into the hall with drawn sword and spoke this verse:

> Boast the battle-eager –
> but, I wonder, know they
> harshly how avenged was
> the hero? – of Njál's burning;
> nor were the gladly giving
> gold-dispensers[1] therefor –
> ravening ravens[2] their flesh got
> raw – repaid grudgingly.[3]

With that he ran to the centre of the hall and dealt Gunnar Lambason such a powerful blow on his neck that his head flew off on the table before the king and the earls. The tables as well as the clothing of the earls were covered over and over with blood. Earl Sigurd recognised the man who had done this deed and said: 'Seize Kári and slay him!'

Kári had been a member of Earl Sigurd's retinue and he was

loved like no other man, and therefore, whatever the earl said, no one arose.

Kári spoke: 'Many are likely to say, sire, that I did this deed in your behalf, in order to avenge the man who was your retainer.'

Flosi said: 'Kári has not done this without cause; he has entered into no settlement with us. He did what was his right to do.'

Kári left the hall and no one pursued him. He and his followers returned to their ship. The weather was good and they sailed south to Caithness and went ashore at Freswick at the home of a worthy man named Skeggi. They stayed with him for a long time.

The men in the hall of the Orkney earl cleansed the tables and carried out the dead man. The earl was told that Kári and his men had sailed south to Scotland.

King Sigtrygg said: 'That was a mighty brave man who did so bold a deed and was not concerned about his own safety!'

Earl Sigurd answered: 'No one is Kári's equal in valour!'

Thereupon Flosi began and told the story of the burning. He told it without bias, and so they believed him.

King Sigtrygg then brought up the matter of his errand to Earl Sigurd and asked him to go to war with him against King Brján. The earl hesitated for a long time, but at length he consented, on one condition. It was that he was to marry King Sigtrygg's mother Kormlod and become a king in Ireland, should Brján be slain. All his men tried to dissuade Earl Sigurd from participating in this venture, but without avail. They parted after Earl Sigurd had promised to join him, and Sigtrygg on his part had promised him his mother and the kingdom. It was agreed that Earl Sigurd should come to Dublin with all his army on Palm Sunday.

Thereupon Sigtrygg sailed south to Ireland and informed his mother Kormlod that the earl had promised to join him and what he, on his part, had promised Earl Sigurd for his help. She was pleased with this, but said that they would have to gather an even larger force. Sigtrygg asked where they might expect to do so. She answered that two vikings were lying off the west coast of Man with thirty ships – 'and so hardy are they that no one can withstand them. One is named Óspak and the other Bródir. You must go and find them and not spare anything to get them on your side, whatever their demands may be!'

Sigtrygg went to look for the vikings and found them off the west coast of Man. Sigtrygg brought up the matter of his errand immediately, but Bródir refused his help until at last Sigtrygg promised him the kingdom and his mother. This, however, was to be kept secret so that Earl Sigurd should hear nothing of it. Bródir was to come to Dublin before Palm Sunday. King Sigtrygg journeyed back to his mother and told her how things stood.

After that Óspak and Bródir conferred, and Bródir told Óspak about his agreement with Sigtrygg, and asked Óspak to go to war with him against King Brján. He added that the matter was of the greatest importance to him. Óspak said that he did not wish to fight against so good a king. Both became enraged and split their forces; Óspak took ten ships and Bródir twenty. Óspak was a heathen and an exceedingly shrewd man. He anchored his ships inside the sound, whereas Bródir lay outside the sound. Bródir had been a Christian and had been consecrated a deacon, but he had cast off the faith and became an apostate. He sacrificed to heathen gods and was greatly skilled in magic. He had a coat of mail no iron could pierce. He was both tall and strong, and his hair was so long that he could tuck it under his belt; it was black.

156

The Portents Before the Battle of Clontarf

One night[1] it happened that a great din was heard by Bródir and his men, so that they all awoke and hurriedly put on their clothes. At the same time seething blood rained down upon them. They held their shields over them, and yet many were scalded. That portent lasted till dawn, and one man on each ship died. They slept the following day.

In the next night there came that same din, and they all started up. Their swords leaped from their sheaths, and axes and spears flew up and battled one another. The men were so hard pressed by the weapons that they had to protect themselves; yet many were wounded, and one man on each ship died. This portent lasted till dawn, and again they slept the following day.

The third night there was the same din. Ravens pounced upon them and beset them so fiercely that they had to defend themselves with their swords and protect themselves with their shields. This lasted till daybreak. Again one man from each ship died. Then they again slept, for the first. When Bródir awoke he sighed deeply and gave orders to lower a boat – 'because I wish to see Óspak.' Then he and men with him got into the boat.

When he met Óspak he told him of the portents which had occurred and asked him to explain what they might signify. Óspak did not want to tell him before he was given a pledge of peace. Bródir gave him this pledge, but nevertheless, Óspak procrastinated until night, because Bródir would never commit a slaying by night.

Óspak then said: 'The blood raining down upon you signifies that you will shed many a man's blood, your own as well as that of others. The great din which you heard foretells a world catastrophe, and you will all soon die. The weapons attacking you signify war, and the ravens which beset you signify the devils in whom you trust and who will drag you down to the torments of hell.'

Bródir was so enraged that he could give no answer. He returned immediately to his men and had his ships set up a blockade across the sound and had them fastened to the shore with cables. He planned to slay Óspak and all his men the following morning. Óspak saw through their plans. He vowed to accept the faith, if he escaped, and to join King Brján and follow him to the day of his death. Then he devised the stratagem of covering all his ships and poling them along the shore and cutting the cables of Bródir's fleet. Bródir's ships then drifted together, but the men on board were asleep. Óspak and his men thus got out of the fjord and sailed west to Ireland and did not stop till they got to Kankaraborg. Óspak told King Brján everything he had learned. He was baptised and entrusted himself to the protection of the king.

Thereupon Brján gathered his forces throughout his realm. They were all to assemble at Dublin the week before Palm Sunday.

157

The Battle of Clontarf

Earl Sigurd Hlodvisson prepared to sail from the Orkneys. Flosi
offered to join him, but the earl would not accept the offer, since
Flosi still had to redeem his pledge of a pilgrimage to Rome. Flosi
offered fifteen of his followers to join the expedition, and the earl
accepted that; but Flosi himself journeyed with Earl Gilli to the
Hebrides. With Earl Sigurd there went Thorstein Hallsson, Hrafn
the Red, and Erling of Stroma.[1] The earl did not want Hárek to
go along, but promised he would be the first to be told what
happened. The earl arrived at Dublin with all his army on Palm
Sunday; Bródir had already arrived with his whole force. Bródir
tried to learn by means of his sorcery how the battle would turn
out, and the answer was this: if it was fought on a Friday, King
Brján would win the victory but die; and if it was fought before
that time, then all who were against him would fall. Then Bródir
said that they should not fight before Friday.

On Thursday a man on a dapple-grey horse came riding up to
Kormlod and her people; he held a javelin in his hand and he talked
for a long time with Bródir and Kormlod.[2]

King Brján had come up to the fortified town with his entire
army, and on Friday the army of the Norsemen issued from the
town. Both hosts arranged themselves in battle array. Bródir
headed one wing, King Sigtrygg the other, and Earl Sigurd was
stationed in the middle.

We are told that King Brján did not wish to give battle on Good
Friday; therefore a shield-castle[3] was set up about him and his army
stationed in front of that. Úlf Hreda headed the wing facing Bródir,
and Óspak with King Brján's sons headed the wing facing Sigtrygg,
but Kerdjálfad stood in the middle and had the banners carried
before him.

Now the armies advanced against each other and there was a
furious battle. Bródir waded through the ranks of his enemies,

felling all who stood foremost, and no iron could wound him. Úlf Hreda then went to face him and thrust at him thrice so hard that Bródir fell each time and could hardly regain his feet. But as soon as he succeeded in getting up he fled to the woods.

Earl Sigurd fought furiously with Kerdjálfad, and Kerdjálfad forged on so fiercely that he felled all who stood foremost. He broke through Earl Sigurd's ranks up to the very banner[4] and slew the banner-bearer. Then the earl got another man to bear the banner, and after that there was another furious battle. Kerdjálfad dealt this man a mortal blow and slew all who stood near him, one after the other. Earl Sigurd called on Thorstein Hallsson to bear the banner, and Thorstein was about to take it when Ámundi the White called out: 'Don't take the banner, Thorstein, for all who bear it will be slain!'

The earl called out: 'Hrafn the Red, you bear the banner!'

Hrafn replied: 'Carry your fiend yourself!'

The earl said: 'Likely it is most fitting that bag and beggar stay together.'[5] Thereupon he tore the banner from the staff and tucked it into his clothing.

Shortly after that Ámundi the White was slain, and then the earl was likewise pierced with a spear. Óspak had advanced through the entire wing of the enemy; he was badly wounded, and two sons of Brján had already fallen. Sigtrygg fled before him. Thereupon the entire host took to flight.

Thorstein Hallsson stopped while the others were fleeing and tied his shoe thong. Then Kerdjálfad asked him why he was not running, too.

'Because I can't get home this evening anyway,' said Thorstein, 'as I live out in Iceland!' Kerdjálfad spared him.

Hrafn the Red was chased out into a river. It seemed to him as though he could see hell down below and as though the devils were trying to drag him down. Then Hrafn said: 'Twice I, your dog, have run to Rome,[6] Apostle Peter, and would run a third time if you allow it!' Then the devils released him and he succeeded in crossing the river.

Now Bródir saw that King Brján's forces were pursuing the fugitives and that only a few were manning the shield-castle around him. So he rushed from the woods, broke through the entire shield-castle, and levelled a blow at the king. The lad Tadk raised his arm to ward off the blow, but the stroke cut off his arm and the king's head. The king's blood ran upon the lad's arm stump and the wound healed immediately. Then Bródir shouted: 'Let it pass from mouth to mouth that Bródir felled Brján!'[7]

Then some men ran after those who were pursuing the enemy and informed them that King Brján had been slain. Thereupon Úlf Hreda and Kerdjálfad immediately turned back. They surrounded Bródir and his men and threw branches of trees upon them. And so Bródir was taken alive.

Úlf slit open his belly, led him round and round an oak tree, and in this way unwound all his intestines out of his body, and Bródir did not die before they were all pulled out of him. Bródir's men were slain to the last man.

Thereupon they laid out the body of King Brján. The king's head had again grown fast to the trunk.

Fifteen of the Burners fell in Brján's battle. There, too, fell Halldór Gudmundarson and Erling of Stroma.

On Good Friday it so happened that a man called Dorrud went outside his house on Caithness, and he saw twelve persons riding up to a women's bower,[8] and there they all disappeared from sight. He went up to it and peered through a window slit, and there he saw women with a loom set up before them. Men's heads were used in place of weights, and human entrails in place of the warp and woof; a sword served as the treadle and an arrow as the batten. They spoke these verses:

> Widely is flung,
> warning of slaughter,
> the weaver's-beam's-web:[9]
> 'tis wet with blood;
> is spread now, grey,
> the spear-thing[10] before,
> the woof-of-the-warriors[9]
> which valkyries fill
> with the red warp-of–
> Randvér's-banesman.[11]
>
> Is this web woven
> and wound of entrails,
> and heavy weighted
> with heads of slain;
> are blood-bespattered
> spears the treadles,

iron-bound the beams,
the battens,[12] arrows:
let us weave with our swords
this web of victory!

Goes Hild to weave,
and Hjorthrimol,
Sanngríd and Svipol,[13]
with swords brandished:
shields will be shattered,
shafts will be splintered,
will the hound-of-helmets[14]
the hauberks bite.

Wind we, wind we
the web-of-darts,
and follow the atheling
after to war!
Will men behold
shields hewn and bloody
where Gunn and Gondol[13]
have guarded the thane.

Wind we, wind we
such web-of-darts
as the young war-worker
waged afore-time![15]
Forth shall we fare
where the fray is thickest,
where friend and fellow
'gainst foremen battle!

Wind we, wind we
the web-of-darts
where float the flags
of unflinching men!
Let not the liege's
life be taken:
valkyries award
the weird of battle.[16]

Will seafaring men
hold sway over lands,
who erstwhile dwelled
on outer nesses;
is doomed to die
a doughty king,[17]
lies slain an earl
by swords e'en now.

Will Irish men eke
much ill abide:
't will not ever after
be out of men's minds.
Now the web is woven,
and weapons reddened –
in all lands will be heard
the heroes' fall.

Now awful is it
to be without,
as blood-red rack
races overhead;
is the welkin gory
with warriors' blood
as we valkyries
war-songs chanted.

Well have we chanted
charms full many
about the king's son:
may it bode him well!
Let him learn them
who listens to us,
and speak these spells
to spearmen after.[18]

Start we swiftly
with steeds unsaddled –
hence to battle
with brandished swords!

Then they pulled the web down and into pieces, and each one held on to what she had in her hands. Dorrud then went away from the window slit and returned to his home, but the men mounted their horses and rode away, six to the south and the other six to the north.

A similar portent was seen by Brand Gneistason in the Faroes.

At Svínafell in Iceland the priest had to remove his stole as blood rained down upon it on Good Friday.

At Thváttá River on Good Friday the priest thought he saw a deep sea chasm open beside the altar, and in it he saw many terrifying sights, and it was a long time till he came to and could sing the Mass.

In the Orkneys this took place: Hárek thought he saw Earl Sigurd with some of his men. Then Hárek mounted his horse and rode to meet the earl. They were seen to meet and ride behind a hill, and they were never seen again. Not a trace of Hárek was ever found.

Earl Gilli in the Hebrides dreamed that a man came to him and said that his name was Herfinn and that he came from Ireland. He dreamed that he asked the man for tidings from there. Herfinn spoke this verse:

> I died where brave men battled:
> brands did sing in Ireland.
> Many a mace did shatter
> mail-coats – helms were splintered.
> Sword-fight keen I saw there:
> Sigurd fell in combat –
> blood billowed from death-wounds –
> Brján fell, yet he conquered.

Flosi and the earl talked much about this dream. A week later Hrafn the Red arrived and told them all the tidings of Brján's battle: the death of the king, of Earl Sigurd, and of Bródir and all the vikings.

Flosi asked: 'What can you tell me of my men?'

'They were all slain there,' said Hrafn, 'but your brother-in-law Thorstein was spared by Kerdjálfad and is now with him.'

Flosi told the earl that he was going to leave – 'for we still have to perform our promise to make pilgrimage to Rome.'

The earl bade him do just as he wished and presented him with a ship and everything else which he needed; he also gave him much silver. Flosi and his company then sailed to Wales and stayed there for a time.

158

Kol is Slain. Flosi's Pilgrimage

Kári Solmundarson told farmer Skeggi that he would like him to procure a ship, and Skeggi provided him with one with all equipment. Kári, Dávid the White, and Kolbein the Black went aboard and sailed south past the firths of Scotland. There they met some men from the Hebrides who reported to Kári the tidings from Ireland and also that Flosi and his men had sailed to Wales.

When Kári learned this he told his comrades that he wished to sail south to Wales, there to find Flosi and his followers. He bade anyone who preferred to part company with him to do so, because he would not conceal from anyone the fact that he considered he had not yet sufficiently avenged himself on Flosi and his men. All chose to accompany him. Then he sailed south to Wales and they landed in a secluded inlet.

That morning Kol Thorsteinsson went to the town to exchange silver for his wares. Of all the Burners he had used the most scornful language in speaking about that deed. He had often talked with a fine lady, and it was as good as agreed that he was to marry her and settle there.

That same morning Kári, too, went to the town. He came to the place where Kol was counting the silver. Kári recognised him and rushed at him with his sword drawn and aimed a blow on his neck. But Kol kept on counting the silver, and his head counted 'ten' as it flew from the trunk.

Kári said: 'Let someone go and tell Flosi that Kári Solmundarson has slain Kol Thorsteinsson! I give notice of this slaying committed by my hand.' Then Kári returned to his ship and told his shipmates of the slaying.

Then they sailed north to Berwick, drew up their ship on land, and journeyed to Hvítsborg in Scotland and stayed with Earl Melkólf that year.

When Flosi learned of Kol's slaying he had the body laid out and contributed much money for the burial. Flosi never was heard to utter vengeful words against Kári.

From Wales Flosi sailed south and started on his pilgrimage. He journeyed south on foot and came to Rome. There he was accorded the great honour of receiving absolution from the Pope himself. For that he gave a large sum of money.

Then he returned by way of the eastern route,[1] tarrying in many towns, presenting himself to great lords, and receiving great honour from them.

The following winter he was in Norway and was given a ship by Earl Eirík[2] for sailing to Iceland. The earl presented him with a great quantity of flour, and many other personages accorded him great honour. Then he sailed to Iceland and made Horn Firth. From there he rode to Svínafell. He had now fulfilled all the terms of the agreement, both in respect to his banishment and his fines.

159

Kári and Flosi are Reconciled

Now it must be told that Kári betook himself to his ship the following summer and sailed south across the sea to begin his pilgrimage in Normandy. He continued south on foot, received absolution, and returned by way of the western route. He again boarded his ship in Normandy and sailed north across the sea to Dover in England. From there he sailed west, around Wales, and then north past the firths of Scotland, and he did not stop until he arrived at Freswick on Caithness and came to farmer Skeggi. He made over his cargo ship to Kolbein and Dávid, and on it Kolbein sailed to Norway, but Dávid remained on Fair Isle.

Kári spent that winter on Caithness. During the winter his wife died in Iceland. The following summer Kári made ready to sail to Iceland. Skeggi gave him a cargo ship; there were eighteen men on board. They were rather late in getting the ship ready for sailing; still they put to sea. They were much delayed by contrary winds; yet at last they made Ingólfshofdi promontory. There the ship was dashed to pieces, but the men were saved. Then a snowstorm came upon them.

Kári's followers then asked Kári what they should do, and he answered that the best plan would be to go to Svínafell and put Flosi's generosity to the test.

Without stopping they then went to Svínafell. Flosi was in the sitting-room. He recognised Kári as he came into the room, jumped up to meet him, kissed him, and had him sit down on the high-seat beside him. Flosi invited Kári to stay with him that winter, and Kári accepted the invitation and they came to a complete reconciliation. Flosi gave Hildigunn, his brother's daughter, to Kári in marriage; she was the same one who had been married to Hoskuld Hvítanessgodi. At first the couple lived at the Broad River farm.

This is the story told of Flosi's end. When he had become an old man he sailed abroad to fetch timber to build himself a hall. That winter he stayed in Norway, but the following summer he was very late in getting ready to sail. People said that his ship was not seaworthy, but Flosi said it was good enough for an old man who was soon to die. He went on board and sailed out into the sea and nothing was ever again seen of the ship.

These were the children of Kári in his marriage with Helga, the daughter of Njál: Thorgerd and Ragneid, Valgerd, and Thórd, the one who was burned at Bergthórshvál. The children of Kári by Hildigunn were Starkad, Thórd, and Flosi. Flosi's son was Kolbein, who was one of the most renowned men in that family.

And here we conclude the saga of the Burning of Njál.

NOTES

CHAPTER 1

1. According to the *Landnámabók*, *Hauksbók*, chap. 304, one of the greatest chieftains of the Rangá River district. There, however, he is listed as the son of Sigmund, the son of Sigvat the Red. There are some discrepancies in the genealogies of the *Njals saga*, but for the most part they are in close agreement with those of the *Landnámabót* and other Icelandic sources. Because of the unusually large number of names occurring in this saga only the important ones will be commented on.

2. The plain between the two Rangá Rivers (Ýtri and Eystri) in south-west Iceland.

3. This abrupt shift of scene at the beginning of the saga is very unusual. These are the Dales, the scene of the *Laxdæla saga*.

4. Hoskuld and his brother Hrút are prominent figures in the first part of the *Laxdæla saga*.

5. Famous legendary king of Denmark.

6. Óláf Peacock and his son Kjartan are important figures in the *Laxdæla saga*.

CHAPTER 2

1. The annual assembly held each summer at Thingvellir (Assembly Plain) northwest of the Rangá River district.

2. By marriage a man 'established himself', and by allying himself with another family improved his influence.

3. The court *(lögrétta)* consisted of 36 chieftains *(goðis)* from the four Quarters of Iceland; but here the reference is merely to the place of assembly on the plain.

4. Each chieftain had his own semi-permanent booth where he was quartered with his followers during the period of the Assembly.

5. The 'great hundred', or 120 in our system; thus, 60 x 120. The reference is probably to ounces of silver. The legal ounce was the equivalent of 6 ells of *vadmál,* or woollen homespun material,

commonly used in reckoning values.

6. Actually Hrútsstead is north of the mouth of the White River. However, west is often used when we would expect north, and east when we would expect south, a custom harking back to Norwegian conditions.

7. This was the usual arrangement in such cases.

8. It is evidently Hrút's own ship and merchandise.

9. Actually south-east.

10. One mark of silver was the equivalent of 8 legal ounces or 48 ells of *vadmál*.

11. A group of islands in south-east Norway.

12. The present Oslo Fjord.

CHAPTER 3

1. Harald Greyfur ruled from 961 to 970.

2. Many Icelandic sources have this incorrect statement. Actually Gunnhild was the daughter of Gorm the Old, the king of Denmark.

3. At the mouth of the Götaelf (Göta River), at that time the border between Norway and Sweden.

4. A typical name for scoundrels of all types.

5. He realises that there is no choice but to obey Gunnhild's command.

6. Icelandic sources stress Gunnhild's erotic nature. According to the *Laxdæla* saga there had been an earlier meeting between Gunnhild and Hrút, which would make this episode more credible.

7. Probably in the morning, which was generally the time for an audience.

8. An anachronism, as stone halls were not built in Norway before the twelfth century.

CHAPTER 4

1. A select division of the king's bodyguard, whose special task it was to track down and dispatch enemies of the king.

CHAPTER 5

1. The relation of Atli's father, but not of his son, to King Hákon the Good of Norway is touched on also in the *Egils saga*.

2. In south-west Sweden.

3. The large lake at the outlet of which Stockholm is located.

4. Jämtland, in central Sweden, at that time paid tribute to Norway.

5. The narrow strait between Sweden and the Danish island of Zealand.

6. That is, the most exposed part of the battle array.

7. The *stafnbúi* was both spokesman and leader in battle.

8. Coastal region in southern Norway.

9. Gudröd was killed in 999 in an attack on Norway. He was the last survivor of the sons of Gunnhild.

CHAPTER 6

1. A difficult passage.

2. At the mouth of the White River.

3. Actually, to the north.

4. Approximately the middle of September, as winter begins at the end of October. The time is later than originally planned (cf. Chapter 2).

5. The north-west peninsula of Iceland with its many firths.

6. Mord addresses Hoskuld as the more respected of the two brothers, but Hrút speaks up immediately.

7. Very likely because she is embarrassed by the presence of so many people.

CHAPTER 7

1. Probably a son of Ozur (cf. Chapter 2), and hence a cousin of Hrút, for whom she has evidently done some favour.

2. There being no partitions in the old Icelandic house, secrecy could be obtained only by going outside some distance.

3. The pre-Christian method of declaring oneself divorced.

CHAPTER 8

1. Hrút's challenge interrupts the legal procedure, but was not sanctioned by law (cf. Chapter 56).

2. cf. the genealogy in Chapter 25.

CHAPTER 9

1. Now known as Fellsströnd (Fell Strand) on the south coast of the peninsula between the Hvamms Firth and the Broad Firth and near the mouth of the Laxá River.

2. One of the two large firths on the west coast of Iceland. The Bear Isles are about 40 kilometres from Under the Fell (now known as Stadarfell). The sea in this region is still noted for its good fishing.

3. Probably from the peninsula of Akranes (Field Ness) in the inner reaches of the Borgar Firth, which was sown to grain.

4. This was rather unusual and justifies her reproaches in the following chapter.

CHAPTER 10

1. He was the son of Bjorn, one of the original settlers.

2. The Bear Firth and the Steingríms Firth are both on the east coast of the large north-western peninsula of Iceland.

3. The elevated dais for the women at the upper end of the hall.

CHAPTER 11

1. The fish were probably stored here after being caught, but it is surprising that the flour was stored so far from home. The author seems to underestimate the great distance of the Isles from the mainland (cf. Chapter 9, note 2).

CHAPTER 12

1. Unknown otherwise, and possibly an invented character.

2. Peninsula on the north-east coast of the Broad Firth. It must be assumed that Ósvíf had moved there from Under the Fell after the marriage of his son.

3. Both at the inner end of the Steingríms Firth.

4. *Fylgja* (plural *fylgjur*), the spiritual doubles of men, sometimes in animal form, which appear on special occasions and are visible to people with second sight. According to popular belief one becomes sleepy at their approach.

5. By covering his own eyes Svan means to blind his enemies through sympathetic magic.

6. Alliterative magic formula in verse.

7. Between Selárdale and the Bear Firth.

8. Alliterative proverb.

9. Alliterative proverb: 'We are all involved.'

10. The usual award, although for freemen of inferior social status a wergild of only 100 in silver is sometimes demanded (cf. Chapters 38 and 43).

11. This refers to an equitable manner of payment (by weighing the silver), as it was rarely minted.

12. That is, Hallgerd's dowry.

CHAPTER 13

1. With the exception of Glúm the members of this family appear also in the *Egils saga,* chap. 29, *LB,* chaps. 35, 109, and in other sources.

2. Their terms were 950–969 and 930–949, respectively. For the duties of the law-speaker, cf. Chapters 105 and 142.

3. Near the mouth of the White River.

4. Engey, an island, and Laugarness, a peninsula, both near Reykjavík.

5. Actually, Hoskuldsstead is directly north of their farms.

6. According to Icelandic law a widow was permitted to betroth herself with the consent of her father or closest relatives.

CHAPTER 14

1. It is surprising that he should have been invited or even tolerated in the company after what had occurred.

2. *cf.* the genealogy in Chapter 1.

3. A small inlet to the north of the Bear Firth.

4. Between Veidilausa and the Bear Firth.

5. One of the many instances of the old Germanic belief that the dead entered a realm in the mountains. One of the best-known legends of the kind is that of the German emperor Frederick Barbarossa.

CHAPTER 17

1. Covering the body in this manner and reporting the slaying distinguishes manslaughter from secret murder.

2. In typical saga style her words and laughter are ironic.

CHAPTER 19

1. A Swede who discovered Iceland in 870.

CHAPTER 20

1. 'Islands of land', in the marshy delta of the Markar River.

2. About 8 miles from Hlídarendi, as the crow flies.

CHAPTER 22

1. One of the large firths on the northern coast.

2. This position opposite the high-seat is considered a seat of honour.

3. In Icelandic law the exact wording is of greatest importance.

CHAPTER 23

1. The valley of the Laxá River.

CHAPTER 24

1. These neighbours who were to testify that Hrút had not returned the money to Unn should have been summoned in the home district. The entire procedure is very brief compared with the description in Chapter 56.

2 The exact wording is given in Chapter 142.

3. *cf.* Chapter 7.

4. The river which flows through the Almanna Gorge and debouches on Thingvellir Plain (*cf.* Chapter 145). An island in the river was the usual site for duels fought at the Assembly.

5. That is, to advance the amount of silver which they did not have at hand.

CHAPTER 25

1. Harald Battle-Tooth and Hrœrek are famous figures of Danish heroic legend.

2. One of the most prominent families in Iceland.

3. The founder of Icelandic historiography (d. 1133).

4. This reference (found in all manuscripts) to an important chief (d. 1245) of the Sturlung Period is worth noting.

CHAPTER 26

1. This is referred to also in Chapter 139.

CHAPTER 27

1. Fosterage was generally offered to children of people of higher social station than one's self; hence it was regarded as an honour shown one.

2. As to Thórhall's proficiency in the law *cf.* Chapter 139.

CHAPTER 28

1. A place not to be located definitely, but somewhere on the south coast.

2. On the White Sea.

CHAPTER 29

1. The present Tönsberg on the Oslo Fjord.

2. All members of the famous line of earls of Lade who had their ancestral possessions in the districts about the Drontheim Fjord.

3. The large island at the mouth of the Götaelf in Sweden.

CHAPTER 30

1. The province of Sweden.

2. Reval, in Estonia.

3. An island in the Gulf of Riga.

CHAPTER 31

1. Died 986.

CHAPTER 34

1. Sigfús was therefore Mord Fiddle's brother.

2. Njál's natural son, not the father of the bride.

3. Hallgerd's father.

4. As our 'pouring', in no way considered below the dignity of the hostess.

5. This *kvithling* (ditty) in *fornyrthislag* meter.

6. A typical gesture of indignation and sudden resolve.

7. Possibly the seating is to indicate her changed rank.

CHAPTER 36

1. The name is now unknown, but the mountain Stóra Dímon, a few kilometres south of Hlídarendi, is probably meant.

2. The right of the defendant to determine the amount of indemnity.

3. The usual wergild for a thrall.

4. He refers to Bergthóra's sons.

5. That is, of the year following.

CHAPTER 37

1. From Bergthórshvál.

CHAPTER 38

1. *cf.* Chapter 17, note 1.

2. The usual wergild for a freeman of low rank.

CHAPTER 39

1. Njál's mother, and therefore closely beholden to the family.

2. A poor pretext after so long a time; the text probably due to some later hand.

3. The wedge formed by the confluence of two water courses.

CHAPTER 41

1. Gunnar's cousin.

2. *cf.* Chapter 12, note 4.

CHAPTER 42

1. *cf.* Chapter 17, note 1.

2. This saw occurs also in Chapters 99 and 134.

3. *cf.* Chapter 44 and Úlf's verse in Chapter 102 for this figure of speech.

CHAPTER 44

I This scene is in the taste of the *Fornaldarsogur*.

2 A frequently occurring motif in the sagas indicating that the weapon will be the death of someone.

CHAPTER 45

1. Very possibly an ironic prognostication of Sigmund's death: appearing in bright red clothes, he is referred to as being already 'red and dead'. 'Elf' is the designation of chthonic beings.

2. The spring Assembly of the Rangá River district.

CHAPTER 46

1. The first bishop of Iceland, who lived a full century after the events here told.

CHAPTER 47

1. Not an anachronism: the farm was named so by Ketil the Foolish, a Christian from the Hebrides, but even before him Irish anchorites had settled there and had a sanctuary.

2. Now called Minna-Hof to distinguish it from the one by the Rangá River.

3 There was such a period in 976, although this does not agree with the chronology of the saga.

4. The reference is to the chieftains Gizur the White and Ásgrím Ellida-Grímsson, under whose protection they had placed themselves and to whom they appeal later on (*cf.* Chapters 49f.).

CHAPTER 48

1. Ordinarily separate from the other buildings.
2. He returns by a different route to escape detection.
3 It is, to be sure, a little strange that the fire was not noticed during the night.

CHAPTER 51

1. In the original an alliterating proverb.
2. On Grímsness, in the Western Quarter.

CHAPTER 52

1. A breed of horses still peculiar to Iceland.

CHAPTER 53

1. Said in irony.
2. A euphemism for saying that he feared for Otkel's death.

CHAPTER 54

1. Of imported cloth; ordinary garments were of uncoloured homespun.
2. And so, perhaps, slippery for horses, so they must dismount.
3. This presupposes the long shields ending in a point, which were hardly used at this time. They were preceded by the smaller, round type.

CHAPTER 55

1. Since Thorgeir Otkelsson was not of age.
2. They counted the wounds and specified who had inflicted each.

CHAPTER 56

1. Law-speaker (1004–1030).
2. Giving him the opportunity to 'challenge' anyone not having the required property qualifications.
3. A technicality, one of the many in which Icelandic law practice abounded.
4. That is, for three years as distinguished from lifelong outlawry.
5. Possibly just a feint on the part of Njál.

CHAPTER 58

1. A favourite sport in old Norway and Iceland. The horses were goaded on to fight with their forelegs and teeth, and their owners often came to blows themselves.

CHAPTER 59

1. *cf.* Chapter 1, note 6.

CHAPTER 60

1. The famous skald (*cf.* Chapter 102).

CHAPTER 62

1. The following prophetic dream is typical of the so-called *Fornaldarsogur* – those of predominantly fanciful, romantic character.

CHAPTER 64

1. Óttar must have died of his wounds.

2. According to old Icelandic law a suit could be handed over or sold as a quasi-asset for another party to prosecute.

CHAPTER 66

1. The *Grágás* states that a slayer may ask the plaintiff for peace (*grid*) at the Assembly. It appears that Gunnar did make the request, whereupon Njál made this proclamation. Mord's questions either reveal his ignorance of the law or the author's desire to explain older legal procedure with which his audience might not be familiar.

2. This is, to be sure, a bit of sharp practice.

CHAPTER 68

1. *cf.* Chapter 20, note 1.

CHAPTER 69

1. It is not too far-fetched to assume that this unusual drowsiness falling on the whole troupe is of magical origin and was superinduced by no other than Njál himself (cf. Chapter 100). Possibly this was covered up by the author in view of the later conversion of Njál.

2. Skarphedin's wife.

CHAPTER 70

1. The first part of this alliterating saw still serves as a motto over countless city halls and courts of justice in Scandinavia.

2. According to *Laxdœla saga* he was his grandfather.

CHAPTER 73

1. He now lists the wound first and the assault afterwards, making two cases of it. This was according to the law.

CHAPTER 74

1. Not because they had been summoned illegally as in chapter 142, but because only five jurors (*bjargkvidr*) were necessary to utter a verdict in behalf of the defendant in this case.

2. This verdict, which may appear unjust to our sense of justice, possibly had the purpose of softening the resentment of his opponents.

CHAPTER 75

1. The great ravine to the west of the Thingvellir.

CHAPTER 77

1. A similar requisition of women's hair for a last stand occurs in a great number of classic sources. Here this motif has found its 'classic' expression.

2. Kenning for 'warriors'.

3. 'Mariners'.

4. 'Mariners'.

CHAPTER 78

1. To her son-in-law, Thráin.

2. Kenning for 'warrior'.

3. 'Warrior'.

CHAPTER 79

1. It was the belief that the warriors slain in battle were gathered for everlasting war-play in Valholl. Accordingly their weapons were buried with them.

2. They are Odin's birds, and their flight is a favourable omen.

3. Luxuriant grass grows on the sod-covered roof of the old Scandinavian house and affords fodder for sheep or goats.

4. It had become morning by then.

CHAPTER 80

1. That is, the fines for Starkad and Thorgeir were determined, and the fine for the attack on Gunnar was deducted from that amount. Mord was to pay the remaining sum to balance the awards.

2. For the slaying of Hróald.

3. cf. Chapter 102.

4. A strange lapse on the part of the saga writer, as he appears again later in Chapters 92, 93, and 109.

CHAPTER 81

1. Many Scandinavians became members of the special guard called 'Varangians' under the Christian emperors of East Rome.

CHAPTER 82

1. The northernmost province of Norway.

2. The seat of the earls of that line, near Drontheim.

3. The strained relation between Earl Hákon and his oldest son is historic and is featured in several sagas.

CHAPTER 83

1. Those with whom Helgi and Grím had sailed.

CHAPTER 84

1. The whole following episode, like those of Chapters 30 and 44, is in regular *Fornaldarsaga* style.

CHAPTER 86

1. The Orkney earls did not pay tribute to Norway until nearly half a century later, and then to King Óláf the Saint.

CHAPTER 87

1. This whole episode is very likely freely invented on the model of later tales.

2. His words recall the sentiment voiced in the Eddic poem *Hóvamól*, stanza 42.

3. This seat, denoting rank, once assigned was kept for a season.

4. The tryst in the dense hazel bushes is a motif common both in the North and in the Romantic stories of the South.

CHAPTER 88

1. She and Irpa are the tutelary feminine divinities of the earls of Lade. They play a role in the *Jómsvíkinga saga*. Hákon's second sight is gained through communion with them.

2. It would seem much more likely that Thráin is tempted to accept the bribe.

3. That is, his former services or the surrender of Hrapp.

4. Another, younger, son of Hákon.

CHAPTER 89

1. According to Icelandic conceptions night killings are murder. This as well as the subsequent escape are standing motifs in the saga.

CHAPTER 91

1. Ironically meant.

2. Grey was the colour of deceit and malice.

3. *cf.* Chapter 44: about equivalent to 'eunuch'.

CHAPTER 92

1. It is altogether unlikely that he would have started out in the evening, especially in winter. Also, in the following narrative the presence of Hallgerd and Thorgerd is forgotten.

2. The ordinary clothing of homespun *vadmál* being dun-coloured.

3. These heraldic figures are, of course, anachronistic.

4. Referring to the death of Hoskuld Njálsson.

CHAPTER 93

1. The bridegroom's contribution which, however, became the bride's property.

CHAPTER 95

1. One of the greatest chieftains in the East Quarter, to which the estate of Svínafell belonged.

CHAPTER 96

1. According to the *tháttr* (story) bearing his name. The *dísir* in this story were a sort of female guardian spirit.

CHAPTER 97

1. It was considered highly improper to broach important business immediately after arrival.
2. As the husband's portion.
3. That is, Njál and his kin. The passage is not entirely clear.
4. The reference is to Njál's support.
5. The famous law-speaker (1004–1030). Before the laws were codified this important office involved the yearly recital of the laws of the land on the Law-Mount.
6. Both headland and farm of this name as well as the farm Ossabœr are not very far west of Flosi's estate at Svínafell.

CHAPTER 98

1. He is Njál's illegitimate son by Hródný.
2. The heathen rite of closing the eyes and nostrils of the departed.

CHAPTER 100

The events of this chapter are told also in Ari's *Íslendingabók*, but somewhat differently.

1. In 995.
2. The greatest chieftain of a district had the privilege of first choice in dealing with merchants from abroad and the right to fix prices. Often Christians and heathens had no dealings with one another.

CHAPTER 101

1. The *prima signatio* was the first step toward conversion. It enabled one to have relations with both heathens and Christians.
2. The section usually called Sída.

CHAPTER 102

1. From the verse we infer that Vetrlidi had attacked Thangbrand with intent to kill.
2. This not unskilful stanza by an unknown skald contains apt allusions and cunning puns difficult to reproduce.
3. Kenning for 'breast'.
4. That is, Gudleif.
5. The hammer is his battle-axe which smites the 'anvil' of Vetrlidi's head.

6. This Hall (Thórarinsson) 60 years later became the foster father of the historian Ari.

7. The famous skald (cf. Chapter 60, note 1).

8. This seems to have been the punishment meted out to offenders against the heathen divinities.

9. Odin's mead is a kenning for 'poetry'; hence its winner is a poet.

10. Kenning for 'warrior'.

11. Farmstead at Reykjaness on the Broad Firth.

12. The mocking terseness of the first two lines has resisted the art of the translator – the last two are generally regarded as later additions. [I cannot agree with Genzmer, who would interpret the first line 'I don't like gods to bark', *Ark. f. n. F.* 1928 (XLIV), 211f.]

13. Because he had been exiled for this and other blasphemy (cf. Chapter 104).

14. At the southern shore of the Bear Firth.

15. Kenning for Thór, as the slayer of trolls.

16. Kennings for 'ship'.

17. Atal is the name of a sea king; hence his kingdom is the sea. Similarly 'the swans'-land' is a kenning for 'the sea'.

18. On the north coast of the Broad Firth.

CHAPTER 103

1. That is, those of the great north-western peninsula of Iceland.

2. Probably because of the iron hoops used to repair it.

CHAPTER 104

1. An error for á Eyum (the Westmen Isles).

CHAPTER 105

1. Thorgeir was still heathen and was probably chosen by them precisely for that reason. He was also universally known for his fair-mindedness; hence his verdict would be acceptable to all.

2. The date was June 24, 1000.

3. Because the horse was sacred to Ódin and its meat was eaten at sacrifice in honour of him, the Church interdicted the consumption of horse-meat. An additional reason was found in the Old Testament ban on eating the flesh of non-cloven-footed beasts. The principle of gradualism seems to have been effective in abating antagonism.

CHAPTER 108

1. The *arvel* is the funeral feast generally celebrated a year after the death of the person who leaves the inheritance.

CHAPTER 109

1. In Iceland this has always been a proof of kindly feeling toward the guest.

2. The reference is to Ámundi's revenge in which the sons of Njál were not involved.

3. *cf.* Chapter 27, where he is called the greatest lawyer.

CHAPTER III

1. Hoskuld's mother.

2. Mord, as one of Hoskuld's slayers, could naturally not be a plaintiff in the suit for the slaying. This 'error' would invalidate the suit.

3. Hildigunn and her people.

CHAPTER 113

1. These genealogies, as well as those of the next chapter, though in the main correct, go back to mythical origins.

CHAPTER 114

1. The heroine of *Laxdœla saga*.

CHAPTER 116

I. On festive occasions the walls were covered with tapestries. Hildigunn wishes to impress Flosi with the solemnity of the occasion.

2. The second and main meal of the day, eaten early in the forenoon.

3. The tables were set up or removed as occasion demanded.

4. Note the threefold symbolic (but obvious) hints to Flosi: the festive reception planned for him as the avenger, the towel full of holes with a piece torn off at the end (alluding to Hoskuld's wounds and her bereavement), and the spreading of the bloody cloak over his shoulders as a dreadful reminder of his duty to avenge Hoskuld.

5. Note the curious mixture of Christian and heathen elements in her adjuration.

6. A frequent alliterative saw.

7. Not to be confused with Hoskuld Thráinsson.

CHAPTER 117

1. That is, the sons of Njál.

CHAPTER 118

1. He points out bitingly the contrast between his own straight-forward way and Njál's deliberate and introspective manner.

2. Not to be confused with the Laxá River in the west.

CHAPTER 119

1. The belief obtained that good luck or the reverse were innate qualities which could be discerned in one's features.

2. This exchange of words between Skarphedin and Skapti, as well as subsequent ones, are the inventions of the author, even though some

of the events alluded to by Skarphedin did occur.

3. His genealogy as well as his heroic deeds are largely fictitious.

4. In central Sweden.

5. The present island of Ösel in the eastern Baltic.

CHAPTER 120

1. One of the greatest chieftains of his time.

CHAPTER 123

1. A palpable anachronism, as is the reference below to a churchyard.

2. In the court there were three rows of benches, the middle row for the *goðis,* the others for the jurors.

3. Ironically, because it makes him think of the cloak of Hoskuld and his death which Hildigunn had wanted Flosi to avenge, and because he suspects an insinuation of effeminacy – which in the North was the deadliest insult.

CHAPTER 124

1. Between the Markar River and the Eyjafell Glacier. Flosi's plan is to avoid the inhabited regions in the west.

2. Nothing is known about these incidents.

CHAPTER 125

1. The hoarfrost-covered horse seems to symbolise Flosi's swift icy-cold plans; the fiery, poisoned arrow, the destructive conflagration to follow. The repetition of the last line(s) is frequent in incantations.

CHAPTER 126

1. *cf.* Chapter 47, note 1.

CHAPTER 127

1. Not to be confused with the famous bishop's seat of Hólar in the North Quarter.

2. It is quite a number for the lonely mountain passes.

CHAPTER 128

1. We hear frequently of secret subterranean passages leading from inside a house to some distance outside.

CHAPTER 129

1. There is a sardonic pun here in the original, in that *baka* means not only 'to bake' but also 'to bask'.

2. Meaning that his chief duty was loyalty to him as the avenger of his father Gunnar, rather than vengeance for the death of Hoskuld Thráinsson.

3. Perhaps (anachronistically) a medieval Christian sentiment about doomsday.

4 Which would befall him if he failed to avenge his sons.

CHAPTER 130

1. Njál.
2. Kenning for 'woman': possibly Hildigunn, Hoskuld's wife, or Skarphedin's wife. The rendering of the second part of this stanza is purely conjectural.
3. Kenning for 'warriors'.
4. Ygg is one of Ódin's names. His gift is the mead of poetry.

CHAPTER 131

1. Since it had been revealed that he had been implicated in the slaying of Hoskuld (cf. Chapter 121).
2. That is, the one on the Eyjafell Mountain.

CHAPTER 132

1. Very likely an anachronism, as the first church was built much later.

CHAPTER 133

1. Attention has been called to the fact that Flosi's dream closely resembles one told in the much-read *Dialogum* of Pope Gregory the Great (d. 604). As it happens, the manuscript fragment of a translation dating from about 1200 was found in the church at Kálfafell, not far from Flosi's farm.
2. For this kenning for 'battle', cf. notes to the Song of the Valkyries in Chapter 157. Here Kári is meant.

CHAPTER 134

1. Flosi's itinerary covers about one-fifth of the Icelandic coast and extends as far as the Vápna Firth, the most northern of the East Firths.
2. A frequently occurring alliterating proverb.
3. The hero of the saga bearing his name.
4. Her dream forebodes Thorvald's death, though curiously the details are at variance with it as told in Chapter 145.

CHAPTER 135

1. Kenning for 'warrior' – here, Kári himself.
2. The author may have copied these legal formulas from some lawbook, unless indeed Mord intentionally lists all types.
3. Northern districts which Flosi had not visited.

CHAPTER 138

1. cf. Chapter 120.
2. The fourth being Hallbjorn.
3. In the original, an alliterative saw.
4. The author (mistakenly) considered it a bribe.

CHAPTER 139

1. *cf.* Chapter 119.
2. Gizur was married to Skapti's sister.
3. There is a slur in this, because 'white' in Old Icelandic had also the connotation of 'white-livered'.
4. In the original, a proverb for which there seems to be no equivalent in English.

CHAPTER 140

1. *cf.* Chapter 119.

CHAPTER 141

1. According to the *Grágás* collection of laws, chap. 81, such a change of allegiance should have been announced at the spring session of the proper Quarter Assembly or else at the Althing itself. It is possible, however, that this regulation did not exist at the time, and it has been suggested that it might have been enacted as the result of just such a technicality.

CHAPTER 142

1. A striking understatement, typical of old Norse saga style.
2. Probably some Mass book, in which case it would be an anachronism.
3. Curiously, this Christian name, taken from the *Grágás* collection of laws, and corresponding to our John Doe, is mechanically retained here instead of the real name of the judge who was to recapitulate the evidence before the jury passed sentence.
4. According to old Germanic custom, a man's first name is his proper name, and his father's name the determinative – exactly the opposite of the modern system.
5. The law-speaker served as the repository of the yet unwritten law.
6. A technical expression, although only five jurors remained. It is curious that this verdict is given before the defence had its turn.

CHAPTER 144

1. And thus bring it before the Fifth Court (*cf.* Chapter 97).
2. The engagement of counsel was considered bribery (*cf.* Chapter 138, note 4).
3. *cf.* Chapter 56, note 4.
4. Consisting of a ring or, later, one mark in silver paid by the person condemned, as alternative of the 'lesser outlawry' of three years' exile.
5. More exactly, of confiscation, held at the home of the one condemned to outlawry 14 days after the conclusion of the Althing.
6. As witnesses of misdemeanours committed at the Assembly itself.

CHAPTER 145

1. *cf.* Chapter 138.

2. The author evidently did not understand Snorri's reply. According to *Íslendingabók*, chap. 3, these men had by crimes forfeited their lands, which then fell to the Althing. Snorri seems to hint that they, as the evil spirits haunting the locality, have stirred up the strife and now hinder Flosi's flight.

3. In Chapter 140. These words show that the author had a written copy before him.

4. From this and other passages in the sagas we know that the meetings of the Althing attracted a certain number of artisans of various kinds.

5. In all probability no church existed there at the time.

6. That is, from the family of Njál.

7. Here, of course, meant ironically.

8. Kenning for 'swords'.

9. The first half of this stanza is difficult, and the rendering therefore purely conjectural.

10. The sword-furbisher possibly also functioned, or was regarded, as such.

11. The laughter must refer to the points made in the first two stanzas.

12. That is, the agreement which is in the making.

13. Because of his awkward attempt at composing in the difficult *dróttkvætt* metre.

14. Because of Kári's refusal to come to terms.

CHAPTER 146

1. That is all we know about this adventure, but the meaning of his sobriquet, Skorargeir 'gorge-spear', alludes to it.

2. Ketil was married to Thorgerd, and Kári to Helga. Both were daughters of Njál.

3. To the sevenfold wergild for Njál, Grím, and Helgi would thus be added half as much again for a total of 10½-fold wergild.

4. Leidólf the Strong.

CHAPTER 147

1. This seems to be the meaning of the original.

2. Not previously mentioned.

CHAPTER 148

1. *cf.* Chapter 139, note 3, for this sobriquet.

2. The central desert of Iceland, now called Sprengisandr.

CHAPTER 149

1. *cf.* Chapter 133.

CHAPTER 150

1. *cf.* Chapter 54, note 3.
2. Of course, ironical.

CHAPTER 152

1. Probably the stretch now called Mýrdalssandr.
2. An alliterating proverb found also elsewhere.

CHAPTER 153

1. *cf.* Chapter 86.
2. Which would be an ignominy for brave men.
3. *cf.* Chapter 95.
4. Several other instances of this custom occur in the sagas.

CHAPTER 155

1 . Kenning for 'warriors'.
2. As scavengers of the battlefield.
3. Ironical for 'paid back for the burning'.
4. Helgi Njálsson.

CHAPTER 156

1. Note the medieval Christian tinge of the following legend.

CHAPTER 157

1. These personages, not introduced before, are taken from the *Brjáns saga*.
2. A 'blind motif', since its bearing is not made clear. Is Ódin the mysterious rider, who gives them baneful advice?
3. Composed of warriors with their long shields.
4. This is the famous 'raven-banner' of the vikings.
5. An alliterating saw.
6. That is, made pilgrimage.
7. Apparently an alliterating reminiscence of some lost lay.
8. More precisely, a house where the women's work was done.
9. Kenning for 'battle'. The same conception, growing out of the interweaving of darts and arrows in the air, is found in the Anglo-Saxon *wīgspēda gewiofu*, 'the web of battle-luck' (*Beowulf* 697).
10. Another kenning for 'battle'. (Thing = 'meeting' or 'assembly'.)
11. The whole line, probably, a kenning for 'blood'. Randvér's banesman was Bikki, the evil counsellor of King Iormunrekk, in whom we may detect Ódin, the instigator of strife between men. 'Fill' is probably used here in the sense of completing the web with

woof and weft; but it might also mean to 'saturate', and so to 'colour'.

12. The batten is the instrument used to beat home the yarn. Much also in this stanza is doubtful.

13. The names of valkyries.

14. Kenning for 'battle-axe'.

15. Granting that 'the web-of-darts' is a kenning for 'battle' (from the cloud, or web, of missiles flying overhead), the meaning of this uncertain line is that the valkyries are urging each other on to 'weave' another such victorious battle as the young king (Sigtrygg) had before.

16. It is for the valkyries to decide the fate of battle and to choose the slain: they have no need of his life.

17. That is, King Brján, who was set upon at the very end of the battle. The earl, Sigurd Hlodvisson, had fallen earlier.

18. A hint to the listener outside.

CHAPTER 158

1. That is, through Germany, whereas the western route led through France.

2. Part ruler of Norway until 1014.

CHAPTER 159

1. The famous law-speaker (1066-1071).